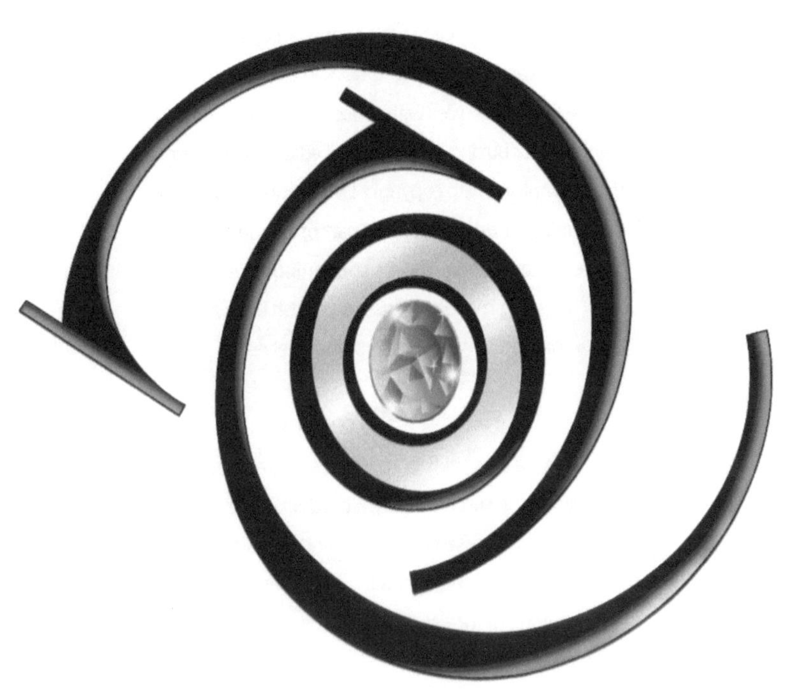

ARCHAIC

Jasmin De Anda

Published by Stargazer Literature
An imprint of De Anda Family Group LLC

ISBN 979-8-9880025-0-5

TABLE OF CONTENTS

CHAPTER 1
The Beginning of Everything

The darkness and silence in the streets were unsettling. It was a week before Halloween and all the houses in the cul de sac were decorated for the holiday— all except one small home at the very end that remained barren. Its bright red door and low, black metal fence brought attention to the place, catching the eye of anyone who walked by it.

The reason why this small house was the only one without decorations is because its owner was not yet accustomed to the human tradition of Halloween. Leanna Blackwood paced in her nursery that night, carrying her ten-month baby in her arms. She was young, aged 22, and had only lived among humans in San Diego for the past three months. She held her son Eric against her chest with his head resting on her shoulder and gently rubbed his back, trying to put him to sleep. Eric looked to the side with his eyes wide open, alert, unaffected by his mother's attempts. She walked to the window and opened it, letting in the cool air. The breeze made her shiver, but filled the room with the fresh scent of wet grass. She glanced over her shoulder to look at Eric, sighing when she saw his open eyes staring into hers. She pressed her cheek against his head and hummed a lullaby, hoping it would soothe him.

Leanna turned to watch the sheer curtains flutter in the wind. She felt blissful as she stared trance-like at the shining stars with her son in her arms. Then a noise outside snapped her back into the present. Her body stiffened, and then the sound of splintering wood made her jump. She moved closer to the nursery door, praying the sound was just her imagination, but when she heard the rumbling in the distance, her heart sank because she knew it was someone downstairs. She felt sick with apprehension as she looked around the room for a safe way out. She had known the dangers of being a sorcerer for too long (to expect anything less than the worst). She

could only assume that whatever was making the ruckus downstairs was there to harm her. As the footsteps neared them, she panicked. Unable to think clearly, she ran to the closet and opened the double doors, setting Eric down at the back. She took the boxes stacked inside and piled them around him as a barrier, hoping it would hide his presence. Leanna's eyes were wide with fear as she prepared to stack the last box. Taking a moment to calm her breathing, she kissed the top of his head. His big blue eyes stared right through her. She tried to reassure herself that he would be fine as she placed the last box in front of him.

The footsteps were just outside the door to the room. She stepped back and closed the closet doors, turning to face the nursery door. Leanna squeezed her hands to stop their shaking, her fingernails digging into her palms. With a bang, the door swung open. What stood in its place surprised her: She had never seen anything like it. In front of her was what appeared to be a man, but not a normal one. He had long black hair tucked behind his ears and strange scale-like patches across his skin. He stood tall, rolling up the sleeves of his dark jacket. Instinctively, Leanna stepped back, crashing into the crib. When he saw the fear in her eyes, he smiled. His footsteps charred the carpet as he walked toward her, leaving footprints behind. She grabbed the crib behind her and tightened her hands around the bars, bracing herself for the worst. The man's red eyes darkened. An orange glow appeared underneath the skin on his neck as if there was a fire inside him and slowly rose to his jaw.

When he was about halfway across the room, he stopped suddenly, his head jerking to the right, his eyes focusing on the floor. He closed his eyes, focusing on his hearing until he realized there was someone else in the room— another heartbeat. Leanna's stomach twisted when she saw the smile on his face as he looked at the closet doors. She moved quickly, putting herself between him and the closet and waved her hand up, making the lamp by the door rise. Then she pulled her hand back, throwing the lamp at the back of his head. The impact did nothing. The man did not even flinch as the lamp shattered against his skull.

"Move," he said flatly. Leanna could not.

"Leave him alone," she pleaded, her voice shaking. The man shook his head,

then lunged forward toward her so quickly she barely had time to react. She tried to shield herself with her powers, but before she could manage anything, he let the fire reach his fist and drove his hand into her stomach. Her breath caught in her throat as she stood still in front of the doors. The only thing holding her up was the hand in the center of her abdomen. He retracted his hand and she fell to the floor with a thud. Her breathing felt broken, as if she had glass shards in her lungs. In seconds, her blood stained the floor. With the little strength she had left, she reached over and clung to his leg, desperate to stop him, but he shook her off easily, without any struggle.

The man opened the double doors of the closet and moved the boxes, throwing them to the side. Eric sat on the floor and looked up at him, his eyes wide with fright. As the man neared her son, Leanna reached out with a shaky hand and pressed it against the carpet. She watched as what was left of her power left her fingertips and sent a string of light that surrounded Eric. The man knew he was too late. The sheer light barrier she'd thrown had already closed— the dome forcing his hand back when he touched it. He tried to break the shield with blunt force, but his efforts were useless. Angered and annoyed, he turned to Leanna, ready to finish her off, but the sound of police sirens distracted him. Instead of ending her life, he turned to the open window and listened to the noise outside. A pair of deep red bat-like wings emerged from his back, the edges frayed and the ends sharp. He took a step toward the window and vanished.

Leanna kept her eyes on Eric, afraid to end her protection spell. Her breathing hitched and her body felt cold as the numbness took over and she knew she was dying. She was terrified as she looked at her son, knowing she was about to leave him just as her parents had left her.

She whispered his name in fear, her eyes rimmed with unshed tears.

Finally, her body stopped shaking and she took her last breath, a single tear escaping with it.

Seconds later, a blue light exited her body through her parted lips, like a ribbon of smoke, and rose gently toward the sky.

Outside in the darkness, a policeman exited a vehicle alone. The soul that had

just risen could not be seen by human eyes, so he remained oblivious to the events that had taken place. The sound of a door closing caught his attention. When he turned, he saw a young man, maybe eighteen, rushing down his yard.

"Are you the one who called about the disturbance?" the officer asked as the young man reached him.

"I heard banging, over there," he said, turning to gesture toward Leanna's home, but when he turned back to the officer, he saw the officer was face-to-face with a man neither of them knew.

The man had brown hair and was dressed in black pants and a blazer over a white collared shirt. The policeman jumped back in surprise, but before he could react, the strange man placed his hands across the policeman's face. His blue eyes turned a foggy white, matching those of the strange man, and he fell into a trance.

"It was a false alarm," the man said. Then his eyes returned to their original blue color and he retracted his hand. The policeman's eyes remained foggy even after the man had finished his spell. Sill in a trance, he stepped back into his car and drove away. The young man stood stunned by what he just witnessed. He was startled when the man faced him, but before he could process what had just occurred, another man in his twenties approached and did the same to him. The young man, in the same trance, made his way back to the home next door as the sorcerer who cast the spell on him watched.

When the man looked to the other houses, several sorcerers who had arrived with him approached the houses individually, their movements almost in sync as they knocked on each door and repeated the memory replacement spell on the residents of each house.

This strange man's name was Cornelius Alewar, but he went by the name "Neil." He was the man in charge, the leader of all sorcerers. He was born and raised in England and, although he appeared to be no older than his mid-to-late thirties, he had lived for well over a century. Neil watched from the sidewalk to make sure nothing went wrong. The man in his twenties returned to his side. He was mortal like the other sorcerers; a man named Theodore Cross. Theo stared at the house, terrified to go

inside. He ran to the front door with Neil watching him. When he reached for the handle, he froze when he noticed the splintered wood and the handle warped and melted. His hand stopped just over the handle and he gave the already open door a gentle push. Its creaking was almost eerie. Theo quietly walked in, unsettled by the silence inside. When he reached the staircase, he felt as if his heart had stopped. Cold sweat formed on the back of his neck, dampening his dark hair. He saw the soul pass just before he arrived, but he did not know whose body he would find. He knew that he would walk into the room to find either an orphaned boy or a heartbroken mother who had just lost her child.

He slowly made his way up the stairs, assessing the damage as he moved. The pictures that once hung on the wall were now shattered on the ground, the broken glass crunching under his feet with each step, and the carpet was still warm where the man had left it charred. When he reached the nursery door, his hands shook as he pushed the door open to find her just as her killer had left her; in a pool of her own blood. His throat tightened as he slowly walked to her and knelt in front of her, his hands shaking as he reached out to touch her. When he saw her cold eyes, he could no longer hold back his tears. They fell down his cheeks freely as he closed her eyes and caressed her brown hair. Then he took her in his arms and held her, brushing her cold cheek with his thumb and squeezing her shoulder.

Neil rushed into the room and stopped at the door. His heart broke at the sight of Theo holding her lifeless body. He swallowed back his tears. Knowing there was nothing he could say or do to ease the pain they were both feeling, he walked to the closet and knelt in front of Eric. Neil stared at the child, relieved he was unharmed.

"Why didn't you see this coming?" Theo asked quietly, his voice thick. Neil kept his eyes on Eric, unwilling to meet Theo's gaze. He shook his head. "I wish I could have… Our minds have always been connected, but by the time I saw what he was doing, it was too late…"

"Why her…?" asked Theo.

Neil stared down at the carpet; his guilt apparent. He pressed his palm to Eric's head and closed his eyes. "I think he may have been after Eric… His father had

the potential to be quite powerful, after all. He may have inherited that potential. It's the only explanation I have at the moment."

"Is it really?" Theo asked, questioning him. Neil removed his hand and stared back at the ground. He took the baby in his arms and got back on his feet, looking down at Theo, who was still on the ground holding Leanna. He knelt next to him and gently placed his hand on Theo's bloodstained hand. He spoke softly to Theo. "We must get Eric to safety… Let the others take care of her body. We will hold a proper service once Eric is safe."

"We can't just leave her here," he said angrily.

"Theodore… she was my daughter," he said with unshed tears in his eyes. "I wish to stay as much as you do, but my priority now is getting my grandson, her child, far away from this."

Theo nodded to show he understood. He took a deep and shaky breath before gently setting her body down on the floor.

Neil carried Eric, and they walked back outside to the car, where another sorcerer was waiting in the driver's seat. Neil and Theo climbed back into the back seat, and the sorcerer drove toward their home. Theo stared down at his bloodstained hands in shock. When Neil noticed, he reached for his handkerchief and handed it to Theo. Theo took it slowly and wiped the blood off his hands, which were still shaking.

"A whole society of sorcerers… You'd think we'd have a better way to get places…"

"Please inform me when you've discovered a faster and more efficient way to travel that does not expose us to humans. Even if we only travel at night, it's a new age. There is always someone with some form of technology eager to expose us to the world."

"The place looks empty to me," Theo sighed.

Neil was confused. He looked out to the streets to see that they were indeed empty. What confused him is that the streets were never empty. Even at night in this neighborhood, someone was always wandering or a group of teenagers out past curfew. Then he looked closely and realized that the streets were not empty but that

the people were not awake. The few citizens on the streets that night were lying unconscious on the ground. By the time Neil looked forward to warn the driver, it was too late. A woman with a white mask, her brown hair braided, jumped out in front of the car and threw it back over her head and upside down onto the street behind her.

Neil panicked and tried to use his power to protect everyone, specifically Eric; Theo did the same. When they landed, Neil was drained of energy. He could barely keep his eyes open but was relieved to see that Eric was safe. He removed his seatbelt and dropped down next to Eric. The woman turned and walked toward the car. Neil did not have the energy to use his power. He desperately tried to wake Theo up, but he was just as drained and would not open his eyes. The woman came close and, with one swift movement, detached the car door and flung it behind her to reveal Neil on the ground; one arm wrapped protectively around Eric.

"Leave him be," he pleaded. The woman reached out to him, waving her hand across his face and putting him to sleep. She took a wide-eyed Eric into her arms and stepped away from the wreck, teleporting away. When the woman materialized at her destination, she staggered forward, and her vision blurred. She fought to keep herself conscious but barely managed. The woman walked with Eric to the doorstep of an orphanage, gripping the rails as she tried to make her way up the steps. When she reached the door with a copper sign that read 'Robin Street Orphanage,' she set Eric down on the steps with a cloth wrapped around him. She gripped the cloth, and her brown eyes became white and foggy like Neil's had been. She whispered a story, then let go. He watched her with large confused eyes. She smiled, then rang the doorbell and vanished, leaving Eric alone.

A young woman answered the door, at first confused by the silence on the other side. Eric's cooing brought her attention to the floor where he lay. Panic and shock crossed her face at the sight of the baby abandoned on her doorstep.

"Oh God," she whispered, kneeling down and taking him into her arms, but the moment she had him she went into a trance, her eyes turning foggy. When the spell wore off and her hazel eyes were clear again, she smiled and closed the door, ready to put the child she was convinced had been in her care for hours to bed.

The woman in the mask appeared near her original location and began to run as fast as she could. She made it four blocks, but when she turned a corner, she was knocked backward by what could only have been magic. The gust sent her airborne until she landed flat on her back on the damp concrete, knocking the wind out of her. Her bones ached from the impact. A few yards ahead, a man walked toward her quickly with a scowl on his face. It was the man who wanted Eric.

This man was Neil's enemy, Malphilus.

Despite the mask that covered his face, she could see his anger. She quickly picked herself off the ground, readying herself for his wrath.

"WHERE IS HE?!" yelled the English man as he reached her, waving his hand so her head jerked to the side and her mask was torn from her face, landing on the damp road.

"Where have you taken him?!" he asked furiously, now standing just inches from her.

"Away from you," she said in spite. Malphilus was seething with rage. He lifted her from the ground in a choke hold without touching her. She reached for her throat instinctively, although she knew there was nothing she could do in her weakened state. "I...don't have...any regrets about what I did..." she whispered.

"Good," he replied. Malphilus let her drop down and turned away. "I shall not have regrets either," he said. Malphilus left her on the ground, and out of the shadows came the man who had murdered Leanna. The man smiled and walked toward the woman with his wings spread wide, his footsteps burning the ground beneath him. The fire within him spread quickly through his body, and he knelt and thrust his arm through her chest, killing her the same way he had killed Leanna. The woman's breath hitched in her throat, and she fell to the ground, her body shaking. In seconds the life faded from her eyes, and her body stilled. Just like Leanna, her soul left her body as a pale blue ribbon of smoke. Malphilus turned to watch the soul ascend to heaven. His head pounded, but he did not move, still staring up at the soul. For just a moment, he looked pained.

"No," he whispered in shock. Then he gripped his head, and his expression

hardened once again. He turned to his men standing nearby, ready for orders, and gestured to the soul.

"You see that?!" he yelled. "That is proof of betrayal! If any of you choose to follow in her steps, I guarantee you will suffer the same fate." He walked to the man with wings, who quickly gripped Malphilus' shoulder and teleported them both away.

Meanwhile, Neil came to, his head aching from the blood that had rushed to his head. When he remembered what happened, he scrambled to drag himself out of the car. When he was out, he took a moment to catch his breath. He looked around, panicked that his grandson was not there. Then, in his panicked state, he caught sight of something at the corner of his eye. Neil froze, turning his head slowly, afraid to look. When he turned his head toward the sky, he was overcome with despair as he saw the pure soul rising to Heaven. He stared at the soul in denial and brought himself to his feet. His head pounded. At first, his senses were clouded, and then he was there, watching the soul rise. He was looking through the eyes of Malphilus, his eyes locked on the soul as he watched through the body of Malphilus. His features shifted from anger to heartbreak as he watched what he thought could only be Eric's soul joining his mother's.

"No…" he whispered in shock. Then, just as quickly, he returned to his own body. Neil sat on the road, his face twisting with suppressed emotions. His breathing quickened, and he turned and hit the car in anger with his fists, his screams echoing in the night, unshed tears rimming his eyes. He forced himself to calm down and took a few deep breaths, then turned to look at the driver and Theo, who still lay upside down in the car.

He did the only thing he could: bring the others to safety. Neil picked himself off the ground and raised his arms, bringing the car with them. He slowly turned it back onto its wheels and carefully moved the unconscious sorcerer to the passenger seat. Then he climbed in behind the wheel and gripped it tightly, applying pressure on the gas pedal and never turning back to look at the soul as the tears fell down his cheeks.

CHAPTER 2
The Light in the Darkness

Eric watched a man he did not recognize reach for him while a woman he did not know stared at him in dread. When he opened his eyes, they were gone. Although their physical forms were no longer in front of him, he found himself looking up at the drawings of those same people. The detailed pictures were pinned to the roof of his bottom bunk. Although he did not know these people, he had dreamt of their faces every night for the past year. So, when the dreams became clear enough to remember, he had drawn them and pinned them above him as a reminder.

Thirteen years had passed, and he had grown to look like the mother he never knew, inheriting her chocolate brown hair and artistic talents. Since he had never shown the drawings to another soul, no one had the chance to notice the resemblance, and he was oblivious to it himself. He only wondered who the sorrowful woman was and why she was in his dreams.

He looked at the time and then let out a heavy sigh: it was time to get up and go into the world he dreaded living in. Eric reluctantly dragged himself from his bed and lazily dressed in the first thing he could grab from his dresser. His routine always began slowly, and he tried to wait as long as possible before walking down the steps to the orphanage cafeteria for breakfast.

Each day was nearly the same. He walked down the steps and was greeted happily by Yvette, the woman in charge. The other children became weary and silent because they all thought he was strange, so they kept their distance. He knew he was different. Somehow, he had always known and eventually came to terms with it. When he was younger, strange things would happen to the things he touched. Objects would suddenly fly across the room at the times when he was angry, and at times when he was happy, he would notice a light on his palms. Sometimes, he wished he could

comfort the children who would arrive, sad or angry, to be separated from their parents, and suddenly a warmth would surround them. He came to realize that he was making these impossible things happen, but no one else knew.

After he discovered what he was, he became afraid of how others would react if they knew or how they would suffer if he lost control. So, he secluded himself to keep both himself and those around him safe.

Although it was impossible not to notice the shift in atmosphere as he entered a room, what he dreaded most was not breakfast, but boarding the bus to school every morning. Each day, Eric took the public bus to his school after deciding it was less painful than the school bus. The moment he stepped onto the vehicle he was faced with the judgmental stares of his neighbors. They all knew who he was because either their own children had told them about him, or they had seen him around enough to know he was strange. They whispered to each other when they saw him, gossiping about what their children had said or what his teachers had mentioned to them. They commented on his strange behavior, like how he spent every day after school at the park and just sat there rather than spending time with the others his age.

Normally, the whispers were noticed but unheard, but for Eric, it was as if their whispers were being spoken directly into his very ears. He could not stop himself from hearing every word. No matter how hard he tried to ignore them, his attempts only made their words louder to his ears. This made the half hour he was forced to spend on the bus torturous and seemingly never-ending, but walking was not an option because Yvette would worry, and he did not like it when she worried. This is why he would spend his leisure time at the local park staring up at the sky. There was no one there to listen to, only the sound of birds chirping and leaves rustling.

When he arrived at school that morning, he began his routine day, attending his classes and complying with the rules so the teachers would have no reason to bother him. He always kept to himself. Every so often, someone would try to include him or anger him, but Eric did not care for whatever insults they would throw, and he had no interest in making friends.

When his fourth-period class ended, he walked to the cafeteria to purchase

his lunch. He took his paper plate of food to leave, but today someone interfered. The girl who sat next to him in his previous class approached him. Unlike many of the other students in his classes, she was quiet and conservative, barely speaking a word, only talking to her small circle of friends. This girl, Patty, walked to him with her plate in hand, her long brown hair covering her cheek.

"Hey, Eric," she said shyly. Her pale cheeks were suddenly flushed with color.

"Hey," he replied.

"Did you start your book report yet?" she asked quickly, as if afraid of the silence.

"Not yet," he said. "I'm probably going to start after school."

"So-umm…. You should come sit with us," she said nervously. "It's just me, Iris, and Tommy, so there's a lot of room." Patty waited nervously for his reply.

"I think I'm going to have to say no. Sorry."

Her smile quickly faded away. "Sorry, I was just-" Eric could see the regret across her features.

"No, no, it's okay. It's not because of you. I just… I just think it's better if I'm alone."

"Oh," she said in surprise. "Well, if you ever change your mind, we hang out at the pizza place down the street after school, so…yeah," she smiled, then left to join her friends. Unfazed by the encounter, Eric walked to the quad and sat at one of the concrete benches to eat alone as usual.

After a long day at school, he walked straight to the park to his usual spot under the trees, ready to relax. He lay back with his arms spread to the sides and closed his eyes so he could escape into his own mind. Every time he closed his eyes, he saw them again, the ones from his dream both staring at him. The cool breeze and the smell of the damp grass were so soothing to him that, before he knew it, he had dozed off.

When he woke up, it was dark. He sighed when he realized he would most likely return to a worried Yvette, ready to scold him for staying out so late. This was not the first time he would return late, so he knew she was most likely sitting on the

steps awaiting his arrival. He shifted, preparing to stand up when he was startled by a noise in the darkness.

He slowly sat up and peeked over the bushes to see what it was. A few yards away, a man was gripping a teenage girl tightly by the wrist and dragging her across the field as she struggled to free herself.

Eric watched as she begged him to let her go, but he ignored her pleas. The man was angry, yelling at the girl to stay quiet, but when she continued to cry, he raised his arm. Before he could swing it her way, he was struck with agonizing pain. Eric gripped his arm to stop the man from hitting the girl, sending surging pain through the man's body. When he released her, the girl stepped back in shock as the man screamed.

Panicked by what she was seeing, she ran into the small patch of trees. At the same time, Eric stepped away from the man, releasing him. The man looked down at the wound on his arm, his face twisting in agony.

"What did you do to me, you freak?" he yelled. By the time the man turned around, the girl was long gone, and this angered him.

The young girl ran through the trees in fear, occasionally looking back to see if she was being followed. One of the times she looked back, she lost her footing and slowed to a stop before she could fall, steadying herself. When she looked ahead again, Neil was standing before her, startling her. Before she could react, he placed his hand on her face and performed the memory enchantment.

"It seems you have lost your way," he said. "It's time to return home." When he removed his hand, the girl walked past him as if she did not see him and made her way home with the enchantment still in effect. A man in a white coat stood behind Neil, his auburn hair peeking out from beneath it. He waited for a command.

"Follow her. Make sure she arrives home safely," Neil said.

"As you wish," the man said before leaving to follow the girl.

Meanwhile, Eric stood with the man, who was seething with rage. The man pulled his pocket knife out, opening it and aiming it at Eric. Eric stumbled back to avoid the weapon, waving his hand forward to unarm the man. The man's hand jerked

as his knife slipped from between his fingers, and he looked down at his empty hand in shock. Pushing his surprise aside, he turned his attention back to Eric, grabbing him by the collar with one hand and putting his other on Eric's arm, raising him from the ground.

Then Neil arrived, forcing himself between Eric and the dangerous man. He pressed his palm to the man's face, knocking him unconscious with another spell. Eric fell back, and so did the man. When Eric hit the damp grass, he looked up at Neil in shock. This was the first time he had seen another person capable of doing the extraordinary things he could.

"Are you alright?" Neil asked.

"I'm fine-" he answered, stopping when he paid closer attention to Neil and realized it was him. The man he had seen in his dreams was standing in front of him. Eric stared in shock, wondering if he was real or if he hadn't really awakened and was still dreaming.

"Are you injured?" Neil asked. He stretched his hand out to Eric to help him up, but Eric crawled backward and stood up by himself.

"You're-" Eric moved as if trying to shake an illusion out of his head. "You're not-" He could not get the words out; he could not believe that the man from his dreams could be standing in front of him. The man with the coat appeared next to them, making Eric jump back in surprise. He eyed Eric curiously, a spark of recognition before he returned his attention to Neil. He let Neil know that the girl had returned home safely. When Neil turned his back to listen, Eric took his chance to run. He made it home, his sore legs barely holding him up. When he arrived, thankful Yvette was not there, he went straight to his room and shut himself inside, throwing himself to the ground. He was frightened but did not want to admit it, not even to himself, as he tried to stop his trembling.

He jumped onto his bed so he could stare at the drawings he had pinned, and sure enough, it was the same man he had just met looking down at him

That night, Eric could not sleep. He spent the night staring at his drawings instead, trying to make sense of what had just happened. There was no way for him to

explain it.

The next morning, Eric was out of bed at dawn, surprised he managed to get up at all. He got dressed quickly and ran downstairs to the front entrance, but just as he was about to open the front door to leave, he was startled by a presence.

"Where do you think you're going?" asked Yvette. Yvette was the closest thing Eric had ever had to a family. She had never treated him differently, and she was the reason he still had his sanity, the reason he could carry on with his "normal" life. Eric froze with his hand over the knob and slowly turned to face her. She was standing by the steps, still dressed in her pajamas with a blanket wrapped around her shoulders. Her pitch-black hair was down, brushing against her cheeks.

"I was just going for a walk."

"At seven in the morning?" asked Yvette, raising her eyebrows.

Eric stayed quiet, afraid he would get himself in trouble no matter what he said. Yvette rubbed her dark eyes to keep herself awake.

"Do you have money with you?" she asked with a sigh. Eric nodded. "Wait here," she ordered. She disappeared into the kitchen, returned with a brown paper bag, and handed it to Eric. "Lunch. Don't stay out too long."

When he left, he did not know where he was going. All he knew was that he needed to clear his head. Dreams are meant to be nothing more than dreams, but if the man he saw was real, what did his dreams mean? Eric wondered if he saw the future or maybe just theirs.

Before he knew it, he found himself by the park again in the same place where he had been the night before. He could not focus as he repeated the memory of what had occurred there in his head again and again, specifically the moment when the man from his dream rendered the attacker unconscious with one swift movement of his hand.

Before he could reach a conclusion, he was distracted by the sound of people arguing nearby. At first, the voices were unfamiliar, but then one quieter than the others spoke. Eric recognized it.

"Just leave us alone," the girl said. Eric looked over in the distance and saw

Patty, Iris, and Tommy with two guys from their school who appeared to be targeting Tommy. He considered ignoring the situation, but when Patty tried to intervene, and one of the guys shoved her back, nearly knocking her down, going after Tommy next, Eric had enough. He rushed to where they were, just as the bully shoved Tommy again. He knocked Tommy to the ground, but when he moved to hit him, Eric grabbed the bully's arm to stop him. The bully quickly turned in an attempt to shake off Eric and punched him in the face. Eric stumbled back and brought his hand to his face, feeling the sting of the hit.

The bully was surprised to see Eric. "The freak actually came outside," he said, laughing. Eric recognized him. It was Jordan, a guy at their school who was always getting into trouble with the APs for backtalk.

"You really have nothing better to do?" asked Eric angrily.

"Mind your own business," Jordan responded.

"Says the guy who's picking a fight. Just go home, Jordan. Or go to the arcade or something."

Jordan was angry, his fist clenching at his side. He turned and punched Eric in the stomach, but when his fist connected, he was sent flying back by a surge of power originating from Eric. Jordan and his friends landed on their backs. When the shock wore off, they slowly got up in pain. They each turned to Eric with wide eyes, but they saw how calm he was. They realized it was him and stared at him. Their eyes narrowed.

"I knew you were a freak," Jordan said before running off with his friends. Eric watched them run, expressionless. He knew the truth would come out someday. When he turned, Tommy was still on the ground staring up at him in shock.

"You okay?" asked Eric, but Tommy did not answer. Eric sighed. When he saw even Patty staring at him in fear, he walked away without speaking. He continued to walk, paying no attention to where he was going until he was alone. When he slowed his steps, he felt the pain in his stomach and the throbbing of his face and stopped to take a breath.

"Does this happen often?" asked a voice, startling Eric. He turned and saw

Neil standing a few feet behind him with the man in the white coat.

"Are you stalking me?" asked Eric.

"It's difficult to ignore a fellow sorcerer. Especially one so young… Although I admit we have been trying to track you for quite a while, assuming you caused all the disturbances."

"Sorcerer… Is that what you call it?" Eric smiled, letting the air escape from his nose.

"We have to call ourselves something since we are not quite as human as others," said Neil.

Eric walked to a nearby bench and took a seat while Neil turned to the coated man.

"Do you mind helping our friend with his injury?"

The man nodded and approached Eric, making him stiffen. When the man with the coat reached for him, Eric backed away slightly.

The man in the coat raised his hands to show he meant no harm. "I just want to help. My name's Aaron, and you are?" he asked, holding out his hand for Eric to shake, which Eric took.

"Eric," he replied. When he spoke his name, Aaron stiffened and he saw Neil's eyes flicker in what he could only assume was sorrow before reverting back to his calm expression. Aaron continued to stare at Eric, holding onto his hand.

"Aaron," Neil called, snapping him from his thoughts. Aaron released Eric's hand and then reached toward Eric's stomach, hesitating.

"May I?" he asked, his eyes still on Eric. Eric stayed still, not turning away as the man pressed his hand to Eric's stomach. He felt a strange warmth. Suddenly the pain was gone, and Aaron backed away.

"How did you do that?" Eric asked, his relief evident.

"I'm an angel," Aaron answered.

"You will have to let the exterior damage heal naturally, but the pain will not return."

"Angels," Eric repeated in disbelief.

"If sorcerers are where you wish to draw the line, then by all means," Neil replied.

"True… I've just never met anyone else like me before you."

"Are your parents not like us?" he asked in surprise.

"I'm an orphan," Eric answered.

"I'm sorry," Neil said. "I believed there were none left unaware of us, but perhaps I missed whoever your parents were… A few groups of our kind choose to live on Earth, but most of our kind reside in a safe haven. A separate world."

"A secret world?"

"Precisely. Would you like to go there?"

The sudden invitation caught Eric off guard. He considered the idea of leaving his town.

"I understand if you need more time to reach a decision. After all, this is-"

"I'll go," Eric answered without hesitation.

Neil was surprised. "If you need a few days to consider your decision thoroughly, the offer will remain."

"No. I want to go," he insisted.

"Are you certain?"

"It's not like I'm leaving anything behind," he answered.

Neil nodded slowly. "I will make the arrangements. Where do you reside?" he asked.

"The orphanage on Robin Street. Do you know where it is?" he asked.

"I can manage."

Eric walked away from them, and Neil let him, moving to speak to Aaron when he remembered something. He called out to Eric.

"I forgot to mention. My name is Cornelius Alewar, but you may call me Neil. What is your full name?"

Eric looked over his shoulder but continued to walk. "Eric Blackwood," he said before returning his attention to the path.

At the sound of his last name, Neil felt his stomach sink and his throat close

up. His body went cold, and he was unable to process what he had just heard. Aaron knew the name as well as he did.

"Do you think-"

"No, no," Neil said in a low voice, shaking his head. "It's a coincidence. It must be."

"He's the same age as he would be."

"I know, I know…" Neil said, closing his eyes and rubbing his head. "I thought he looked like her," he said quietly.

Unaware of the gravity of his name, Eric ran home to the orphanage feeling light as air, stopping on the way to let it all sink in. When he arrived an hour later, he was surprised to see Yvette sitting by the entrance waiting for him. When Eric stepped through the front door, Yvette stood and smiled at him gently.

"That man you met with? Neil? I got a call saying the adoption paperwork went through. He's waiting for you in your room."

Eric was confused but not surprised. He knew that Neil must have done something to create the illusion that all the necessary formalities had been completed; he was just unsure how. Eric walked to the top of the steps. When he reached his bedroom, he found Neil lying in his bed, staring at his drawings. Neil seemed distant as he studied the drawings, his hand tracing one of Leanna. Eric observed him, confused by the expression he wore. Neil seemed saddened but not shocked as he expected him to be seeing his face pinned to the bunk.

When Eric entered the room, Neil seemed to feel his presence and turned to look at him.

"Where did you get these?" he asked.

"I drew them," Eric answered. Neil rose from the bed, holding the drawing of the woman, who Eric still did not know was Leanna. Eric continued. "I started having these dreams of you and her. I couldn't remember most of them, but they started getting clearer, so I drew them."

"What were the dreams of?" asked Neil, still staring at the drawing of Leanna.

"Not much. You're both just… staring at me. I can never hear you guys."

Eric could see how focused Neil was on the drawing. "Who was she?" he asked. Neil reacted to Eric's question as if he had just awakened from a dream.

"She was my daughter…" he answered quietly. Eric stared up in confusion: the man looked too young to be the father of the woman in the picture. Neil continued, looking up at Eric. "Her name was Leanna… Blackwood."

Eric was not sure how to react. "Blackwood?"

Neil nodded slowly. "Assuming you are who you claim you are, which I have no reason to doubt… she was your mother."

Eric had noticed the sad tone each time Neil had said the word was. "…was?" he repeated.

"Her life was taken from her years ago…" he said. "On that same night, you were stolen from us." Neil could no longer look Eric in the eye as he spoke. "You were just an infant… We were sure you were dead."

Eric looked at the woman in the drawing more closely, shocked he had been dreaming of his own mother.

"They said my parents died in a car accident."

Neil shook his head. "Then they were given false information. Clearly, you were meant to be hidden from us." Neil set the drawing back on the bed. "I'm sorry, I think this is all too much for both of us." He stood, fixing himself. "Let's pack your belongings. We can figure this out once you're settled in. The others will wish to see you."

Neil helped Eric pack the few things he had into a suitcase and took it, carrying it down the stairs with Eric following close behind. When they reached the bottom of the steps, Yvette was waiting for them.

"Thank you for everything," Neil said to her, shaking her hand. "I'll wait outside," he said to Eric before leaving.

Yvette smiled at Eric. He could see she was emotional. She pulled him into an embrace. "Don't forget about me, okay? You spent thirteen years here. I'm basically your mother, so make sure you come and visit every once in a while." She stepped back, and he saw her ivory skin flushed with color.

Eric walked out the door, turning to wave goodbye. As promised, Neil was outside with the luggage in hand.

"Ready?" Neil asked.

Eric nodded. "Yeah…" he said nervously.

Neil headed down the street with Eric following close behind. They walked only a few blocks side-by-side with Aaron until they reached a place without people. Aaron walked in front of them and turned to face Eric and Neil, placing a hand on each of their shoulders. When he touched them, Eric felt disoriented for a moment but quickly regained his senses, realizing that the scenery around them had changed. What was originally an alley was suddenly a different street in front of an old house. Eric looked around, confused by the change, unsure of what had just happened or what he was feeling.

Neil looked at him and smiled. "It takes some getting used to. Excuse us for one moment," he said, pulling Aaron to the side. He lowered his voice, but Eric could still hear them.

"When you arrive, do not tell a soul about today. Not even Evangeline." Eric wondered who Evangeline could be, but he saw by the look on Aaron's face that she was someone not to meddle with.

"You know I can't lie to her."

"Only for today. I only wish for him to have a chance to settle in before he's bombarded."

Aaron sighed, stressed by the request. "She'll see right through me."

"Then avoid her, go for a stroll, or perhaps a surprise inspection."

"Only for today," Aaron said with a sigh.

Neil smirked. "Thank you."

Aaron nodded and took a few steps back before disappearing.

"Where did he go?" asked Eric.

"Angels were blessed with the power of teleportation. They were given wings not to take them through the skies but to let them travel more quickly than humans. It's simple for them to take another across the world, but traveling through dimensions

with a passenger is quite taxing."

"What?" is all Eric had to say. With every question that was answered only came more questions. He had witnessed an angel teleport, but now all he could wonder was what wings Neil was referring to when he saw none on Aaron's back. He did not even dare ask what Neil meant by crossing dimensions.

Neil could see the confusion on Eric's face. "You have much to learn, but give it time."

Neil entered the abandoned house and walked straight to the basement, making sure Eric followed. When they reached the bottom of the stairs, he stopped in front of a solid wall and reached for Eric's hand. "The portal won't recognize you. You won't be able to pass through unless I take you with me." Eric grabbed onto Neil's arm and nervously followed Neil as he walked slowly through the solid wall as if it was not even there. On the other side of the wall was a small windowless and doorless room with white walls. Neil turned to face Eric, still holding onto his arm.

"Do not let go of me and, no matter what, stay calm. We'll be there soon," said Neil. At first, Eric was confused, waiting for something to happen. Then suddenly, something flowed toward them from every corner of the room. The substance materializing from the solid walls resembled a silk sheet, a metallic silver. When it reached them, it began to wrap around them. Eric tried to stay calm, but it was difficult when the substance swallowed them whole. Eventually it covered them and Eric saw nothing but darkness.

CHAPTER 3
Luxwick

The darkness made Eric nervous, but luckily it was only seconds before it released them and returned to its place in the walls. At first, Eric believed he was in the same room as he had been in before. Then he noticed small changes: the walls were now slightly blue and glossy; there was a closed door to his right that was not there before. The small room was sleek, but the trim moldings were antique a geometric hand-carved design. Neil released Eric's arm and walked over to the door, placing his hand on the gold handle but not turning it. He looked back at Eric.

"Ready?" he asked.

"Not really," Eric answered, still unmoving.

Neil gestured for Eric to come closer with the hand that still gripped his luggage. "Do not be afraid. We won't be doing anything today other than getting you settled. I do not wish to overwhelm you."

Eric nodded nervously. He joined Neil at the door and waited for him to open it.

"Welcome to Luxwick," said Neil, and then he opened the door. Eric followed Neil out and found himself at the center of a beautiful Victorian-style town. They were standing on the rooftop of a small building staring out at a crowded town where people were filling the streets. The sky was different from the one on Earth, no longer blue but lavender. The clouds were a beautiful golden champagne color, misty in appearance.

"What is this place?" asked Eric, mesmerized by the beauty.

"It is a safe haven that was created for sorcerers. It stands separate from Earth, in its dimension."

Eric followed Neil down a set of stairs leading in the opposite direction of the

town. Separating the portal from the town was a tall black metal fence. Just on the other side of it was a smaller, closed-off portion of the town. Houses and apartments were lined up along the left side, while on the right, a large and very wide building took up most of the space. At the furthest end of this space was a beautiful Victorian building with an octagonal tower and a balcony with a gazebo roof. The building was mostly white with pale blue trim and intricate details, highlighting its craftsmanship. For example, even from where he was standing, Eric could see the wood-carved angel wings just above the main entrance, painted a pale blue.

There were people all around him. Some were dressed in casual attire, the same style as on Earth, while others wore suits similar to the ones business people wore on Earth, but their jackets were longer and kept open. It was clear Earth still had an influence on this world, but its Victorian roots remained, however subtly. A majority of the people who walked throughout the area wore the same white-hooded coat as Aaron did. The women wore loose coats, longer at the back with three points, one on either side and one on the back. Blue embroidery lined the edges of the sleeves as well as the bottom trims of the coats. The men also wore the coats, but theirs were slightly shorter and even in length all around. The curious thing was that they all seemed to be dressed in seemingly modern clothing, with clear influences from various time periods, such as rounded collars, thin striped patterns, and palazzo pants.

Neil walked Eric to one of the two-story homes along the left side and unlocked the door to let him in. He found himself in the living room after stepping through the door. The walls were painted beige, and the floors were covered in white tile that resembled wood. The room was furnished with dark mahogany furniture, which was well kept but had not been replaced since the 1920s. Eric stared at the ornaments, especially those with only decorative purposes, like the candlesticks on the walls despite the overhead lighting. Eric noticed the lack of personal touches like photographs. It made the room feel like a museum rather than a home.

"Would you like anything to drink?" Neil asked.

"Just water, please," Eric replied.

Neil left him, stepping through the first door on the left side of the room,

which Eric assumed led to the kitchen, and returned with two glasses of water. He handed Eric one and then took a seat on the couch, where Eric joined him.

"I'm sure you have questions," said Neil. "Ask me anything you'd like, and I will answer as best as I can."

Eric thought about what he would like to ask first.

"I wanna' know more about you. You said you raised my mom, but you don't look old enough," he said.

Neil nodded and took a deep breath before he answered.

"My full name is Cornelius Henry Alewar. I was born and raised in a small town near London, England, in 1835. Although I am not your biological grandfather, I am one-hundred-and-eighty years old. I ceased aging when I was thirty-five."

"You're immortal?" Eric asked in disbelief and was answered with a nod.

"I cannot die. There have been attempts, but none were able to take my life from me."

"Is everyone like you? The sorcerers, I mean."

"Not quite. There is one other like me. We have shared a link since birth. Even the angels were puzzled by my existence when we first met."

Eric somewhat grasped the situation, but there were questions that lingered in his mind. Before today, he was the only proof that he knew that the impossible existed. He had no trouble accepting that there were things bigger than him, more impossible to him. It actually brought him comfort.

Neil placed his glass on the coffee table, straightened his back, and looked down at his hands, barely making eye contact with Eric. "Your mother… her parents, her birth parents, were killed when she was very young. I took her in and raised her as my own from the age of six." After Neil's explanation, the mood became sullen. He continued to look down at his hands. It was clear that, although thirteen years had passed since her death, he still struggled to think of her without brooding on what he had lost. "She… she was a wonderful person. When she had you, all she wanted was for you to live normally, but normalcy seemed impossible to her under my roof. Because of me, she knew of every minor disturbance, each attempt Mal-," Neil cut

himself off, keeping the name from Eric. He shook his head. "Each moment I looked over my shoulder, she seemed to look with me. She wished to raise you away from it all." Neil took a deep breath to keep himself composed. "We believed… it would be safe, that she would be hidden, but we were wrong, and she was taken from us."

"And my dad?" Eric asked in a low voice.

"Your father…" Neil shook his head in disapproval. "He was a very troubled young man. We were forced to exile him to Earth shortly before you were born. We had hoped that if he lived amongst humans, he would learn from his mistakes. Unfortunately, he lost his life soon after. The report stated he was trespassing… There are people in this world who are unable to put aside their bad habits. Unfortunately, he was one of them."

Eric gripped his glass tightly in his hands, alerting Neil to his tension.

"I think that's enough for today," Neil said, standing from the couch. "Let's go upstairs and get you settled in your room."

Eric stood and followed Neil upstairs. When they reached the second floor, they entered an open room with a seating area in the center. There were two doors on each side of the room. At the back was a tall dresser with photos and candles on it, making up an altar. Neil walked to it slowly with Eric next to him.

When Eric was close, he examined the altar. The dresser was a dark mahogany, matching the furniture downstairs. A white lace table runner covered its surface. The photo on the far left was of Leanna and a boy as teenagers. Next to it was a photo of her taken while she was pregnant, lying on the couch on her side with her hand on her large stomach, a blue teddy bear against it. At the very center of the altar was a photo of her holding a newborn baby Eric. She was staring at the camera with joy, her cheeks flushed, and her hair damp with sweat at her roots. Candles of different heights filled the empty spaces.

Neil walked past the altar and gripped the door handle. He stiffened, hesitant as he looked down at his hand on the knob. Finally, he opened it and flipped the switch.

The room had a full-size bed with a light blue comforter with a butterfly pattern along the edges. There was a white desk next to it with a small lamp and a

closet on the far left of the room. The walls were beige and practically barren, only a poster of an impressionist painting above the bed. Neil set Eric's luggage by the door.

"This was your mother's room," Neil explained. "Now it will be yours."

For Eric, seeing the remnants of his mother left a strange impression. It was clear to him the emotions and the memories they signified for Neil, but to Eric, they were the objects and photographs of a stranger.

"The bathroom is just next door, and I am directly across the room if you need anything," Neil said, still standing in the doorway.

"Thank you," Eric answered without facing him.

Neil nodded and headed for his room. When he was halfway across the room, he suddenly stopped with his eyes focused on the ground, deep in thought. He turned to Eric.

"Eric," Neil called out, hesitant. "We should have searched for you... I... should have searched for you." Neil's guilt was clear. He avoided eye contact at first, but when he looked up, Eric could see the sadness and guilt in his eyes. Eric did not know what to say, taken aback by the hurt Neil carried. From the little he was told about that day, it seemed it was not Neil's fault. Eric said the only thing that came to mind. "You didn't know..."

Neil stared at Eric for a moment until Eric ended the encounter. "Goodnight," he told Neil, shutting the door and leaving Neil alone.

Eric spent the remainder of the afternoon wandering the room, taking note of each remnant of his mother. When he opened the desk drawer, he found it filled with colored pencils, some used while others were untouched. Although the closet was mostly barren, he found the tattered sketchbooks his mother must have used. It did not take long for Eric to unpack his belongings, the items doing nothing to change the room. If it were not for his own sketchbook on the desk surface, there would be no impression he was ever there.

When night came, he fell asleep right away. He could tell it would take no time to adapt to his new surroundings. That night, he had another dream of a face he had not remembered before, one of a young woman with a braid and a mask covering

her face. She stared at him from the ground, then her head jerked to the side, and her mask flew off, but he did not have the chance to see her face before he woke. Eric quickly tossed the covers aside, unwilling to spare even a second before the dream could fade. He pulled the colored pencils from the desk drawer and opened his sketchbook, hoping to finish the drawing before he could forget her. By the time he finished, two hours had passed, and it was half past two in the morning. He did not have the energy to put himself back in bed, resting his head on the desk's surface instead.

That morning, Neil woke just before seven. Thirty minutes later, he was dressed, cleaned up, and ready to start the day. He walked to Eric's room, barely opening the door to check on him. When he noticed him asleep at his desk, he entered the room quietly and approached him, making sure not to disturb him. He reached for the blanket on the bed and was about to drape it over Eric, but when he saw the drawing under Eric's hand, he hesitated. He could see the braid and the mask peeking out from the sides of Eric's hand. It was the woman who had taken Eric thirteen years before. Eric stirred and slowly came to, rubbing his eyes.

"I'm sorry, I didn't intend to wake you," Neil said, still staring at the drawing.

"What time is it?" Eric asked, letting out a big yawn.

"It's just past seven… Did you draw this?" asked Neil. Eric looked down and moved his arm away from it, remembering waking up in the middle of the night.

"Yeah, I had another dream," Eric answered. "Why?"

Neil reached for the drawing, sliding it closer to him. He stared at it, his thumb brushing the one-inch scar at the corner of her mouth.

"What's wrong?" Eric asked, noticing his fixation.

Neil shook his head. "It's just… This is the woman who took you from us, but… I know her." Neil struggled to process the new information. "She served…" Neil cut himself off, once again stopping himself from saying a name Eric had not yet heard. "She was against us, but I don't understand why she would take you only to hide you."

Neil stared at her eyes, analyzing her expression, but he only saw determination, which confused him further.

"Maybe she knew something you didn't," he said.

Neil thought about it and then removed his hand from the drawing. "Perhaps," he said quietly. Neil backed up and then took a deep breath, hoping to shake the thought which had just entered his mind. "Alright. Get dressed. We have a long day ahead of us. Come downstairs when you're ready. I'll start breakfast."

Neil left Eric alone in his room. Eric stared at the drawing, then slipped it into one of the desk drawers with the rest of them.

After breakfast, Neil walked with Eric to the tower building. When they entered through the double doors, which were propped open, the room was buzzing as people rushed in different directions, all focused on their tasks. Eric looked up at the high ceilings and the beautiful pillars along the walls, then down at the floor. The ground was covered in white ceramic tile flooring with gray marble-like details. At the center of the room was an open space with no furniture, just an emblem.

Eric realized it was the same emblem embroidered onto the back center of the coats, which nearly every person in the room was wearing. The room was elegant, its furniture matching the outside in light colors, making the space appear brighter.

Eric watched Neil approach, someone, telling them something. Then Neil took Eric deeper into the building, straight to an elevator, and pressed the button for the fifteenth floor. When they reached their floor, directly across from the elevator was a set of mahogany double doors. Neil opened them, revealing that they were on the balcony floor.

Directly at the center of the room was a large round table that seated ten people. Behind the table were two sets of small steps on either side, leading to a ledge three feet higher and surrounding the lower level. Rails along the ledge separated the

two levels. The second-level walls were lined with bookcases and on the far side of the room was an arched open entryway that led to the balcony. The balcony rails were the same smooth metal as the ones in the room. The room was octagonal like the tower, but the balcony that stuck out was half an octagon.

"What is this building for?" Eric asked.

"This is the base for the angels assigned to watch over Earth. This is our conference room, where we discuss classified information. The balcony overlooks the headquarters."

Eric walked past the table and headed up the steps, straight to the balcony. The view was breathtaking. He could see everything Neil had described and even more beyond the headquarters fence. People walked amongst each other, and the gold-and-violet sky above them was even more beautiful in the morning. Neil stayed on the lower level by the entrance. Eric was so relaxed by the view and fresh air that he was startled when the double doors opened behind him.

Two people burst into the room. One was the angel Eric had met the day before, Aaron, and the other was a woman. Just like him, she had auburn hair and hazel eyes and wore a white coat. She looked to be the same age as Aaron, her late twenties. The woman walked straight to Neil, anxious and expectant, nearly crashing into him, while Aaron followed close behind, more relaxed. Neil stopped her, gently grabbing her by the shoulders.

"Is it true? Is he here?" she asked anxiously. Neil smiled at her.

"He's been alive this entire time," he said quietly. The woman smiled in joy and relief, then looked past Neil's shoulder, seeing Eric standing by the rails, watching them. She looked back at Neil.

"Is that him?" she asked. When Neil nodded, she rushed past him and up the steps, stopping just inches from Eric. She seemed taken aback at the sight of him. Neil and Aaron were close behind her. She stared at Eric, who was stiff and nervous.

"You look like your mother," she said.

Neil walked to Eric and put a hand on his shoulder to relax him.

"Eric, this is Evangeline. She is Aaron's sister." When Neil spoke the words,

something flickered in Evangeline's eyes. She looked to her brother, who avoided her eyes, then returned her attention to Eric, clearly noticing the lack of an introduction to Aaron. Eric knew then they had been referring to her. Neil continued. "They are both angels, and they were close to your mother."

"It's nice to meet you," Eric said.

"Likewise," Evangeline said.

Seeing the coat again made Eric wonder. Aaron noticed the question in Eric's eyes. "What do you want to know?" he asked. His question caught Eric off guard.

"Oh- I was just wondering about the coats," Eric said nervously.

Evangeline smiled. "We've always used enchanted clothing to make us look human when we go out. The coats were an upgrade at one point." She looked at Aaron, nodded, and then the two removed their coats. Their wings slowly materialized from their backs, and Eric was mesmerized. Instead of having soft white feathers, they appeared thin and delicate, a soft blue color. It was as if they were a projection of light, creating an illusion of feathers that resembled intricate ice crystals layered over each other in the shape of a bat wing.

"Wow…" said Eric. Evangeline and Aaron put their coats back on, making the wings disappear. "And the logo?" he asked.

Neil answered. "It is a sign of allegiance. It is the emblem an old friend, and I designed when we first settled here in the early 1900s. Two C's next to each other, surrounding a blue gem."

"What do the letters stand for?"

"For our names. Cornelius and Carlisle."

"Who's Carlisle?" Eric asked, regretting it almost immediately. He could tell Carlisle was a sore subject.

Neil swallowed, considering his answer. "He died a very long time ago," he said.

Evangeline stared at Eric as if she feared he would disappear if she looked away. Then she remembered something and turned to Neil. "Does Theodore know yet?" she asked. Eric silently wondered who Theodore was.

Neil's expression went blank, as if he had forgotten about Theo until that moment. "I suppose now is the time to inform him…"

"Does he-" her eyes darted to Eric before returning to Neil. "Have you told him? About Theo, I mean."

Neil shook his head. "I will tell him on our way there."

"He's going to be shocked, maybe even upset," she added quickly, clearly worried. "Maybe I should tell him."

"Not without all the information," Neil replied. Neil noticed Eric watching their interaction uncomfortably, having no idea who they were discussing or why he would be upset. Evangeline noticed as well.

"Maybe Eric should stay here with us… while you tell Theo the news." Evangeline asked Eric, "Would you be fine with that? Waiting here with us?" As she asked him, he could see how hopeful she was that the answer would be yes.

Eric nodded. "I can wait here," he told Neil.

Neil left Eric with Evangeline and Aaron.

"Why don't we sit out on the balcony?" Evangeline suggested with a smile.

"Okay," Eric replied, but as Eric made his way up the stairs, he heard Aaron react in pain.

"You know why," Evangeline hissed at him before he could respond.

Eric pulled a stool that was against the wall and moved it to the balcony while Evangeline and Aaron did the same, the three of them taking a seat across from each other.

"I assume you're wondering about Theo," Evangeline observed.

"Who is he?" Eric asked.

"He was a close friend of your mother's," Evangeline explained. "He was…" she seemed hesitant to continue, looking out at the view. Aaron took over.

"He was there the night they found your mom and when you were taken."

Evangeline swallowed, avoiding Eric's gaze. Eric could not decipher her reaction, wondering if it was somehow guilt. She shrugged her feelings away, a smile appearing on her face. "Enough of that. You don't know us, but we'd like to know

you."

Eric spent the next hour answering their questions, but his answers were vague. Eric was not accustomed to such conversations, and Aaron could sense he did not feel comfortable sharing the details of his life. All it took was a look for Aaron to relay the message to Evangeline that it was time to shift the focus, so she told Eric about them instead.

"Aaron and I were the first angels sent to observe your grand-," she cut herself off, noticing Eric was uncomfortable with the title since he had only just met Neil. "To greet Neil. This was…" she thought back, trying to place the year, looking to Aaron to help her remember.

"1970, sometime in the winter," Aaron answered.

"It was our first task as angels to shadow Neil and his operations.

"How old are you guys?" Eric asked.

"Well, our bodies are twenty-eight, that was the age we were at our rebirth, but if we go by date of birth, then we are both seventy-five," she smiled while Eric stared blankly. "We're twins."

The answer only gave Eric more questions, which made it difficult for him to know where to begin.

"Maybe we should hold off on the history of angels," Aaron interrupted.

Aaron and Evangeline spoke of his mother and their relationship to her. They described her as kind, enthusiastic, and very artistic. Eric was relieved to have the conversation shift to her, but he wondered what Neil could be doing with the man called Theo.

CHAPTER 4
Old Wounds

After leaving Eric in the capable hands of Evangeline and Aaron, Neil made his way to the elevator, taking advantage of the silence to decide how to break the news to Theo. Neil often tried to shake the memory of the night they found Leanna as Theo clung to her, but it would always haunt him.

Just across from the building with the tower where the angels worked was another building, one story but large. The building did not have many windows, and in comparison to the tower, its beige walls and solid metal doors were quite plain. Neil stepped through the main entrance, navigating through the tiled hallways, ignoring each door he passed. He had a specific destination in mind. He knew that Theo would not be at home at this time of day but in the training room, and the moment he heard the familiar sounds on the other side of the door, he knew he was right.

Neil knocked on the door and was immediately met with Theo's voice inviting him in. He let himself in as Theo raised his palm toward the target he had mounted on the wall in front of him. He pulled his arm back, bending at the shoulder, and watched as the throwing knife that had pierced the target's center removed itself, flying straight until the handle had reached his waiting palm.

Although it was his day off, it was no surprise that Theo had decided to spend his free time practicing with his weapons. No matter how skilled he became, he never seemed to feel it was enough. After depositing the knife back into the open case next to him, Theo faced Neil, noticing he had not spoken since entering.

"Is there an emergency in the village?" Theo asked, unable to think of another reason for Neil's visit.

"No, but. I do have something important to share," Neil said cautiously.

Noticing the seriousness in Neil's tone, Theo straightened, waiting for him to

continue.

"The other day at nightfall, there was a powerful disturbance about an hour's drive from the portal."

"The one you and Aaron went to check out?"

Neil nodded. "When we arrived, whoever caused it was no longer there, but while we were searching the area, we came across another sorcerer, a young boy… He ran off, but we were able to locate him yesterday."

"You came here just to tell me about some kid messing around out there?"

Neil struggled to find the right words.

"What aren't you telling me?" Theo demanded, growing as concerned as he was impatient.

"The boy… he's an orphan, thirteen years old, with no knowledge of our existence." He could not stall any longer. "His name is Eric." Theo winced at the sound of the name. "Blackwood," Neil finished.

Theo's breath hitched as he stared at Neil, waiting for him to say it was some cruel joke, but he never did.

"You're not serious…" Theo said, afraid to feel hope.

"I'm being very serious," Neil replied.

Theo shook his head. "You said you saw him murdered."

"I watched…" Neil's voice drifted before he continued. "I watched a soul rise, accepted by the heavens. I watched it rise through his eyes," he said, practically hissing out the word 'his.' "I believed it was my grandson, but it appears I was incorrect."

"You're wrong. He probably sent some fake to mess with us."

"He shares a strong resemblance to her," Neil said. Seeing the struggle in Theo's eyes, he offered proof. "Allow me to show you," he said, holding out a hand to Theo, which he hesitantly took.

The light spread from Neil's palm onto Theo's, and their eyes both turned foggy as they watched the memory. Neil only showed him his face as he had just seen that day. Suddenly Theo broke his hold, pulling his hand away as he jumped back,

rubbing the back of his neck, something he only did when he was anxious.

"It's really him?" Theo asked, with a tremor in his voice.

"Eric is alive," Neil confirmed.

Perhaps it was the shock that kept Theo from celebrating, or simply that reality had not yet set in, but he only stood, holding his hand to his neck and his eyes focused on the ground. Neil wished he could give him more time to come to terms with the good news as well as accept that they'd had no way of knowing he had survived, but there were more pressing matters to discuss.

"He's not safe here," Neil said, waking Theo from his trance. "Malphilus cannot know he is with us."

"He's just a kid… Why would he come after him?"

"Revenge… rages… perhaps to taunt me," Neil guessed. "He has not been familiar to me for decades. I am unable to fathom the thoughts which consume his mind… Yet he seems to know each and every one of mine."

"What do you want me to do?"

Neil glanced at the case behind Theo, which held his knives, and when Theo saw where his eyes had settled, he could predict the request.

"You want me to train him?" Theo asked in surprise.

"My biggest regret is that I did not offer the same to Leanna. I was so protective of her that I only left her defenseless in the end, without the tools or the skill to fight… I won't make the same mistake with her son."

Theo nodded, understanding.

Neil and Theo went to Theo's office and drafted a plan, a schedule of sorts. They felt it was best to begin by building Eric's stamina and strength, and then they would move on to self-defense, beginning with the basics. Theo would be the only one working with Eric for an hour each weekday, even once Eric started to school.

"Are you signing him up for school?"

"The schools are on leave for the holidays beginning next week. Even so, I don't plan on enrolling him for the next term. He will take his courses online until next year, so he has time to assimilate."

Neil knew it was time to retrieve Eric when the sun began to set.

"Eric is still waiting with Evangeline and Aaron. It's time I return home with him," as Neil began to leave, he hesitated at the doorway. "Would you like to meet him now?" he asked cautiously.

Theo's eyes widened in what could only be described as fear. He once again rubbed the back of his neck, swallowing.

"I think it'd be better if we meet tomorrow," he answered, trying to keep his voice steady to hide his nerves.

Neil nodded, understanding his hesitance, and then walked back to the tower to retrieve Eric. When they reached their bedroom doors, Eric was just about to shut himself in his room when Neil called his name.

"There's someone I'd like you to meet tomorrow," he told him.

"Is it that guy Theo?" Eric asked.

"Yes," he answered. Neil gestured for Eric to come to him, approaching the altar. "Theo is a friend," he explained. "He was very close to your mother." He reached for the photo of Leanna, and the boy, which Eric now realized must be Theo. "They met as children and were always quite fond of each other's company. This picture is from the first day of their final year of high school. Your mother wanted to commemorate the day."

"But he works with you?" Eric asked.

"He joined the moment he was of age, his eighteenth birthday."

"What does he do?"

"He was recently promoted. There are instances where things get out of hand both on Earth and in Luxwick, things in our area of expertise that others are not equipped to handle. It could be an unstable source or one of our kind wrecking havoc. Whatever the situation may be, Theo runs the operation, deleagating."

"And I'm meeting him tomorrow?"

Neil nodded. "As I said, he was close to your mother… Even if he was not, there are certain skills he has more expertise in that I wish for him to teach you."

Eric realized what he was saying. "You want him to teach me to fight?"

"Only to protect yourself," Neil said quickly, making it clear he did not want Eric to participate in anything violent when it was unnecessary.

With the agenda explained, Neil let Eric turn in for the night. Instead of sleeping, Neil sat at the edge of his bed, deep in thought, occasionally focusing on listening in on Eric. When Eric's breathing deepened, letting him know he was asleep, he quietly entered Eric's room. Eric lay under the covers with an arm wrapped around his pillow. Neil quietly made his way to the desk, opening the drawer to reveal the drawing of the woman in the mask. He stared at it, his finger brushing over the scar by the woman's mouth once again, then he slipped out with it clutched to his chest.

Neil locked up, knowing Eric would be safe so long as he remained asleep in his room, and walked to the angel tower, which even at nightfall was bustling. He rode the elevator, returning to the conference room where Aaron and Evangeline waited, seated at the table.

Without a greeting, Neil approached them, placing the drawing down in front of them.

"Recognize her?" Neil asked. They both studied the woman in the photo, trying to place her. When Evangeline's eyes settled on the scar, her eyes widened with familiarity.

"Is that... Ivy?" she asked.

"I believe so."

"I don't get it," Aaron said. "Why are we looking at a picture of Ivy?"

"Eric drew this the other night, from a dream, a memory. She is the woman who stole him from us."

Everyone quieted as they realized what it meant for Eric to dream of her, and the room grew tense.

"The soul..." Evangeline whispered, connecting the dots as Neil had.

Neil nodded solemnly. "It must have been hers."

"Do you have the memory?" she asked, knowing the answer when his face fell. "Can I see it?" she asked. Neil tightened his grip on the chair he had been clinging to, nodding reluctantly. "Where do you keep them?" she asked.

"In my dresser... bottom drawer."

Evangeline stood, vanishing. A minute later, she appeared again with an old wooden chest in her arms and gently placed it on the table. Glancing at Neil as if searching for any arguments before she opened it, revealing dozens of glass orbs, an inch in diameter. Blue light swirled inside each one. She looked to Neil again for guidance.

"Number six," he told her, his eyes glued to the table. Evangeline carefully removed the orb and turned her hand, so it lay in her open palm. Neil approached her, covering her hand with his, so the orb was sandwiched between their palms. Neil glanced at Aaron, who shook his head, indicating he did not wish to participate. Neil focused on their hands, watching as the light expanded, slipping through their fingers and surrounding their joined hands like a blanket of fog. Their eyes turned white and foggy, all while Aaron stood to the side watching them.

Neil and Evangeline watched the memory of that night as Neil had seen it through his eyes, beginning with the moment the woman they now knew was Ivy stepping onto the road. He slowed it, and Evangeline spoke while they remained in the memory.

"She looks nervous," she said. Reluctantly, Neil focused on her features as Evangeline was doing. He saw she was right; Ivy did seem nervous. The clarity of the memory made it clear that he had paid more attention to that night than he was willing to admit. Her hands shook as she raised their car, the memory blurring in the moment when Neil had focused his energy on protecting Eric. They watched as she approached the overturned car until she rendered Neil unconscious. Then the memory ceased, and their eyes returned to normal. Evangeline kept her eyes on Neil. "It was definitely her," she said.

"I don't understand," Neil said. "Her soul was accepted, meaning her intentions were deemed pure, so why hide him from me?"

"It doesn't matter," Aaron said. "What matters is he's alive, and he was somewhere safe. We can worry about why Ivy did it later..."

Knowing Aaron was right, Neil decided to put his questions to the back of

his mind for the moment.

"Tomorrow, I am introducing Eric to Theo. I will have an hour to spare if they begin their training immediately. We can investigate then."

Aaron nodded, and with that, he disappeared.

Without Aaron there, Neil slipped into one of the chairs and let his shoulders slump in defeat.

"What is it?" Evangeline asked, recognizing his posture as one riddled with guilt.

Neil shook his head. "Nothing of importance."

Evangeline studied him for any clues as to what ailed him when she finally reached her conclusion. "You think you should have known."

"Known what?" Neil asked, hoping she would drop the subject.

"That it was Ivy who was killed." When Neil did not respond, Evangeline sighed, knowing there was nothing she could say to get through to him. "Wallowing in the past won't do you any good," she told him. "Sometimes, we just have to accept that there are things we can't know at any given moment. Maybe even the reasons Ivy was taking him could have been meant for good."

Neil chucked, startling Evangeline. "Eric said something very similar about Ivy possibly having more information than we did."

Evangeline smiled. "Smart kid." She approached Neil, resting her hand on his shoulder. "You should get some rest," she told him.

The next day, although Neil was well rested, the questions about that night still weighed heavily on his mind. He struggled to keep his focus away from such questions, even as he sat across from Eric at the breakfast table.

Neil spent most of that morning in his bedroom, reviewing his memory. He was watching the one with Ivy again when he was shaken from the memory by a sound. Neil looked up at his open door and saw Eric retreating from it.

"Eric," Neil called. Eric froze, turning back to face him.

"Sorry, I didn't know you were busy," he said.

"Eric, there's no need to apologize. I would like you to feel comfortable approaching me for anything you need. After all, I am your grandfather." Neil noticed the way Eric seemed uncomfortable each time Neil pointed out he was his grandfather. He expected it was because no matter how much Neil wished for such a relationship, it did not change the fact that they were still almost complete strangers. He imagined their lack of a blood connection or the fact that Neil's inability to age would make that relationship all the more difficult to achieve.

"What did you need?" Neil finally asked.

Eric hesitated. "I was wondering if you have wi-fi here."

Neil struggled to suppress a smile. "The password is written on a paper on the refrigerator," he told him.

"Thanks," Eric said before rushing off.

Neil smiled to himself, suddenly remembering what it was like to have a teenager under his roof. He remembered how Leanna had begged him for a laptop when she was fifteen, as if it was the most important thing in the world. His reminiscing quickly turned to sadness as he realized she would always be so young in his memories. In just nine short years, Eric would be the age she had been when she was taken from him.

When the afternoon came, Neil knocked on Eric's door to find him still on his phone.

"Ready?" he asked, referring to his introduction to Theo.

"Yeah, sure," Eric answered hesitantly.

The walk to base was quiet. Neil led Eric, who remained three steps behind him. He knew Eric must not be comfortable meeting another new person, but he needed him to meet Theo, and he knew that Theo desperately needed to see Eric with his own eyes. Neil did not bother knocking when they reached the door to Theo's office. He had told Theo to expect them. The moment they stepped through the door, Theo scrambled up from his seat, his chair rolling back so suddenly that it slammed into the wall.

For the first minute, no one said a word. Neil watched Theo as he tried to

process what he was seeing. He watched Theo's eyes redden, and his hands shake ever so slightly as he stared at the young boy he could not deny was Leanna's. Finally, Theo walked toward them, and Neil reached back for Eric, placing a hand on his back to gently push him forward.

"I'm Theodore, Cross," Theo said as he raised his hand toward Eric. "You can call me Theo."

Eric reached for Theo's hand, shaking it. "Eric."

"I know," Theo said, finally smiling with a shaky breath.

"Why don't we take a seat," Neil suggested. Neil, Eric, and Theo spent the next two hours with introductions. Theo told Eric how he and Leanna met when they were children. At first, Eric was uncomfortable in the room with two people who cared for him far more than he did for them. But the more Theo and Neil spoke of his mother, the more curious Eric became. He eventually asked questions of his own about his mother. With each story Theo shared, his eyes lit up, although there was no disguising the pain lingering behind the excitement. Neil knew it had been a long time since they had spoken of Leanna, as both were too weighed down by their grief. Having Eric back made them realize how much time they had wasted focusing on their loss when they could have celebrated the life she had lived.

When Neil saw how their postures had relaxed, and their smiles became more natural, he thought it was time to use the opportunity.

"Would you mind watching Eric for a few hours? There are some things I need to take care of."

Neil could tell by the way he stiffened that the thought of them being left alone made him nervous, but even so, he agreed.

Neil stood outside the portal, waiting.

"Where to?" he heard Aaron ask as soon as he and Evangeline arrived. Both were no longer in their coats, having temporarily exchanged them for more subtle coats, their wings still hidden by enchantments.

"The orphanage."

Aaron nodded in understanding and reached for both his sister and Neil. Seconds later, they appeared in the alley just behind the orphanage. Neil listened for any movement while Aaron and Evangeline searched their surroundings.

"No one saw us," Neil confirmed.

"Is anyone inside?" Evangeline asked, gesturing toward the orphanage.

"Yes," Neil said as he made his way around the building. Neil walked up the front steps and was just about to knock when he froze. His body locked; something having distracted him.

"What's wrong?" Aaron asked.

Neil did not answer him since he was unsure of the answer himself. Lowering his hand, he searched the front door and was suddenly struck with a familiarity. Neil tried to focus, searching for something, when his eyes locked on the doormat below his feet. He stepped back and knelt, gently pulling back the doormat to reveal the concrete slab, almost completely smooth except for a stone embedded at the center. Aaron and Evangeline glanced at the rugged blue gemstone in confusion, but Neil seemed familiar with it. He brushed his thumb over the stone and watched it react, glowing from his touch. The stone matched the one on Luxwick's symbol. He smiled, only the soft exhale indicating his amusement mixed with his frustration. Neil tossed the doormat back in place and stood suddenly, storming past Aaron and Evangeline, who chased after him.

"Was that celocus?" Evangeline asked.

"What's celocus?" Aaron asked, but Evangeline ignored him, continuing to question Neil.

"It was, wasn't it? That's why you never felt him."

Neil stopped suddenly, his head jerking toward Evangeline. "Not here," he warned.

With a huff, Evangeline grabbed him by the hand, pulling him to the nearest vacant area she could find, and teleported them just outside the portal for privacy. Aaron appeared moments after.

"Why was there celocus on the cement like that?" Evangeline asked.

"Can someone please tell me what celocus is?" Aaron asked, still calm but beginning to grow annoyed.

Neil sighed. "It shields magic, hides it," he explained quickly before turning to Evangeline. "It was once traditional. Households in which sorcerers resided would place the stones to signify that, as well as to keep from overwhelming others with their power. But that was before Luxwick."

"Didn't you ever consider that some of the stones would still be on the properties?"

"We displayed them proudly on our front doors Evangeline, never embedded into the ground. Regardless, it doesn't matter. That slab is fresher than the concrete surrounding it.

"Wait," Aaron interrupted. "Then Ivy put it there?"

"She must have," Neil concluded. "One just large enough for the property," he sighed. "If he had not used power at that park, I never would have felt him."

With each answer, the puzzle grew more confusing. Aaron and Evangeline waited patiently for Neil to wrap his head around the revelation. Finally, he reached a decision.

"We must retrieve it. It's a long shot, but I don't wish to chance any traces that could be on that stone."

Evangeline nodded and took Neil back to the door. He lifted the mat and pressed his palm to the cement, cracking it apart. Evangeline picked the stone up, and Neil patched the surface. Without a word, they returned Neil to one of the rooms in their headquarters where he could work in peace.

The following week moved slowly for Neil, but he was relieved to know Eric would be kept occupied. Although he would have much rather continued to get acquainted with the teen in his care, his desire to understand why the last thirteen years were stolen from him was far more important to him. Knowing Eric would train with Theo and be looked after by Aaron and Evangeline, Neil put himself to work.

Neil stood in the padded room with the stone on the table in front of him. He

circled it, trying every trick he could think of to learn more of where it came from, but on day seven, he had not made any progress and was growing exhausted.

"Why are you still coming here?" he heard a voice ask.

Startled, Neil turned to see Evangeline watching him. Noticing his flinch from when she spoke, Evangeline sighed, knowing the answer.

"You're not making any progress," she concluded.

Neil sighed. "The stone is too old. If there was any trace of Ivy, it's long gone." Dejected, he slumped against the wall, staring at the celocus.

"Is Eric progressing with his training?" he asked.

"You could ask him that yourself." Neil nodded but said nothing more. "Have you spoken with him? Cared for him?" she asked.

"Of course I have."

"I don't mean the formalities." Evangeline joined him against the wall. "I'm not asking if you've checked on his health or if you've kept him fed. I'm asking if you've gotten to know him." When Neil said nothing, she continued. "He's been here a week already. Do you know his favorite color? Or his favorite dish? Do you know about his school life or how he got the tiny scar on his chin?"

Neil closed his eyes, each question weighing on him, but Evangeline went straight to her point.

"It's time to give up on the stone. Stop using it as a distraction to keep yourself away and from knowing your grandson." She paused, allowing her words to sink in. "He's not going anywhere." Without another word, she left Neil there to stare at the floor.

Neil stood in the conference room, looking out at Luxwick. He pulled the stone from his pocket, tracing the jagged edges with his thumb. He knew Evangeline was right. He should have given up on the stone days ago. He was not still on the subject because it was useful, but because he was afraid to lose the distraction. He pocketed the stone again with a sigh and gripped the railing, thinking of Leanna like he always did. His beloved daughter, not in blood but in bond, yet he avoided the life

she created out of fear.

Neil stood, contemplating the questions he felt he should ask Eric at dinner later, when suddenly he was distracted. His blood ran cold as he felt power nearby, unstable power, and immediately knew exactly what it was.

CHAPTER 5
Training Session

Eric and Theo jogged on the treadmills of his private gym, their usual warm-up. When they were finished, Eric moved to go straight to the stationary bike as he had done each day when Theo stopped him.

When they first began their exercises, the atmosphere was uncomfortable to say the least. Naturally, Eric had been uncomfortable with Theo since he did not know him and had rarely ever spent time with others while on Earth. Theo's constant looks and fidgeting only made matters worse. Although they did not speak much, they had fallen into a steady routine. Theo had explained that before they began self-defense, Eric needed to build up his stamina.

"Your endurance is impressive," Theo said as he stopped Eric from going to the bike. "I think we should just dive right in if that's okay with you."

Eric noticed how Theo seemed to tiptoe around him. It made him wonder if it was because of his relationship with his mother or if Theo simply was not used to teens.

"Yeah, sure," Eric said quickly.

Theo nodded, grabbing a water from the small fridge and tossing one to Eric.

"Hey," Eric said suddenly, causing Theo to look at him. "Uh… How did you know my mom?" Eric asked, fiddling with the water bottle.

"We were friends," Theo answered quickly. "Met her when I was a lad." Noticing the confusion on Eric's face, he smirked. "When I was a child, sorry. We were about six years old. Inseparable ever since."

Eric noticed how the tension seemed to vanish from Theo with just the mention of his mother.

"Were you guys ever…"

"No," Theo answered quickly. "We were m- friends. We were the best of friends." Shaking away the memory he almost lost himself in, Theo approached Eric. "We should get started."

Theo began with simple maneuvers, taking things slowly. He taught Eric how to free himself from someone's grip and how to block. Soon enough, they were sparring, Theo always stopped his gloved fists so they would never hit Eric the times he missed the block, so that Eric could get used to the movements. Eric was tense as he struggled to bring his arms up to the right positions on time. Although he knew Theo was keeping his hits light and that the forearm guards he wore would keep him from getting hurt, he still couldn't help his nervousness.

On the seventh day, Theo and Eric were on their third sparring session, and although Eric was nowhere near comfortable yet, he had at least stopped feeling so nervous.

"You're doing great," Theo said between hits, his words feeling empty to Eric, who did not believe he was improving. Yet he couldn't help the slight excitement he felt from hearing the praise.

They continued when something Eric had never expected happened. When Theo swung his arm again, Eric nearly missed the block again when he suddenly brought his arm up, catching the hit. Instead of simply blocking and continuing, his entire body tensed. He felt the surge just as he had the day his classmate had punched him in the stomach. He stiffened as the power surfaced in an instant and sent Theo flying backward, straight into the wall, before he fell to the ground in a heap.

Eric's heart raced in panic as he watched Theo groan in pain on the ground, rolling onto his back as he cradled his arm. Eric's body suddenly felt weak, his skin clammy. He expected the look on his face must have been terrible when Theo turned his head, and his pained expression changed to panic.

"Hey, it's okay," Theo said quickly, trying to calm Eric. He clenched his jaw as he shifted until he was sitting upright in an effort to conceal his pain.

"I'm sorry," Eric wanted to say, but his throat felt too tight.

Theo let out a shaky breath. "It's alright, I'm alright," Theo continued to say

to Eric, but the words did nothing to assure him.

Neil suddenly rushed into the room with Aaron behind him.

"What's happened?" he asked quickly, stopping to take in the scene. Theo on the ground clutching his arm to his chest, and Eric frozen in place, completely pale.

"It's nothing," Theo explained quickly. "Just a wee accident is all."

Aaron rushed straight for Theo, taking his injured arm from him so quickly that Theo was unable to stop the cry of pain, which made Eric flinch. Theo quickly shut his jaw again.

"It's broken," Aaron said, immediately beginning to heal him.

It took minutes for Aaron to mend the broken bone. Neil had not even realized he had crossed the room to Eric and was gripping his shoulder in comfort. Eventually, all that was left behind were the bruises. As soon as Theo was healed, he rose to his feet, stretching his arm to show Eric.

"Look, see? Good as new. No harm done," he told Eric quickly.

Eric looked from Theo's face down to his arm. "I'm sorry," Eric finally said, making Theo sigh.

"It's not your fault. It was just an accident."

Despite the reassurances, it was clear they did nothing to ease Eric's guilt. Aaron quietly took Eric home, returning a few minutes later with Evangeline by his side.

"He's resting," she told them. "What happened?" she asked Theo who was stretching his bruised arm.

"We were sparring, just some light hits. I was teaching him to block. He finally managed to block one of my hits, and I went flying," Theo explained.

Neil rubbed his face. "I felt the energy from the tower. Unstable…" His jaw was tense as he spoke. "I should have known. He's never been able to use his magic openly. It's only natural he won't have full control."

"Then we shift the training to magic," Theo said confidently.

"Training with you will temporarily be on hold."

"I can handle a wee bit of magic Neil," Theo said, slightly annoyed. Neil planned for their sessions to cease.

"I'm aware of that, but this situation is uncommon. Eric is inexperienced but quite powerful. You saw how he reacted to your injury. I think it's best I handle the situation, but if you truly wish to continue, then have him do endurance exercises only until he is in control."

Theo silently agreed, understanding, but Neil could tell from his tension that he felt he should still be the one training Eric.

The next day, Neil led Eric into the same room where he had been agonizing over the stone's origins, except now the table was gone. Entering the room, Eric was surprised at the simplicity of it. Storage cabinets lined the walls, and the space was divided straight down the middle by a wall with a large glass window, making it resemble an interrogation room. Except rather than the mirrored side with the metal table, the glass was transparent on both sides, and on the other side, there was nothing but padding on the walls.

Neil led Eric straight to the padded side.

"Because of your lack of exposure to magic, your body is trained to defend itself," Neil explained. "At any sign of danger, even fear itself causes you to use your abilities on instinct. My goal is to help you gain control. You need to be able to use your powers on command and suppress them when they are not needed."

"How do I do that?" Eric asked.

"I will use magic against you— nothing dangerous, just simple orbs of light. Although you are aware they will cause you no harm, your body can only distinguish the fact that it is magic. I need you to focus your energy and relax your body. I want you to get this so you can have control over it.

Eric nodded, but understanding did not stop him from being nervous.

Neil stood on the opposite side of the room from Eric, rolling up his sleeves.

"Ready?" Neil asked.

"Yeah, I guess," he answered. Neil smiled reassuringly and took a few more

steps, widening the distance between them.

Neil raised his hands to his chest, hovering his palms across from each other. A soft orb of blue light formed in the space between his palms. Neil let the light float, then swung his arms forward and sent the light toward Eric. The first orb evaporated into nothing before it reached Eric. Eric was surprised. He felt his body react the moment the orb disappeared.

Neil threw one orb after the other at Eric, speeding up and sending them out as quickly as he created them.

"You must relax your muscles. Convince your subconscious that there is no threat."

Eric tried to focus as Neil continued to attack. Neil smiled when he realized the orbs were getting closer to Eric. He continued and watched as Eric's barriers continued to shrink. Suddenly, Eric's concentration was broken, and his body tensed; when the next orb reached him, it was as if all the magic he had suppressed was released at once. His barrier expanded from his body quickly in one blow. Neil turned to face the wall and shielded himself, bringing his arms up to cover his face. The glass panel shattered into fragments from the impact, the shards falling in every direction, clattering against Neil's shield.

Once the damage was done, the room was silent as Neil peered at Eric.

Eric stood still with his eyes focused on the ground. He felt hazy; his body suddenly felt heavy. The only thing he could hear was the pounding in his ears. When he took a step forward, he lost the strength in his legs and stumbled, putting his hands out in front to catch himself before he hit the ground. Eric sat still, leaning forward with both palms on the floor as his vision faltered.

Neil rushed to check him, quickly removing his phone on the way and hitting his speed dial. Evangeline was rushing through the door before Neil even hit the ground next to Eric,

"Are you alright?" Neil asked as he knelt down.

"Yeah," Eric said, his vision finally clearing up. "I'm just really tired all of a sudden."

Neil pressed his palm to Eric's forehead and felt the heat from his skin. "You used too much power in such a short time. You're feverish."

"You need rest," Evangeline said. She reached for both Eric and Neil and teleported them to Neil's house. Neil helped Eric to his feet, guiding him up the stairs. When they reached his room, Eric practically collapsed onto the bed, sitting on the edge.

"Rest for now. Magic uses energy. You are powerful, but you are also young. You haven't had the time to exercise these abilities, so your body isn't capable of handling your full power."

"I'm sorry," Eric said.

"Eric…" Neil said with a sigh. "Everyone in this world has had years to practice and learn what they are capable of. This has always been our lifestyle. You cannot expect to catch up in just one week.

Eric said nothing, only managing to nod.

Neil left Eric alone to rest, knowing there was nothing else to say. Eric spent the rest of the day and night in bed. The next morning, although his fever was down, Neil and Evangeline insisted that he rest so his strength would be fully recovered before they continued training. So instead, Eric began one of the mathematics workbooks Neil had put aside so Eric could see if he was at the standard of the school in Luxwick he would eventually attend.

The next night, when Neil went to check on Eric, he found him fast asleep in bed with an open textbook on his chest. Neil gently removed it from Eric's hands and closed it, placing it on the desk, and left Eric to sleep.

When Neil closed the door, he leaned back against it in defeat. About to walk to his bedroom to sleep himself, he stopped when his eyes landed on the closet next to Eric's room. Neil entered the closet, quietly shutting the door behind him. He flipped the light switch and stared at the dust-covered room filled with boxes. Many of them were filled with items he'd collected over the years which held memories of his long life, but the ones he focused on were those with Leanna's name scrawled across the sides. Those were the items he could never bear to get rid of. He pulled a small dusty

wooden box from one of the shelves and sat on the soft rug, placing the box down in front of him. He opened it to reveal a stack of photographs.

Carefully, he took the first photograph in his hands and turned it over. It was one of him and Leanna when she was eleven years old. They smiled at the camera, sitting on the living room couch. The second photo was of Leanna and Theodore when she was fourteen on their first day of school that year. Leanna leaned against Theo with her arms around his waist while Theo smiled shyly at the camera with his arm around her shoulder. The next was of Leanna when she was seven, fast asleep on the living room couch, tightly embracing her stuffed bunny.

Neil sighed as he looked at the photographs, each picture breaking down his walls. They reminded him of the years she never got to live.

Next to the photos were a handful of memory orbs. With shaking hands, he picked one up randomly and let himself be lost in the memory. As he relived the happy memory, a tear slipped from his eye. When he could no longer take the pain, he stopped the memory and tossed the orb back into the box, shoving it aside. He threw himself onto his back and stared up at the ceiling. He was there for a few minutes until he mustered up the energy to pick himself from the ground. When he looked down at the open box again, he noticed something underneath the photographs. Neil moved the photos out of the way and picked up the delicate handmade bracelet. It had small, circular wooden beads interlaced on thick brown thread. Neil stared at the bracelet and then looked at the matching one on his wrist. He was deep in thought as he twirled the beads between his fingertips. That night he left Leanna's bracelet on Eric's nightstand for him to wear.

The next morning, Eric was well rested but unwilling to get out of bed. He sat in his room half-dressed and stared straight ahead at the closed door. To him, the short eight days had made him feel like a failure. But when he looked at the drawing of his mother pinned to the wall above his desk, he convinced himself he needed to keep trying.

By the time he stepped downstairs, Neil had breakfast ready.

"Good morning," Neil said, smiling. "Egg, toast, sausage, and bacon are on the table. Eat whatever you like."

Eric took a seat across from Neil and filled his plate. Although Neil always seemed cautious around Eric due to them still being strangers, he noticed Neil was particularly strange that morning.

"I was thinking we could go to see a film today," Neil said as they cleared the table. "If you're interested, of course."

"Sure," Eric answered, uncomfortable by the invitation. He could not help the relief he felt to have a day off from training.

The clinking of the plates and silverware was the only sound as they made their way to the kitchen.

Neil cleared his throat. "Is there anything in particular you'd like to see? I haven't visited a theater in ages, so I'm not sure what types of films there are at the moment."

"We can just pick one when we get there."

"Yes, of course..." Neil agreed. The rest of their cleaning was spent in awkward silence.

As promised, Neil took Eric to a cinema on Earth, believing the familiarity for Eric would be better. Neil was pleased to learn that a movie was the perfect remedy. As they made their way back to Luxwick, Eric was surprisingly more talkative than usual as they discussed the spy thriller they had just seen. Neil found himself laughing along with Eric, making him realize he should have waited with the training until after Eric was settled in.

The next few weeks passed more smoothly and peacefully. With both Eric and Neil unaccustomed to celebrating Christmas and New Year's, the holidays passed without either realizing it. Fortunately for Neil, Eric did not seem to mind. Neil spent as much time as he could spare with Eric, learning everything he could just as Evangeline had pushed him, and he was glad she had. He knew Eric's favorite color was blue, and his favorite dish was the spaghetti Yvette would make in the fall.

Although Eric did not have much to share about his school life, Neil had learned that he was particularly skilled at literature and (of course) enjoyed drawing with colored pencils.

"Can I start training again?" Eric asked Neil one day at the dinner table in the second week of January. Initially, Neil had planned to push training until the summer, but when he saw the gleam in Eric's eyes, he could not say anything but yes.

When Neil and Eric arrived at the training room, Eric stared at the glass he had broken, which had now been repaired. Without a word, they began.

Neil again formed an orb of light and aimed it at Eric. Just as expected, it evaporated before coming close to Eric.

"Focus on relaxing. Your body only reacts because it believes you are in danger, and your magic is reacting."

Eric tried to relax, but his body tensed with every blow.

"Deep breaths," Neil reminded him.

Eric closed his eyes and took deep even breaths. There were moments when he could feel the amount of energy he was using lessen. It was as if his power, his shield, was an elastic band being stretched out. When he could draw back that power, it loosened, but he could not pull it back completely. At the same time, with every blow, he could feel it pull further apart as if a crank was turning, twisting it more and more.

After two hours of repeating the exercise, there was little to no progress, and Eric was exhausted. The same thing continued for days, and the confidence Eric had felt when he had asked to train dissipated as he grew more impatient.

When Neil noticed Eric stagger on the sixth day of training, he stopped. "That's enough for today," he said, moving to open the door. "You need rest. If you wish, we can continue in the afternoon, but you need a break."

Eric sat on the ground and leaned back against the wall to rest his legs. When they returned home, Neil poured a glass of water and brought it to Eric at the table.

"It's not working," Eric said.

Neil took a seat next to him. "It's only been a few days. It takes time to see

results, but I'm sure-"

"It's been a week!" Eric said, and in his outburst, the glass of water shattered and his eyes widened. Eric stared at the broken glass and the water flowing off the table as he tried to calm himself. He stood quickly and rushed for the front door.

"I'm going for a walk," he announced as he left.

Eric wandered through the town of Emispro, which was just outside the Luxwick headquarters. The sound of laughter drew him to the large fountain in Emispro's town square. There he found a dozen children running along the fountain, scooping water with their hands and tossing it at each other. Watching their joy helped ease Eric's agitation, reminding him of the orphanage, specifically of the young children who were always uncritical.

The sky was clear and more of a golden orange than its usual violet since their sun was at its highest point. The light warmed his skin, and the breeze carried the smell of the water across the quad.

Eric approached the fountain, sat on the stone ledge, and looked down at the water. For a moment, all his thoughts stopped as he stared at the rippling water. The feeling of cold water splashing against his neck brought him back to reality.

A girl aged about five stood next to him, water dripping down her black hair and her cheeks. "Sorry," she whispered nervously, her fingers twisting the ends of her braids.

Eric smiled, and the girl smiled back in embarrassment. She slightly dropped her shoulders.

"Want to see something cool?" Eric asked. The girl nodded. Eric turned to face the fountain completely, submerging his feet into the water and patting the spot on the fountain's edge next to him. The girl sat down. Once she was seated, Eric reached out to the water with one hand but did not touch it. He focused his energy on it and raised his arm, making a portion of the water rise. He drew it up until he had a blob the size of a baseball, then raised his other arm and moved his hands apart, stretching the blob into a long rope. Eric focused as he made the water brighten and glow blue. The other children gathered and watched in awe. When he let the water

drop back into the fountain, the other children immediately began to imitate him. They each tried to make the water rise but struggled. The little girl did her best but could only manage to raise a water droplet the size of a quarter before it fell. She grew more agitated with each attempt.

"It takes practice," Eric told her reassuringly. She continued to try with the other children.

"When did you learn to do that?" asked Neil, startling Eric. Neil joined him, taking a seat on the fountain edge with his torso turned to face Eric.

"There was this kid at the orphanage. His name was Charlie," Eric explained. "Yvette told me his mom was a drug addict, and when it got bad, social services took him and brought him to her. When he got there, he didn't want to talk to anyone. Yvette tried getting him to play with the other kids, but she couldn't get him out of his room. I tried too, and I ended up using magic in front of him one time. I started with small stuff like turning on the lamp from the other side of the room, stuff like that, and it got him to smile. He was still really shy and didn't talk much, but it cheered him up, so I started practicing more."

Neil smiled. "It's extraordinary."

"They're really easy tricks," Eric said with a shrug.

"That these children here are struggling to replicate because they have never attempted them before," he said. Eric knew he was referring to his training.

Eric sighed. "It's not the same thing."

"But it is," Neil insisted. "You never needed to practice such control in your life because you are young, and instincts have always been enough. Control is like learning to walk or speak or ride a bicycle. It may seem simple, but to someone who has never done so, it takes time and requires patience and practice. Then once you learn, you will never forget. The others your age can do things you cannot because it is second nature. That does not change that you are attempting to master it in weeks when it took them months. This is the first step. Once you master it, everything else will seem almost effortless, although time-consuming."

"So don't give up is what you're saying."

Neil nodded. "You can only fail if you stop trying."

Eric thought it over. He looked at the children who were still struggling to make the water rise. "Okay… Let's get this over with."

Although Eric was still reluctant, he was ready to stop being so hard on himself. When they entered the training room for the second time that day, Eric reached his spot in the room and shook his arms in an attempt to loosen himself up.

"Ready?" asked Neil.

Eric smirked, shaking his head. "Let's just start."

Neil formed the first orb and spun it in his hands, launching it. Eric tried to relax, but after half an hour of failure, he realized something. His focus was misplaced. Instead of trying to stop something he could not see, he tried to focus on wanting the orb to hit him. The entire time he had been wrongly trying to lower an invisible shield.

Eric stared straight at Neil. He relaxed his body and hoped for the orb to reach him, trying to convince his body that it wished for the impact. He felt something he had not felt before, the imaginary elastic loosening. His body gradually became lighter until he felt the pressure deteriorate into nothing. Then he felt the orb pass through him, and it surprised him. It felt light and airy, like a fog. His eyes widened, and he looked up at Neil, who was smiling widely and laughing in relief.

"Congratulations on completing your first lesson, Neil said.

"Finally," Eric said as he threw himself to the ground and rolled onto his back with his arms outstretched.

"You haven't mastered it yet. You will need to practice until it becomes instinct, but after that, you may continue your physical defense training with Theodore, and I will begin teaching you defense with your abilities."

"Great," Eric said sarcastically.

"On your feet. I believe celebration is in order. Perhaps a film."

"A movie sounds great right now," Eric said.

Neil held out a hand to Eric to help him up, and they left the training room together.

"I just need to let Evangeline know we are leaving," Neil said as he dialed

her. "Evangeline- Successfully, actually. We were just about to…"

When Neil's sentence was cut, Eric turned to see why. Neil's entire body tensed as if his breath had been stolen. His eyes bulged, and the phone fell from his hand. Eric could hear Evangeline's frantic shouts but was too shocked by Neil. Neil let out a shriek of pain and fell to the ground with his hands on his head, knocking Eric from his stupor.

"What's wrong?" Eric asked, panicked.

Neil did not answer, his breathing labored. He opened his eyes, but his eyes darted about frantically as if he could not see Eric at all.

"What do I do?" Eric asked, but Neil said nothing. He only gripped Eric's arm to lean on him but was unable to speak.

Evangeline rushed into the room. "Eric, what happened?" she asked. Eric turned at the sound of her footsteps to answer but was stopped when Neil screamed "NO!" Confused, Eric watched as Neil stilled, his eyes turning dark, pinning him while Evangeline stood motionless.

CHAPTER 6
Malphilus

Neil was experiencing something he had not felt in years, looking through the eyes of someone else. He could see the pavement and two hands that were not his, flat on the ground for support. His head ached, and the sound of car horns and chatter echoed in his ears.

He could faintly hear Eric's panicked question, but what he heard next was as clear as day. He heard Evangeline call Eric's name.

"NO!" he screamed, but it was too late. He was no longer in control of his own body, nor could he see through his eyes or hear through his own ears. Someone else possessed him.

Eric felt the chill run through his spine when Neil's eyes met his, no longer familiar. Neil suddenly lunged forward and grabbed Eric by the neck, pinning him to the ground and choking him. Neil tightened his grip, and Eric struggled to breathe, thrashing underneath him. Evangeline rushed forward, desperately trying to pry him off, but Neil did not budge.

"AARON!" she screamed out in panic.

Suddenly Aaron was there as well, trying to pry Neil off as Eric began to see spots, straining to breathe.

"Let go of him!" He heard Aaron demand.

Finally, Eric felt Neil's grip loosen and his breath rush in. His body spasmed as he desperately took in oxygen, coughing.

"You should be dead!" he heard Neil yell. Eric tried to sit up, reaching for his throbbing neck.

Aaron and Evangeline threw Neil against the wall and pinned him by his

shoulders.

"You have to push him out, Cornelius!" Aaron shouted.

Neil continued to thrash, then suddenly, he stopped, and his rage turned to fear, followed by guilt when he looked at Eric. He stared at him, sitting on the ground, coughing to try to catch his breath and calm down.

"Is he gone?" asked Evangeline.

Neil nodded quickly. His eyes were still fixed on Eric. Evangeline looked into his eyes, then nodded at Aaron and they both released him.

Eric weakly slid himself to the opposite wall and collapsed against it, throwing his head back and closing his eyes. His breath still shook.

"Let me see your neck," Aaron said to Eric. Eric removed his hand slowly and looked at Aaron; the movement caused him to wince. Aaron examined his neck then eased his pain, but bruises still formed.

When Eric looked to Neil again, Neil felt sick at what he saw. Eric was frightened and at the same time confused as expected. Evangeline knelt next to Neil, gripping his hand.

"It's not what you think," Aaron told Eric quickly. He grabbed his head, forcing him to look at him instead of Neil. "That wasn't him."

"Then who was it?" Eric asked hoarsely before trying to clear his throat.

"Malphilus," he heard Neil answer, his voice shaking. Eric seemed unsure if Neil had spoken a name or a creature, but before he could say more, Aaron shook his head.

"Not now," he said. "When does Roman get back?" he asked Evangeline.

"A few hours."

Aaron sighed and nodded at Evangeline who approached him and Eric. She rubbed Eric's arms before moving her hands to the side of his face. "We will explain, but until then you should rest." Blue light sprung from her hands and suddenly Eric was asleep, his head slumping forward against her shoulder. Aaron picked him up and teleported to take him to bed.

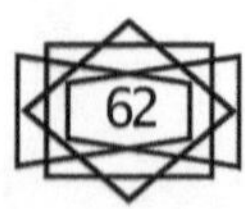

Neil couldn't look at Evangeline. Instead, he stared at his shaking hands, consumed in his guilt. Evangeline's hands appeared, taking his, but he kept his eyes downcast.

"This wasn't you. This was him," she said quietly.

Neil responded with a slight nod, but her sigh let him know she was aware he did not believe that. She moved her hands to cup his face, forcing him to look at her. "You have to believe that this wasn't your fault... If not for yourself, then for Eric." Without another word, she stood and walked out to leave Neil to think.

Neil leaned back against the wall, closing his eyes to ease his pounding head.

Two hours later, Neil sat in the conference room, his eyes fixed on the door. The only other soul in the room was Aaron who waited by the balcony. At the sound of the doors, Aaron was suddenly at Neil's side. Evangeline entered with Eric next to her, his eyes still drowsy from sleep. The way Eric stiffened at the sight of Neil made his heart sink. Neil looked at the table, unable to look Eric in the eye as he was guided to the seat next to Neil.

"Evangeline said it wasn't you."

Neil's head jerked to look at Evangeline who only nodded. With a sigh, Neil explained. "It was my body... but it was not my mind in possession of it."

Eric considered this before asking, "What does that mean?"

Neil swallowed nervously. "Do you remember? On the night I brought you home, I explained that there was one other like me. Someone with whom I share a link?"

Eric nodded.

"Well, that person is a man called Malphilus," Neil spoke slowly, but he knew he had no choice but to speak of him. "When we were young, we were able to feel each other's thoughts only when we were asleep. I believed they were simply dreams. Then it began to happen when I was awake."

"Like mind reading?"

"Not quite... We have moments where we..." Neil struggled to explain. "At

first, it was as if we shared a mind; his senses overlapped with mine. Then we were able to see and feel what the other was feeling. When we connect, for a moment, we switch bodies. What occurred earlier was that. I was in control of his body while he was in control of mine."

Neil finally locked eyes with Eric. He was not sure what he was searching for in his eyes. Did he wish for Eric to believe him or to run?

"Is it just with him?" Eric finally asked.

"Yes… There is no one in this world like us."

Eric fidgeted in his seat. "How often does it happen?"

Neil shook his head. "It's hard to say. It could be multiple times a day or we can go days, months, even years without an occurrence. I believed the link was broken until moments ago."

Eric nodded, but continued to fidget.

"Is there something you want to ask?" Aaron asked.

Eric shook his head. "It's nothing."

"You can ask anything. It's better if there are no secrets."

Although Neil did not entirely agree, he nodded.

Eric took a deep breath, summoning his nerves.

"Was it him?"

Neil did not need to ask to know what Eric was referring to. He wanted to know if Malphilus killed his mother.

"Yes… Only not through me."

"Why?"

Neil looked at Eric with a pained expression, tears threatening to spill though his eyes. "I wish I knew," was all he was able to say.

Eric stared at Neil, relaxing, the change in posture making Neil relieved. The sound of the doors opening again forced Neil to look away as he composed himself. When he looked up, he saw it was Theo stepping through them. Neil assumed Evangeline had invited him to the meeting.

"Am I interrupting?" he asked, taking in the room.

"No," Neil answered quickly.

"Does it have anything to do with why I was invited to this emergency meeting?" he asks.

"Unfortunately."

Theo took his seat when another person unfamiliar to Eric entered the room. He wore the angel coat like the others. The man was tall and lean, his hair short and pitch black. His eyes were pale blue, icy, and his skin clean shaven. Neil tried to hide his smirk when he noticed Theo roll his eyes at the sight of him. The man did not look pleased, an expression most would say was the only one he was capable of. When his eyes met Eric's, his gaze was almost piercing, causing Eric to stiffen. Neil placed a hand on his shoulder, ready to defend him.

"Why is there a child here?" he asked, informing Eric that he was English.

Neil sighed, not surprised by the man's immediate hostility. "This is my grandson, Eric."

"So, you're the one they found," the man muttered. Neil ignored him, continuing with his introduction.

"Eric, I would like you to meet Roman, a member of our Council alongside Aaron, Evangeline, and I."

Remembering his manners, Eric opened his mouth to speak, but Roman did not give him the chance.

"Are we letting children attend official meetings now?" he asked, gesturing not only to Eric, but to Theo, who seemed amused by it.

"He will only observe today's meeting," Neil answered. Roman only grew more irritated.

"And why should they receive special treatment?"

Aaron cleared his throat, gaining Roman's attention. "Because this matter concerns him more than any of us."

Roman did not argue, his silence indicating he would drop it. Neil silently thanked Aaron for speaking up. Although the angel Roman was often in disagreement with Neil and Evangeline as well, he had never argued against Aaron. Neil believed it

was out of respect. Roman averted his eyes, ready to commence the meeting.

"What so urgently required my presence a second after my return?"

Everyone looked to Neil, waiting for him to share the news with Roman and Theo.

"It appears the connection is not as severed as we previously presumed."

Roman's expression remained unchanged, but Theo was agitated.

"So, the snake still lives," he bit out through his clenched jaw.

"Have you reported this to Cyrus?" Roman asked, causing Neil to tense.

Neil shook his head. "It only happened a few short hours ago. It was only a moment, but long enough to inflict damage," he said, his eyes darting to Eric briefly.

Confused, Theo looked at Eric more closely, his eyes immediately settling on the bruising around Eric's neck. His agitation turned to rage.

"Are those hand marks?" he asked, his voice raised.

"Theo," Aaron warned.

"You're telling me the bastard tried to strangle him and we're just sitting here on our hands?" He practically yelled, nearly jumping from his seat.

"Theodore!" Evangeline yelled.

Theo's head snapped toward her. When she subtly gestured to Eric at the table, Theo's expression softened. He took a deep breath, closing his eyes until he had his temper under control.

"Eric's presence was revealed and he was targeted, but we are already taking extra measures," Neil assured him.

Roman muttered something that no one heard but caught everyone's attention.

"Do you have something to add, Roman?" asked Neil.

Roman looked up from the table with a smile of disbelief.

"Tell me you're joking."

"I assure you there is nothing humorous about this situation," Neil responded, his patience wearing thin.

Roman straightened. "In the event of your connections, the proper action is

to report to Cyrus. Yet you called this meeting because you believe, what? That the most powerful sorcerer in the world was set off by the existence of a child? You are wasting your time focusing on such a trivial matter."

Eric was so thrown by what Roman had said, he did not even notice the name he did not recognize.

"Evangeline, will you please return Eric to his room" Neil said, his voice hard. Agreeing, Evangeline ushered Eric away.

Neil's gaze became stern and intimidating. "If you believe this to be trivial, then clearly I have not informed you well." He watched Roman's smile fade. "Knowing he failed is enough. Malphilus despises loose ends. His failure to murder my grandson will surely motivate him. The man has remained silent for over a decade while we have cleaned up his old messes. Imagine what he may attempt now?"

Roman knew he had made a mistake. The humor left him completely. "Then what do you suggest we do?"

"Keep our eyes open and our ears listening. We've grown far too comfortable in his absence. We must be ready for anything."

Evangeline returned, staying off to the side of the table.

"We must bring this to Cyrus' attention," Roman said.

Neil sighed. "I know." Neil knew Theo was confused by his state at the mention of Cyrus. Theo did not understand the sadness mixed with fear and stress that seemed to take Neil just by the mention of Cyrus' name.

Evangeline said, "I'll tell him next week. If he wants to see you then, he'll tell us."

"No," Roman insisted, "he needs to be informed immediately."

"Next week, Roman," Evangeline said. She did her best to reassure Neil. "Next week. It can wait until then."

Neil nodded. "Next week."

Roman was not amused, but did not argue with the decision.

The meeting was dismissed, and the sound of chairs dragging across the tile floor broke the tension in the room and it was only seconds before Roman was gone

again.

Neil stayed where he was and watched Evangeline move across from him.

"Thank you," he said to her.

"It's the least I can do. Considering I'm the idiot who forgot what it looks like when Malphilus is with you."

"You couldn't have known. It's been ages. The connection was more intense than it usually is."

She smiled at him sadly. "You're right. You should probably have a code word for whenever it happens. So we know when to shut up."

"Any ideas?" he asked, holding back a smile.

"No, but I will let you know when I come up with something humiliating," she joked.

The sound of a throat clearing surprised them, alerting them that they were not alone. Theo stood off to the side, his hardened expression diminishing their temporary ease. Neil's smile faded as he remembered what happened to Eric.

"Was he trying to hurt him or kill him?" Theo asked.

"Kill," Neil managed to answer.

With his anger threatening to spill again, he took a deep breath and nodded. "Right," he said. "I'll get back to work then."

"I can take you," Evangeline offered, but Theo shook his head as he was leaving. He needed to be alone.

Evangeline stepped toward the door. She looked back at Neil. "Get some rest," she ordered. "And no wallowing in your guilt. It won't help him." Then she vanished.

Neil reached into his pocket, removing the celocus stone. He stared at it, remembering how just a few weeks ago, it was the most concerning matter. But as he turned it, something caught his eye. A small spot, nearly invisible, where the color was different. Neil jumped out of his seat and rushed to the elevator, stopping on the third floor.

On the third floor of the angel building, there was a storage facility. Off to

both sides of the elevator were changing rooms as well as hangers of wardrobe for angels and sorcerers to check out. Uniforms, office wear, and other sometimes-necessary disguises filled the hangers. Neil walked straight past them to the counter that split the room in half, walking past the sorcerers there with a wave. Moving past the walls of shelves and storage drawers, he stopped in front of a sorcerer at his desk and placed the stone in front of him.

"Cornelius," the sorcerer said, surprised. "How can I help you?" he asked.

After speaking to the sorcerer, Neil learned his hunch was correct. The stone did come from their own storage room, containing the serial number to prove it. What he did not expect was the name linked to its check out.

"Are you sure?" he asked.

The sorcerer nodded. "It was checked out thirteen years ago by Leanna Blackwood."

Eric paced in his bedroom, unable to sleep and with no desire to leave. For the first time since he was strangled through Neil, Eric was truly alone, free from observation. He could feel his walls beginning to crumble. He felt his body shaking and his heart racing and it frustrated him. When Eric lived at the orphanage, he always felt himself to be strong. No matter what hardships he faced or how others belittled him, he had never been emotional. But now he clenched his fists as he tried to fight the tears, but it was no use.

"Stop," he told himself angrily, frustrated by the quivering of his own voice. Despite his strong will, tears still rolled down his cheeks one at a time. When he felt the first tear reach his neck, he knew it was no use. Eric threw himself to the bed and curled into himself, his forehead to his knees.

Neil returned home, unsure of what to do with the information he had just received. His imagination could not answer the question of why his daughter was in need of the celocus. Sending a text to Evangeline to alert her of the new information, he stopped in front of the altar to stare at the pictures of Leanna. Neil hesitantly

approached Eric's door, quietly opening the door to peer inside. He found Eric fully clothed on the bed. When he approached him, he immediately noticed the tear stains on his cheeks, letting him know Eric had been crying.

"Oh, Eric…" he whispered.

Neil carefully removed Eric's shoes and lifted the covers over him. His eyes fixed on the bruising on Eric's neck, he gently caressed Eric's head.

"I'm so sorry," he whispered.

Neil stood and turned the lights off. As he was leaving, a sound stopped him. The whisper was so quiet, it was amazing he heard it at all.

"I'm okay," Eric said in his drowsy state.

Neil knew he was lying, but said nothing, leaving Eric to rest.

CHAPTER 7
The Weather Room

With January coming to an end, things once again settled. Evangeline had managed to keep Roman from reporting the connection to Cyrus. Each time Cyrus was mentioned in front of him, Eric wondered who he was and why Neil seemed to loathe discussing him. Eric decided it was time he found out.

Eric had asked Neil about Cyrus once, but the subject was changed quickly. He considered asking Evangeline but he had gathered from watching her interactions with Neil that the two shared a closer relationship, and therefore, he doubted she would be willing to share with him. With Roman seeming unapproachable, that left Aaron and Theo, but Eric still harbored some guilt for breaking Theo's arm. His decision made, he walked to the angel tower, knowing that Neil was occupied elsewhere, although he did not know the details.

When Eric stepped into the angel headquarters, it was bustling with activity as usual as angels and sorcerers sat at their desks, making reports of earth's activities, answering calls, and other things Eric did not yet understand.

Searching the first floor, he saw no sign of Aaron. Noticing that the angels and sorcerers seemed too occupied with their work to mind his presence, he decided to seek out Aaron himself. Eric took the stairs to the second floor and saw the doors were closed with no sign of light shining through. He was about to continue his way up when he heard something on the other side of the door. Eric approached the doors carefully, opening them as quietly as he could. Across from the doors, in the wide-open space of the darkened room was light. In the open space, what appeared to be clouds floated, above them a bright floating sun, not nearly as bright as Earth's real one. On the ground within a large frame was water, like the ocean, Eric realized. The people in the room did not seem to notice Eric had joined them as they studied the

simulation.

To his left was a long row, a counter with monitors where angels filled the seats in front of them, their backs to the simulation. Their focus was on the large screen on the wall with lists of what appeared to be coordinates and weather reports. "5 mph wind, light rain," Eric noticed the words that were next to one of the coordinates listed. Between the counter and the screen was a large table with a monitor Eric could not see from where he was standing. The same setup was to his right. In front of him at the center of the room with his back to him was a woman angel with a tablet in her hand. Her hair was brown, tied in a messy bun at the top of her head.

"What is the next location?" she asked, with a thick Spanish accent.

One of the other angels read her coordinates which she quickly typed into her tablet and Eric watched in awe as the projection changed to a town Eric did not recognize.

"What is the current magical activity?" she asked.

"Low activity," someone answered.

The woman turned left to look at the list of coordinates, still not noticing Eric who stayed against the doors.

"Projected weather patterns?" she asked.

"At this time of year," someone began to say. Eric watched one of the angels search for something on his monitor. "It's the rainy season. If we aren't careful, they're at risk for a hurricane."

The woman nodded, turning back to the town's projection, her eyes crossing Eric this time. She stiffened at first, her green eyes filled with questions until she seemed to come up with her own answers. She smiled at him and then returned her attention to the projection.

"Let's start with half a percent and see how much we can release there. If there is anything left, we can spread the remaining power in Asia."

Clicking something on her tablet, she watched the drizzle begin and continued to work, watching the drizzle pick up until it became a storm. The sun above it almost faded completely.

"Point eight percent, nothing more," she turned to the closest angel to her right who sat at one of the monitors. "Can you finish up the cycle Laura?" she asked, and was replied to with a nod.

Her work temporarily finished, she turned back to Eric. Her professional demeanor seemed to disappear as she smiled wide and Eric watched as a wave of energy seemed to surface.

"You must be Eric!" she said, approaching him. "You look so much like your mother. I was not able to meet her, but I've seen photographs in Theo's office. I heard you were brought here. Did you come alone? Well clearly you did because I don't see Neil or Evangeline or anyone, unless you know someone else here." She spoke quickly and energetically, never giving Eric a chance to respond. When she saw his expression, she laughed. "Sorry, I'm just very excited you are here. It's very nice to meet you. My name is Esme," she said, holding out a hand which Eric shook.

"Were you exploring?" she asked excitedly. Eric was about to answer when something on the screen caught her eye and her excitement turned to annoyance. "Remy!" she called, walking closer to the screen.

"¿Por qué no has despejado esto?" she demanded, reverting to Spanish. One of the male angels responded, exasperated.

"You know I don't understand you when you talk to me in Spanish," he told her.

"It's not my fault you were too busy lounging around Paris to learn it."

"Au moins j'ai appris le français," he muttered just loudly enough for Esme to hear it. Eric guessed he spoke in French.

"Moi aussi," she replied smugly. Remy sighed in defeat and Esme gave the order, this time in English. "Get that first line off the board already."

Rather than argue with her, the angel Remy got to work.

When Esme returned her attention to Eric, her joyous demeanor returned. "Sorry about that. Work things." She waved her hand, gesturing to the rest of the room then reached past him to hit a switch by the door which caused the blinds on the back wall to open, the natural light shining through the windows.

"What work are you guys doing?" Eric asked.

Esme eyes lit up at his question. "All of this is new for you. How exciting!" She grabbed Eric by the arm, pulling him closer to a barely visible projection and pointed at the sun. "You see that?" she asked.

"The sun?"

"Yes. But you see, the sun is not just what humans believe it is. Long, long, ago, a titan created the earth and everything on it, but one day when that titan died, he disappeared and all of his power became the sun."

"The sun was a god?" Eric asked.

"No, not a god, a titan. Much more powerful than Cyrus. His father."

Eric had received some of the information he sought without having to ask. He now knew that Cyrus was a god.

Esme continued her lesson. "But you see, that power doesn't just go away. It keeps growing and all of that power that it releases has to go somewhere."

"You control it?"

"No one can control it. We can only…" She searched for the right word, "Guide it. No one can be sure exactly how much power is released, but our job is to do our best to figure out how that power can be spread."

"What happens if you mess up?" Eric asked.

"That sun is what keeps the Earth alive. It's what gives it rain and wind, but when there is too much in one place, bad things happen. Too much power makes chaos. That is how things like earthquakes and tsunamis happen."

Shocked, Eric stared at the projection, thinking of the natural disasters that had destroyed homes in the past.

Esme's expression softened. "We aren't perfect. Sometimes there is more power than we thought there was and so tornadoes and floods still happen, but things could get much worse. We get the reports and make the calculations so that the angels who work in Heaven can do their best to make it come out alright."

Eric turned to look at the screen of coordinates and weather reports thoughtfully.

"What about here in Luxwick?" he asked.

"Cyrus powers Luxwick. Our job is not needed for it because he controls his power."

"But we get weather too," Eric pointed out.

"Yes, but we get to have fun!" she said as she pulled him to the other side of the projection where there was a small podium with knobs and a schedule clipped there as well. "Think of it as an allowance. We have a certain amount of time we can have any of these weather cycles in Luxwick, so we stick to the usual seasons. Snow in winter, rain going into spring, things like that."

"What kind of person is Cyrus?" Eric asked suddenly, desperate to learn more of the mysterious god.

Esme hesitated. "I have not met him personally. Most do not meet him until they are needed."

"Neil doesn't like him," Eric said.

Esme seemed to be uncomfortable with his questions, but did her best to answer them. "It's not that he does not like him..." she began to explain. "Their relationship is... complex. What Cyrus needs from Neil can be very... unpleasant."

"So, Neil just doesn't like it when he needs him?" Eric concluded.

"You should really be asking your abuelo these things," she said. Eric knew enough Spanish to know she had said grandfather.

"Eric," a voice suddenly called. Eric stiffened at the sound of Neil's voice. When he looked up, he saw Neil standing by the doors. Eric suddenly felt guilty for prying and hoped it did not show on his face as Neil approached them.

"You shouldn't wander around on your own," he told him.

Esme rolled her eyes. "He's thirteen Neil. You worry too much."

"I see you've met Esme."

"Yes, he has, and it is about time he did," Esme said, her annoyance showing clearly on her face as she checked something on her tablet.

Unphased by her attitude, Neil responded. "I thought it best that he had time to get settled before facing you," he mocked.

Esme's jaw dropped. "I am a delight!" She turned to Eric. "Do not listen to a word he says about me. It is all lies."

Amused, Neil told Eric. "I am only teasing. Esme is our most dedicated and reliable comrade."

"That is more like it."

The sudden sound of an alarm forced their good mood away. The alarm was followed by a flashing red light above the door.

"Remy! ¡Que hiciste!" Esme yelled.

"I didn't do anything! Whatever it is came out of nowhere," he assured her, clearly having understood her sentence from frequently hearing it.

Esme left Eric and Neil and approached the screen, also checking her tablet. "We need to send out the scouts," she said.

Suddenly, Neil was reaching for his head. When Eric saw how he gripped his head in agony, unable to keep his back straight, he paled. Neil barely managed to look up at Eric, his skin already clammy from fighting the connection. "Go," he urged Eric with a whisper. Before Eric could react, he was pushed back, forced behind Esme who shielded him. Every angel in the room stood completely still, their eyes fixed on Neil. They seemed to forget the siren, understanding that the threat in front of them was more important as Neil's features steeled. They knew he was no longer present in his own body.

In his panic, Eric lifted his hand. A shield formed around Neil, forcing some of the angels to step back.

"Keep it steady," Esme said quietly, her eyes never leaving Neil.

Neil, who was now possessed by Malphilus, smiled when he noticed Esme shielding Eric as well as the tense expressions of every angel in the room. He looked up at the barrier which surrounded him and reached out to touch it. His hand bounced back, making him laugh.

"Am I so frightening?" he asked calmly.

"Not frightening. Just annoying. You are a bug we look forward to squishing," Esme told him angrily.

Malphilus laughed. "Esme, is it?" If Esme was surprised he knew her name, she did well hiding it. "I am not someone you can easily squish."

"I enjoy a challenge."

Malphilus glanced up at the flashing alarm, a smirk on his face. "Then I'm sure you will enjoy this one."

He winced in pain and his expression softened. He immediately searched for Eric, relaxing when he confirmed he was safe. When Neil noticed the barrier, he seemed more relieved.

"It's alright. It's me," he assured them.

Eric lowered his defenses, allowing the shield to dissipate.

"Cucaracha," Esme muttered, stepping aside.

Something about the look on Esme's face told him something was wrong, something more than the inconvenience of Malphilus' presence.

"What did he say?" Neil asked.

Esme sighed. "He left us a gift," she told him, glancing at the siren.

CHAPTER 8
Dreaming of You

Eric opened his eyes to the night sky. The cold winter breeze sent chills down his spine. He sat up, feeling the grass beneath his palms, and realized he was at the park where he had spent so many afternoons before. Eric was confused. He tried to remember when he left Luxwick, but the only thing he could recall was going to bed. His stomach was in knots as he looked around, searching for a familiar face or sign to tell him how he had gotten there. He scrambled to reach for the cell phone Neil had given him, but realized it was not in his pockets. He looked down at what he was wearing, surprised, because it was nothing he'd had in his closet. The plain gray T-shirt clung to his skin and the gray sweatpants felt rough and uncomfortable.

He quickly jumped to his feet, realizing he was barefoot when he felt the dewy grass wet his feet. He turned to walk to where the street normally was, but was surprised to find himself facing the front of the school he used to attend. Eric stared at the school gates.

"This isn't right," he said to himself. Eric squeezed his eyes closed. He wondered if he was hallucinating, but when he opened his eyes again, the school was still there, three miles closer than it should have been. Eric entered the school grounds. They were empty and silent, not surprising considering the late hour, or at least he believed it was late. Something about the pitch-black sky completely lacking in stars made Eric wonder if it was really night, but the shining moon told him otherwise.

He walked through campus, looking all around him. He could not shake the feeling that he should go to one of the classrooms. When he reached the first classroom door, he carefully pulled it open and stared into a pitch-black room. It was like looking into an abyss; no end in sight. Even the ground in front of him was swallowed in darkness despite the moon casting its light from behind him. Eric slowly reached in

and watched his hand disappear completely in the darkness. Trying to ignore his fear, he took a step inside.

When Eric was inside, he was confused that although the room remained pitch-black, he could see himself. Eric looked down at his hands, examining their color, wondering why he did not disappear in the dark. When his uneasiness did not fade, he felt the need to get out of the room, but when he turned toward the door, he realized it was gone and he was now standing in complete darkness.

"I'm dreaming," he said to himself in disbelief. Eric walked aimlessly, searching for anything that could lead to an exit. After a minute, he felt as if he was going nowhere. He stopped and held out his palm, focusing on it. He imagined light radiating from it, illuminating the room. He focused, trying to summon the light like Neil had done during training. It did not work. Annoyed by his failure, he sighed and threw his hands to his sides. The sudden motion caused something unintentional to occur instead. A dim light shot from his palm, straight to the ground. When he looked down, on the ground in front of him was a flame the size of a baseball. The flame was unusual, blue in color, yet not spreading. Eric slowly knelt down then lay flat on his stomach so he was able to get a closer look at the flame. He stared at it, keeping his face only a foot away. He waved his hand over it but felt no heat. Then he carefully ran his fingers through it and was surprised he felt nothing from its touch.

"Hello?" a voice called out faintly, startling Eric. He stood up and searched the darkness frantically. He saw no one, but the voice continued to echo in his space.

"Anyone there?" the voice called out again, closer this time. Eric turned toward the sound, and saw what appeared to be a man in the distance. Eric stepped forward when the blue flame spread and formed a circle around him, blocking his path. Afraid to step through it, he stayed still and instead let the man come to him. The man came close enough for Eric to see him clearly, but Eric did not recognize him. He was about the same height as Theo, if not slightly taller. His hair was short and a dirty blonde color, and his eyes were blue. He was light skinned but not pale, and he appeared to be in his mid-to-late thirties. The man stood a few feet from Eric, twisting a dark blue thread that hung from the end of his long sleeve around his index finger.

"Who are you?" he asked.

Eric hesitated. His body tensed out of nervousness. The man must have noticed, because he raised the corner of his mouth into a smirk. "I won't bite," the man assured Eric. "I promise."

Eric stared at the man and summoned up the courage to answer. "Eric," he said. "What's your name?"

The man thought about his answer. He averted his eyes to the floor and his eyebrows furrowed. "...James?" he said, but he seemed uneasy. His eyes were fixed on the flames that surrounded Eric.

"You don't sound sure," Eric pointed out. He tried to keep his voice even, but it still came out shaky.

"That's because I'm not," James said. "Not a hundred percent, anyway..." James' eyes trailed back up until he was making eye contact with Eric.

"Do you know where we are?" Eric asked.

James looked around at the darkness then shook his head. "I'm not sure," he said. "I just woke up and I was here... Then I found you."

"I have this feeling that we're not really awake," Eric said.

"Like a dream?" James asked. His tone remained flat, making it difficult for Eric to read his emotions.

"I don't know," Eric said, shaking his head.

James looked down at the flame again. He knelt in front of it but kept his distance. "How did you do that?" he asked

Eric shook his head. "I don't know. I've never done it before, it just happened," he explained.

James looked up at Eric with disappointment in his eyes. He slowly straightened his legs without breaking eye contact with Eric. He walked forward slowly until he was just inches away from him. His presence was intimidating as he stared at Eric with curiosity, making him feel trapped as he looked down at him. They said nothing to each other. Then suddenly, they heard a strange rumbling and turned in the direction of the noise.

Eric suddenly opened his eyes and was awake. He was startled and could hear his heart pounding in his chest. He was floating four feet above the surface of his bed. Once he realized where he was, he plummeted, bouncing off the soft mattress. Once he had calmed down, he jumped to his feet and walked to his desk. His chair slid from the impact as he sat down.

With the face he just saw so fresh in his mind, Eric opened the drawer and pulled out his sketchbook and colored pencils, the pencils clattering across the surface. He drew James exactly as he remembered him. The memory was so vivid that he questioned whether or not it was really a dream. When the drawing was finished, he gently picked it up and examined it. Even on paper, he felt as if his stare was piercing him; as if James could see right through him.

"Who are you?" he whispered to himself.

Eric jumped when he heard a door close, realizing Neil was home. He rushed to put away his colored pencils and hid the drawing of James under his mattress. There was a soft knock on his door.

"Come in," Eric said.

Neil opened the door, keeping one hand on the frame and his other on the handle.

"How are you feeling?" Neil asked.

"I'm okay," Eric answered.

"Let me know if that changes," Neil said. "That is what I am here for."

Not wanting to worry Neil, Eric only nodded. He could see how exhausted Neil was. The dark circles made his blue eyes appear brighter and his skin was pale. Neil ran a hand through his hair to smooth it out and nodded. He seemed worried and distracted. Although looking at Eric, his mind was clearly elsewhere.

"Did something happen?" Eric asked.

Neil hesitated. "I just received some new information. Nothing for you to concern yourself with yet," he said, only making Eric more curious. "I've called a meeting with the Council, so I won't be home until nightfall. Theo will be home if you need anything."

"Theo isn't part of that?" Eric asked.

Neil shook his head. "He is too young. Cyrus prefers it to be just me and the angels he selected. We will only bring in Theo if we believe the new information concerns our kind."

At the mention of Cyrus, Eric thought back to the information Esme gave him on the god. He struggled to keep himself from pestering Neil for more information.

"Well then, get some rest. I will see you at dawn," Neil said.

"See you tomorrow," Eric responded before Neil closed the door.

When Eric was sure that Neil was gone, he let out a breath, ran out the door and went straight to the training room, sealing himself inside. Something about the alarm, the message from Malphilus at that moment, and the growing stress Neil seemed to be experiencing made Eric more desperate to have full control of his power.

That morning was not the first time he had awakened floating in the air, but he had never known how to do so on command. He sat on the ground and focused. Eric closed his eyes and imagined himself slowly rising from the ground. He focused on making himself lighter, but nothing happened. If anything, he felt heavier than before.

He stretched his legs and lay down so he was flat on the ground with his arms out. He closed his eyes, trying to relax his muscles, and again imagined himself rising, slowly. For a moment, he thought he felt a gap form between his back and the ground, but it was only seconds before he fell again. He groaned. It would be a long afternoon before he could accomplish his goal, but he was determined to make himself useful.

Meanwhile, in the conference room, Evangeline and Aaron were waiting for the others to arrive. Aaron stood behind the table and leaned back against the rails between the steps, lost in his thoughts. Evangeline sat at the table with her eyes fixed on the doorway. She fiddled with her bracelet, rubbing the silver wings between her thumb and index finger.

"Should I have gone with him?" Evangeline asked.

Aaron's head jerked up to look at her. Her eyes remained on the door.

"He's dealt with the connection since way before we were born. I know you're worried, but he'll be fine."

"I know… He just seemed a little shaken this time."

"I think he's just more worried after what he did to Eric."

"What Malphilus did," she responded hastily.

Aaron smirked, his eyes softening. "That's what I meant," he assured her, knowing she believed he was accusing Neil.

"Sorry," she said, not once looking away from the door.

Aaron took a seat next to her, blocking her view of it.

"What is it?" she asked.

"You're worrying too much."

Before Evangeline could respond, the sound of the double doors opening startled them. Roman entered the room with Neil and they both took a seat at the table. It was clear that Neil was drained of his energy and his body dropped onto the chair like a weight. It had been a long few weeks, and his connections with Malphilus were taking more of a toll on him than usual, even affecting his sleep. The dark circles under his eyes were impossible to ignore. His usually upright posture was now a slouch and he rested his elbows on the table for support.

"I apologize for calling another meeting so soon, but I have something important to share."

"Is it about the alarm?" asked Evangeline.

Neil leaned back in his chair, closing his eyes. "Unfortunately, yes," he answered. He leaned forward again on the table, resting his arms and intertwining his fingers. "Whatever set off the alarm was no accident, but a message."

Roman leaned forward. "You aren't suggesting that Malphilus was behind it, are you?" he asked. "Not every terrible thing that happens in the world can be pinned on him, Cornelius."

"I am not assuming anything, Roman. I know it was him. Just as the alarm went off, we connected. He called it a gift and I am bringing this to your attention because we must prepare for the worst. We cannot let him blindside us, not again."

Roman stood from his chair. "It's a shame we're missing half the Council at a time like this, but we must continue regardless." Roman made eye contact with Neil. "Is it under control?"

Neil took a deep breath and nodded. "For now," he said.

Roman nodded. "I will go speak to my team on the matter."

"Thank you," Neil said.

Roman nodded.

"I'll go with you," Aaron said, standing up. They left the room together. When the double doors closed, Neil hunched over the table and pressed his forehead to his joined hands and sighed. His head ached and he could feel pressure in his ears.

Evangeline walked over and gently pressed her hand to the top of his head. Neil felt the pain slowly fade from her touch. Relief washed over him and his muscles relaxed. When the pain was gone, he reached for her hand without looking up from the table.

"Thank you," he said, gently squeezing her hand. "I needed that."

"Happy to help," she said.

Neil let go of her hand and leaned back in his chair. Evangeline turned to face him. "You deserve a good night's rest," she told him.

Neil shook his head. "Not until I can wrap my head around this."

"What could he be planning?" she asked.

Neil turned his head to her. "I wish I knew."

In the training room, Eric grew frustrated. He threw himself back and rested against the wall, trying to slow his breathing, closing his eyes so he could rest for a moment. What felt like seconds passed, but when he opened his eyes again, he was in a room he did not recognize. This time he was not so surprised. He looked around and groaned, wondering when he fell asleep.

Eric cautiously stood up and looked around the room. Once again, he was dressed in a gray T-shirt and sweats. Despite being more prepared this time, the uneasiness did not pass. The room was ten-foot square and empty. It had white walls

and white carpet that felt rough under his bare feet, but had no windows and the air smelled like ash and smoke. A single door was directly in front of him. It opened for him, revealing the darkness.

"Here we go again," Eric said with a sigh.

He stepped through. This time, he fell through what he thought was solid ground, landing on his side in the darkness. He groaned from the impact and rolled onto his back with his hand on his side.

"I thought dreams weren't supposed to hurt." Eric muttered to himself.

"Maybe it's a nightmare," said James, startling Eric. Eric jumped onto his feet. As he stood, the blue flame appeared, forming a circle around him again. He saw James, standing a foot outside the circle. James looked down at the flame ring. "Is that really necessary?" he asked.

Eric looked down at it. "I don't think I'm the one doing it," he said. He looked up at James again. "How come you're here every time I close my eyes?"

"Why is it that every time you close your eyes, I find myself here?" James asked instead of answering. Eric was baffled, making James smile. He chuckled as he paced and faced Eric again. His eyes were lifeless, his lips a straight line. "You believe this is a dream, but it may not be. Maybe one of us isn't real or perhaps one of us is dead. Did that thought ever cross your mind?"

"I think I would know if I was dead."

"What makes you so sure? You can't know what death feels like unless you've experienced it before. Have you ever died, Eric?"

"I guess that's true," said Eric. James smiled again and stepped closer.

"Then again, what do I know?" said James. "I'm just the stranger in your head." They stared at each other, their faces only inches apart.

"Who are you?" asked Eric.

"I don't know yet," he answered.

They heard the rumbling again, more powerful this time. They turned their heads quickly at the sound. Then Eric was awake, a warm hand on his shoulder. Theo was crouching in front of him.

"Hey," Eric said tiredly. He rubbed his eyes with his right hand.

"Morning, sunshine," Theo said as he straightened his back. "How long have you been in here?"

Eric peered at the clock through the glass window. "About two hours."

"What are you doing here this early?"

Eric shrugged. "I had something I wanted to try. I don't remember when I fell asleep," he said.

Theo sat down next to Eric, against the wall.

"What were you trying?"

"I was just trying to see if I could make myself float," he answered.

Theo's eyebrows furrowed. "Levitation?" he asked, surprised.

Eric nodded. "Sometimes I wake up at night and I'm staring at my ceiling and then all of a sudden, I just drop. It always happens in my sleep, but I can't figure out how to do it while I'm awake."

"Why the sudden urge to try?"

Eric shrugged. "I just want to control it, I guess."

Theo sighed. "Well, I've never tried levitation before; never had a reason to. So how about we figure this out together. Sound good?"

Eric nodded. "Okay," he answered.

Later that night, after an unsuccessful day, Theo walked Eric home, reassuring him by pointing out that neither of them had succeeded and it would take time to accomplish their goal. Eric went to bed, falling asleep the moment he hit the mattress, which was where Neil found him when he returned home. He covered him before heading to bed himself for another sleepless night.

He stopped at Leanna's altar and stroked the beads on his bracelet as he looked at the photo where she held her newborn Eric. "Don't worry," he whispered. "I will protect him with my life."

That night, Eric had another strange dream, but not a lucid one this time. In the dream, Eric was standing in the middle of an open road. The sky was white and

the air was filled with a thick layer of fog. The scenery did not change no matter how far he walked. After a while it began to snow, but when the delicate flakes stuck to him, they did not melt. Eric examined them closely. When he tried to brush the flakes off his jacket sleeve, they only smeared, staining the cloth gray. He realized it was not snow falling, but ash. Eric inhaled the tainted air through his nostrils, then exhaled out his mouth. Smoke escaped from his lips and clouded his vision.

CHAPTER 9
Answers

When dawn arrived, Neil stared up at the ceiling after another sleepless night. Although he had not told anyone of his current insomnia, even he knew the effects were beginning to show. After his routine of breakfast with Eric, he walked him to Theo's then rushed straight to his own task.

Sitting in one of the spare training rooms, he stared down at the celocus gem in front of him. His focus was on the energy it gave, but he knew his goal would be fruitless. Although he could feel what it was meant to do, he knew that thirteen years was far too long for there to be any traces of anything else left.

"You needed me?" asked Aaron the moment he appeared.

"I'm getting nowhere with this stone. It's time we get information the more traditional way."

After meeting outside the portal, Aaron was confused when rather than taking Aaron's hand to provide him with a location, Neil walked straight outside.

"Where are we going?" Aaron asked, following him.

"Next door. If I remember correctly, this will be your first meeting with him, correct?"

"Meeting with who?" Aaron asked.

"Harrison, of course."

Aaron thought back, but the name did not sound familiar. Neil stopped walking and looked back at Aaron, realizing he did not know who he was speaking of.

"I assumed Evangeline would have told you about him."

"She's met him?" Aaron asked in surprise.

Neil smiled. "Yes, a few times. Shall we go?" he asked, gesturing to the front door. Neil and Aaron walked directly to the home next door. Neil rang the doorbell

and a woman answered. She was in her late sixties and had caramel-colored skin and jet-black hair down to her chin. She smiled when she saw Neil and tucked a loose strand of hair behind her ear.

"It's good to see you, Cornelius," she said, opening her arms to give him a welcoming embrace.

"It's good to see you as well," he responded. When she stepped back, she noticed Aaron. Neil introduced him. "This is Terra. She is Harrison's sister."

Aaron shook her hand. When they touched, he looked surprised for a moment before his expression reverted back to normal.

"Is Harrison home?" Neil asked.

"Yeah, he's in his study. You can let yourself in."

Aaron followed Neil straight ahead and up the stairs. When they reached the white door at the end of the hall, Aaron closed his eyes and concentrated on what was on the other side. Neil knocked and was answered by a deep rugged voice. "Come in," said the voice.

Neil opened the door slowly. Harrison was at a mahogany desk against the back wall, leaning back into his chair, reading a book. He closed it, setting it down on the desk before looking up at his guests, smiling at Neil. Harrison stood from his chair, hugged Neil and then stepped back.

"You haven't aged a day, of course," Harrison said laughing. "Me, on the other hand…" Harrison pressed his hand to his face, "…I look old enough to be your father now." He turned to Aaron and reached out to shake his hand. "I don't believe we've met. I'm Harrison."

Aaron shook Harrison's hand. "Aaron."

Harrison smiled. "You must be Evangeline's brother. I've heard so much about you."

Aaron's smile disappeared, and he raised his eyebrows, making Harrison laugh.

"You don't have to worry. She's only said good things."

"I'll have to confirm that with her," Aaron said.

Harrison walked to his desk, picked up the book, then slipped it into an empty space in the bookcase. "So, what brings this visit?"

Neil approached the desk as he slipped the folded handkerchief from his pocket, unwrapping it. "This," he said, laying the cloth on the desk with the celocus now exposed.

When Harrison stared down at the gem, he was awed by the sight of it.

"Celocus," Harrison said. "I haven't seen a fresh fragment in ages- well, ages for me at least." He picked up the stone, still in its handkerchief so he could get a closer look. "Are you in need of more?" he asked.

"Actually, I wondered if you could examine this fragment."

"Why?"

"Because of where it was found," Neil explained. Harrison waited for Neil to continue, so he did. "The stone is from our own storage. It was checked out by Leanna, but we discovered it beneath a doormat at an orphanage. More specifically, the orphanage where Eric resided."

Understanding why Neil brought the stone, Harrison quickly pulled a box from his desk to safely store the stone in. "I'll have it brought in for radiometric dating."

"Radiometric what?" Aaron asked.

"Methods to determine the age of the stone."

"Why would we need to know that?"

Neil answered, "Because celocus is not naturally occurring, although the stone is natural, the effects remain dormant until activated and the process is specific. The dating can possibly help me determine when the stone was placed."

Harrison nodded. "The dating will help me narrow down the time of which its mutation was activated."

"Thank you, Harrison," Neil said.

"We both know if this was the only thing on your mind, you would have just sent the stone with one of the other sorcerers, so tell me Neil. What else do you need?"

Neil sighed. "The weather team's alarm was triggered and Malphilus seems

to be the cause."

"So, keep my eyes and ears open is what you're asking."

"Precisely."

Harrison nodded. "Should I be expecting a fight soon?" Harrison asked.

Neil tensed at the thought. In the end, he shook his head. "I don't think so, but we should be prepared."

Harrison nodded and ran his hand through his thick gray hair, smoothing it back only so the strands could fall to the sides again.

"Is everything well?" he asked.

"Well with what?" Neil replied.

"With Eric, of course," he said.

Neil nodded. "As well as I could hope, considering the circumstances. He's adapted more quickly than expected, although we had a recent incident…"

"Have you told him everything there is to know?" Harrison asked.

Neil shook his head. "I have told him what he needs to know and nothing more." Neil noticed the disapproving look in Harrison's eyes. He continued, "It's for the best. The less involved he is in all of this, the better. He is already much more involved than I would like him to be."

"Shouldn't he know what's happening in your world? After all, he is living in it."

Neil said nothing at first. "He is young. There is no reason for him to know."

Harrison walked to his desk and sat in his chair. "You should tell him, so he can be prepared for anything. If you don't, his ignorance could get him killed. You told Desmond everything, didn't you?"

Neil's expression was suddenly a mixture of pain and anger, but he kept his tone controlled. "Now is not the time to discuss this," he told him.

Harrison shook his head, knowing Neil would not let the conversation go on.

"Make sure you bring Eric next time, so I can officially meet him."

"I will," Neil promised.

Once they had parted ways with Terra, Aaron walked Neil to the portal

building but stopped him before he could go in.

"Harrison is human?" he asked.

Neil was surprised at the question. "She really has not told you anything about him?"

"I've never heard of him, let alone a human who knows about our existence," Aaron explained. "I can't figure out why she never told me."

Neil sighed. "I don't believe this is a matter of trust, Aaron, but caution. We both know the laws against humans knowing of our existence."

"And why would she have to be careful with me?" he asked. Because Aaron and Evangeline were twins, they had always shared a close connection. Angels were more often born as only children, so they had no one to personally confide in apart from their mothers, as they learned from about the angels they would someday become. Aaron and Evangeline however, had each other. The thought of Evangeline keeping a secret from him did not compute.

The corners of Neil's lips went up, but not enough to form a smile. "Aaron, when is the last time you and Evangeline were truly in private?"

The question helped the situation make sense to Aaron. "Roman…" he said.

Neil nodded. "We both know he is quite the enforcer. If he learned of Harrison and Terra, he would wipe them of their memories no matter what the consequences of their mental states."

"And why do they know?" Aaron asked.

Neil thought back to the time when Harrison and Terra were just children, frightened and broken as they gripped the body of a woman.

"I met them when they were young. I cannot recall their ages. There were two rogue sorcerers causing havoc and their mother was caught in the crossfire. They witnessed the entire conflict. We did not have contact with angels yet, so we were unable to save her."

"Wouldn't it have been better to take their memories then? So they wouldn't have to remember something so horrible?"

Neil shook his head. "I thought the same, but they begged me not to. Harrison

was too young to understand what was happening, but Terra somehow knew what I was about to do. She had caught a glimpse of one of the other sorcerers doing the same to a civilian witness. She believed that the terrible memory of their mother's death would be better than a false one. I brought them with me to Luxwick and gave them a home. When the angels arrived, they thought it would be best if they lived on Earth, so I helped them get the home next to the portal. They manage the house for us to help us keep our claim on it. They only come to Luxwick on official business so that it is easier for me to conceal the fact that they are human."

"What kind of business?"

"Harrison spent his life studying magic. He has his shop where he crafts with glass and metal, but when needed, he creates our tools, weapons, and sometimes armor. He knows what stones can suppress magic and what materials can withstand certain spells. Terra owns a few shops in the area, so she helps with delivery from human vendors."

Aaron thought back, remembering seeing Terra walking with Neil through town once. "How do you hide that they're human?" he asked.

"They carry cadeea when they visit Luxwick."

"The gemstone?" Aaron asked.

Neil nodded. "It radiates the same energy as we do. To angels, they will feel like sorcerers." Neil checked his wristwatch. "We should return now." He looked to Aaron. "You should take Evangeline to Earth. Spend some time away from Luxwick so she is able to answer your questions."

Aaron smiled. "I'm just trying to figure out what she told them about me."

Neil laughed. "I assure you, only good things."

"I still don't believe you."

Neil turned away laughing and walked to the portal. At the other side, he met Aaron, who was now standing with Evangeline. Evangeline smiled when she saw Neil. When Aaron left, she walked with Neil.

Evangeline fiddled with her winged bracelet as she looked at Neil. She appeared lost in thought as she looked at the growing circles beneath Neil's eyes,

despite having so recently relieved him of his headache. She knew he had not had another 'visit' from Malphilus, so she wondered why he was still so tired.

"What is it?" Neil asked.

Evangeline fixed her expression. "Just spacing out."

Just as they were reaching the training rooms, Neil smiled. "I suppose I should warn you," he said.

"Warn me about what?"

"I introduced Aaron to Harrison. He is quite upset that you never shared his existence with him. I did my best to excuse you, but why did you never mention him?"

"I don't know. It never came up."

"Well, he's going to suggest you two go out for a walk on Earth, so when he ambushes you, it is best you pretend you were never warned."

When Eric woke the next morning, after leaving his bedroom, he noticed Neil's door was slightly open. Eric quietly walked over to Neil's room and carefully pushed the door open just enough to see inside. Neil looked exhausted. He was asleep in bed, lying on his back with his head turned to the side. The covers were tucked under his arms. Eric was surprised to see Neil sleeping so soundly, but even more surprised to see Evangeline there.

Evangeline sat on the edge of the bed and had her hand pressed to his head, a warm light radiating from her palm. When Eric looked in, she noticed him and turned to face him. Evangeline tucked the loose strand of the auburn hair that covered her face behind her head and smiled at Eric. She raised her index finger to her pursed lips to signal him to stay quiet. Then she disappeared.

Eric quietly closed Neil's bedroom door and walked down the stairs. When he reached the bottom of the steps, Evangeline was waiting for him on the couch.

"Good morning," she said.

"Good morning," Eric replied.

"I snuck in to check on him," she explained. "He doesn't seem to be sleeping, so I thought it would be good to help him get some rest."

"Are things always this stressful for him?" Eric asked.

Evangeline considered before answering. "He always worries. It's part of the burden that comes with immortality. He's lived longer than the rest of us, so he feels responsible for everyone's safety. Malphilus being out there puts him on edge, but it usually doesn't affect him to this extent." Evangeline stood and smiled at Eric, hoping to leave behind the subject. "Come on. You're having breakfast at Theo's."

Eric stepped forward and took Evangeline's outstretched hand and watched the scenery change from the living room to Theo's front door. Eric had never been to Theo's house before. All he knew was that the door in Theo's office led to his house. When Neil realized Theo would be spending most of his time training, he had his house built right outside and made sure they built a hallway that attached to the office building.

Eric found it difficult to conceal his laughter when Evangeline pulled a key from her coat pocket and unlocked the door to let them in. She grinned in response.

"Old habits," she said. "Plus, he told me to stop popping in."

Theo's house was surprisingly welcoming. When they stepped through the front door, their steps seemed to echo at first on the tile floors of the living room. The layout was very similar to Neil's house but with slight variations. Theo's home was more open, the kitchen and living room both visible from the entrance. Instead of a dining table, he had a bar-height counter with chairs and there was no second story.

The walls were light gray and most of the furniture was wood that had been stained gray, with the exceptions of the couch and two lounge chairs, which were black leather. The cushions and lamps were a deep red, Theo's favorite color. Eric was captivated by the paintings on the walls. On the wall to Eric's right where the television was mounted were four paintings that hung on either side, all evenly spaced out. One was of the Luxwick sky at sunrise, the second was of the angels' wings, the third was a wolf covered in snowflakes, and the final painting was of a lake. Eric recognized the medium as acrylic, which he had tried once before but stopped when he realized how much better he was with colored pencils. Each painting had a style that resembled that of Claude Monet. On the wall behind Eric was a painted tree that covered the entire

living room wall. In place of the trunk was the front door with the branches extending from either side. On the wall, multiple photos were hanging in metal frames. Eric did not know all of the people smiling in the photographs but there were a few faces that caught his attention. Some of the photographs showed people he knew: Aaron, Evangeline, Neil, and his mother Leanna.

"Leanna…I mean, your mother, did the decorating," Theo said as he walked out from the hallway. He had been working in his office before they arrived. "When Neil gave me the key to the place, I moved in some furniture, but she thought it needed to be more personal. Before I knew it, she showed up with art supplies and was covering the floor with sheets."

"She did all this herself?" Eric asked.

Theo smiled. "I told her she didn't need to do anything, but she wouldn't take no for an answer. I helped where I could, but it was more her barking orders at me."

Evangeline smiled. "You say that like you ever said no to her before," she said.

Theo looked slightly offended. "What's that supposed to mean?"

Evangeline laughed. "As hot-headed and stubborn as you are, in the end she had you going along with her every whim. She always got her way with you."

"That's rubbish." Theo tried to think of an example, but then realized he could not think of anything. "Christ," he muttered before turning away.

The entire time Theo was cooking breakfast, Evangeline intervened and commented every time she thought he was doing something wrong.

"How would you know, you don't even eat," Theo said when Evangeline told him he put too much pepper on the eggs.

"You don't eat?" Eric asked, surprised.

"Not since my rebirth, but I used to eat in my human life," she told Eric quickly before returning her attention to Theo. "Which is how I know that was too much pepper."

As Theo and Evangeline continued to argue, Eric remembered how Evangeline had mentioned their rebirth once before. She had told him that she and

Aaron were twenty-eight at the time of their rebirth and twins. Now with the added information that she'd had a human life, Eric realized that she and Aaron must have been humans before they were angels. Although Eric still had questions, such as if all angels were once human, he was unable to ask before Evangeline left.

"Focus." The word echoed in Eric's head each time Theo repeated it. They sat in the training room together with their legs crossed, Eric's eyes closed.

"Relax your body like a rag doll. Don't let it tense up," Theo said.

Eric tried to relax, but nothing happened. He opened his eyes and sighed.

"You're getting frustrated," Theo said. "Getting stressed will only make it worse."

Eric nodded and took deep breaths.

"I'm going to try it myself, Maybe, if I manage to do this, it will be easier to show you," Theo said.

Theo closed his eyes and relaxed his muscles. He focused on his breathing, imagining himself as a balloon filling with air as he inhaled. He pressed his palms to the ground and his body became lighter. Eric watched Theo rise until he was floating a foot above the ground with his hands out as if air was escaping from his palms. He stayed in the air for less than a minute, then slowly came back down, landing with a thud.

"Okay, so now we know it's possible," he said.

"What did you do?" he asked.

"Magic for us is like walking. It's like waving to someone or drawing a picture; you just do it naturally. When you walk somewhere, you don't stand there and tell yourself to move one foot in front of the other. You just do it without thinking about it, which is probably why you've only ever levitated in your sleep."

"How do you do something you've never done before without thinking about it?"

"You just feel it. Don't focus on completing the task, focus on your surroundings. You're trying to float like a balloon, so feel the air, feel your weight."

Eric tried to do as he was told. He let his mind go blank and felt the air in the room as it cooled his skin. His first successful attempt was not as graceful as Theo's. He jerked up into the air like a puppet being yanked up on strings. He rose three feet and then came crashing back down, landing on his side. Theo tried to suppress his laughter as Eric rolled from his side and onto his back.

"At least you levitated," Theo said, his laughter now erupting and making Eric laugh too.

After an hour and a half of practicing, Eric managed to get two feet off the ground and hold himself there for two minutes before he fell again.

"That's good, you're making progress," Theo said.

Eric nodded to show he understood, then Theo's phone beeped. He slid the cell out of his pocket and checked it, sighing.

"I have to leave," he said. "You good with walking home by yourself?" Eric nodded and watched Theo leave.

Eric contemplated continuing to practice but decided to go home and watch a movie. He was halfway to the door when his legs gave out. He crashed down and when he opened his eyes, he was on the balcony of the conference room.

He was asleep once again. Eric groaned in annoyance and pushed himself off the ground. When he was standing, he looked out onto the balcony briefly, not wanting to waste any time, then headed straight to the door so he could be swallowed by darkness.

"James?" he called out.

"Back so soon?" he heard James say in the distance. At the sound of his voice, the blue flame circled around him. Eric turned to see James standing just a foot outside of the circle.

"You really don't like me, do you?" said James while staring at the flames.

"What is this? Why do I keep ending up here with you?" Eric asked. It was the third time he had seen James in just a short time so he was growing impatient for answers.

James shrugged. "I'm just as in the dark as you are," he said, then smiled.

"No pun intended."

Eric wanted to throw something at him, but there was nothing. It was just him and James with the blue flame between them. They stood in silence until James broke it.

"There's a fire coming," he said quietly.

"What?" Eric asked, despite having heard him.

"It's just a thought that keeps popping into my head," he said, shrugging.

Eric remembered the smell he noticed every time he fell asleep just before seeing James.

"Every time I close my eyes, wherever I end up, it smells like ash and smoke," he said. He looked up at James, his eyebrows furrowed in confusion.

"Maybe they're trying to tell us something," James said.

"They?" Eric asked.

James shrugged. "Someone. Whoever keeps sending us here, probably?"

"Tell us what?"

"You said you keep smelling ash. Well, I keep seeing fire, so maybe someone's trying to warn us."

"Why would someone try to warn us about a fire? Compared to everything else that keeps happening in my life, a fire doesn't feel like a big deal."

"You're thinking too small," James said. "Fires don't just happen, people start them."

"Why would a pyromaniac be our problem?"

James laughed and Eric stared at him in confusion. Finally, when James saw the look on Eric's face, he stopped and smiled.

"You're still thinking too small," he said. "The fire I keep seeing, there's no way a normal person could cause that much damage." Eric still did not understand. "Hold out your hand," said James, but Eric hesitated.

"Come on. Just stick out your hand outside the circle so I can show you what I see," James insisted.

James continued to hold his hand out, and Eric reached outside the circle and

took it despite the sickening feeling in his stomach. The moment they touched a strange rush went through his body. Suddenly, they were no longer in darkness. The scenery changed around them, bringing them to a place Eric did not recognize. The earth burned beneath the flames and the sky was thick with smoke, nearly blinding them. He could barely make out the silhouettes of thrashing figures and screeching. Through the smoke, Eric saw the silhouette of a man, but he could not make out his face. The man's face appeared to be glowing like fire and dark wings emerged from his back.

Eric's stomach twisted when the man turned. In his fear, he pulled back his hand from James' grasp using so much force that he knocked himself down onto his back. The second he pulled away from James, they were back in the darkness and Eric was on the ground in the safety of his blue barrier. James stood outside the circle and lowered his hand, staring at Eric without emotion.

"What was that?" asked Eric.

James bent down, so he was eye level with Eric who was now sitting on the ground. His concern showed in his eyes.

"I don't know what it means, but it's like I said before: There's a fire coming and someone's going to start it," he said.

"Who could do something like that?" Eric asked.

"More like what?"

The rumbling they always heard woke Eric up again. He opened his eyes and quickly sat up. He was on the ground of the training room where he had collapsed. Two hours had passed, but for Eric it was only a few minutes. He went home to grab the laptop Neil bought him, then rushed to the balcony to research.

He tried to research anything he could think of that could be relevant. Lucid dreams, the blue flame, but there was nothing on Luxwick's public search databases and Earth's proved to be just as useless, which did not surprise him considering that to Earth, the supernatural did not exist. In the end, he closed his laptop and leaned back against the rails to look up at the sky.

"This is a place of business, not a lounge," said a voice, startling Eric. He saw it was Roman standing at the door. He walked up the steps but kept his distance.

"I like to come here to think," Eric explained. Roman seemed to only have one expression: constant disapproval. He took his responsibilities very seriously and that seemed to mean that nothing was ever good enough.

"Well don't make a habit out of coming here. There is a meeting here in two hours so make sure you're out before then," Roman said. He turned to leave, but Eric stopped him.

"I was wondering if I could ask you about something," Eric said nervously. He realized there was no better person to ask than someone who did not care about him.

"What?" Roman asked.

"Can you keep it a secret?"

"Only if I feel it is irrelevant."

Eric did not like the answer, but he knew it would have to do. "I've been having this dream," he said carefully, not wanting to share too much. "I've had it three times in a row. It's always different, but there's always this blue fire. It makes a circle around me. I was wondering if it could mean anything."

Roman thought about it. "Does the flame give heat?" he asked.

"No. It just protects me. I think."

"I don't know much about a heatless blue fire, but blue is usually linked to spiritual power. It's why our wings are blue as well as the souls of both sorcerers and angels. I don't know if that helps you."

"Thanks," Eric said, nodding.

"You should tell Neil. There should be no secrets kept from him." Roman said before leaving.

When Neil woke up, he looked at the time. At first, he believed he had been asleep for two hours. When he noticed the date, he realized he had not slept for two hours, but twenty-six. Neil sat up in bed, shocked that an entire day had passed. Then he thought and understood. He picked up his cell from the nightstand so he could dial.

"Bedroom. Now," he said sharply, hanging up once the words were out of his

mouth.

Evangeline appeared by the door and switched the light on.

"Did you put me to sleep?" Neil asked in disbelief.

"Of course," she said. She crossed her arms, leaned back against the door and smiled. "You're so stubborn sometimes that I had no choice."

"I've lost an entire day."

"And you're better off without it," she said. "Neil, you're allowed to rest every so often. You are allowed to rely on us sometimes. Immortality, and all, you still need to sleep and eat like a mortal does."

"Not when my own body can't be trusted. Not with Eric in the next room," Neil said, agitated.

Evangeline tensed. "That's what this is about? You're not sleeping because you're afraid he'll take over?" When Neil did not answer, she knew she was right. "You could've told me. We both know there are plenty of precautions we can take to make sure nothing happens to Eric, without sacrificing your physical state."

Neil sighed, unable to admit she was right. The day's rest made him feel much better than before.

"I'll be downstairs," she said before heading out the door.

Neil got dressed and was headed for the door when he felt a dull ache in his head. His body was rested enough to keep the pain at bay, but he still knew what it meant. He locked his bedroom door, hoping to keep Eric out, then sat on the bed and waited.

First, he heard his voice speaking to him, taunting him.

—You never answered," Malphilus whispered. —Did you like my gift?"

"I'm still unsure what it is," Neil answered.

—You'll have to ›gure that out yourself," he replied.

When the switch happened, Malphilus sat in Neil's body. He did not try anything, he simply stared at the wall with cold, dead eyes.

Meanwhile, Neil saw floorboards under his feet. They were old and warped, squeaking as he shifted. He could feel the thick dust on his skin. When he looked

straight up at the end of the wall, he recognized the sight. There was a large dent at the center of the old wooden wall and a picture frame he knew originally covered it lying shattered on the floor, covered in a thick layer of dust like the floor beneath it. At first, he thought his mind was messing with him, but he knew the room too well to mistake it for anywhere else.

Neil walked to the frame and turned it over enough for him to see the faded and damaged photograph that was still inside it.

He knew where Malphilus was.

CHAPTER 10
The Burning Earth

Neil sat on the edge of his bed lost in thought. He knew where Malphilus was and the thought frightened him. He recognized the dent from when he once lost focus and accidentally caused a nearby vase to slam into the wall. He had placed the picture frame there to cover the damage.

Neil let the aching in his head settle before he joined Evangeline and Eric downstairs at the table. The room had a lingering smell of bacon and although Eric was at the table, there was no sign of Evangeline.

Eric noticed Neil's eyes searching the room. "She's in the kitchen," he told him.

Neil walked into the kitchen, pushing the swinging door open. Evangeline was cooking breakfast, standing in front of the counter, cracking eggs into a bowl.

"Evangeline, I can cook my own breakfast," Neil insisted.

"I know," she said, but beat the eggs she had just cracked in the bowl. "Can you bring me the pepper?" she asked.

Neil smiled and added the pepper to the bowl himself. When he put the pepper mill back in its place, he realized he did not hear her mixing anymore. When he turned around, she was watching him.

"What did you see?" she asked, her voice thick with concern. She spoke quietly so that Eric would not hear.

"How did you know?" Neil asked.

"Your eyes," she said. "You may be smiling but you can never hide the worry in your eyes." She continued to mix the eggs as she spoke. "Aaron gets that same look when he's hiding something from me."

Neil considered telling her what he knew, but he shook his head. "Not here,"

he said. "We need to have another meeting. Soon."

Evangeline hovered her hand over the pan to check the heat. "Is it that serious?" she asked.

Neil shook his head. "Nothing dire. I would just rather discuss this with everyone present."

Evangeline nodded in understanding. "I'll tell the others after breakfast."

After Evangeline finished cooking, she retrieved two plates to serve it. Neil was amused by how comfortable she was, walking around the kitchen as if it was her own, reminding him of when she had done the same for Leanna every so often. She grabbed a small pill bottle from a drawer and tossed it to Neil. He caught it and looked at the bottle of pain medication in his hand.

"I know you aren't going to let me heal you right now, so do us both a favor and at least take human measures for that headache."

Neil shook his head. "I'll be fine."

Evangeline's eyes narrowed. She filled a glass with water and held it out to him. "Take the pills before I shove them down your throat."

Neil took the glass of water in defeat and swallowed one pill so she would leave him alone, but when she raised her brows, he took three more and sighed. Smiling, she picked up both plates before leaving the kitchen.

"Good luck today," she told Eric, ruffling his hair as she walked past him and teleported away. Eric smiled and tried to smooth down the strands of his hair back in place.

"Are you progressing with Theo?"

"A little."

"I'm sorry I am unable to join you again."

"It's okay. I know you're busy. Besides, that's one less person watching me land on my face."

Neil smiled. "Evangeline mentioned something about levitation," he said. "Why the sudden interest?"

Eric finished his orange juice and set the glass back down, shrugging. "I keep

floating in my sleep. I got kind of tired of waking up just to fall. That, and I don't like that I can only float in my sleep."

"The subconscious is often more powerful. I guarantee most of the skills you will acquire will begin as accidental ones."

Eric nodded.

Once Neil and Eric finished cleaning up in the kitchen, Neil insisted that he accompany Eric to the training room. When they arrived, Theo was already there getting the extra protective padding ready. He had the knee and elbow pads laid out for Eric. Theo stopped when he heard the door open.

"Good morning," he said.

"Good morning," Neil and Eric responded. Eric walked into the padded room so he could warm up.

"How are you feeling?" Theo asked Neil. "You know, with the whole connection side effects?"

Neil smiled. "I was put on bedrest for over a day. I feel I've already missed too much."

Theo laughed. "The world will keep turning even if you decide to take a vacation sometime. You should have more faith in us."

"It's not a lack of faith, just an unwillingness to sit on the sidelines. Especially not with matters involving Malphilus."

Theo nodded. "Just don't overdo it, old man."

Neil laughed.

Theo smiled and put his gloves on. "You staying for training?" he asked.

Neil shook his head. "I need to discuss something with the Council. I'm going there now."

"Need to know?"

"When the time is right, yes. For now, it's going to have to stay between the Council and me."

Theo nodded to show he understood. "Ever think about letting sorcerers onto the Council?" Theo asked.

Neil shook his head. "You know Cyrus would not approve of anyone he cannot monitor."

Theo shrugged. "Worth a shot," he said. "Good luck."

Neil waved goodbye and left, heading straight to the conference room for the meeting where Aaron, Evangeline, and Roman were waiting for him.

"What's the emergency?" Roman asked. Neil shut the doors behind him and took a seat at the table across from them.

"It's regarding Malphilus," Neil explained.

"Was there another connection?" Roman asked stiffly.

Neil nodded. "For the third time, this morning when I awoke, but that isn't what I would like to share," he said. "I know where he is."

The room became tense.

"Are you sure?" Aaron asked.

"When we switched places, he was in an old house. At first, I presumed he was hiding in whatever abandoned building he had found, but I recognized it."

"It could just look similar," Aaron said.

Neil shook his head.

"I know the location because I used to reside there. I'm certain of it. It was the house I lived in during the 1800s. I lived there briefly before I met him in person. Everything is exactly as I left it."

"It's most likely a trap," said Roman.

"I am aware of that." Neil rubbed his temples.

"Where is the house?" Roman asked.

"Seattle," he sighed. "If he's staying there, we need to keep our guard up. He's too close."

Roman quickly slid his chair back and stood up.

"Where are you going?" Neil asked despite already knowing the answer.

"To see Cyrus as I was meant to," he said. "We've kept this from him too long and it's time I stopped letting distractions prolong it."

Evangeline rose to her feet too. "Roman, is this really necessary?" she asked.

Neil shook his head. "It's alright, Evangeline. He's right."

Roman nodded and straightened his coat. "I will make sure it's clear we can manage your situation. It may convince him to wait before he summons you."

"Thank you."

Roman headed for the door when Evangeline called out to him. "I'll go with you," she said as she walked after him, giving Neil a look of reassurance. Only Neil and Aaron were left in the room. Neil let out a heavy sigh once he knew Roman and Evangeline were gone.

"He couldn't have picked a worse time to come out of hiding," Neil said while rubbing his face with his hands. He sat back in his chair and looked over at Aaron, who was leaning forward against the rails with his back to Neil. "When will the others be back?"

Aaron stared out over the balcony. "Some time in November, assuming all goes well."

Neil leaned forward and rested his elbows on the table. "Malphilus finally tries to draw us to him and we're missing half our Council members." He shook his head in disbelief. "It's as if he knew."

"The home is in Seattle. Did he live there with you?"

Neil stared at the table, unable to find the words. Although he was silent, the sadness he felt was clear in his eyes. He was reminiscing about the past, recalling memories both good and bad, all the memories that were lost.

"Briefly, yes. When he came to stay with me, I purchased a larger property so he could have a bedroom rather than a couch." The words came out dryly, each word weighing on his conscience.

"He knew Carlisle?"

Neil hesitated, but then nodded. "Closely."

Aaron sat next to Neil. "Do you plan on sharing this information with Theodore?"

"Do you think I should?" Neil asked.

Aaron shook his head. "No," he said. "He's too reckless when it comes to his

emotions. I think if you tell him you know where Malphilus is, he'll try to go after him. Everything he does is for Leanna, and Eric's safety being threatened is more of a reason for him to go after Malphilus."

"You don't believe we can convince him to be cautious?"

"He may be older, but when it comes to Leanna he turns back into the reckless teenager he was when you invited him in."

Neil sighed heavily. "You're right. We'll keep this information between us until Evangeline and Roman return and we can discuss other options. Hopefully it will be easier to keep Theo calm if he has something he can help with by then."

Aaron nodded, then stood. He gripped Neil's shoulder then left.

Neil spent the next half hour sitting in the conference room to clear his head. He looked down at his arm and pulled his sleeve back, so he could see the jagged scar on his arm. He traced it with his thumb and lost himself in the memories. Then his eyes fixed on his emblem at the center of the table until he grew irritated with himself and left, deciding this time would be better spent with Eric.

When he arrived at the training room, Eric was wearing a helmet along with the matching knee and elbow pads. He stood upright on the mats and took deep breaths as he tried to lift himself off the ground like a balloon. Soon enough, he was rising from the ground slowly and steadily. Once he was two feet off the ground, he opened his eyes and smiled at Theo. It was clear that this was the most progress he had made so far: He was beaming with joy. Eric continued to smile, even when he crashed down onto the cushioned floor. Theo laughed and helped him up. Eric removed his helmet then his elbow padding as Theo praised him, ruffling his hair.

The sight of them happy made Neil think of a future that could never happen. He imagined what it would have been like if Leanna were alive and wondered if it would be similar to what he was seeing. He thought that maybe Theo would have been very involved in Eric's upbringing, only Leanna would have been there as well, openly praising her son. The fantasy left his mind once Theo and Eric noticed him outside, watching them. Eric ran past Theo and pushed through the door.

"Did you see?" Eric asked Neil.

Neil nodded. "I walked in just a minute ago, so I managed to see your accomplishment. You are doing spectacularly."

The compliment made Eric's smile wider. It was the first time since he had arrived that he had acted his age.

Theo came up behind him, placing a hand on Eric's shoulder. "You should have seen him yesterday. He was practically bouncing off the walls. I almost had to wrap him in bubble wrap," Theo said, gesturing to the helmet and padding.

"It wasn't that bad," Eric said, trying to conceal his embarrassment.

Theo cleared his throat and pointed at the slight dent in the ceiling in the next room. "You're lucky I brought you that helmet today," he said.

Eric's face turned bright red with embarrassment. In an attempt to hide it, he took the chance to remove his knee pads while his face cooled down.

"How is your energy?" Neil asked.

"Good, I think. I don't feel as tired as I did yesterday."

Neil smiled. "Now that you are using your abilities regularly, your body is adapting to them."

"Good," Eric said. "I want to get stronger."

Neil noticed the determination in Eric's eyes and it made him proud, but he also could not help but worry.

"There's no need to rush," Neil said.

Eric nodded. "I know. I just want to be ready," he explained.

The three of them walked together to Theo's office so he could put everything away. Just as Theo was dropping the helmet into the chest he kept in the room, Esme appeared.

"We have a problem," she said. Without wasting a moment, she looped her arm around Eric's then reached for Neil and Theo, teleporting them all to the weather floor where the alarm was going off again.

"What caused it?" Neil asked.

"I don't know. I sent the scouts again, but they still have not come back with answers," she said quickly, gesturing to the map wildly. She turned to some angels

who were gathered around one of the monitors. "Muevete! Necesitamos esa ubicación!"

"English! Please!" They heard Remy yell.

Esme turned to him. "We need to get our asses moving and track that location."

An angel suddenly appeared, calling for Esme's attention.

"We found something. A fire."

"Try again, fires are caused by humans."

"The scouts are sure of it," the angel replied.

Esme stared at the angel and when she realized he was serious, she turned to Neil. The concern on Esme's face matched Neil's, both aware something was wrong, but what they did not realize was that Eric's expression matched theirs as well.

Eric's heart sank with dread when he heard the word 'fire.' James' words echoed in his thoughts. *There's a ›re coming…*

"I should take a look," Neil said.

"I'll go too," Esme said. "Someone get me a camera!" she shouted to the room as she rushed to one of the monitors. Neil turned to Theo who understood what was needed.

"I'll get a team together," he told Neil, immediately heading for the door.

"Remy, go with him!" Esme called out.

Remy stood, exasperated. "You know, I do in fact know how to do my job."

Esme replied with sarcasm laced in her voice. "Well, it's good that you know that, but I don't see you showing me." She returned her attention to Neil. "I'll meet you outside the portal in twenty minutes."

"Eric, go home for today," Neil told him.

Eric shook his head. "I'm going with you," he insisted.

"No, you are not," he argued.

"I just want to see what happened, so I can know what to look out for," Eric explained. "I won't do anything stupid, I swear."

Neil kept shaking his head as he struggled to answer. When he saw that Eric

genuinely felt he needed to go, he gave in. "Fine, but you stay in my line of sight at all times. Do you have your phone?"

Eric nodded quickly. Neil sighed and pulled his wallet out of his pocket and handed Eric a fifty-dollar bill. "Just in case. I'd rather you have something in case we get separated," he said as Eric put the money in his pocket with his phone.

When they stepped through the portal, dozens of angels stood in the building, each partnered with a sorcerer. Aaron stood to the side with Theo.

"Do you have the address?" Aaron asked as Neil and Eric stepped out of the house.

"I've got the location!" yelled Esme as she appeared, a camera hanging from her neck and her tablet in hand. She passed the tablet to Aaron so he could share the location with everyone.

Aaron briefed the angels. "When we get to the scene, sweep the area for anything unusual. Heal everyone you can. If the damage is permanent, try to at least relieve them of their pain."

Theo gave his orders to the sorcerers. "The fire made the local news, so when you get there, be discreet until the press leaves. Don't let any officials leave without removing their memories of us and alter the memories of anyone who gets healed. We want to make sure we get witness statements from everyone who's there."

Neil stepped in. "We are unsure what this is yet, but we wish to avoid a panic. We need them to be honest with us about what they saw. Make sure they feel heard otherwise they may cower if they experience any shame. We will stay until all civilians have returned to their homes or have been transported to a hospital. Understood?"

They all responded that they did.

"Alright then. Stay together and keep alert. Whatever caused the fire could still be nearby. See you there," Neil said.

Each pair vanished one by one until the only ones left were Neil, Eric, and Esme. Esme transported them next to Hopkins Library, just a few blocks from the apartments where the fire was located. They could already see the thick smoke from where they stood. They walked four blocks. When they turned the corner, the

apartment building was smothered in a thick layer of smoke and the fire department was struggling to put out the flames. Three ambulances were on the scene. The people who were rescued from the fire sat on benches or in the ambulances as the paramedics checked their wounds. The area was blocked off to keep members of the public away and police were taking their statements since it was a suspected arson. The familiar scent of ash and smoke flooded Eric's nostrils as he stared at the scene in horror.

James' voice repeated in his head.

There's a › re coming…

Before, it had been nothing but a dream. Seeing a fire just after receiving the warning from James made the threat very real. What James had shown him was much worse than what he was seeing, and the thought terrified him. Eric tried to put on a strong face, knowing that if Neil saw through him, he would send Eric straight home. Eric followed Neil and Aaron closer to the scene. As they approached the barrier, a police officer cut them off.

"Excuse me, sir, please stay behind the barriers," he said with an arm outstretched to block Neil.

"I apologize, the station should have called you by now. I'm Cornelius Alewar," Neil said, holding out his hand.

The police officer was confused, but he shook Neil's hand. He was about to give his name but his eyes turned foggy and he fell into a trance. "We are meant to be here," Neil said steadily, keeping eye contact with the officer. "We are investigating the arson for research purposes and the young boy with me is a witness." Neil let go of the officer's hand and they walked onto the scene. Eric watched the officer stand in his trance for a bit longer before he was completely conscious again.

"Did you use mind control?" he asked.

Neil shook his head. "We cannot control people. We can alter or add to their memories, but it's only effective with humans. I've only convinced him that we have spoken before. Later, I will make him think he never saw us."

"Can all sorcerers do that, or just you?" Eric asked.

Neil's eyes narrowed. "It is a skill available to every sorcerer," he said.

"Although I would prefer it to be a skill you won't need in the near future."

When they arrived on the scene, everyone had scattered. The angels carefully made their way around the building without being seen by humans. Neil monitored everyone, making sure there were no issues. All Eric could do was stay close to Neil and watch. The air was thick with smoke, making it difficult to breathe. At first, Eric was distracted by the sight of the people so broken because they had lost their homes. Eric sympathized with them. Then he noticed a shadow entering the building. Eric went to the side of the building and reached for the door's handle, wincing when he touched the hot metal. Eric forced the heat radiating from the handle to disperse until it was cool enough for him to touch. When he turned, he saw that Neil and Aaron had not noticed him wandering off. Eric quietly entered the building, the thick smoke nearly choking him. His instincts caused him to create a barrier around himself so the smoke could no longer reach him. When it was clear enough for him to see down the hallway, he saw the shadowed figure across the hall walk up the stairs and disappear.

Outside, Theo walked over to Neil.

"So far, no one's seen anything."

"Are you certain?" Neil asked.

Theo nodded. "Most of them were knocked out from the impact. Some of them said the halls were filled with smoke in seconds. It was all too fast for any human to notice what was happening."

Neil sighed. "We keep going. Hopefully we can get to those who have been taken to the hospital. They may know something."

Theo agreed. Then he looked concerned.

"What is it?" Neil asked

"Wasn't Eric with you?" he asked.

Neil realized that Eric was no longer behind him and the color drained from his face.

"Eric?" he called out.

Meanwhile, Eric was walking toward the shadowed figure. The steps

squeaked and groaned under his weight with each step he took. He reached the third floor, where the smoke was thickest. Just as he was about to go up the next flight of stairs, he heard a noise. Someone was crying. The sniffling was faint but it was coming from a nearby room.

When he reached the room, the fire there was dying out, but the smoke was still thick. Eric closed his eyes and focused so he could pinpoint on the source of the sound. He realized it was coming from a closet in a child's room. When he opened the closet door, he found a girl about seven years old, curled up in a ball, covered by the clothing hanging from the rods. Eric moved the clothing to the side and gently shook her. At first, she did not respond, but eventually her eyes opened just barely, and she stared up at Eric hazily. She rubbed her eyes, wiping away the moisture on her cheeks.

Eric smiled at her. "Hey, it's okay."

The girl's eyes widened as she tried to look past him. "The monster…" she whispered. She shook and coughed.

Eric tried to reassure her. "It's okay. There's no monster. I'm getting you out. Get on my back so I can carry you, okay?"

The girl nodded weakly. When Eric turned his back to her, she climbed up, wrapping her arms around his neck and gripping his shoulders. He felt her head rest on his shoulder as he stood. When he left the room, he watched the embers from the flames go out before they could reach them. Finally, he reached the door he had originally come through and stepped outside.

Eric had barely taken three steps outside the building when Neil, Aaron, and Theo, along with a paramedic, were already running to him. Eric stiffened when he saw Neil's furious expression.

"Do you have any sense of danger?" he fumed.

"I know, I know. I shouldn't have gone inside," Eric spoke quickly. "But it's a good thing I did because I found her."

Neil looked at the little girl clinging to Eric. The paramedic held out his arms to take her. After a reassuring nod from Eric, she let the paramedic take her to the ambulance.

"Why were you in there?" Neil yelled.

"I thought I saw someone," Eric explained. "I could handle it. I made sure I was careful. The smoke didn't even touch me."

Aaron grabbed Eric's hand and turned it over to reveal a slight burn on his palm. "Not completely careful," he said before healing Eric.

"That happened before I got inside," Eric explained.

Neil ran his hand through his hair and tried to calm himself down. He groaned and looked at Eric. "Next time, you tell me you're leaving and take someone with you. Do you understand?"

Eric nodded.

Neil sighed and then turned to look at the young girl who was being checked by the paramedic. She sat in the ambulance wrapped in a blanket and an oxygen mask on her face next to a woman who was slowly regaining consciousness on a gurney, presumably her mother.

"Recklessness aside… You did well," Neil admitted.

"That was deadly!" Theo said, his cheery tone confusing Eric as he used his Irish slang. Neil gave him a look of disapproval, causing Theo to retreat. "Neil's right though. It was stupid going into a burning building alone." When Neil turned back to Eric, Theo gave Eric a quick thumbs up so that Neil would not see him and then he walked away.

Eric tried to hide his smile. "She was hiding in a closet."

Neil was confused. "Why would she hide from a fire?"

Eric shook his head. "I don't think she was hiding because of the fire. She looked scared when I found her… She said something about a monster."

Aaron turned to Neil. "A witness," he said quietly. Neil nodded and approached the girl and her mother.

"Sorry to disturb you." Neil held out his hand to the mother who was now sitting upright, and she shook it. "My name is Cornelius. I was wondering if I could ask your daughter some questions. We believe she may have seen the arsonist."

The mother spoke softly to her daughter, who was clinging to her. "Sweety.

Can you tell the man what you saw?"

The girl stared at Neil nervously.

He knelt to be eye level with her. "It's alright. I only wish to stop the monster. Can you tell me what you saw?" he asked her.

"There was a man…" she whispered.

"A man?" he asked, and she nodded. "What did he look like?"

"He- he was on fire. He had wings…" she said.

Her mother hugged her to soothe her. Neil quickly put a hand over each of their faces and erased their memories.

Eric watched the girl in horror. The memory of the figure James had shown him invaded his thoughts. He saw it again, the figure with wings whose skin glowed like fire.

Once the fire was completely out, Eric followed Neil and the others into the building. Everyone scattered to look for clues as to what had caused the fire. Eric started where he had found the girl and searched the hallway outside the apartment. On the landing was a spot on the floor that was particularly charred. Eric looked down at the ashes so he could discern the shape underneath.

"Footprints," he whispered.

Neil, who was coming up the stairs, froze when he heard Eric. He joined him and looked down at the charred shape of the sole of a shoe. He remembered the last time he had seen something similar: the night Leanna was murdered.

"Aaron!" Neil called out and he joined them.

"What kind of creature can conjure fire?" Neil asked.

Aaron stared at the footprint, trying to make sense of it.

"We were raised to believe the only supernatural beings in the world are sorcerers, angels, and Gods," Aaron said. "As far as I know, only the Gods are capable of manipulating the elements."

"We must find out what Malphilus got his hands on," Neil said. "We need to leave immediately."

Esme took photos of the footprints as well as the rest of the fire damage.

When they arrived at Luxwick again, Neil and Eric parted ways. Neil was too distracted to notice that Eric was not returning home.

Eric ran straight to the training room and sealed himself in. He stood at the center of the room and exerted his energy until his body grew heavy. When it was too much of a struggle to keep his eyes open, he leaned back against the wall. When his breathing evened, he closed his eyes. When he opened them again, he was outside the building where the fire was, and he knew he was asleep.

Eric walked straight to the door and let himself into the darkness. The door shut behind him and he let the darkness swallow him. He walked aimlessly, searching for James, but saw no one.

"James?" he called out. When there was no answer, he kept walking. "James!" he called out louder. Eric stopped walking and looked up ahead to see if James was arriving yet.

Just then James stood directly behind Eric, nearly breathing into his neck.

"Boo," James said, startling Eric. Eric jumped forward and turned around to face James. The blue flame instantly shielded Eric, forcing James to jump back.

James raised his arms in surrender. He smiled. "Sorry about that." He walked as close to the barrier as he could. "You rang?"

"There was a fire today," Eric said.

James' smile left him, and he stared at Eric with concern. "Was it the one I showed you?" he asked.

Eric shook his head. "It was smaller," he explained, "but people got hurt. There was a girl who said she saw a man on fire. I think it was that guy you showed me," Eric said.

James' eyebrows furrowed.

Eric continued, "Neil doesn't know what he is. The angels don't even know what he could be."

"What are you asking me?"

"I was wondering if you know. Since you saw that the fire was coming."

James paced back and forth in front of Eric. "You want to know what he is?"

he asked.

Eric nodded.

James stopped in front of Eric and smiled. "The answer is right in front of you. You're just too blind to see it."

"A man on fire with wings isn't really much of a hint," Eric said.

James laughed. "It's more of a hint than you realize. Think of a species you already know exists. Just think about it. Have one?"

"Yeah," Eric said, thinking of sorcerers.

James nodded. "What does society believe about people like them? What is their kind like in the stories? Are they different?"

Eric thought and nodded, considering the sorcerers in the stories who use spell books and wands to do magic and dress in different clothing.

"So, what's the difference between the truth and the tales? It's all a bit animated, isn't it?"

"They added things," Eric answered.

"The stories evolved over time. Do you ever wonder why?"

Eric stared silently, unable to understand where James was going with the conversation.

James smiled. "Humans prefer things to be kept simple, correct? The thought of people like them doing crazy things isn't exactly a comforting idea. So, they changed the stories. They made them different from them."

Eric stared at James in surprise, suddenly aware of the point he was making.

"I know what he is, but the story changed so I don't recognize him."

James clapped his hands together, the sound echoing in the darkness.

"Exactly." James walked around the blue flame barrier, circling Eric. "What do we know that has wings and the ability to conjure up a flame from its own body?"

Eric thought back to the fantasy books he used to read. He realized that the man could only be one thing. He looked up at James. "Dragons..." Eric said, almost whispering.

James smiled. "Bingo. Dispiteous creatures."

"Dispiteous?"

"It means cruel, malicious. I'd say the word suits a monster that burns all."

Before Eric could ask anything else, the loud noise overpowered them, and he was awake, still leaning against the wall.

"Dragons," he whispered to himself. Dragons... He said it over and over again, so he would not forget.

Neil and Aaron had gone straight to the conference room. Neil stood on the balcony overlooking Luxwick while Aaron paced behind him. They stayed silent, trying to fathom what they had just seen.

Neil buried his face in his hands. When he looked back up, he stared at the sky. He released a heavy sigh and focused on feeling the cool wind against his skin. He watched the people walking far below him, all focused on their tasks.

"I don't know what he found," Neil said. "I don't have the slightest idea what he has gotten his hands on and it is frightening..."

Neil straightened his back and turned to face Aaron.

"Cyrus will know," Aaron said.

Neil shook his head. "I'm not even sure Cyrus will be willing to tell us."

"Cyrus keeps a lot of secrets, even from us. If he's been keeping us in the dark about this, it's for our own good," Aaron said. "If we doubt his intentions, nothing good will happen from that."

Neil nodded. "Yes, I know," he paused. "I apologize. I've been on edge since witnessing that fire."

Neil walked down the steps to the table and took a seat. Aaron followed and sat down as well.

"What's weighing on you?" Aaron asked.

Neil shook his head. "The fire reminded me of something." He looked up at Aaron. "It resembled the night Leanna was killed."

"How?"

The memory repeated itself in Neil's head. He visualized when he had first

entered the house. The sinking feeling he had when he walked up the steps returned.

"The sole print Eric discovered. I remember stepping into Leanna's home and seeing the same charred prints on her steps. The front door handle was melted in." Neil shook his head as if trying to shake the memory away. He closed his eyes. "I think whatever caused the fire was there that night." When he opened his eyes again, Aaron was deep in thought. "What is it?" Neil asked.

"It's just… strange," Aaron explained. "We spent thirteen years waiting for him to strike, waiting for him to do something. Then everything happens all at once? Finding Eric, the connections, and now this creature, whatever it is. Then there's the fact that all of this happens when half our Council is busy somewhere else?"

"You think he planned this?"

"No. I just feel like he's using the situation to his advantage. The first connection you shared with him in thirteen years happened after you found Eric. Do you think he found a way to stop them all those years and then decided to turn it back on now?"

Neil considered it. "I suppose it's possible. I've never attempted it myself, but I cannot fathom how that would be an option. If it was, then I imagine Cyrus would have put it to good use by now."

The double doors opened and Roman and Evangeline entered, both looking serious. Evangeline looked guilty. Neil sighed, knowing what she was going to say.

"He wants to see me," Neil stated.

Evangeline smiled sadly and nodded. "I'm sorry. I tried to convince him to wait, but he thinks it would be too risky."

Neil nodded and rose from his chair. "It's alright. It's better that we do this as soon as possible, especially in light of recent events." He straightened and smoothed out his blazer.

Evangeline became concerned. "Recent events?" she asked. She looked to her brother.

"We'll explain on the way," Aaron said.

"You're coming as well?" Neil asked Aaron, surprised.

Aaron nodded. "I think it's better if we all go. It's a good time to tell him what we saw and maybe get some answers."

Neil nodded. "Well then, we shouldn't keep him waiting."

Neil quickly sent a text message to Eric to let him know where he was going and that he would be gone for three days at most. He told him that Esme and Theo would be there, then left the conference room with the others close behind him.

By the time Eric had awakened, Neil and the Council had left Luxwick to see Cyrus. It took Eric a few seconds to recall the conversation he had just had with James. When the grogginess had faded, he jumped to his feet and clumsily pulled his cell phone from his pocket, ready to call Neil. When his screen lit up and he read the message, the color drained from his face. Three days seemed like too much time for information to go unheard. He slipped his phone back into his pocket.

He needed to tell someone that the monster the girl saw was a dragon, but there was no one around. He considered Esme, but assumed she would be busy trying to balance whatever damage the fire had caused. Then he remembered that Theo was not part of the Council and should be home.

When Eric arrived outside Theo's home, Theo was locking the front door behind him. Eric instantly hid behind a wall around the corner, although he was not sure why. His instincts simply kicked in; before he knew it, he was spying on Theo. When Eric peered around the corner, he saw that Theo was carrying a duffle slung over his shoulder. Theo tossed his keys back into his pocket and checked his cell phone, most likely reading the same message from Neil that Eric had received. Theo slipped the phone back into his pocket and looked around as if to make sure no one was watching him before taking off in the direction of the portal.

Eric ran home and went to his room. He could tell by the size of the duffle that wherever Theo was headed, he most likely planned to stay overnight, so he grabbed the backpack he kept stored in his closet. It was filled with money, clothing, and other necessities that were packed in case of an emergency. Neil had insisted they take precautions in case something happened. Eric grabbed the backpack and ran to

the portal. When he arrived, he saw Theo a few yards away, speaking to one of the sorcerers. His instincts told him that Theo was up to something and that he should follow him without being seen.

It was not long before Theo had disappeared behind the door to Earth. For a moment, Eric hesitated before stepping through the portal himself. Eric quickly typed a message to Neil:

I saw Theo go to Earth. I don't think he wanted anyone to know, but I think he might be getting himself into trouble. I know you're with Cyrus, so you won't see this until later, but I'm following him. I can make sure he doesn't do anything stupid and I'll text you when I figure out what he's doing. Don't worry, I'll be careful.

He was not sure when Neil would see the message, but once it was sent, Eric set his phone to vibrate and slipped it back into his pocket.

CHAPTER 11
Loose Ends

Theo arrived on the street, then headed for the main road, where he made a left. Eric's heart hammered in his chest as he followed him.

Theo walked a few miles until he reached a bus station and boarded a bus. Eric snuck aboard without Theo noticing. At first, Eric was not sure where he was going, but the further they traveled, the more familiar his surroundings became. Eric noticed the street signs and realized they were entering the town where Eric grew up. Theo got off and headed to the center of town. The sky was darkening. When there was only a dim orange light over them, Theo walked into the nearest hotel. Eric kept his distance and leaned against the outside wall. He closed his eyes and concentrated, trying to hear what Theo was doing inside.

Theo was paying for a room for just one night. When he heard the sound of the elevator, Eric entered the hotel himself.

He was greeted by the woman behind the front desk.

"Welcome to Starling Resort," she began, but Eric stopped her before she could continue her welcome routine. He put a hand over her face and watched her eyes go blank and foggy. He knew he had her in a trance.

"The man who just checked in is my uncle. I emailed you about him yesterday. I'm throwing a surprise party for him and you agreed to text me if he checks out before seven." Eric let the false memory play out in his head as he created it, making sure it registered in her mind. He lowered his hand, wrote down his number on the small pad at the desk, and handed her the paper. Her eyes focused on him again and she smiled, taking the paper.

"Okay, I'll let you know," she said.

"Thank you."

"Good luck with your surprise party," she told Eric as he left.

Eric left the hotel grateful that the memory replacement worked and relieved that Theo chose to spend the night in a town Eric knew, because that meant he had somewhere to stay the night. Eric's breathing was unsteady the entire walk as he tried to calm down. Eventually, he stood in front of the orphanage and rang the doorbell.

Seconds later, the door swung open and Yvette stood in front of him. Her dark hair was tied up into a ponytail and she was ready to turn in for the night, dressed in her sweats and a T-shirt. When she recognized Eric, she quickly pulled him into her arms and hugged him. He smiled as he returned her embrace. She took a step back to look at Eric as if she had not seen him in years.

"How are you already taller?" she asked. Before Eric could respond, she was pulling him through the door and leading him to the dining table to sit down. "How are you?" she asked.

"Good," Eric said, suddenly feeling shy.

"It's really good to see you, but what brings you by this late?" she asked.

Eric hesitated, knowing he could not tell her the truth. "My friend Theo and I are going somewhere, and we stopped at a hotel for the night, but I wanted to come here instead."

Yvette was suspicious. "Why didn't he come with you? We have the room," she asked.

"He wanted to catch up on some work," Eric explained.

Yvette still did not seem to believe him but she let it go. "Well, bring him next time. It would be nice to meet this friend."

"I will," Eric promised.

"So, what's on your mind?" Yvette asked.

"What do you mean?"

"Eric tried to keep himself from smiling, but the corners of his lips lifted. The realization that Yvette really had been a mother to him made his heart flutter.

When Eric did not answer, Yvette continued. "Are you in trouble?"

Eric shook his head and she relaxed.

"It's my friend. I think he's going to do something stupid," Eric explained.

"And who is this friend exactly?" Yvette asked.

"His name's Theo. He was close with my mom."

Yvette's eyes widened at the mention of his mother. Before he could continue, she said, "Your mom? You found people who knew her? How?"

Eric's stomach twisted in knots when he realized he had revealed something she did not know. He had forgotten that Neil had simply come and adopted him. Suddenly he was not sure if his family information was something to be kept secret. He hesitated, but eventually said, "Yeah… It turns out that Neil, the man who adopted me, knew her. He said he was her step brother." The lie came out naturally, but he felt guilty. "He didn't know about me until a few months before he showed up. That's why it took him so long to come and get me."

Yvette let the news sink in, then smiled at Eric. "I'm happy for you," she said. "So, what's this about your friend Theo? What's going on?"

"He's been going through something. Neil's out of town and he's going to be gone for a few days. I was going to go see him and I saw him leaving, so I followed him. I think he's going to do something that might be dangerous for him and I don't know what to do," Eric explained.

"Have you told Neil?" she asked.

"I sent him a text, but his phone doesn't get any service where he is so he's not going to see it until he's on his way back."

Yvette nodded to show she understood his dilemma. "Do you think he can be reasoned with?"

Eric considered his answer. "I don't know. All I know is that I can't leave him alone."

Yvette smiled. "It should be the other way around. Eric, you're thirteen. No one is going to expect you to be the responsible one, not anymore. Not where you are."

"I know, but…"

"Not used to being a kid?"

"I guess not."

Yvette gave his arm a reassuring squeeze. "You step back and don't do anything stupid, and if you do, don't sweat it, just learn. Whatever this man is doing, if it turns out to be wrong, it's on him to fix it, not you. Understood?"

Eric hesitated before nodding.

"Good. Now let's go get some sleep. Your old room's vacant again, so let's get you some food and then I'll grab you some sheets and we'll call it a night."

When Yvette finally went to bed, Eric settled in his bottom bunk and stared up at the top bed. Seeing the boards bare reminded him that this was not his home anymore. He reached up and felt the smoothness of the wood against his fingertips. Sleep came easily. When he opened his eyes, it felt strange to him that he did not wake with the fresh memory of his mother's face, or Neil's for that matter. This was where he'd first seen them, in his dreams. Before they became real.

It was five in the morning when Eric was up and ready to go. He sat on the edge of his bed and zipped his backpack closed, then waited. His sheets were already neatly folded and piled next to him. Eric stared straight at the wall, lost in thought.

Minutes later, the vibration of his phone called for his attention. He saw the message from a number he did not recognize.

Hey, it's Teri from Starling Resort. Your uncle has just sat down for breakfast and has informed me that he will be checking out soon.

Eric quickly replied to thank her, then stood up and slung his backpack over his shoulder. Eric made sure the note he was leaving Yvette remained visible on the pile of sheets before quietly making his way down the stairs. When he reached the front door, he was about to turn the handle when he heard a familiar sound: Yvette clearing her throat behind him. Eric froze with his hand hovering over the handle. He slowly turned to meet the all-too-familiar look he had gotten every time he tried to sneak out of the house or come back late.

"Leaving so soon?"

"How did you hear me? I thought I was really quiet this time."

Yvette crossed her arms, leaned back against the staircase railing and smirked. "Eric, do you know how many angry teenagers I get a year? My ears are trained." Yvette straightened her back. "I can't stop you, can I?"

Eric shook his head.

Yvette looked worried, but she pushed back her concern and instead walked to the kitchen and returned with a brown paper bag. She held it out to Eric. When he hesitated, she shoved it into his arms.

"I am trying my best not to drag you back home. The least you could do is accept my help."

Eric smiled, took the paper back and slipped it into his backpack. She stepped forward and pulled him into a hug. "Be careful," she whispered before they parted ways again.

Ten minutes later, Eric was back in front of the hotel room waiting for Theo to emerge. His phone buzzed in his pocket.

He just asked me to call him a cab. Would you like me to call one for you as well?

Eric asked her to call one for him and continued to wait. Soon after, a cab pulled up and Theo climbed inside, then a second cab pulled up for Eric. The driver was a woman in her fifties who turned and smiled at Eric.

"Where to?" she asked.

"Can you just follow the cab in front please? My uncle's in it."

The woman nodded and started the meter. Eric watched the cab Theo was in drive three cars ahead, making sure not to lose sight of it. Twenty-five minutes later, they pulled up to a car rental place. Eric paid the cab driver and followed Theo to the counter, making sure to keep his distance. Once he was positioned behind a wall, he let his senses take over. After spending years not wanting to hear what other people were saying, he never imagined he would be doing the opposite, trying to hear every word that left Theo's mouth. Eric listened in as Theo paid for the car and as the employee told him he would bring it out front. Eric went to the back of the building

and followed the employee to the rental car. Eric quickly climbed into the trunk when he was not looking and waited. Seconds later, he heard the engine come to life and felt the car moving as it was driven to the front for Theo to take.

The vibration of the car was soothing, or maybe he was just tired. Eric made himself comfortable in the trunk, lying back and staring up at the emergency handle until he finally drifted off. When he opened his eyes seconds later, he was no longer in the trunk, but in his bed staring up at the ceiling.

The lucid dreams were no longer a surprise to Eric. Now that they were becoming routine, finding the differences between dreams and reality were easier. In this case, the mattress did not feel like the one he slept on each night, but was rough like the trunk where he had just fallen asleep. When he sat up, he noticed the walls were odd, somehow perfect, because he could not remember each hole and bump vividly enough.

Instead of questioning what was happening, he simply stood up and looked for the door he was supposed to go through to find James. This time, there was no open door. When he turned the knob of his bedroom door, it did not budge, and when he opened his closet, all he found was his wardrobe. Eric stood in the room wondering if the dream was different this time or maybe there was no James to find; or at least he did until he felt a breeze. When he turned around, he was staring at his now open window with the curtains fluttering. There was nothing outside but pitch-black. Eric grabbed his phone from his desk, turned on the flashlight, and approached the window, then reached out and released the phone from his grip and watched it fall until he could no longer see it. Eric sighed and let his arms fall forward so he was leaning on the window's ledge. He shook his head in annoyance.

"Any chance you could just come to me this time?" he yelled into the darkness. His voice echoed in the nothingness. "Maybe send a ladder?" When he received no response, he turned around, hoping maybe another door would open. Another gust of wind hit him and when he turned around, he caught a glimpse of something yellow just below the window. When Eric looked out, there was not a ladder as he had requested, but a long slide connected to the window frame.

Eric smiled, stepped over the ledge, and slid down. When he reached the bottom, James stood ten feet in front of him with his back to Eric.

"A slide?" Eric asked in disbelief as he approached him. The blue flame lit a circle around him right on schedule, separating him from James.

"I thought it would be more fun. I don't trust ladders," James said. He turned around, standing just an inch from the blue flame.

"Why not?"

"They're shaky and you never know what someone might do at the bottom of one," he said, his tone turning cold and his expression hardening. "For one moment you're on top of the world and in the next, you're lying face down broken because someone decided to kick it out from under your feet."

A chill ran down Eric's spine as James spoke. He tried to swallow the lump that had formed in his throat. "It sounds like it's people you don't trust, not ladders."

James let out a laugh and shoved his hands in his pockets. "I suppose you're right." James stepped back and watched Eric for a moment, studying him. "Trouble in paradise?" he asked.

"There's always trouble," Eric told him.

James sat down and patted the ground next to him. Eric sat too, the blue flames still between them.

"What situation have you found yourself in today?"

"Well, right now, I'm sleeping in a trunk," Eric explained.

"No room in the backseat? Maybe on someone's lap?" he joked.

Eric smiled. "I'm not supposed to be there."

"So, you're stalking someone."

"More like spying…. I think he's going to do something stupid."

"And you're trying to stop him?"

Eric looked down at his hands and nodded. "I guess I thought if I could keep watching him until Neil gets back, maybe that would help."

"Who's Neil?" James asked.

Eric's eyes widened and his body tensed, making James laugh.

"Do not fret. I'm not asking for his life story; I'd just like to know who it is you're referring to."

Eric could not relax. He hesitated, but tried to convince himself that nothing bad would happen if he shared a few details.

"He's my grandpa."

"And you call him Neil?"

"We just met in December. I didn't even know he existed before then."

James' expression softened. For the first time, Eric thought he looked genuine. "Congratulations on reuniting."

Eric stared at him. "Who are you?" he asked.

James said nothing at first, then he parted his lips to speak, but before he could utter a single word, Eric woke up with a thud and was back in the trunk of the rental car.

Eric rubbed his eyes, allowing them to adjust to the darkness, and let out a big yawn. The image of James smiling was still fresh in his mind. Having a stranger in his head reminded him of Neil and the mind of Malphilus. He wondered if it was the same with him and James. During their first conversation, there was something that frightened Eric, something James had asked.

"And you're trying to stop him?" Him. He had not told James the person he was spying on was male.

Theo sat behind the wheel, focused on the cars in front of him. The road was not busy because it was the middle of the week. Tiring of the endless chatter, he shut off the radio, but the silence drove him just as mad.

When he saw the sign for the next rest stop, he pulled in, hoping a break from the long hours on the road would help him. He checked his phone and there were no alerts from Eric. Theo's instincts told him something was wrong. You're just being paranoid, he told himself.

Theo ran his thumb across the back of his phone, feeling the soft rubber against his skin almost therapeutically. Finally, he unlocked his phone and opened Eric's name on the contact list. His thumb hovered over the call button until he pressed

it and lifted the phone to his ear.

When the first ring broke the silence, it startled Eric and confused Theo. Theo moved the phone slightly away from his ear and realized the ringing was behind him. Eric' who had forgotten to silence his phone, scrambled to stop the noise, not letting it finish the second ring, but it was too late. Theo had already heard it.

Theo slipped his phone in his pocket and leaned forward, gripping the steering wheel with both hands and pressing his forehead to it, then swore under his breath, hoping he was only hearing things. He exited the vehicle and walked around to the trunk, opening it. Sure enough, he found Eric on his back, squinting up at Theo as his eyes adjusted to the sudden light.

"Bloody hell, Eric! What-" Theo rubbed his face with his hands, seething with anger, but tried to calm himself. "Care to explain your presence?"

Eric was stunned into silence.

"Get up before someone sees you! I don't need you getting me arrested for kidnapping!"

Eric quickly climbed out of the trunk.

"Get in the car. Now!" Theo snapped. Eric obeyed and climbed into the passenger seat. Once they were in the car, Theo waited for an explanation, but Eric said nothing.

"Okay. Let's start with the obvious question. Why were you in the trunk of my rental car?"

"I- uh," Eric stammered, "I followed you from Luxwick."

"Why?"

Eric did not want to answer because he knew it would get him sent home. "I followed you because I know where you're going."

"And where do you think that is?" Theo asked.

"To wherever Malphilus us."

Theo tensed. "You think I'm going after Malphilus?"

"I know you are. It's the only reason you'd wait until Neil was gone. Because he'd probably stop you."

Theo sighed and leaned back. "You can't be here, Eric."

"I'm not going home without you."

"Why are you doing this?"

"Because I know you don't have a plan. I mean, what are you going to do anyway? What if he is there?"

"If he's there, then I take him out."

"He's immortal."

"Nothing truly lives forever. Even gods can be brought down."

"That doesn't mean you can kill him. Even I know this is a stupid idea. If stopping him was easy, Neil would've done it a long time ago."

Theo laughed dryly. "This is ridiculous. I can't believe I'm arguing with a thirteen-year-old."

"A thirteen-year-old who stalked you for hours without you even knowing."

Theo's jaw clenches. "You have your phone with you?"

"Yeah."

"Good. Look up where the nearest station is so I can send you on a bus home."

"Send me back and I call Esme and have her drag you back home instead."

Theo examined Eric to see if he was serious. "You wouldn't."

"I know you don't want to go back, so the only way you're getting to Malphilus is if you take me with you."

Theo clenched his hands on the steering wheel. "You do as you're told. Understand?" Theo asked.

"Yes, sir."

Theo sighed, turned the key and drove off.

"Where are we going anyway?" Eric asks.

"Seattle."

"Why Seattle?"

"Because that's where Neil lived."

"Neil lived on Earth?" Eric asked.

"Luxwick didn't exist when Neil was born. It was given to him. Our ancestors

were human at one point."

Eric let the information sink in. An awkward silence settled as they silently continued the drive, only the sound of the car distracting them. Eric stared out the window, watching the scenery blow past him.

Theo did not handle the silence well, squirming until he finally asked Eric, "You got any tunes on there?" he asked, pointing to Eric's phone.

"Yeah," he answered.

"Good. The silence is driving me mad. Do me a favor and put something on?" Theo said as he opened the center console and handed the available cord to Eric.

Eric plugged in his phone and hit shuffle. Soon after, the speakers filled the car with the opening instruments of a famous Fleetwood Mac song. The familiar sound made Theo smile. He reached over and turned the knob to raise the volume.

"I haven't heard this song in ages," he beamed. "I'm surprised you know it. I was half expecting you to put on some pop song or whatever it is kids your age are into, but you actually have good music. Where'd you hear this?"

Eric barely suppressed a smile, pleased with the praise he was receiving. "Fleetwood Mac is Yvette's favorite band. She played me some of their songs."

"Who's Yvette?" asked Theo.

"She's the one who raised me at the orphanage."

Theo nodded in understanding. "Your friends listen to the same stuff, or just you?"

"I didn't have any friends."

"Why not?"

"Because it was too dangerous."

Theo suddenly pulled over, surprising Eric, and turned to face him.

"Are you telling me that you didn't have any friends because of your powers?"

Eric nodded.

Theo leaned back and rubbed his face, sighing. "Christ, Eric. Was it really so bad that you had to keep to yourself?"

Eric remained calm, having come to terms with being alone long ago. "It wasn't at first," he explained. "I had friends at first. Then when I was in second grade, weird things started happening. This one time I wanted a box from my room and I couldn't reach it and all of a sudden it was flying at me. Stuff like that kept happening. I didn't even know it was me at first. Then me and my friends were playing on the monkey bars and he accidentally kicked me, and he just went flying and I felt it. He broke his arm when he hit the fence. That's when I finally figured out that it was me and I just couldn't control it."

"You isolated yourself?"

"Not completely. I still talked to people, but I stopped hanging out with anyone after school or during vacations."

Theo turned the key and started the car again. "Well, that's going to change," he said before driving off.

"How?" Eric asked.

"Once Neil and I get you to the level of the rest of the lads your age, I think it'll be time for you to start school. Then you can start making friends."

Eric stared at Theo. "What are the schools like in Luxwick?" he asked.

Theo furrowed his brows and glanced over at Eric. "What do you mean what are they like? They're schools."

Eric's cheeks flushed in embarrassment. "Right," he said.

"What were you picturing?"

Eric shrugged. "I don't know… Harry Potter?"

Theo laughed. "Sorry, mate, no potion classes and flying broomsticks for you. Unfortunately, school is practically human."

"So, I still have to learn math?" Eric asked in annoyance.

Theo nodded. "Sorry to crush your spirit," he joked.

Eric sighed. "I hate math and science."

Theo laughed. "Don't worry. It's a little more fun for us than it is for the humans since we don't have as many safety concerns as they do."

Hours passed by and they kept their stops to a minimum, only pulling over

for bathroom breaks and meals. After the sun set, Eric's eyelids began to feel heavy. Theo must have noticed because minutes later, he was pulling into a parking spot in front of a motel.

"Did you pack for the nights?" Theo asked.

"Yeah. I grabbed my emergency bag," he told him.

"Alright," Theo said as he cut the engine. "Wait here. I'll book us a room."

Theo stepped out of the car, locking it behind him. The wind howled; he wrapped his jacket tighter around himself before heading to the front desk. Eric watched him in the well-lit room as the man at the front desk slid the sign-in sheet to him.

Observing the area, Eric noticed that it was mostly vacant. Only three other cars were in the parking lot and the street lights barely lit the area. A dim glow in the distance caught Eric's eye. When he turned, the glow was gone, but he saw the silhouette of a woman. Eric stared at her and wondered what she was doing out in the middle of the night. Then the silhouette changed. Something emerged from the girl's back, widening her silhouette. Eric realized that they were wings, like those he'd seen on the man in the vision.

Before he could react, Theo was tapping on the window, startling him.

Eric looked back to where the girl was standing, but she was gone.

Theo knocked on the window again. "Come on already. It's Baltic out here," he said.

"What?" Eric asked, perplexed.

Impatient, rather than explain what he meant, he shook his head. "Just get out here."

Eric broke out of his trance and stepped out. The wind took his breath away. He grabbed his backpack and slung it onto his shoulder, then followed Theo to their assigned motel room, pleased by the welcoming warmth inside. The room was small but comfortable. Two twin beds were well made against the wall directly across from the door. On the left side of the room was a bathroom door. Theo tossed his backpack onto the bed closest to the bathroom and Eric did the same with the remaining bed. He

kicked his shoes off and pushed them under the bed then climbed on top, happy to be out of the car.

"You need to use the toilet?" Theo asked Eric.

"No."

"Righty then. I'm going to hop in the shower then," he said. He picked up the remote from the TV stand, tossing it to Eric. "I'll just be a few minutes."

After scrolling through the available channels, Eric settled on some science fiction film he had never seen, then changed into his pajama bottoms and waited for Theo to finish his shower. As promised, he only took a few minutes, then returned in a pair of gym shorts and a tank top, toweling his hair dry.

"What film is this?" he asked as he settled onto the bed.

"I don't know, but it looks old."

Theo tossed the towel next to him and laid back.

"Do you have a plan?" Eric asked. Theo was caught by surprise, having forgotten his objective for a moment. A heavy silence fell between them. When Theo did not answer, Eric asked a different question. "Why do you want to fight him so bad? I mean, I get that he's a bad guy, but isn't Neil the one he's after?"

Theo sighed. "It's not something I feel comfortable discussing with you."

Eric fiddled with a loose thread on the end of his blanket. "He..." he began, drifting between words. "He's the reason I'm- I was an orphan..." Eric looked up at Theo. "Plus he tried to strangle me," he said, his throat tightening and his heart pounding at the reminder. "I think we're way past keeping me out of it."

Theo looked at Eric's neck, reminded of when it was covered in bruises, and nodded.

"You've just answered it," Theo said. "That man is a menace. He keeps threatening the people I care about and I can't just stand aside and let him keep going."

Eric tugged on his mother's bracelet, rolling the beads between his fingers. "I get that," he told Theo. "But if Neil says he's dangerous, shouldn't we listen to him? Shouldn't we be careful about him?"

"Neil does what he does because he's worried about everyone all the time,

but since what happened to your mum, he's been playing it too safe. The snake hid for thirteen years and so far, he's made all the moves. At this rate, we're never catching him."

"Do you even know what he looks like?"

Theo shook his head. "I'll know him when I see him."

"He knows what we look like."

"What?"

Eric sighed. "I've haven't seen him either, but he's seen all of us, right? Through Neil?"

Theo nodded. "I suppose that's true. Why?"

"He knows what we look like, but we don't know what he looks like. We aren't like Neil. We can't feel when someone uses magic. We might have already met him without knowing it was him."

Theo let out a sigh. "You really know how to make a man paranoid," he joked.

"I just don't think you're being smart about this."

Theo leaned back against the headboard. "You're right," he said.

Eric continued to stare at his mother's bracelet. He glanced over at Theo, who was focused on the television.

"What was she like?" Eric asked quietly.

Theo turned his head toward Eric. He did not need to ask who Eric was referring to. Theo looked at the young boy across from him and was saddened by the thought that he never knew the wonderful person who was his mother.

"She was…" he was at a loss for words, "...wonderful. Kind, considerate, but also stubborn when she felt she needed to be. I'd say you inherited that side of her."

Eric smiled. "Feels like everyone is."

Theo looked at Eric's wrist and focused on the bracelet he was still fiddling with. "She loved making things," he said. Theo reached for the thin cord around his neck and pulled it up, revealing a pendant at the end of it. He removed the necklace and held it up by the cord to show Eric. It was a sterling silver pendant, an inch and a

half in diameter, and in the shape of a shield. He tossed it to Eric, so he could get a closer look.

"She made that. Gave it to me the day Neil invited me to join them in their headquarters. She wanted me to have something to commemorate it."

Eric examined the perfect shield pendant. On the front was their emblem, engraved into the silver with a blue gem at the center. On the back was a personalized engraving:

Theodore Cross

Be sTrong

And Cour Ageous

05.19.96

"How did she make it?" asked Eric, staring down at the pendant in awe.

"Harrison taught her," he answered. Eric turned to Theo for clarification, because he had not yet met Harrison. "You don't have a clue who I'm talking about, do you?" Theo asked. Eric shook his head. "He's a friend, a human friend. He's a blacksmith, but he's also a jeweler. He's retired now, only helps us out when we need it and does some repairs on the side every now and then, but she said he showed her how to make it and helped her with the polishing."

"That's so cool," he said before handing the necklace back to Theo.

"It is," he said. Theo put the necklace back around his neck and tucked it under his shirt.

"I didn't think you guys made friends with people who aren't like us."

"We don't," he said, winking. "It's against the rules for humans to know what we can do, and we agree with that rule, but some people are exceptions. Neil found Harrison and his sister Terra when he was a wee lad. Both were newly orphaned. Terra was too young to care for her brother, so he took them in and eventually bought the house next to the portal and moved them there. They've been helping us ever since. Terra doesn't live there anymore, but she's still there all the time."

"What happens if a person does find out about us?"

"We wipe out their memory of us," he explained. "Or at least, that's what we're supposed to do. Anyway, I heard you're a pretty talented artist yourself."

"Yeah, I guess," Eric said shyly.

"What's your skill?"

"I draw with colored pencils."

"Any of them there?" he asked, gesturing to Eric's phone on the night stand. Eric nodded and opened his photos.

"Before Neil found me, I used to dream about him and my mom. I thought they were just dreams, but I guess I was remembering them a little. When he told me she was my mom, I got really happy, so I took a picture of my drawing after he got me a phone."

Eric opened the photo of the drawing he had of his mother. He smiled at the drawing, then passed the phone to Theo so he could look at it. Theo was impressed. "This is...amazing."

"Yeah, well I had a lot of free time to practice."

Theo smiled. "You're just like her."

Eric enjoyed hearing he shared similarities with the mother he would never meet. It made him feel closer to her. Then he was reminded of another person he would never meet.

"And my dad? What was he like?" Theo tensed at the mention of Eric's father. Noticing Theo's reaction, Eric continued. "I know what happened to him because Neil told me, but I don't know anything about him. I was wondering if you would tell me... I don't even know what his name was."

Theo looked down at Eric's phone again, at the photo of Leanna. "His name was Desmond Collins," he said.

"His last name wasn't Blackwood?"

Theo shook his head. "No, it wasn't. Blackwood was Leanna's family name. They were never married, and Desmond passed on before you were born. Leanna thought it would be better for her to pass on her family name completely, so you're

named after her fathers."

"Fathers plural?" Eric asked in surprise.

"Theo's eyes widened. "Were you never shown your birth certificate?" Theo asked. Not waiting for Eric to answer, he continued. "Eric Cornelius Blackwood, named after the man who helped give her life and the man who raised her. She actually wanted your first name to be Cornelius, but Neil told her it would be cruel to give you what he thought was such an outdated name," he joked. "Anyway, she felt it was wrong for you to have his name, so she gave you hers."

"Did you know him?" asked Eric.

Theo sighed, "Yeah, I knew the bloke."

"You didn't like him," Eric pointed out.

"He wasn't so bad, he was just… trouble. Your mother and I met him when he moved to our school. She was fifteen, he was seventeen, same as me, and she was smitten with him from the second she saw him. He was a good man when he wanted to be, he just couldn't break his habits."

"What did he do?"

"He was a conman, a thief. When he found out your mother was pregnant, he robbed one of the markets for money, but he was caught. He injured three of the officials, nearly killed the shop owner…" he said sullenly.

"Why was she with him?" Eric asked.

Theo shrugged. "She didn't know. We knew he had problems with authority, we just didn't realize how bad they were until it was too late."

"Was she happy?" he asked. "When she was with him?"

Theo thought back. "There were bad days of course… but bad days make for better days," he said with a thoughtful smile. He shook his head. "That was what she said every time I asked her that same question."

Theo looked at Eric, who was sullen from the discovery of what kind of person his father was. "We should get some sleep, get an early start in the morning," he said.

Eric nodded. "Okay,"

The next morning, Theodore rose bright and early. When he opened his eyes, he turned his head to see Eric fast asleep in the other bed. Theo quickly climbed off the bed, keeping his footsteps light as he gathered his things. He pulled the notepad from the nightstand and wrote:

I'm sorry, but I need to go alone. Call Esme, have her come get you. Don't come after me.

He slid the note to Eric's side and quietly stepped out of the room, but realized his plan had failed. Theo jumped back, his side hitting the door, and rubbed his eyes. Eric stood in front of him, leaning against the car with his arms crossed.

"Why aren't you inside, sleeping?" he asked in annoyance.

Eric smiled. "I knew you were going to try to leave without me, so I snuck out early and stuffed pillows under the blanket."

Theo sighed. "This isn't a game. You can't come with me, not for this."

"You can't go alone," Eric insisted.

Theo raised his voice, "Would you just…" he stopped, closing his eyes as he tried to calm himself down. He spoke again in a steady voice. "You're just a kid."

"And you're just a guy."

"What do I have to do to make you go back?"

"You have to come back with me," Eric replied.

In the end, Theo did not have it in him to argue anymore, but he also could not turn back when he had come so far. He and Eric sat in silence as they drove.

"Neil's going to freak," Eric finally said.

"By the time he gets back, we'll be halfway home,"

"Evangeline's going to be mad," Eric pointed out.

The mention of Evangeline made Theo grimace. "Yeah, I might have to go into hiding for a bit."

"Is she scary when she's mad?"

"You better believe it. The woman looks younger than me, but she's twice my age and she'll never let me forget it."

"What about Aaron?"

"Worse," he said. "He doesn't get angry, just disappointed."

"He guilt-trips you?"

"First it's a lecture, then he shuns you," he said.

Eric smiled. "Yvette does the same thing."

"You miss her?" Theo asked.

Eric looked out the window. The breeze from the air conditioner hit his face, spreading the scent of pine air freshener. He nodded. "Sometimes," he said, "but I can still go see her."

Theo nodded. "Anytime you find yourself in need of a visit, you just let us know and we'll get you there."

They fell into reminiscing. Theo told stories of his adventures with Leanna, and Eric recalled his times with Yvette. With each hour that passed, Eric felt closer to Theo and his mother. They only stopped for gas, bathroom breaks, and meals. By the time they reached Seattle, it was nearly nightfall.

When they reached the state line, Eric's heart sank at the reminder of where they were going. He reached for his healed throat, remembering the pain he felt when the monster attacked him. Eric opened his phone, but was disappointed he did not have any new alerts.

Theo hesitated but eventually nodded. "I need to," he said.

Eric nodded. "Okay," he said. Then he opened his phone and stared at Neil's name, watching the blinking blue line on the message bar. He sent a text to Neil.

We just got to Seattle.

Sending the message did not make him feel any better because it would not make a difference. Neil was still out of range, and Theo was only minutes from making a huge mistake.

When he felt the car slow, his heart beat faster. Theo parked the car and stepped out.

"We'll be on foot the rest of the way."

Eric did not pay much attention to where they were going. He was so occupied with trying to calm himself down that he could not register every crosswalk and street sign into his memory. He was not even sure how long they had walked. Was it five minutes, or twenty? Before he knew it, they had stopped, and found themselves in a vacant alleyway.

"Is this it?" Eric asked in confusion. He tried to find something out of the ordinary, but it was only brick and debris.

Without a word, Theo turned to face him, and Eric felt a surge through his body before he fell backwards. A tingling sensation knocked the wind from his lungs. Theo caught him before he hit the ground and gently lowered him, sitting him upright against the wall. Eric was awake, but he could not move. He panicked as he sat there immobile, his heart hammering in his chest and his breathing difficult to control.

"It's alright. Stay calm," Theo said quickly. "I've paralyzed you temporarily. The spell will wear off in about an hour, two at most."

Eric tried to speak, but his lips would not move.

Theo smoothed Eric's hair back, then pulled a beanie from his backpack, sliding it onto Eric's head. "When the spell wears off, call Esme and have her come fetch you. Don't go looking for me." He removed his jacket and wrapped it around Eric. "I should've done this back at the motel. I wish I'd thought of it then."

He stood up and leaned back against the wall, shaking his head. "I'm sorry, Eric, I just can't have you there with me. It's too dangerous."

Eric watched Theo move out of his line of sight. His entire body shook as he tried to break free from the spell.

Theo left Eric there, knowing he would be home in just a few hours. He knew where he was going, and he knew he had to go alone. Fifteen minutes later, he stood in front of an abandoned house in a desolate area. When he moved forward onto the old wooden steps, they creaked under his weight. He reached the door and gently

pushed it open. The rough texture from the chipped paint scratched his fingertips. When he entered the house, he felt swallowed in the darkness. The dust in the air was almost suffocating and the whole house creaked with each step. When he reached the hallway, he turned and focused on the damage on the wall, the dent Neil had made. He closed his eyes and let his senses take over. Then he heard a creak behind him. Theo quickly used his power to pull the broken picture frame from the ground and launched it at the shadowy figure standing at the other end of the hallway. The figure dodged and threw a lamp at Theo, but Theo ducked, letting the lamp smash against the wall.

Theo ran toward the figure and brought his palms together. A ball of foggy light formed between them, then he thrust his arms forward and let that light hit the figure, which he could now see was a man wearing a white mask. The man fell down on his back and slid into the wall behind him. Theo pulled shards of glass from the broken frame and threw them down at the man. The man screamed as the shards hit his legs.

Another figure ran behind Theo, but before he could react, something cold went into his right upper arm and was pulled out just as quickly. The pain made him shriek. Theo turned to see another sorcerer, a female this time, wearing the same type of mask, manipulating the knife, which was now covered in his blood. She attacked him again, but Theo threw his arms in front of himself and formed a shield, deflecting the knife. He managed to take the knife, but just as he turned it on her, a ball of light hit him on the back of his head and he fell forward. Theo lay on the ground as the woman grabbed him by the back of his head and forced him to sleep.

CHAPTER 12
Into the Fire

The first thing Theo felt when he came to was the pulsating in his right arm. The pain arrived soon after. The next thing he felt was the cold hard surface under his body. He tried to move, and realized he was lying on his stomach on the ground. He opened his eyes, but the light blinded him. He moved to push himself up, but his arm throbbed under his weight, and he fell right back down. Theo rolled onto his back and reached for his wound. His vision was just beginning to focus when the lights pointing down on him blinded him again, making his head throb. He looked around, realizing he was in a concrete room. He tilted his head back and glimpsed metal bars, showing him he was in a cell.

"Nice, Theodore. You really made a bag of that," he muttered to himself.

"You sure did," said a female voice.

Theo pushed himself up with his good arm until he was sitting. He looked to the other side of the cell bars. Sitting in a chair against the wall was the woman who stabbed him at the house. She stared at him, now without her mask. The woman had reddish-brown shoulder-length hair tied back neatly in a low ponytail. Her nose was thin and her gray eyes almond-shaped. She looked around the same age as he was, maybe younger. She wore a smug smile, her legs crossed and her hands rested in her lap.

"You watching me sleep?"

"Don't flatter yourself. I'm just making sure you stay breathing. If the boss wanted you to be a corpse, I would have just left you in a dumpster," she said.

Theo looked down at her mask, which was on the floor by her feet. He gestured to it. "Aren't those part of the dress code around here?"

"They're to hide our faces from the humans we walk among, not the dead

man walking–well, bleeding in your case."

"Hey, this dead man walking has a name."

"Not an important one," she said.

"Why? Because it makes us people?"

"You are such a hypocrite," she said with some venom in her voice. She leaned forward, resting her elbows on her knees. "You're sitting there judging me for what? For not trying to start a conversation? I didn't see you trying to start a conversation with the guy you used as a dart board. His name is Oscar, by the way, in case you're curious."

"I'm not the one working for a maniac."

"Neither am I," she said before leaning back in her chair.

Theo scoffed, but decided to keep his mouth shut. He observed her: her clothing was clean and professional, business-like. She was dressed in a navy-blue pants suit, but with a pair of sneakers.

"You look too…professional to be a minion."

She scoffed. "You talk about us as if we're just mindless drones."

"Aren't ya?"

She ignored his statement. "I do have a day job which I am missing since they called me in for pest control. Trust me when I say that I would rather be there instead of babysitting you until the boss gets here."

"If you're going to insult me the whole time, the least you can do is give me a bloody first aid kit."

She ignored him.

Theo sighed. "How long do I have to sit here before the roach arrives?"

She furrowed her brows. "Who do you think is coming to see you?"

"Malphilus, of course."

Her eyes widened, and she laughed. "You aren't serious," she said. "No. You're way below his paygrade."

Theo's heart stopped. "You said your boss was coming."

The woman raised an eyebrow. "And by boss I meant the rank above mine."

"Who would that be?" Theo asked.

The woman smiled. "You'll see for yourself soon enough."

"You're telling me you have a ranking system?" he asked in disbelief.

The woman rolled her eyes. "We are civilized, we're not savages. We didn't just elect a leader and move on, all that does is get you people who will eventually commit treason. Do you guys have just one person giving all the orders?"

"Fair point," he said.

Theo sat and waited as the woman watched him in silence. The cell only had one exit and the woman was sitting next to it. He knew he could not use his powers there. When he was young, he learned about the rare gemstones and how they affected sorcerers' abilities; he recognized the gleam within the iron bars as the orange stone, seraphinum, that suppressed magic.

Suddenly, he saw a soft glow coming from the other side of the door, gleaming through the cracks. The woman looked at the glow as it dimmed again. She smirked and turned to Theo.

"He's here. Do yourself a favor and don't touch the bars," she told him.

The door opened slowly and a man entered. It was the man who killed Leanna, although Theo did not know this because he had never seen him. The only person from their side who had was too young to remember his face. The man looked the same as he did that night thirteen years prior. He still wore the same dark clothing and there were no new blemishes on his skin. The only proof that any time had passed for him was the fact that his hair was slightly longer.

The sound of the metal door slamming shut between them echoed in the small room. The man kept his eyes on Theo, eager to study his prisoner. Theo stared at the strange scales on the man's face. When the man noticed this, he smirked. "Is it not rude to stare anymore?" he joked, speaking in an accent Theo had never heard before. "What is your name?" the man asked. Theo stayed silent so the man turned to the woman.

"Theodore Cross, but his friends call him Theo," she said, surprising Theo. His reaction seemed to amuse her. "We're a lot more resourceful than you think."

"Thank you, Lydia. I'll take it from here," he told her. Lydia nodded and stepped out of the room. On her way out, he called out. "Make sure no one bothers us!" Then the man brought his attention back to his prisoner. "My name is Borrit," he told him.

Theo kept his lips sealed, unwilling to engage.

"Giving me the silent treatment?" he asked, growing impatient. He glared at Theo, and an orange glow ignited under the man's skin, beginning at his neck and slowly rising to his jaw. The sight of it sent a chill down Theo's spine.

"Who are you?" asked Theo.

Borrit smiled and let the glow extinguish. "He speaks," he joked. Borrit looked down at the scales on his hands and watched them glow from his heat. "I do not know…" he said. "no one told me. I cannot remember my beginning, but there is this…fire inside me. I am…" he tried to find the words, "…something ancient." He let his bat-like wings emerge from behind his back. Theo stared at the wings in shock. Borrit's eyes glowed briefly. "He told me you were coming, but I did not think you would be so foolish."

"Who told you?" Theo asked.

"Malphilus."

His name made Theo tense. Borrit chucked. "What did he do to make you seethe with such rage?"

Theo ignored his question. "Did he create you?" he asked.

Borrit rolled his eyes. "Fine. I will go first," he said. "No. He released me."

"From where?"

"The fiery place down below that the immortal man guards."

Theo paled. "Hell," he almost whispered.

"Is that what it's called?" Borrit asked.

"That's not possible. There's only one doorway to hell and it doesn't lead here."

"No conventional doorway."

"What does that mean?"

Borrit smiled. "It means there is no handle to turn. Are they all stupid like you or are you special?"

"Are you all this arrogant?" Theo replied. Theo was weakening from the blood loss. His skin was losing its color and there was cold sweat on his forehead. He applied pressure to his wound as best as he could, but his hands were shaking, and the blood was seeping through his fingers from his lack of strength.

Borrit's eyes narrowed as he looked at the wound. "You just arrived so I do not want you dead so quickly."

"Why is that?"

Borrit smiled. "We have not had any fun yet."

Borrit knelt so he was eye level with Theo. Theo could see the coldness in the eyes that were staring straight at him "I am already disappointed you came alone. I was hoping the boy had come with you. We were expecting him too."

Theo tensed at the mention of Eric.

Borrit laughed. "You were supposed to bring him with you."

"He's just a kid," Theo growled.

Borrit tilted his head and smirked. His eyes glowed. "I do not like unfinished business."

Theo felt as if his heart had just stopped and fallen from his chest. "What?" he whispered. Unfinished business… the words echoed in his head. He knew what Borrit meant, but he did not want to admit it to himself. He did not want it to be true. He remembered the burnt footprints on the steps the night of Leanna's death, the doorknob melted in, but he pushed the memory to the back of his mind.

Borrit studied Theo's reaction and was entertained. "I wanted to finish the job I was given. To deliver him, the boy."

Theo's stomach sank at the confirmation of his fear. "You killed her…" he said aloud.

"Be more specific."

"You killed Leanna…"

Borrit stared, his expression unchanging. "Oh, you mean the boy's mother."

His eyes darkened. "She was just in the way."

Theo lunged at the bars. "SHE HAD NOTHING TO DO WITH THIS!" he screamed. He was overcome with anger, desperate for revenge. All this time, he had been searching for her killer, but his search had been misplaced. He was looking for the wrong monster. Now he was in a cell just inches from the one who took her life, yet the monster was just out of reach. Theo tried to tap into his power, but the gems in the bars weighed him down. Borrit felt a slight pressure on his body from Theo's desperate attempts seeping through. He was angered by the feeling of magic, so he reached through the bars, grabbing Theo by the shirt and pulling him close, slamming him forward into the bars. The impact knocked the air from his lungs. Theo struggled to break free. When his shirt tore, Borrit grabbed him by the throat with his left hand instead and squeezed.

"I can end your life this second if I please," he said angrily. Borrit's skin glowed from the fire rising in his throat. His clothing began to burn and the fire spread to his free right hand. He raised his glowing hand and grabbed Theo's side with it, applying pressure on his wound, and burning him instantly. Theo screamed in agony as Borrit cauterized the wound. When the pain was too much, Theo's world turned black and he fell unconscious.

Theo woke up with a start. His side ached terribly. He rolled off it and reached for it, but the tenderness of his skin made him cease his movement.

"You really pissed him off," said a woman. Theo looked up to see Lydia back at her post. "I warned you about getting too close to the bars, although I guess in this case you gained something from it. No more bleeding out."

Theo groaned and pushed himself up, leaning back against the wall.

Lydia continued, "What were you trying to do, anyway? Escape? Or are you just suicidal?"

Theo tilted his head back and closed his eyes, ignoring her. He was angry and exhausted, and hoping to drown out the sound of her voice.

Lydia rolled her eyes. "You complained when I gave you the silent treatment

and now you're giving it to me. You're a hypocrite."

"Your boss is a monster," Theo muttered.

"Definitely a hypocrite," she sighed. "You saw fire and wings and suddenly he's a monster. He's not any different from the angels you seem to worship."

Theo glared at her. "The difference between the angels and that man is that my comrades don't go around murdering people."

"Death in a war is unavoidable and inevitable."

"That's your argument? Death is inevitable?" Theo raised his voice. "That doesn't justify the deaths of INNOCENT PEOPLE!"

"Get off your high horse. None of us are innocent in this war!"

"SHE WAS!" he yelled. Theo pushed himself up to his feet and leaned on the wall for support. His body ached from the movement and his head pounded, but he said nothing. "He murdered an innocent woman…" Theo's voice cracked. He took a deep breath to regain his composure. "He killed her…" he told her.

"Who? Your lover?" she asked mockingly. "She was probably hiding something from you. She probably wasn't as innocent as you think. Did you ever think that was a possibility?"

Theo shook his head. "No. She was my best friend," he said. "She was only twenty-two and she was kind and kept away from all of this because she never belonged in this chaos… She was safe from all of it until that monster…went and murdered her in her own son's nursery."

Lydia kept her eyes locked on Theo's. "You're lying," she said.

"I wish I was," he said softly. "Now he's after her son… He's just a kid who didn't even know angels existed until last winter, and he's already being hunted by the people you so proudly follow." Theo slid to the ground; his trembling legs no longer able to support his weight. He gripped his side and closed his eyes, trying to catch his breath.

"We have innocent people too," she said softly.

Theo sat quietly, contemplating what he should say next. He looked up at Lydia, looking her in the eyes so she could know that what he was about to say next

was genuine. He said, "Then let us help them."

She broke eye contact with him and whispered, "We don't need your help."

"Never said you did," he replied calmly. "What made you join his crusade?"

She hesitated. "I was born into it, just like you were born into yours."

He shook his head. "I didn't know Malphilus existed until I was eleven. I never knew the details until I was eighteen because that's when I joined the guard. Neil doesn't believe in burdening those who don't want to be burdened."

"Then why are you on their side?" she asked.

"I chose on my own. I was never once told how to feel or how to think. Malphilus was my enemy because he hurt the people I care about, and I've seen the pain he's caused others." He paused to study her reaction. "Can you say the same? That your opinion of us is your own?"

Lydia sat frozen in her chair, not wanting to give away what she was feeling for the first time since she joined the crusade. Doubt. Possibly even guilt for the things she had done for her people and for herself.

She watched Theo drift back out of consciousness.

Theo had a dream—not an escape from the nightmare that had just unfolded, but an extension of it. In it, Leanne stood in Eric's nursery terrified as the white door opened, revealing Borrit on the other side. He slowly neared her, his neck glowing from the heat within him. He smiled sinisterly then lunged at her, grabbing her by the arm and thrusting his hand into her abdomen. She screamed in agony as her flesh burned underneath his fist.

Theo woke to the sound of his heart pounding in his ears. He tried to catch his breath by counting the beats. When his breath was finally even, he realized that his guard was no longer at her post. He sat alone in his concrete cell, waiting for his nightmare to end.

In the alley, Eric was still paralyzed. His body shook as it attempted to fight the paralysis. His energy was being drained from his body. He tried not to fight the paralysis, aware that it would wear off on its own, but his body refused to obey hum.

An hour had passed and he was exhausted, struggling to keep his eyes open. He wondered if Theo was alright. He hoped that Neil had arrived home early and seen his text. These were all fantasies to him, fantasies that were likely to remain just that. As more time passed, he was regretting not calling Esme when he had the chance. If he had just contacted her when he noticed Theo leaving, he would not be in this situation.

Eric was not sure how much time had passed but he was exhausted. He sat with his eyes closed, desperately trying to conserve his energy. Then he felt something cold touch the skin on his hand. When he opened his eyes, he saw the soft white flakes floating to the ground and settling on his clothing. He sighed and closed his eyes again, praying that Neil would come home early. Thirty minutes passed and the snowflakes were dampening his clothing, but he felt something else too. His heart jumped and his breath quickened; the spell had worn off. Eric was weak from the fight his body had put up. He moved to stand, but his arms and legs shook so badly that he immediately fell back onto the snowy ground. He crawled forward but only moved inches before he flopped back down. He had reached the end of the alley, but there was no possibility of him reaching the road, let alone wherever Theo was.

With what little energy he had left, he reached into his pocket for his cell phone, but it was not enough. Just as he felt the smooth surface on his numbed fingertips, his eyelids drooped and he lost consciousness. As soon as his eyelids closed, he was in the dream world once again, only this time it was different. This time, the setting was the motel room he and Theo had spent the night in. Before he could look around for the entrance, the room flickered in and out. He panicked and struggled to control his breathing.

He did not understand why, but he felt fear. His heart beat more rapidly, and his hands trembled. He gripped his wrist to stop the shaking.

He looked around until he finally saw James standing in front of him, a large distance between them.

"What's wrong with you?" James asked. "Too much caffeine?"

Eric stayed where he was, not moving, and said nothing, unable to speak.

James looked concerned. "Eric?" he called out, taking a few steps closer so he could see him more clearly.

Eric fell to his knees, unable to hold his body up. James had a look of realization.

Eric tried to speak between his quick breaths. "What- What's- h- happening?" he asked.

James stared at him with worried eyes, unmoving. "You're dying," he answered quietly.

Eric's eyes widened in fear and his panic worsened. He grabbed his chest, unable to calm down, and fell to the floor, the blue flame fluttering around him.

When Theo opened his eyes again, he was unsure of how much time had passed. When he looked ahead, he noticed that Lydia's chair was vacant. He shifted, bending his knees, and looked down at the burnt handprint that would scar his skin. He knew the future was grim because of his own stupidity and wondered if he deserved to face Neil again, if he even made it out alive.

He was left alone with his thoughts. He knew Neil would come for him and that was the last thing he wanted. He did not want to be the reason they were put in danger, especially since they did not know what they were up against.

When he finally looked up again, a figure startled him. In the doorway stood a young woman around eighteen years old. A pair of large blue eyes stared straight at him. They were strange. They were human eyes, not red like Borrit's, but her pupils were oddly shaped, slightly narrow. Dark locks rested on her shoulders, making the blue of her eyes stand out more. Yet she was not human, nor sorcerer. He could see scales across her face, neck, and bare arms. She entered the room slowly, closing the door behind her. She eyed Theo curiously, her wings spreading out from behind her, revealing that she was indeed the same species as Borrit.

"Who are you?" he asked.

She did not answer, but continued to study him. She neared the bars one step at a time in long black pants and knelt in front of him. The way she moved and watched

him made Theo feel that she was as young as she looked. Finally, she turned her attention to the bars. She reached for the lock and held it in her hands. He watched in suspicion as she tightened her grip on the lock and pulled it until it snapped open.

Theo's eyes widened, and he stood up slowly as she opened the cell door, her eyes still fixed on him.

"What are you trying to do?" he asked.

Once again, she did not answer, but instead let herself out of the room leaving the door wide open. Theo wondered if it was a trap or if she was trying to help him. He took a wary step forward, leaving his cell. His side throbbed with each step he took. When he stepped through the door, the girl was waiting on the other side. He stopped next to her.

"Are you helping me?" he asked.

She thought for a moment, then nodded.

"Thank you," he said.

Theo staggered until he reached a nearby set of stairs and was relieved when he saw a natural light shining through the bottom of the door. He reached the steps and was about to go up when he heard a female voice behind him.

"Not yet," she said.

He turned around and saw it was the girl who was speaking to him. "Why not?" he asked.

When she did not answer, he turned and continued up the stairs. He was only three steps closer to the door when she appeared in front of him, stopping him in his tracks.

Theo jumped back, nearly falling down the steps. "You can teleport?" Theo was bewildered by her ability. He had never heard of a species with that capability other than the angels.

The girl furrowed her brows, confused by his question. She seemed unfamiliar with the term. When he realized that she had nothing to say, he tried to get past her, but she blocked him and shook her head.

"Please let me through," he practically begged, exhausted and desperate to

get home.

She shook her head. "I can't. Not yet," she said and pointed to her left.

Theo followed her hand and saw she was pointing to another door. Although he was out of the cell, he did not have the energy for a spell. Knowing he was unable to get past her, he walked back down the stairs and over to the door she had pointed at. When he reached it, he turned to look at her to confirm and she simply nodded. When he opened the door, he groaned at the sight of stairs leading down.

"You want me to go deeper?" he asked in frustration. She said nothing, only staring at him. He took a deep breath. "I'm going to regret this," he whispered to himself.

The girl led him to a dimly lit basement. On the other side of the room was a white curtain. Theo could smell something almost metallic, like copper, in the room. He approached warily, unsure if he wanted to know what was there. When he reached the edge of the white curtain, the girl took a few steps back and gestured to it.

Theo stepped forward to look. Behind the curtain was a gurney where a man lay unconscious hooked up to a machine. Blood was being drawn from one of the man's arms, while he received a blood transfusion into the other.

"What the hell is this?" Theo asked. He walked closer to the unconscious man who was kept breathing by a ventilator. He reached over to examine the blood bag, but as soon as he touched it, she grabbed his arm to stop him. Her grip made his body tense. She shook her head and moved to press a switch on the machine, releasing his arm.

"You have to wait," she said.

"Wait for what?"

"For him to wake up," she said.

Outside in the cold, Eric lay in the snow, still unconscious in the dream world. He was on the ground in the darkness, his body shaking uncontrollably. The flame flickered around him and he was terrified.

"I-I'm s-scared," he said as he tried to control his shivering.

James took a deep breath. "Listen to me," he said as calmly as he could. "You can't stay here. You have to wake up, because whatever is happening, it can't be good."

Eric shivered. His heart pounded. "I-I can't," he said in between panicked breaths. Suddenly they both felt a cold breeze. James was confused. His breath escaped as a white fog and he rubbed his arms.

"Where are you, Eric?" he asked in confusion. Snow began to fall from nothing and settled around them. James stared up at the soft flakes with terror in his eyes. "You're outside," he whispered in shock. "He looked down at Eric. "Eric, you need to wake up before you freeze to death!"

Eric did not respond, he only continued to shake along with the ground, his eyes wide with fear. James crouched next to Eric. He reached to touch the back of his head but stopped just inches from it and let his hand hover. "Listen. Your power will keep you from freezing for now, but it won't last forever. You can't stay asleep or you'll never wake up." He lay on his stomach with his head next to Eric's, his hand still hovering as if he was afraid to touch him. "Wake up, Eric," he said. "Wake up!" he said again, this time more demanding.

The snow began to cover them both and the ground shook and moved. James suddenly grabbed his own head in pain and his breath quickened. "WAKE UP!" he screamed in Eric's face, and it worked.

Eric opened his eyes and found himself back in the cold, shivering. He looked forward and waited for his eyes to adjust. He put his hand deeper in his pocket and slid his phone into his hand. He brought the phone to his eyes and unlocked it. He wanted to call Esme, but realized he had no signal.

Eric cursed his terrible luck. He tucked his phone into his jacket so it would not get wet and focused on keeping his eyes open.

This was the first time Eric had seen the snow and he was not sure he would ever want to see it again. It was cold and wet and uncomfortable, despite its beauty.

CHAPTER 13
Escape

In a lower level of the Angel Tower in Luxwick was an arched door without a handle, its stone frame flush against the wall. The room remained empty, but guarded, hidden from the civilian sorcerers for their own sakes. The stone frame was more important than it appeared to be: it was not just any door, but a door to Heaven.

The wall within the frame slid open slowly, revealing a bright opening. From that opening, Evangeline stepped out first. She went through the portal and turned around, waiting for the others. Next came Roman, who stepped forward then turned around as well.

Neil stumbled out of the portal next and practically fell into Roman's arms, who had been ready to catch him. He grabbed Neil by the waist, draping Neil's arm around his neck to support his weight. Neil was exhausted, his head pounding. He was pale, and his legs shook as he struggled to hold himself up. Aaron exited the portal entrance almost immediately after Neil. Neil waved his free hand to close the portal, and it darkened, reverting to its original appearance once again. Aaron quickly moved to support Neil from the other side and Evangeline stepped forward and took his head between her hands, soothing whatever pain she could.

Neil let out a breath of relief.

"Let's get you to bed," she said, taking a step back. Neil nodded weakly, desperate to rest. Evangeline took Roman's place, so he could leave to check on the other angels. She and Aaron teleported Neil to his bedroom and gently lowered him onto the bed's edge, so he could sit. He moved his hands to his sides to keep himself up, his arms shaking. Neil said nothing as Evangeline removed his shoes and Aaron helped him take off his coat. He sat there like a hollow vessel with his eyes closed to keep himself from falling back. Aaron and Evangeline helped him into bed, pulling

the covers over him.

Aaron turned to his sister. "I'll meet you in the conference room."

She nodded and watched him vanish before sitting at the edge of the bed. Neil lay on his side with his eyes open, but his eyelids drooped. She looked down at him in his fragile state and wished to take the pain he had just endured voluntarily for their sakes. She stroked his hair, using her power to relax him so he could sleep and to bestow him with good dreams. His body relaxed, and he started to drift off but before he did, he raised his right arm and reached for the hand that stroked him. When he felt it beneath his palm, he let sleep take him. She smiled and moved his hand back to his side.

When she went to the conference room, Aaron was waiting for her on the balcony.

"Is he asleep?" he asked, feeling her presence behind him.

"Peacefully," she answered. She joined him and looked out at Luxwick, "This time was worse."

Aaron placed a comforting hand on her shoulder. "It only feels that way. I don't think I'll ever get used to it either."

Evangeline leaned forward on the rails and rubbed her head.

"Headache?" Aaron asked.

"Just a little. I'm worried… Cyrus didn't find anything in his memories," she said.

Aaron shook his head. "Nothing new," he confirmed.

"It feels like we're getting nowhere."

"We'll stop him eventually," Aaron said. "We should go check on Eric. I didn't hear him in the house."

Evangeline nodded in agreement. "Let's see if he and Theo are in the training room first." She teleported there, but found the room empty. When Aaron appeared by her side, she said. "His place maybe?" Once again, they both teleported to a room with no one in it but them. She looked around in suspicion. "Where's Neil's cell phone?" she asked nervously.

"It should be in his dresser."

"I'll meet you back at the conference room."

Evangeline teleported to Neil's bedroom, where he was still deeply asleep. She quietly walked to his dresser and opened it, taking his cell phone in her hands. When she unlocked it, she saw the message alert and clicked on it to open the messages, seeing they were both from Eric. Reading the messages filled her with dread. She looked over at Neil, then back at the messages, hoping her eyes were deceiving her, but it was true. Theo had gone after the enemy, and Eric had followed.

Theo sat on the floor of the basement-level room with a hand on his side. He sat patiently on the ground, waiting for the unknown man to wake from his slumber. The dragon girl who had insisted he wait stood to the side, her large eyes fixed on Theo, as if making sure he did not leave.

"Who is he?" Theo asked, breaking the silence. She looked away from Theo and approached the unconscious man slowly, her gaze lingering on the blood bag.

"I don't know," she said.

Theo forced himself to his feet. "Then why am I…why are you helping him?"

She turned, making eye contact with him. "Because he's innocent. You guys help people who are innocent, right?"

He walked over to the end of the gurney and leaned on it, trying to make out the girl's motives. "What makes you think that?" he asked.

"I heard you talking to Lydia," she said.

"And him? How do you know he's innocent?"

"Because he's not like us," she explained.

"Us?"

"Me and you. He's not what we are."

"He's a human?"

She nodded. "Borrit took him.

"Why would he want humans?"

"To use them."

Her vague answers were frustrating, but Theo realized she did not know how to explain what she knew.

"What is he doing to him?" he asked.

She hesitated. Several emotions crossed her face: Guilt. Worry. Fear.

"I can't tell you. Not yet," she said.

"Why not?"

"Because he'll know."

She looked so young and afraid that Theo did not have the heart to interrogate her. He sighed and changed the subject. "Why do I have to take him? Why not just teleport him yourself?"

"I can't."

"Why not?"

"Because I don't know how," she admitted.

Theo did not know what to say to that. He knew that an angel could not teleport to a place they had never traveled to, which is why they were encouraged to travel during their early life, but he did not understand how this girl could not travel to just any town in her head and take it from there. She looked young, but not young enough to be incapable of finding a hospital or a civilian to help once she was out. Then he realized that she was acting young; younger than she looked.

"How old are you?" he asked.

She looked at him puzzled.

"Do you know what I'm asking you?"

She shook her head.

"I'm asking how long you've been alive. How many years?"

The girl looked confused at first, then turned away as if remembering something. Her face twisted as she searched her thoughts for the answer. "I don't know," she said hesitantly.

"How long have you been here?" he asked instead.

Her eyes went blank once again as she searched for the answer. "Always, I think," she finally replied.

Theo nodded, not surprised by her answer. He wondered how she came to be, but he was pulled from his thoughts when the machine began to make noise. Theo's head jerked toward the sound of the beeping, suddenly paranoid that someone would hear it.

"What's happening?" he asked.

The girl remained calm and stared at the man on the gurney. "He's waking up," she said. The man jerked suddenly and reached for his throat in panic. He desperately tried to remove the breathing tube and his eyes opened wide as he struggled, letting out choked noises. Theo ran to the man's head and removed the tube as quickly as possible. Once it was out, the man coughed and coughed, struggling to control his breathing. He rolled onto his side. The man was panicking in his groggy state. When the gurney shook from his movement, Theo pinned his arms down, trying to still him.

"Whoa. You're alright. Take it easy," Theo repeated the words until the man steadied his breathing. Once he was still, Theo backed away, slowly releasing the man's arms. The man blinked, his hand instinctively covering his eyes from the blinding light above him. He rubbed his eyes and threw his head back.

"You good?" Theo asked.

The man looked at Theo, squinting. "Please don't tell me I'm in Ireland," he said in response to hearing Theo's accent.

"What's wrong with Ireland?"

"Nothing, nothing," he said quickly. "It's just…far."

"Well, rest assured, we're somewhere in Seattle or Washington at least."

The man tried to sit up, but struggled, his arms shaking under his weight. Theo helped him sit upright. "But where am I?" the man asked.

Theo frowned. "Unfortunately, I don't know." He helped the man off the gurney and onto his feet. He struggled to stand but managed with Theo's help.

"What do I call you?" asked Theo.

The man's breathing was heavy. He looked at Theo and wondered if he could trust him, then remembered how insignificant a name was in his current situation.

"Shawn," he said. "My name's Shawn."

"Theo."

Shawn nodded. "Nice to meet you. Now let's get the hell out of here."

Theo nodded and looked over at the girl. "Lead the way," he said. She stared at them, then her eyes went wide and she stiffened. The look on her face worried them both. "What's wrong?" Theo asked.

"Someone's coming. I can hear them," she said quietly. Before they had a chance to react, she was reaching for them. She grabbed them both by their shoulders, then teleported them to another concrete room.

Shawn gasped loudly. "What the hell just happened?"

Theo ignored him. "Where are we?" he asked the girl.

She hesitated. "Basement," she said.

"But we were in a basement."

"A different one."

"Okay, but how do we get out?"

She looked at them with wide eyes, frozen in fear. "I can't help you," she told them.

Shawn walked toward her. "What do you mean you can't help us?"

"He will know," she said. Then she pointed at the wall ahead of her. Theo turned around to see what she was pointing to and was surprised when he saw the panel to a crawl space. "Through there. Hurry," she said.

Shawn moved to grab her. "Wait," he called out, but she disappeared before he could reach her. Shawn let out a shaky sigh and ran his fingers through his hair. "This can't be happening," he whispered to himself.

While Shawn panicked, Theo searched for something to help them reach the panel. When he noticed the wooden crates stacked along the wall to his right, he rushed over and grabbed one and placed it just beneath the panel. He stepped onto the crate and pushed open the panel. The wood piece was heavier than he expected and his muscles strained as he carefully slid it aside. He turned to call Shawn over and saw him pacing, muttering to himself. "Shawn," he called out. Shawn continued to pace,

grabbing at his hair. "Shawn!" Theo called out, slightly louder this time, but trying to keep his voice down to avoid unwanted attention.

Shawn turned to look at Theo. "This is crazy," he said, waving his arms wildly to gesture at everything around them. "We don't have time for this now."

"Well, I'm sorry I'm not coping with this as well as you are!" he whisper-yelled.

Theo groaned. "This is why I don't fraternize with humans anymore," he muttered to himself. "This situation is absolute cac, but it's my bloody life and right now, both of ours are at risk. So, if you want so desperately to get back to your simple life, then you better get your arse moving."

Shawn took a deep breath and walked over to join Theo. "Okay, okay, I'm coming."

Theo climbed into the vent and Shawn followed. They crawled through the dark crawl space quietly, hoping to remain unnoticed.

Theo maneuvered through the crawl space slowly in order to avoid making noise. He kept going until he was at the end of the space, reaching another panel. She turned so that Shawn could see his face, signaling for him to stay quiet. Theo lay his head on the panel carefully and focused his hearing, listening until he was sure there was no one in the room below. He lifted the panel and set it aside, then maneuvered so he could swing his legs down. His side throbbed with every movement, but he managed to drop to the ground. He was now standing in what appeared to have once been a storage room, the shelves bare and dusty.

Theo waved for Shawn to join him then searched every inch of the room for anything he could use as a weapon. If he was not worried about making noise, he would have used his power to snap a piece from the metal shelves.

"Where are we?" Shawn asked.

"Still below ground. Can't tell how far."

Theo reached for the door and froze, hearing something.

"Hide," he whispered. Shawn rushed behind one of the shelving units and dropped to the ground while Theo flattened himself next to the closed door. The door

opened slowly inward, covering Theo. A sorcerer entered slowly. Theo moved quickly, not letting the sorcerer have any time to think as he hit him with whatever power he could muster, stunning him before punching him. Theo barely managed to catch the sorcerer before he hit the ground, placing him down gently before dropping to the ground himself. He clutched his side in agony as he took a moment to catch his breath.

Shawn rushed out from his cover to Theo's aid.

"You okay?" he asked, glancing at Theo's injury.

Theo nodded. "Check for weapons," he told Shawn, gesturing to the unconscious sorcerer.

Shawn found a sheathed dagger on the sorcerer's belt and held it out to Theo who shook his head. "You keep it and stay behind me," he ordered as he pushed himself to his feet.

"I don't know how to fight," he told him.

"I'm not asking you to. Your only job is to stay alive. I promise you I will get you out of here, then all of this will just be one bad day," Theo told him as he approached the open door.

Shawn gripped the dagger tightly and sighed. "Bad days make for better days," he said.

Theo froze at the sound of the familiar quote, the quote Leanna said to him each time he would ask if she was happy. The same quote he had just told Eric at the motel.

"Where did you hear that?" he asked.

"What?"

"That quote. Where did you hear it?"

Confused, Shawn shrugged. "From a neighbor I think, way back."

Theo stared at Shawn until he remembered. He had seen Shawn once before, briefly thirteen years prior when he wiped his memory the night of Leanna's death.

"You called the police," he said.

Shawn grew more confused, but before they could continue their

conversation, a red flashing light startled them. Theo looked up at the silent alarm and cursed.

"Stay behind me," he ordered before rushing out of the closet.

CHAPTER 14
No One Left Behind

Evangeline appeared in the conference room. "We have a problem," she told her brother urgently. She showed him the messages on Neil's phone.

"How old are these?" he asked.

"He wrote that they reached Seattle five hours ago."

"Did you try calling him?"

"It goes straight to voicemail," his voice shook in distress. "What do we do?" she asked.

"We go after them, of course."

"That's not what I'm asking," she said. "I'm talking about Theo. He went after the enemy on his own. Roman would never let us use the time needed for a rescue mission, not without reporting us to Cyrus as well, not for a circumstance caused by rebellion."

Knowing she was right, Aaron rubbed his temples and tried to think of what they could do next.

"So, we don't tell him, and we go after him alone," he suggested.

Evangeline's jaw dropped. "Break protocol?"

"Not break it, just delay it. Roman and Cornelius are the only members of the Council not present. Cornelius is unconscious and Roman is out of reach. That makes it our call."

"That's a technicality," she said.

"I thought you'd love the idea."

"Of course; it just isn't something I thought you would do."

Aaron smirked. "You're all corrupting me," he joked. "Besides," he continued, "Eric's with him and we just got him back. We can't lose him and we can't

give him up. We could even argue that he could be used against Neil."

Evangeline nodded and instinctively reached for the chain of her bracelet to soothe her worries. "We have to bring him back before he wakes up," she said. "We can't let him go through this. Not again."

"So, we agree. The matter is too important to waste time by calling a Council meeting. It's urgent, and we have to leave right away because not going after Theo puts our information at risk," Aaron said.

"Agreed… but how do we locate them without Neil?" she asked. "Seattle is a big city. We don't have time to search it and we can't sense magic like he can. Unless we run into one of Malphilus' followers, finding them will be like looking for a needle in a haystack."

Aaron sighed. "We can't just stand here and ponder either. We have to start searching."

"I know someone who can help us," she said suddenly.

"Who?"

"Harrison."

Aaron remembered what Neil had told him, of how Harrison had studied everything there was to know about magic.

"Let's not waste time, then."

Aaron and Evangeline traveled to Earth and went to Harrison's home near the portal. Evangeline knocked on the door and Terra answered. The smile on her face quickly turned to surprise when she saw who her guests were.

"Evangeline. What's wrong?" she asked.

"We just need to speak to Harrison about something. Is he home?"

Terra nodded. "He's in the dining room. Come in," she said, stepping aside to let them through. Evangeline and Aaron went into the dining room, where Harrison was sitting with a sketchpad in front of him.

When he saw them, he removed his reading glasses and set down his pen. "Something tells me you're not just visiting," he said with a worried smile.

Evangeline mimicked his expression. "I wish it could be under better

circumstances," she said. "Theo has gone rogue and Eric went after him. They both left two days ago, and they haven't returned. We just found out."

"I'm actually surprised this day didn't come sooner. What do you need me to do?" he asked.

"We know they arrived in Seattle a few hours ago, but we don't know where they are. We were hoping you could help us narrow the search."

Harrison nodded and stood, waving for them to follow him as he headed up the stairs to his study. He walked straight to his bookcase. When he found the book he was looking for, he opened it to a page in the center of the book and nodded when he found the information he sought.

"I have what you need," he told them. He closed the book and took them back downstairs, leading them to the basement. The blue Celocus stone glowed on the doorway.

"Please close the door behind you," he requested.

Aaron did as he was told and closed the door. He felt a sudden wave of energy hit him. When he did not follow them down the steps, Evangeline stopped as well. She watched her brother as he gripped the wall and took a deep breath, his eyes wide. She placed a hand on his arm.

"It's the celocus. There's so much magical energy in this room that he had to fill the frames with celocus to coat it properly. It packs a punch at first, but you get used to it," she said.

Aaron followed her down the stairs to the dimly lit room where Harrison searched for what they needed, reading the labels on the two-by-three-inch drawers that covered the back wall.

He opened a drawer and removed a metal cuff. It had a dark green metallic stone that covered the center band.

"What is that?" Aaron asked.

Harrison carefully turned the cuff in his hand. "This is a very rare stone," he said. "It took me decades to track it down and this is the only one I was able to find. Rumor has it that this was the stone that absorbed the most of Adan's power."

"Adan, as in the god who guards Hell?" Aaron asked.

Harrison nodded. "Yes, your uncle I suppose. The stone reacts to the energy of a sorcerer. It heats up when it's near, so it's no wonder why there isn't any around anymore. The constant exposure before Luxwick… most of it would have broken down eventually, but this is your best chance of finding Theo and Eric."

Aaron nodded. "Thank you," he said as he reached for the cuff.

Harrison stepped back, keeping it out of Aaron's reach. "Oh no. You're not using it, I am," he said.

"It's a simple rescue mission. The stone will be returned to you, but we can't put you at risk by bringing you with us."

"You don't have a choice," he explained. "Your energy signature is too similar. The stone may not react to you, but it won't work if you're too close. You'll only confuse it."

Evangeline began to worry. "Harrison, we don't know what we might find if you run into anyone who works for him."

"I won't," he said. Harrison looked at Evangeline and Aaron and smiled reassuringly. "I've been in this world for a very long time. I know how to keep my head down. Just drop me off somewhere in Seattle and if the stone reacts to anything, I'll call you."

The siblings hesitated, unsure if the risk was worth it, but they had no choice. Evangeline surrendered. "Fine, but if you encounter anyone, you can't speak to them. Once we have a location, we bring you back home."

"Once you have a location, I go and get a coffee until you have them."

"Harrison-."

"You never know when you might need the extra help," he argued.

Evangeline sighed. "Alright then. Just stay public," she insisted.

"Of course."

Aaron stepped forward. "Are we ready, then? We can't waste any more time."

Harrison nodded and reached for Evangeline's hand. She took it and looked over at Aaron. "The basement under the apartment Roman lived in before his rebirth.

It's usually abandoned, and we can't afford to be seen by civilians without a sorcerer to erase our encounters."

Aaron nodded and vanished, and Evangeline followed close by with Harrison. Luckily, the basement was empty.

"You should go back to my home," said Harrison. "You stand out too much with those coats. You might as well wait there. Make yourselves comfortable."

Harrison went up the stairs, exiting the basement. When he was halfway up, he stopped and turned to them. "We'll find them, so don't worry. I know what I'm doing." Then he left them alone in the dark. Evangeline glanced at Aaron before teleporting back to Harrison's basement. Aaron followed and they took a seat on a bench against the wall.

Harrison walked out of the building onto the street and was reminded of how large Seattle was. He looked around at the tall buildings and the crowded streets and took a deep breath.

"You can do this," he told himself. He pulled the cuff from his pocket and placed it on his wrist, pulling his sleeve down to cover it. Then he walked forward and began his search, hoping to feel the heat consume his arm.

Harrison walked through the streets of Seattle, dissatisfied by his lack of progress. The cuff had not changed temperature at all and he was beginning to lose hope, but he did not give up because Aaron and Evangeline were depending on him.

Harrison reached an area that was more desolate. Something drew him to a set of buildings on the outskirts. Call it a gut instinct, or perhaps fate, but he knew he should investigate. He reached the sidewalk in front of the buildings and the cuff began to react just outside an alley opening. The stone heated the metal of the cuff, warming his skin. The temperature was barely warm, but noticeable nonetheless. Harrison smiled to himself and quickly rang Evangeline. He spoke before she could say anything. "Have Terra search the address I'm about to message you. Hopefully you've traveled somewhere nearby," he said, then hung up and messaged them the address.

Evangeline looked down at the text in relief and ran up the stairs with Aaron

right behind her.

"Terra!" she called out. They found her in the living room with the television on. "Can you search this address for us, please," she asked, handing Terra her phone. Terra went to Harrison's study and used his laptop to search for the address, showing Aaron and Evangeline the results.

Evangeline smiled and pointed to a nearby building. "There. The pizza parlor that mom took us to." She thanked Terra, then teleported to the pizza parlor and ran south with Aaron until they saw Harrison. He pointed to the alley.

"They must be somewhere in that direction. The signature is strong, so it should be nearby."

Aaron immediately transported Harrison back to his home before he could argue against it and then he joined Evangeline again.

"Let's go get our boys," she said.

They sped through the alley.

"I can actually feel them," Evangeline said. Aaron nodded in agreement, feeling the strong magical energy as well.

"There must be a lot of them," he said with concern.

Evangeline continued to move in the direction from which they felt the magical energy without hesitation. When the energy stopped increasing, she stopped in confusion. She looked around at the frost-covered concrete and the solid brick walls and shook her head. "We're standing right at the center of it," she said.

Aaron saw something strange on one of the bricks. He approached carefully, noticing the small symbol etched into one of the bricks, camouflage among the various scratch marks. The symbol looked almost like a flame. He reached to touch it, but stopped at the sound of a slight echo beneath his feet. Evangeline heard the noise as well and they turned to each other in surprise.

Aaron took a few steps back and looked down at where he was standing. He knelt and brushed his fingertips over the ground, wiping away the snow to reveal a manhole cover and pushed it off to the side, revealing a ladder. He climbed down and found himself in a small concrete room. Evangeline followed him down the ladder,

pulling the manhole cover back into place, leaving them in darkness.

The pitch-black room brightened as two sets of beautiful wings began to materialize. Evangeline and Aaron stood with their coats removed, their wings slowly visible.

"So much for being inconspicuous," Evangeline said.

"We wear his symbol on our backs. We'll be noticed either way; might as well have our eyesight."

Evangeline nodded in agreement. She turned to the door next to them. "Let's go. We've been gone too long already."

Theo rushed out of the storage room with Shawn close behind him and watched as two masked sorcerers rushed in the room. The first one immediately used his power to throw knives at Theo, who barely managed to block them with a shield. When the sorcerer reached him, he fought him only to be tackled by a second sorcerer. Theo used his power to throw himself back out of the fray then raised the knife, throwing it into the neck of the sorcerer who was the farthest away. Then, returning his attention to the one closer to him, he kicked his legs and pulled him to the ground, knocking him unconscious. Theo struggled to catch his breath as Shawn pulled him to his feet.

They ran through the doorway and found themselves in a hallway where another sorcerer immediately crashed into them, knocking them back into the room. Theo used his power to push Shawn away, but the sorcerer hit Theo's wound and Theo screamed in agony. Theo was out of energy, unable to do anything as the sorcerer raised his blade in the air and aimed it at Theo.

Suddenly Shawn was there, tackling the sorcerer who twisted his body as they crashed into the ground. The moment they hit the ground, Shawn thrust the dagger down, stabbing the sorcerer in the abdomen. The sorcerer waved his arm but stopped in pain as Shawn rolled off him in shock. Theo kicked the sorcerer from his position on the ground to knock him unconscious.

For a moment, Shawn felt a mixture of pride that he had just saved Theo, as

well as shock that he had committed violence, but the moment was brief. A sharp pain in his side brought him out of his trance. His breathing caught as if the air was stuck in his throat and each breath brought him pain. When he looked down, he finally saw where the pain was coming from. The sorcerer's knife was in his side. Blood spread from the wound, staining his white clothing. He pressed his hands to the knife's grip, but they were shaking. He fell to his knees.

Theo crawled to Shawn and waved the door shut. Shawn's hands shook as he reached for his wound, but Theo stopped him. "Leave it," he said. He gently grabbed the soft cloth around the knife and pulled it, tearing it until the wound was visible.

"Is it bad?" Shawn asked.

Theo looked down at the wound. "You'll live," he said.

Shawn let out a humorless laugh. "Don't sugarcoat it," he said, trying to keep his tone steady. He took a few breaths in exhaustion. "It already hurts less, and I know that can't be good."

"Wasn't trying to. I have friends who can fix you up, but for now you need to stay breathing."

Shawn nodded, breathing heavily. "I've only known you for like ten minutes, but I'll take your word for it."

Theo looked at Shawn in concern, noticing how pale he was. He stood, hooking his arms around Shawn and dragging him to the storage room, hoping the cover would buy them some time. Shawn groaned as he moved him. Theo looked to the closed door in the other room, suddenly not sure either of them would survive when he still had no idea how close they were to an exit and no way to search for one and defend them at the same time with Shawn bleeding out.

"Your neighbor…" Theo said, as he grabbed one of the metal shelving units and dragged it to the door in the other room. "Tell me about her."

Struggling to stay conscious, Shawn was perplexed by the question. He spoke slowly, his words slurring.

"She was… nice. Always let me hang out when my parents were yelling…"

Theo knocked the shelf on its side and wedged it against the door before

returning to Shawn whose eyelids were now drooping. He snapped his fingers in front of Shawn's face.

"You have to keep talking. How well did you know her?"

"We weren't… close. She moved…"

Theo's heart sank as he remembered the moment he wiped Shawn's memory of calling the police that night. He knew another sorcerer would have returned to make the neighborhood think Leanna had simply moved away.

Shawn sluggishly turned his head so he could see Theo.

"W-why aren't you l-leaving me?" he asked as he began to shiver.

Theo kept his eyes on the blocked door, unable to look at Shawn as the memory of Leanna's body invaded his thoughts as well as the moment he had faced her killer. "I'm tired of failing," he said.

The sound of footsteps in the distance made Theo tense. He raised his hands, creating a barrier to help keep the door closed in case the shelf wasn't strong enough.

Shawn closed his eyes in frustration. "Just go. I-I'm just…dead weight."

"You can still make it."

Shawn sighed. "My family…"

"Don't start," Theo cut him off. The door shook as someone tried to break it down. Theo kept the barrier up, sweating as he struggled.

"I've got twin boys at h-home," Shawn whispered. "I need you to go so you can tell my wife…"

"Save your breath, because I'm not telling them anything." Theo told Shawn. Suddenly whoever was trying to break the door down stopped, but Theo kept his barrier up. He wondered why they had stopped, but his question was answered the moment he felt the heat. A glow started from the center of the door, spreading as it burned, the door crumbling. Theo stood in the doorway of the storage room and moved the barrier to cover himself and Shawn, knowing the walls would do nothing to stop what was coming.

Borrit entered the room, charring the concrete floor with each step. Borrit was angry, but when he saw Theo, his scowl turned into a smirk and the fiery glow in his

neck spread to his jaw and his eyes smoldered.

He opened his mouth, revealing the fire within him. Theo somehow knew his barrier would not be strong enough to stop Borrit's fire from killing them, but he couldn't bring himself to give up.

Borrit opened his mouth, revealing the fire within him. Theo closed his eyes and tensed. He felt the heat close in on him but the burning never came. Instead, a new light swallowed him, a warm comforting blue glow enveloped him and a pair of arms wrapped around him. The first thing he heard was her scream before his eyes focused on her auburn hair. He realized who had saved him from the flames. Evangeline stood with him, her arms wrapped around him and her wings spread wide, shielding both their bodies. She screamed as the fire hit her wings, eating away at the icy feathers and dulling her glow. When the fire stopped, Theo stepped out from her safety and sent his magic at Borrit with what power he had left, knocking him back through the burnt doorway. Aaron rushed into the room, shocked at the state of his sister's wings, which were now blackened on the surface.

"We have to go," she said as Aaron reached them. Aaron reached for Theo's arm when Theo backed away from him.

"Wait! I'm not alone," he said.

Theo rushed to Shawn and pulled him off the ground. Aaron turned to Evangeline. "Can you teleport?" he asked.

She nodded. "I can make it outside," she said before vanishing.

The heat spread again as Borrit reentered the room, looking angrier. His fire began to spread again, but just as he was about to release it, Aaron grabbed Theo and Shawn and teleported them both just outside the entrance. The three of them stood on snowy ground, the soft flakes falling on them.

"Can you heal him?" Theo asked Aaron.

Aaron nodded and knelt next to Shawn. He carefully removed the knife, then lifted the fabric, exposing the wound and pressed his hand to it. Shawn barely winced. Aaron focused his energy on Shawn's wound and let a soft blue light spread underneath his palm. Shawn felt the burning on his skin and tried to hold in his scream.

But eventually the pain faded and was replaced by a warm and comforting sensation.

Shawn took a deep breath as Aaron stepped away from him. Shawn looked down at the spot where his wound had been and was amazed by the scar that replaced it. He laughed in relief and threw his head back. "Thank you," he whispered. As Theo helped Shawn to his feet, still supporting his weight, Aaron searched for Evangeline. She stood only a few feet from them in an open spot in the alley. Her wings were spread out and the snowflakes were coating them. She stood with her eyes closed as the cold flakes soothed the burning. When she heard their steps next to her, she opened her eyes and looked to Theo.

"What was he?" she asked quietly.

Theo stared at her charred wings, which were now covered in a thin layer of snow. He shook his head. "I don't have a clue…" he told her.

Evangeline sighed and carefully slipped her arms into the sleeves of her coat, concealing her wings. "Where's Eric?" she asked.

Theo's body went rigid, confused by the question. "Didn't he send you after me?" he asked.

Evangeline grew nervous. "I saw the messages he left on Neil's cell. He said he was with you."

Theo furrowed his brows, sure that the paralysis would have worn off hours before. He stepped forward, his pace quickening with each step until he was running, the others following after him. When he reached the area where he'd left Eric, he stopped, searching around. His face paled when he saw a hand sticking out from around the corner.

"Eric!" he yelled. Eric lay in the snow, a thick layer of it covering him. Theo quickly brushed the snow off and shook him. "Eric, wake up!" he shouted. He shook Eric again, relieved when he opened his eyes, although just barely.

"What did you do?" Aaron yelled as he reached them. He picked Eric up off the ground, taking him into his arms.

Theo was a nervous wreck. "I-I just paralyzed him is all, so he wouldn't run after me. He should have been back on his feet hours ago."

Aaron stood with Eric in his arms just as Evangeline and Shawn reached them.

"Oh my God, Eric," Evangeline said when she saw his pale face and his limp arms.

"We have to get him to a bed," Theo said. Theo grabbed Aaron's arm and they teleported just outside the portal house. Eric was passed to Theo and the guilt ate away at him when he felt Eric sagging in his arms. Aaron and Evangeline left for Luxwick and Theo ran into the house with Shawn close behind him.

"Grab onto me," Theo said as they reached the portal's entrance.

"What?" Shawn asked.

"We need to go through the portal. It won't recognize you, so you need to grab onto me. NOW!"

Shawn did as he was told.

"Stay relaxed," he told Shawn as the door closed behind them. Aaron was waiting for them, ready to grab them and teleport them to Eric's room. Theo placed Eric on the bed. Eric's eyes fluttered open as he landed on the soft mattress. He released a pained breath from the movement.

Aaron grabbed Eric by the arm.

"He was outside for too long. This is going to hurt," he said before letting the glow spread from his palms, beginning to heal Eric. It wasn't long before Eric regained consciousness, but this also meant the pain from being healed while awakened as well. Eric screamed and thrashed. "It hurts!" he cried between screams.

"It will be over soon," Aaron assured him. Eventually, Eric's thrashing slowed, and his body stilled as he lost consciousness. Aaron sighed. "He's passed out from the pain." He finished healing Eric and stepped away from him, relieved it was over. He stepped back and sat on Eric's desk chair, exhausted by the events of the day. Theo collapsed onto the floor, against a wall. He stared at Eric who was now asleep, the color returning to his face. Evangeline stood in the doorway.

"Where are we?" asked Shawn from behind her, bringing everyone out of their thoughts.

Aaron groaned. "Roman is going to have my head on a platter," he said, burying his face in his hands.

Theo closed his eyes and rubbed his face. He glanced at Shawn.

"It's a long story."

CHAPTER 15
Secrets

Theo and Aaron sat in Eric's bedroom, where Eric laid unconscious on the bed. They both stared at Shawn and wondered how to handle the situation they were in. Evangeline retrieved dry clothing from Eric's closet and handed the pile to Aaron.

"He needs to get out of those wet clothes," she said.

"I'll join you in the living room when I'm finished."

She looked down at Eric, stroking his hair before leaving the room. Theo stood from the ground and followed her, but Aaron stopped him.

"Don't go too far. We have a lot to discuss."

Theo nodded without turning around, following after Evangeline with Shawn close behind.

Aaron closed the door and proceeded to strip Eric of everything but his underwear, quickly exchanging each soaked garment for the dry clothing Evangeline picked out. Once Eric was dressed, he retrieved a towel from the bathroom and removed as much water as he could from Eric's hair and neck, hoping to make him more comfortable.

Eric did not stir.

Aaron carefully covered Eric and smoothed his damp hair back, away from his forehead, and left him to rest, making sure to close the door before joining the others in the living room.

Shawn sat on one end of the couch and Theo sat on the other end with his elbows on his knees. Across from them Evangeline sat stiffly in a chair she'd pulled from the dining room table. Aaron could feel her pain despite her attempts to hide it from them. They each looked up at Aaron when he entered the room. Aaron focused on Shawn.

"Why was there a human with you?" he asked.

Theo straightened. "He was there, hooked up to a machine…"

"We can't have him here."

"I know that, but we can't send him home. Not before we've had a chance at a proper conversation."

"I'm not suggesting we send him home. I'm only pointing out that if Roman realizes we have a human here, we won't have the choice not to."

Evangeline thought for a moment. "I can get some cadeea from Harrison for now," she suggested. Before Aaron could suggest that he go instead, she was already gone. He groaned in frustration.

"What's cadeea?" asked Shawn, reminding Aaron he was in the room.

"It's a gemstone. It will give you an aura similar to other sorcerers- at least for now until we can return you to Earth."

Shawn's eyes widened. "I'm sorry, I'm still adjusting to this whole situation. We're not on Earth? Wha…what is this place? Like an alien planet?"

Shawn stopped talking when he saw Theo shaking his head.

"Sorry, it's just… a lot."

Evangeline returned and walked to Shawn, handing him a thin chain with a small green and black gemstone. "Wear it around your neck. Keep it under your shirt," she instructed. He did as he was told. "Don't lose it," she told him before returning to her seat.

"I need an explanation Theodore," Aaron said.

Theo nodded. "I thought I could get to him. I didn't think Eric would follow me. I don't know how he knew where I was going," he said.

"He may be young but he's smart. He probably saw you leaving and put two and two together."

Theo repositioned himself, but his movement made him wince. Aaron noticed Theo's injury. He stepped forward and grabbed Theo by the arm, pulling up his shirt and pressed his hand to his wound, healing it. Theo clenched his jaw during the healing process but relaxed when the wound became a burn scar. Aaron examined the curious

shape of the burn, noticing it resembled the shape of a palm. Then he remembered how the creature breathed fire.

"Was this him?" Aaron asked.

Theo nodded. "He didn't want me to bleed out too soon," he explained.

Aaron turned to Shawn. "And why were you there?"

"Someone grabbed me. One of those things, I think. I didn't see it, but I felt it, the heat before I blacked out."

"He was unconscious when I found him. They were giving him some kind of blood transfusion."

"A transfusion? For what?"

Theo shook his head. "I don't know. She didn't tell me."

Evangeline's attention was caught by the mention of another person. "She?" she asked.

"The girl who helped us."

Neil opened his eyes slowly, grabbing his head when the pounding in his ears began. He glanced at the clock on his nightstand and noted it was nightfall. He wondered if he had been asleep for a day or longer. He slowly pushed himself up and stretched to soothe the aching in his muscles.

His visit to Cyrus felt worse than usual, but then again, he always thought that. The routine which only he and the Council know brings a pain he forgets until he is called to return. Neil slowly stood up, grabbing the nightstand until his vision cleared. He stepped away to flip the light and proceeded to get dressed. When he walked to retrieve his phone from his dresser, he was surprised when he realized it was not there.

Neil left his room and walked across to Eric's room. Before he could reach it, Aaron appeared in front of him.

"Aaron?" he said in surprise. If it had been Evangeline in front of him, he would have assumed she was there to check on him, but Aaron would never be there for such a reason. "What is it?" he asked.

"There was a situation..."

Before Aaron could say any more, Neil pushed past him and into Eric's room. At first glance, it appeared as if Eric had only gone to bed and nothing more. But the more closely Neil looked, the more he realized that was not the case. He noticed the lack of color in his skin, except for the redness of his forehead and cheeks. When he reached for Eric, he noticed he had a fever.

"I healed him, but he needs time to break the fever on his own."

"Healed from what?!" he hissed, turning back to Aaron.

"Hypothermia," Aaron whispered.

There was no need for Aaron to explain any more. Neil's senses kicked in and he heard the voices downstairs. He rushed downstairs and locked eyes with Theo. When he saw the guilt in his eyes, he snapped, rushing to Theo.

"What did you do?" he yelled, grabbing Theo by the collar. Aaron grabbed Neil, pulling him back.

"Cornelius, calm down."

"You want me to keep calm? I left for two days and he went after the snake, didn't he?"

"I couldn't just sit here and do nothing..." Theo said.

Aaron glared at Theo. "This is not the time for petty arguments," he said, then stepped between the two of them. "We have more important things to discuss!"

Neil kept his eyes on Theo, seething.

"When will you choose to grow up..." Neil said tiredly.

Theo stayed quiet at first, taken aback by the disappointment in Neil's voice. "When will you choose to stop running?" he asked quietly.

The atmosphere was heavy as Theo and Neil stared at each other. It was clear there was a suppressed anger between them, finally coming to light.

"Aaron's right, Neil," Evangeline said. "We have more important things to discuss than Theo's recklessness."

Neil wanted nothing more than to pull Theo into a room and continue to scold him, but when he saw the fear in Evangeline's eyes, he calmed down.

"What happened while I slept?" he asked.

"I went after the snake and found the devil instead," Theo replied.

Neil did not look at Theo, but closed his eyes, wishing he could end his nightmare. "Not here… Conference room in five minutes," he said. Aaron took Theo and Shawn to the conference room, leaving Evangeline and Neil alone.

Neil walked to the couch across from Evangeline and collapsed into the cushions.

"How did he get hypothermia?"

"Theo left, and Eric followed… Theo didn't want him there when he faced him so when they were close… He said it was just a simple paralysis spell but…"

"His body fought it until he collapsed," Neil finished.

She nodded. "You should go easy on him. His intentions were good. He was just too eager to realize it was a trap."

Neil considered her words, his eyes fixed on the stairs. They both sat in silence while Neil gathered his thoughts. "We should go to the conference room now," he said. Evangeline reached over and Neil took her hand and they were transported to just outside the conference room. He took back his hand and opened the double doors, where Aaron, Theo, Shawn, and an angry Roman waited, none of them seated.

Evangeline joined Roman and Aaron. "I take it Aaron's caught you up?" she asked nervously.

Roman glared at her. In a hushed voice he said, "We will discuss your misconduct after this meeting." She nodded, knowing there was no avoiding it. Roman looked over at Shawn. "Who is this?" he asked. It was at that moment that Neil had finally noticed him as well. It brought the realization of how tired he was. He looked at Theo, waiting for an answer as well.

"A witness," Theo said.

Neil looked at Shawn, studying him. Despite his exhaustion, he was quick to realize that he was human.

"His residence is on Earth," Neil explained, knowing Roman would send him away if he knew he was human. "He will be with us until he is no longer needed."

Neil looked at Theo and took a deep breath. "Now… Tell us everything. From the moment you first encountered this 'devil'…" he then looked to Aaron, "to the moment when you two became involved."

Theo nodded and began his story, starting from when he encountered Lydia and Oscar in Neil's old apartment, describing the events that led to his capture.

"The girl Lydia kept watch outside my cell. She's the one who told me Malphilus wasn't there," he explained.

"What do you mean he wasn't there?" asked Neil.

Theo shrugged. "He wasn't there. She told me the one who works for Malphilus would come to see me." Theo shook his head as he thought of Borrit. "Something came to my cell, someone. That… thing's name is Borrit. He's the one who set the fire on Earth."

"Show him to me," Neil demanded.

Roman moved to stand with them. "Show me as well. I'd like to be on the same page as the others."

Theo closed his eyes, bringing the memory to the surface. He pictured Borrit when he first described what he was, the fire rising from within him, his feet burning the ground he stood on. Then he joined one hand with Neil's, and the other with Roman's, feeling the memory flow to them. Roman and Neil's eyes widened in shock, their irises fogging from the magic. Neil gasped at the sight of the creature, unlike anything he had seen before, while Roman stood in shock. Theo stepped back, ceasing the memory, and waited for Neil to react.

Neil stood with his eyes wide. "What is he?" he asked as Roman returned to his place in the room.

"He said he doesn't know, said he was something ancient, that Malphilus freed him. But that's not even the crazy part," he said. "He said he was freed from Hell."

Evangeline shuddered at the thought of the creature from Hell and Aaron shook his head. "No, that's impossible," he said in denial.

"Well, that's where he said he's from. Unless you have a better idea as to

where he crawled out from, I'm taking his word for it."

"That's absurd. Hell is a place of dark magic, not mysterious creatures. Cyrus would have informed us of such a threat if it existed," Roman said.

"Bollocks, Roman, again with the Cyrus argument? The man's lived for millions of years. You really think he's sharing every detail with you?"

"Of course not, but we showed him the fires and he informed us that there was no such creature capable of starting them."

"He's not always going to tell the truth," Theo said. "Even gods have secrets."

CHAPTER 16
Dragons

While Eric was unconscious, he found himself once again transported to the dream world. He opened his eyes and stood in the alley, the sight of it making his stomach twist. When he looked up, he saw the familiar darkness in place of the morning sky. To his left, deeper in the alley, a metal door was propped open. He walked through it, letting himself get swallowed by the pitch-black room.

"James?" he called out.

"You're alive," said James from behind him.

Eric turned around and saw James ten feet away from him, looking relieved. When he took a step toward him, the familiar blue flame circled Eric.

James smiled. "Some things will never change," he said. "You frightened me. I thought you were somewhere out in your reality, buried in the frost."

Eric said nothing, only staring at him in suspicion.

"Cat got your tongue?" smirked James. "Or is this the silent treatment after helping you during our last meeting?"

Eric stared at James. "You knew," he said.

"Knew what?" asked James casually.

"That I was a sorcerer. You told me my magic would keep me from freezing. How did you know I can use magic?"

"Is that what made you so jumpy?" He pointed to the flame on the ground. "That fire shows up every time you see me, you talk to a strange man every time you close your eyes, and I show you a man on fire and none of it fazes you," he said.

"Does that mean you're one too?" he asked.

James looked down at his hands, appearing lost in thought. "In here I can... do strange things..."

"And out there?" Eric asked.

"I don't know yet," he answered. James walked forward, stopping just in front of the barrier. "If I ever wake up, if I ever escape from this place… we should meet."

Eric hesitated, but eventually nodded slightly. Then something different happened. Instead of the screeching sound ripping them apart, James simply disappeared, leaving Eric alone in the darkness. Eric looked around, wondering if he was supposed to wake up. The temperature rose, but the source of the heat was unclear. He stood still, trying to focus his hearing on his surroundings. The temperature continued to increase, making him uncomfortable. It was focused on his back. Eric felt the sweat on the back of his neck. He turned slowly and was frightened by what he saw. The man he had not seen since he was a child appeared: Borrit.

Borrit stood in front of him with his eyes glowing, a wide and sinister smile on his face.

Eric jumped back at the sight of him and stumbled.

He opened his eyes in his dark bedroom, his breathing quick and his heart pounding. He thought of Borrit. He did not know who he was, but was reminded of something important. Eric jumped out from beneath the covers. He opened the drawer of his nightstand and grabbed folders containing his drawings, tossing them onto the bed. When he found the oldest folder, its red cover faded and peeling from age, he opened it and rifled through the old crayon drawings until he found the one he was looking for.

He slipped on his damp shoes, took the drawing and ran out of the house to Angel Tower. When he reached the lobby, a few angels stopped to look at him, but he paid no attention to them, sprinting directly to the elevator, too out of breath to dare attempt the stairs. When the elevator doors opened on the top floor, he approached the double doors and was about to open them when he heard Theo's voice.

"He said he was freed from Hell," he heard him say. Eric pulled his hand back, not wanting to interrupt the conversation as things grew heated. Instead, he sat

outside, listening to them argue about Cyrus, waiting for a good moment to enter the room. Then another topic caught his attention.

"There's something else…" said Theo. "When I was in that cell, when he spoke to me, he told me something I didn't want to be true." Eric listened as his voice grew thick with anger. "He was the one who killed her… He killed Leanna."

The only sound in the room was a frustrated grumble Eric could only assume came from Roman. However, the others in the room were completely silent. Eric's stomach sank and he looked down at the old drawing of Borrit.

"No…" Neil finally whispered. "No, it was Malphilus." To Eric, it sounded as if Neil was trying to convince himself of that but was failing.

"I thought he was lying too," said Theo. "But then I remembered… The handle melted in, the charred footprints on the stairs. It was him that night."

"No," Neil said again.

Unable to listen anymore, Eric opened the double doors, startling everyone. They stared at Eric, who stood frozen in the doorway, the drawing still pressed to his chest. "I think he's right," he said quietly. He walked slowly forward, stopping in front of Neil and held out the slightly crumpled sheet of paper. "I drew this when I was little," he told him. Neil took the paper from him. "I used to have nightmares a lot, of him. I just remembered."

Neil's hand shook as he placed the child's crayon drawing of a man with dark wings and glowing eyes at the center of the round table for everyone to see.

"It's him," said Theo.

"I know what he is too," Eric continued.

Everyone looked at him in surprise, waiting for him to continue.

"He looks like us, but he has wings covered in scales, his eyes glow, and he can breathe fire. Someone told me that stories change. The more people tell a story, the more the details change until they end up with something that looks completely different." Everyone looked at him in confusion, not sure what his conclusion would be. "He's a dragon," he said. "He's where the story came from, just like how witches and wizards came from sorcerers."

Everyone in the room looked as if they wanted to argue, but they did not because they knew he was right.

"Holy shit…" Shawn muttered, reminding them that he was there.

Evangeline slid the drawing closer to her. She traced the wings and remembered their shape. "I think it's time we call someone who will give us some answers," she said. She did not have to clarify who she was referring to when she looked at Aaron.

Aaron nodded and rummaged in his inside coat pocket until he found an old flip phone. He opened it and stared at it. He pressed the dial button, then the speaker button and placed it at the center of the table, then took a seat. After three rings, a woman answered.

"Hello?" said an older woman.

"Hello, mom," said Aaron.

There was silence on the other end of the line that made Aaron and Evangeline smile sweetly. Evangeline stepped forward and gripped Aaron's shoulder. The woman, who Eric now saw was called 'Olivia' on the contact screen, finally spoke. "It's lovely to hear your voice. What is the reason for your call?" she asked.

"We have a situation on Earth with something we've never seen before."

"What do you need from me?"

"Cyrus says he has no information for us, but we were hoping you might be able to answer our questions more… thoroughly. We were wondering, what do you know about dragons?"

She paused, taking it in. "Dragons don't exist," she told them.

Aaron turned to look at Evangeline and she took the seat next to him.

"We saw them ourselves. The fire inside of them. We need the truth," she paused. "I need to know why they look like us."

There was a long silence followed by a shaky sigh. "I'm available right now if someone can come get me," Olivia finally said.

"On my way," said Aaron. He vanished, then Olivia hung up. Evangeline looked over at Eric.

"You should be resting," she told him.

"I want to be here. I want to know about them," he said, pointing at the drawing.

Evangeline was concerned, but she let it go, gesturing to the seat across from her and Eric seated himself.

Barely a minute had passed when Aaron walked through the double doors with a woman in her sixties, their mother Olivia. Olivia was average height and wore her long white hair in a loose braid. When she entered, Aaron helped her remove her coat and pulled a chair for her next to Evangeline. The two exchanged a small smile and everyone was soon seated.

Olivia spotted Neil and smiled. "You must be Cornelius," she said.

He nodded. "It's a pleasure to make your acquaintance. Although I do wish it were under lighter circumstances."

"I agree." She turned her attention to the other individuals in the room, her eyes lingering on Eric for a moment before turning to Evangeline. "You said you saw the creature you're referring to?" she asked Evangeline.

Evangeline nodded. "We all have," she explained. "He looked like us, but there were scales across his skin and his eyes glowed." She lost herself in the memory. "He could breathe fire, but the detail that troubled me was his wings." She locked eyes with Olivia. "They were dark red and frayed, but their shape is exactly the same as ours…"

They could all see the fear in Evangeline's eyes.

"Does Cyrus know?" Olivia asked.

"No," answered Neil. "But it's important we know what we are facing."

Olivia knotted her fingers together. "It's not surprising that he didn't share their existence with you. Not many of us know of these creatures."

"Why is that?" asked Evangeline.

"Because they are an old species. Older than ou… than yours."

"Older than sorcerers?" asked Neil.

"Not sorcerers, angels."

Everyone in the room was astonished to learn there was a species created before the angels, or that sorcerers came before them.

Olivia straightened her back. "Has anyone ever told you the story of how the gods created their system? Heaven, Earth, and Hell?" When everyone in the room stayed silent, she continued. "Cyrus and his brothers once all lived in the heavens together. They felt responsible for keeping the peace, so they would each take turns visiting Earth to check on the animals that resided there. One day, the youngest brother, Adan, came down to Earth to carry out his duty. He stayed for weeks. When he returned to give his update, something unexpected had happened. He fell in love with it all. He fell in love with humanity."

"If this is before the angels existed," said Roman, "then this would have been when the humans were still primitive, when written language was barely a concept. How could such creatures pique his interests?"

Olivia smiled. "He didn't fall for them because of their intellect, but their compassion. He fell in love with their mortality and their strength."

"What does this have to do with the dragons?" asked Neil.

"After Adan's visit to Earth, he wished to retire from his duties and reside on Earth. When he told his brothers of his desires, they belittled him for having such thoughts and he returned to his responsibilities. Even so, he still wished to live among humans, so he decided that if he was no longer a god, they would have no reason to make him stay. He discarded his immortality along with his power."

Neil was stunned. "That's not possible," he said.

"He found a way," she said.

"But he guards Hell," Aaron pointed out.

Olivia nodded. "Indeed, he does. You see, that much power does not simply vanish. When he performed the ritual on himself, all his power flowed down to Earth. It affected many of the humans; it changed them." She looked Neil in the eyes and continued. "His power made the humans evolve, and those who could withstand the change became sorcerers."

"The birth of a new species," Neil said.

"Unfortunately, many of the humans were not so lucky. There were those who were negatively affected. Dragons were created as well, and they were vicious and callous creatures. When Adan witnessed the chaos he had created, he took back his power, but that kind of change could not be undone. All those who had been turned could not be turned back. They knew the dragons could not be made human, and they were the ones to be affected by his immortality. Something that powerful could not be destroyed easily, so Adan created a place to contain them. He created Hell to keep them from harming anyone and he vowed to guard it, desperate to redeem himself. After the incident, they agreed that the sorcerers could not be left to themselves, so Cyrus decided to watch over Earth and he created the first generation of angels to help him."

"Then something's not right," Roman said, "because clearly one has escaped."

Olivia looked at Roman. "He shouldn't have been able to. There is no doorway from which he could have escaped. Adan would have noticed if someone escaped. It's likely the reason Cyrus did not feel the need to inform you of such creatures."

Roman stood quickly and headed for the door.

"Where are you going?" Aaron asked.

"To speak to Cyrus," Roman said, teleporting before anyone could stop him. Aaron sighed.

"I hope I've answered all of your questions," she said.

Neil nodded. "Yes, we appreciate your honesty. Thank you for coming on such short notice."

Olivia smiled. "It's my pleasure. If there's anything else you need to know, you know how to reach me," she said, standing from her chair. Aaron stood as well.

"Ready?" he asked.

She nodded, then reached over and gave Evangeline's shoulder a gentle squeeze. Evangeline managed to keep a smile on her face, despite the pain on her back, but Aaron noticed, keeping silent so that Olivia would not worry.

Eric silently wondered why the exchange between Olivia, Aaron, and Evangeline was so formal and distant despite them calling her their mother.

Aaron teleported with Olivia so he could send her home, leaving everyone else in the conference room. Neil stood and leaned against the table.

Shawn who spent the entire time silently listening rubbed his face.

"Taking it all in?" Theo asked.

Shawn groaned. "This is too much crazy for one day."

Finally, without Roman in the room, Neil looked at the complete stranger sitting in the room. "I've been meaning to ask this. Who are you?"

Shawn stood nervously and shook Neil's hand. "I'm Shawn," he said.

"Neil," he said in return. Then he turned to Theo. "Care to explain how we ended up with a stranger in our midst, a human no less?"

"I found him while I was inside. He was kidnapped, strapped to a gurney. I don't know what they were doing to him."

Neil turned to Shawn. "Your captivity. How much do you remember?" he asked.

Shawn shook his head. "Nothing really."

"We will have to remedy that," he said, making Shawn nervous. He turned to Theo. "I assume he will be staying with you?"

Theo nodded. "I've got the spare room."

"Just… keep him out of trouble."

"I thought this thing," Shawn said, feeling the stone hanging from his neck, "was supposed to keep people from knowing I'm human."

"It will," said Neil.

Theo explained. "He's just too experienced for a stone to fool him. I know he doesn't look it, but he's an old man." He pointed to Eric, "That's his grandson, actually- Not by blood, but he raised his mother."

Shawn's eyes widened.

Ignoring Shawn's surprise, Neil looked at Theo with a serious expression. "Don't forget I am still furious with you for the trouble you caused everyone in this

room. Store the memory of Borrit quickly before it fades, and get our guest settled in before Roman gets back."

Theo's smirk faded and his stomach sank. He turned to Shawn. "I'll catch you up once we get to my place," he said quietly. Before he could leave, Neil stopped him.

"Please escort Eric to his room as well." Eric opened his mouth to argue, but Neil silenced him with a glare. "You are in need of more rest, and don't you dare argue with me because you are in just as much trouble as Theodore at the moment. We will discuss the reasons your actions were both reckless and idiotic in the morning. Are we clear?"

Eric who had shrunk back in his chair nodded and stood, following Theo and Shawn out the door. Neil and Evangeline were left alone in the room. Neil rubbed his eyes, seething with anger. For the first time in years, he lost control. He slammed his fist on the table. The bang from the impact echoed in the room and a chair slid out, slamming into the wall behind it. Neil froze with his fist still on the table and opened his hand, pressing it to the surface. He took deep calming breaths with his eyes closed.

"Why must the furniture always suffer?" Evangeline asked, hoping to lighten the tension.

He breathed in and out slowly until his heart rate slowed, then opened his eyes, still staring down at the table. "I'm sorry, I-."

"You shouldn't apologize. If anyone deserves to lose control, it's you."

Evangeline stood from her chair, Neil watching her. She stepped away from her chair and carefully pushed it back in, her movements stiff. When she straightened her posture, she realized Neil was staring.

"What?" she asked.

"What happened to your back?" he asked.

Evangeline stared at him in surprise. "Nothing," she answered calmly, hoping he would not see through her act.

"Don't lie to me," he said quietly. "You've barely moved. I can tell you're in pain."

Evangeline smiled sadly, wondering why she tried to hide it. "When Aaron and I found Theo, that creature had summoned his fire. I managed to shield Theo, but the attack turned out to be more damaging than I was expecting."

Concern was etched on his face as he walked around the table and held an open hand out to Evangeline. "Show me," he said.

She took his hand and let him lead her up the stairs. They stood in the middle of the open floor and she let go of his hand and removed her coat, careful not to let the fabric drag down her back. She draped the coat onto the rails and waited for her wings to materialize, the soft glow reflecting onto his face. Evangeline stood still as Neil stepped around her until he was behind her, so he could see the damage for himself. He gasped at what he saw. He stared at the wings that he remembered as beautiful, shocked by the blackened feathers frayed at the edges and the burns at the center.

She did not turn around but chose to break the silence. "It will take time, but they will heal soon enough. I can feel them healing already."

Neil walked back in front of her and took her hand between his. He took a deep breath and his eyes glowed for a moment before she retracted her hand quickly.

"Don't. I'm fine," she said.

"You do the same for me nearly every day."

"That's different. I make your pain disappear at the expense of minor energy. What you're doing is transferring it to you. I don't need you to do that."

"Then let me share the load," he insisted.

"I can't heal you if there's no damage," she said.

Neil smiled. "I know."

He held both hands out again and waited. When she saw that he was not wavering, she gave in and placed her hands in his, watching as his eyes began to glow as he relieved her of some of her pain. Her shoulders relaxed almost immediately. When it became bearable, she pulled her hands away again and he smiled.

"You said half."

"I needed to try."

She couldn't manage to suppress her smile at first, but it faded when she

noticed the look in his eyes.

"Your turn," she said.

Neil raised his eyebrows. "My turn for what?"

"What's weighing on your mind?" She grabbed her coat and carefully put it back on, then sat on the steps and patted the ground next to her.

Neil sighed and sat with her. He ran his fingers through his hair, smoothing it back. "I always believed it was him," he said quietly.

"Who?" she asked.

"The one who..." Neil's voice broke. He tried to keep his composure but struggled. "The one who killed her. I thought her death was by his hand, but now..." she shook his head. "Malphilus is cruel, but he's efficient. When I thought it was him, I had the peace of mind knowing she at least did not suffer, that her death would have been quick, but now..."

Neil stared down at the bracelet that Leanna had once gifted him and clenched his fist. "All I can think now is of how afraid she must have been. Watching that creature break into her home and enter the room where her child slept..." Unshed tears filled his eyes and he held his breath, willing them to stop.

Evangeline said nothing at first, allowing him time to calm himself before she tried to provide comfort and reassurance.

"I can't say she wasn't afraid because no one can know that, but there is one thought we can cling to," she said. "She protected Eric until the end, and that's something to take pride in. She passed on and his soul didn't follow. She was able to pass on knowing that she kept him safe." She placed a comforting hand on Neil's arm. "So, we can't know if she was afraid, but we at least know she was strong... Just like you raised her to be."

Neil stared at her for a moment, then nodded, taking in her words. He faced forward again, resting his elbow on his knees, and buried his face in his hand. He took the arm that Evangeline was holding and moved it back, grabbing her hand and giving it a gentle squeeze, which she returned.

They sat on the steps together, no clue as to what the future would bring them.

Unwilling to let the past go.

CHAPTER 17
Nightmares

After the meeting, Neil could not bear to return home, not yet. He sat in the conference room alone until late, staring up at the night sky. Evangeline once told him to put his faith in them because resting for a day would not make the world stop turning, and she was right. Technically, the world did keep turning, but the events that took place were not welcomed. He looked back at the clock on the wall and knew if he expected to have any energy for what was to come, he had to rest, even if it was just for an hour or two. He walked through the town, which was peaceful during the night, and paid no attention to his surroundings, his only goal being to return home.

When he entered the house, all was quiet. He walked straight up the stairs, hoping that Eric was safely asleep in his bed. To his relief, when he opened Eric's door, he saw him sleeping soundly with the blanket wrapped tightly around him.

Neil went to bed feeling his age for once. He sat on the edge and stared down at the floor, wondering if his decisions had been the right ones so far. When he found Eric, he had originally felt relief that his grandson had been alive and well, and pleasure that he would be able to protect him in Leanna's place. Since then, Eric had been strangled and nearly frozen to death and Neil began to wonder if he would have been better off hidden on Earth. He shook the thought from his head, remembering that if he had not found him, Malphilus eventually would have. He went to bed that night, the anger inside him softening to a dull roar, knowing that he would release it in the morning once he'd had his talk with Eric.

Like most mornings, Neil was up before the sun rose. He walked downstairs and made himself a cup of coffee, then sat on the couch and switched the television onto their news.

Neil was not the only person awake while the sky was still dark. Theo stood

in his office with a target on the wall across from him. In his hands were throwing knives. He threw them one at a time, hitting the center of the target each time. After a few minutes, he switched to magic, letting the knives circle him in the air. He waved his hands and watched them shoot past him and straight to the wall. He stared at the target, a clear sign of his skill, and wondered if anything he did would ever be enough. Every time he felt he had earned Neil's respect, he felt he lost it just as quickly. He sighed and walked to the target, grabbing the three knives and returning them to their cases, then left the office, ready for a cold shower.

In the guest room, Shawn lay sound asleep in the dark for the first time since he was taken. When Theo woke him up in the basement of Borrit's base, Shawn had only remembered the night he was taken and nothing else. He was plagued with nightmares and tossed and turned in his sleep, unable to get comfortable. His dreams were filled with fire and darkness. They became so unbearable that his eyes opened and he jumped up to a sitting position, gripping the blankets next to him. His arms were shaking, and his breathing was rapid as he focused on the blankets in front of him, finally realizing he was in a safe place. Shawn lifted his arm and wiped the cold sweat from his forehead with the back of his hand. He took slow, even breaths until his heart rate slowed.

Theo, having heard Shawn's panicked breathing, rushed into the room.

"You alright?" Theo asked.

Shawn nodded, although he was far from alright. He sat on the edge of the bed with his feet on the ground. "There's something I've been wanting to ask you," he said. "I just haven't had the guts to."

Theo joined him on the bed. "Ask away."

Shawn took a deep breath. "What's today's date?"

Theo was confused. "February 9th", he told him.

Shawn's shoulders sagged in defeat. He leaned forward, resting his elbows on his knees, and taking his head in his hands.

Theo spoke carefully, not waiting to add to Shawn's stress. "What day was it when you were taken?" he asked.

Shawn straightened his back. His eyes were red from unshed tears. "August 2nd," he finally said. "I missed their birthday." He covered his face just as the first tear escaped. Theo gripped his shoulder in an attempt to comfort him.

"How old did they turn?" Theo asked once Shawn was calm enough to speak again.

"Four," he answered.

"You said they're both boys?"

Shawn nodded. "Hunter and Matthew."

Theo stared at Shawn, wondering if he should give him time to recuperate or if he should get straight to the point and spare him reliving the pain. Shawn could feel Theo's stare. "You want to know about the nightmare, don't you?" he asked.

Theo smiled sadly. "I need any information you can give me..."

Shawn nodded and wiped his damp cheeks with the back of his hand. "I still can't remember all of it, but... I think I remembered something."

"Which part?"

"When they first grabbed me." Shawn tried to focus. "But it's still hazy. I can't tell what was real."

"Neil will want to hear this." Theo stood, patting Shawn's shoulder gently. "Why don't I give you time to get decent and we can go and see him," he suggested, leaving Shawn to himself.

When Shawn first entered the bathroom, he did not recognize his own reflection. He stepped up to the mirror and stared at his face, which was thinner, with a long, scruffy beard. His brown hair was long, greasy, and untamed. Twenty minutes later, he was relieved to see a face he recognized in the mirror.

Theo called Neil and was told to meet with him outside the portal entrance to Earth. He walked with Shawn there, where Neil was already waiting.

"You said you remembered something?" Neil asked.

Shawn nodded. "I told Theo before that I remembered being in the parking lot, the heat... Well, last night I think I remembered these flashes, I think not long after

I was taken… but now that I'm awake…"

"They're gone."

Shawn nodded.

"Your memories Shawn, they may be important. We need to know what you saw."

Shawn's shoulders sagged. "I can't go home yet, can I?"

"If we were to return you home now… I'm not confident we would be able to keep in contact with you without endangering your family. Ultimately, the choice is yours, but I do hope you will consider staying for the time being."

Shawn considered this. "That… monster… He's still out there, right?"

Neil nodded.

"My kids are out there…" He appeared to be shaking a horrible thought from his head. "If my memories can help you catch him, I'm in."

"Thank you," Neil said.

"Where are we going?" asked Theo.

"To meet with Harrison."

When they arrived at Harrison's home, he was already waiting for them. He answered the door and guided them to his study.

"I've brought the ingredients up. I thought it would be more comfortable here," he told them when they reached his study.

"Ingredients for what?" Shawn asked.

Neil gestured for Shawn to sit on the small leather couch. In front of the couch was a small coffee table with a cast iron incense burner, a matchbook, some dried sage, and what looked like flakes of salt. Neil moved the chair from Harrison's desk across from the couch.

"You told us you remembered something in a dream, but the moment you woke, the memory was gone. Your memories from the time of your captivity may have been suppressed. I believe I can help guide you so you may recover them."

"Like with hypnosis?" Shawn asked.

"Not quite. You see, hypnosis is unreliable for recovering memories. Often,

hypnosis can only lead to the reinforcement of false memories. We, however, have an advantage."

Neil gestured to the items on the coffee table. "The items on this table all hold their own symbolic meanings for a reason: sage for wisdom, and quartz for healing. When combined with our magic correctly, they can have wondrous capabilities on the mind. They will ensure the memories you recover are genuine."

"How does this work exactly?"

"We sorcerers have certain capabilities involving memories. The sage will be burned with the quartz for you to inhale. You will then lie on the couch and I will use my abilities to put you in a trance. Think of the moment you remember, the moment you were taken. The rest will be in your hands. I must warn you… the memories are guaranteed to be unpleasant. If I see you're overwhelmed, I will wake you."

Shawn took a moment to prepare himself. When he was ready, Neil added the sage and quartz to the cast iron and lit the match, letting the sage begin to burn before dropping the match in the cast iron. He passed it to Shawn who began to inhale the fumes then took it back. Shawn lay back on the couch and Neil placed the cast iron close to him.

"Close your eyes," Neil instructed.

Shawn did as he was told and Neil placed his hand on his head and used his magic.

When Shawn ›rst closed his eyes, he only saw darkness. Then he felt a warmth on his head and the darkness changed to a hazy blend of colors. Just as Neil instructed, he thought of the moment he was taken.

Shawn had just gotten off work and was walking through the dimly lit parking lot. Not a soul was in sight as he ›shed his car keys from his pocket. Just as he removed them from his pocket, his hand slipped and the keys clattered to the ground. He crouched down to retrieve his keys when he felt heat. It was at this moment when Shawn regained his lucidity. Shawn hesitated as he reached for his keys. He felt the heat grow more intense. Unlike when this moment actually happened, his awareness

made him more afraid. He wished to leave before he could regain any more memories, but when he remembered how important it was, he pushed his fear aside. He picked up the car keys just as he had done before and continued to walk, but before he could reach his car, someone intervened. A woman with a white mask appeared in front of him, and then everything went black.

The next moments for Shawn occurred in flashes as he went in and out of consciousness. He was dragged through a hallway, his head throbbing. He heard sounds of distress. The cries and screams caused his fear to spike as he struggled to regain his bearings. He struggled against the hands that dragged him, but he was weak, and their grips never loosened. He lost consciousness again.

The next time he was awakened by a high-pitched sound. He opened his eyes and saw the cold concrete beneath him. When he lifted his head, the metal bars came into focus. He wondered what the sound was that woke him as it continued to pierce his ears. When he finally pushed away the drowsiness, he realized that what he was hearing was screaming. Shawn fought the exhaustion, trying to assess his surroundings. He realized he was in a cage, barely large enough to sit up in. He searched for where the screaming was coming from, taking in the scene around him. He was in a room filled with cages, a person in each one of them. Some were unconscious, some were weakened, and others were wide awake and terrified. Finally, he found the source of the screaming, a woman being pulled from one of the cages by two people in masks, sorcerers. The sorcerers, tired of her screaming, used their magic to knock her unconscious. He watched them drag her from her cage until she was out of sight, and he could no longer fight his exhaustion.

The next time he woke, it was to the sound of his own cage opening. He had no recollection as to how long he had been there. The sorcerers approached him and he pushed himself back, adrenaline powering his body. He struggled as the sorcerers pulled him from the cage. No longer able to take the memories, what remained overwhelmed him in flashes. He felt heat, heard screaming, felt his body bruised…

Then he was awake.

CHAPTER 18
Haunted

Aaron and Evangeline stood in Theo's living room, waiting for Theo and Neil. She stood in the living room dressed differently than usual. Her usual clothing, which was light and formal, yet comfortable, had been exchanged for a pair of dark wide-legged pants, a white-collar shirt, and a blazer.

"Shouldn't you be healing?" Neil asked Evangeline when he arrived.

Aaron nodded. "My thoughts exactly."

Evangeline rolled her eyes as she adjusted her blazer. "Spare me the looks of concern. The damage is mostly gone, I'll be completely healed in a few hours."

"Your health should always be put first," Neil said, making Evangeline narrow her eyes.

"My own words being used against me."

"You're the one constantly pestering me about my health."

"Oh, so now you listen," Evangeline snapped, making both Aaron and Neil smile, but their moment of peace was broken by the sound of the door opening. Theo strolled in, dressed in a suit.

"It's strange seeing you without the coat," he said.

She smiled, looking down at herself. "I swear I didn't even recognize myself in the mirror. I haven't gone to earth on business since the '80s. Did you get the badges?"

Theo held up the two badge cases in his hand. "Two fake FBI credentials, one for each of us, directly from our friends at the tower."

He handed Evangeline her badge and she studied it and slid the badge into her pocket.

"What's your plan?" Neil asked Theo.

"We'll drop by where Shawn was taken and see if we can get our hands on any security footage, although it's unlikely. Afterwards, we'll take a look at Shawn's family just to make sure they're safe."

Neil glanced at the closed door to the guest room. He lowered his voice. "How is he?"

"He's alright," Theo answered. "Completely knackered, but fine. He feels bad for not giving us more."

"Because of him, we now know that Malphilus has more humans in cages. We can try again when he's rested, but he has already given us plenty."

Theo nodded in agreement.

Evangeline and Theo stopped by the parking lot where Shawn was taken where there was only one security camera on the building where he would have been in sight. Just as they expected, there was no footage from that night. Their next stop was Shawn's home.

Theo checked the address Shawn had given him and found somewhere nearby for Evangeline to teleport them. They watched the family home for signs that they were there, hidden on the rooftop of one of the neighboring homes. The sound of laughter caught their attention and they followed it, reaching a place where they could see the backyard.

Shawn's children ran around the yard with a Labrador retriever as they appeared to be attempting to take a toy from its mouth. Theo smiled in relief until he spotted the mother on the swings watching her children. The woman sat with her dark hair unkempt, tied back in a bun. Although she was smiling, her eyes looked very tired.

"She has dark circles under her eyes," Evangeline whispered. "It doesn't look like she's been sleeping."

"No… but he'll be home soon enough."

"How many others do you think are out there, burdened by the disappearance of their loved ones? Who knows what Malphilus has done to them…"

"That's what we have to find out." He watched the family for a moment

longer. "We should go." When Evangeline said nothing, he looked at her and noticed she was lost in thought. "Evangeline," he called again.

Evangeline and Theo left the rooftop and walked to the first desolate area they could find before teleporting. When they arrived, Theo looked around in confusion because he did not recognize the area. They were standing behind a small warehouse that appeared to be abandoned.

"Where are we?" he asked.

"Sunnyvale, my hometown. There's something I need to check."

Evangeline walked out from behind the warehouse and onto the street with Theo following behind her.

"Check what?"

"When you told us what Shawn said, about the cages, I remembered something from when I was a teenager. I think it may be connected."

Theo was baffled. "The idea that they were around before Leanna died is crazy enough, but you think they could've been around back then too?"

"I didn't say it was definitely him, but I can't say it wasn't. I'd rather not leave any stones unturned."

Theo nodded in agreement. "I'll let you lead the way, then."

Evangeline and Theo walked six blocks to a quiet street. "Okay, we're here."

"You mind filling me in?"

"When I was in high school in 1956, there was an incident at our local diner, a huge fire. There were only two people there, who both worked in the kitchen. The man we're going to see is called Stephen. He was the only one there when the fire department arrived. He suffered from severe burns on his left side and his brother Josh went missing. The fire spread so quickly that the police thought it was arson, but I think it may have been Borrit. I remember Stephen was so terrified after it happened. No one would tell me the details, but they said he had a mental breakdown, maybe lost his mind."

"How old were they?"

"Stephen was seventeen and Josh was fourteen."

"You think he'll still remember?"

"I checked his records. I had to make sure he was still alive. His health is weak, but he doesn't have any mental illnesses. If I'm right and he saw Borrit, there's no way he would forget it. Anyway, you might have to use a memory spell if he recognizes me."

"You knew them?"

"They went to high school with Aaron and me. We were sixteen at the time."

Theo looked at the house Evangeline was staring at and nodded. "Let's go talk to him, then."

Evangeline and Theo approached the small gray house and Evangeline rang the doorbell. A woman in her twenties answered. "Can I help you?" she asked.

Evangeline smiled and removed her badge to show the woman; Theo did the same.

"Sorry to bother you, I'm Agent Clark, this is my partner, Agent Gibson. Is Stephen Gates here?"

The woman grew worried at the sight of the (false) FBI credentials. "Y-yes. He's inside, what do you need?"

"I can assure you, Ms..."

"Susan," she answered.

"He's not in any trouble. We'd just like to ask him some questions about something that happened when he was a teenager. May we come inside?"

A gruff male voice answered from behind her. "Let them in," he said.

Susan stepped aside, letting them in. "He's in the living room," she said.

Evangeline and Theo entered the living room, where the seventy-six-year-old Stephen Gates was sitting on the couch with his television remote in his hand. He silenced the television as they came in. Evangeline and Theo introduced themselves. A look of recognition passed over his face as he shook Evangeline's hand.

Evangeline took a seat on the arm chair and Theo sat in a chair that Susan brought him. Susan was about to take a seat on the couch next to Stephen when he stopped her.

"Susan, do you mind leaving me alone with them for this?"

Susan looked at him for a moment then nodded. "I'll go run some errands. I'll be back in an hour."

Stephen smiled at her and nodded as she left. When the door shut, he looked at Evangeline. "Why would the FBI need to know about a fire that happened sixty years ago?"

"We're working on a similar case. It's just a hunch, but I think it may be connected. I know the official story, but I'd like to know your side," Evangeline explained.

Stephen shook his head. "Well then, you know what happened. There was a fire and my brother went missing."

"Your brother was taken," Evangeline said.

"That was never confirmed."

"You saw it, didn't you?" she asked him.

Stephen stared at her for a moment then shook his head. "I hit my head on something. When I came to, he was gone."

"Is that what happened, or is that what you were told to say?"

Stephen sank back into the couch cushions, agitated that they were making him remember such a horrible time in his life. "That's what happened."

"Stephen, I need you to tell me the truth about what you saw that night."

Stephen stayed quiet and looked down at the ground. "Just what are you expecting me to tell you I saw?" he asked.

Theo leaned forward. "A monster," he said.

Stephen looked up in surprise, his eyes wide with fear.

"We've seen it too," Theo continued. "A winged beast that breathes fire."

Stephen was shocked. He shook his head, unsure of how to respond.

"We just need to know what happened that night," Theo said.

Stephen looked at him and nodded. "We were working the night shift together," he began. "We were getting ready to close up when he went out back to take out the trash. I thought he was taking his time, so I went out to get him and I found

him speaking to a man. He had long dark hair, covering his face and he was on his knees, looking down at the ground. Josh was standing a few feet in front of him. He was a mess, covered in dirt. Then I saw something come out of that man's back. I thought I was crazy, but when you said winged beast..."

"Is that when he was taken?" Evangeline asked.

Stephen shook his head. "No. When I saw that man's wings and I saw this glowing on his hands, I yelled at Josh to get inside. We both ran in and I locked the door, but he just burned through it. Before we knew it, the whole place was on fire and we couldn't get out. I tried to fight him, but he just burned me. I almost passed out from the pain."

"Did he just take Josh?"

Stephen thought back to when he was lying on the ground in pain, his brother standing in front of him trying to protect him. "I told Josh to run but he didn't. I remember... that monster standing in front of him and his face was glowing, then another man showed up."

"There was someone else there?" Evangeline asked in surprise.

"Yes," Stephen said. "It was a man, a normal man, I think. The last thing I remember is him walking up to us and then I was knocked out."

"Can you recall what he looked like?"

Stephen shook his head. "He was wearing a mask."

Evangeline and Theo were shocked; there was only one man it could have been.

"Do you know something?" Stephen asked when he saw the looks on their faces. "Do you know who it was?"

Evangeline hesitated. "I think so. Thank you, Stephen, this is exactly what we needed."

"Please," Stephen begged. "If you find out what happened to him, please reach out to me. I need to know what happened to him." Theo looked over at Evangeline, wondering if she planned on ordering him to wipe Stephen's memory of their visit. She finally nodded to Stephen and he exhaled in relief. "Thank you," he

said.

Theo wrote down Stephen's number as he said it aloud and they left him. Once they were out the door, Evangeline leaned back against it and sighed.

"You sure it's a good idea?" Theo asked. "Letting him remember today?"

Evangeline shook her head. "You saw the look on his face when you mentioned Borrit. The memory's been eating away at him since it happened, I can't take that peace from him."

Theo nodded in agreement and Evangeline teleported them to the house with the portal.

"Are you going to report this to the Council now?" Theo asked.

Evangeline considered it. "I think we should tell Neil first, in private."

Evangeline teleported and Theo went through the portal and straight to his office. By the time he arrived, Evangeline was already there, waiting with Neil. She was already back in her angel coat.

"What's this about? Was there a problem with Shawn's family?" Neil asked.

Theo shook his head. "They're safe."

"Then what is it?"

"We made another stop while we were on Earth," Evangeline said. "There was something I wanted to check, but we learned more than we were expecting."

They told him everything, starting from what Evangeline remembered and ending with Stephen's recounting of the fire.

"Borrit has been free since the 1950s?" Neil asked.

"Yes," Evangeline said. "But that's not what surprised us. Stephen said there was another man who arrived soon after. He said he was wearing a mask."

"Malphilus?" Neil asked in just above a whisper.

"The way he described him, it sounded as if Borrit had just sprung up from Hell."

"Malphilus may have found a way to open a door."

In Theo's home, Shawn sat on the couch exhausted, watching a movie with

Eric. They both sat on the couch quietly when Eric faintly heard the sound of footsteps. "I think Theo's back," he said.

"He is?"

"I can hear footsteps."

Shawn said nothing at first, just nodding, accepting that Eric was telling the truth. "So, you can hear him coming… cool."

Eric smiled. Then, when he heard two sets of footsteps, he focused his hearing to listen to the conversation between Neil, Evangeline, and Theo. When he heard Evangeline say that she believed it was the 1950s when Borrit first escaped Hell, he was surprised. Eric stood up and grabbed his jacket from next to him.

"I'm going home. I was never here, okay?"

"Wait, why?" Shawn asked, but Eric was already out the front door. Eric ran home and grabbed his laptop. The next half hour was spent researching, typing in every possible word combination he could think of in hopes of finding a clue about Borrit in the 1950s. After watching every old video he could find, he was about to take a break when he remembered what Evangeline said about the fire. Eric searched for information about the diner fire. After twenty minutes, he found the story in an online newspaper archive. Then he was able to narrow his search, looking for anything strange that could have happened in 1956 that could be linked to Borrit and Malphilus. He found an image linked to a forum about strange occurrences throughout history.

Eric read the forum article: March 3rd, 1956. Teen claims to have seen a man rise from the dead. Eric scrolled down to see the black and white image, showing the silhouette of what looked like a man on the ground. Eric recognized the silhouette emerging from the sides of the shadowed man: Borrit's wings. Eric scrolled down to see the caption under the image; it said: Riverview Cemetery, CA.

He quickly searched the address and wrote it down along with the details of the article. When the front door opened, he quickly closed the browser and shut off his laptop, then grabbed a book from his desk and jumped onto the bed, opening it to a random page in front of him. Not long after, Neil opened the door and Eric looked up from his book.

"I have to meet with Roman soon. Have you eaten lunch yet?" Neil asked.

Eric shook his head. "Not yet."

"Do you mind taking Shawn out, then? Theo and I will be too preoccupied and I suspect he could use the fresh air."

"Yeah, I'll go over there." Eric stood and grabbed his jacket from the chair. He had no plans to tell Neil what he had learned, hoping to redeem himself by gathering more information.

CHAPTER 19
The Lighthouse

When Eric opened his eyes, he found himself lying on his back, staring straight up at the sky. He was in the alley where he had nearly frozen to death, the snow falling in soft flakes. Only instead of the pale sky, he was staring up at darkness. Still exhausted from his last visit, he took his time to walk out of the alley until it disappeared behind him along with the snow.

Eric stood alone, confused by the lack of a flame barrier, or James to accompany it.

"James?" he called out.

He never received a response, but what he did hear was wind. He listened closely, trying to distinguish the sounds he was hearing. He felt the breeze, and was surprised by the almost salty smell that accompanied it. Eric walked toward the sounds, spotting a light in the distance. As he approached it, he realized what he was hearing was the crashing of waves on a beach.

Along the shore, which was really just the black surface, he spotted someone standing with their back to him. At first, he thought it might be James, but the figure was clearly a woman. He could barely make out her figure, his eyes squinting in an attempt for a clearer image. Suddenly, wings sprung from her back. He froze, examining the dark bat-like wings, just like the ones on Borrit's back.

Eric looked down, taking comfort in the lack of blue fire.

Am I safe? He wondered, believing the flame was normally there to protect him, even if he did not understand it.

When he found himself just a few yards away from the girl, he stopped. Her brown hair was loose, a few strands moving in the wind. She spread her wings as if stretching the muscles within them.

"Hello?" he called out. She turned suddenly, her shoulders stiffening, and the tips of her wings pointing at him. It was only then he realized how sharp their edges were. He raised his hands defensively, taking note that the blue flame still had not circled him.

"Sorry…" he said carefully. "I didn't want to scare you."

Her big blue eyes studied him. Eric did not know it, but he was facing the dragon girl who helped Theo escape. She seemed puzzled by him, making him wonder if it was simply the forces of nature bringing him to strangers in his dreams. Finally, her features relaxed.

"I'm Eric," he said. When she did not answer, he looked to her wings again, then to the scales on her skin.

"You're… a dragon?" Eric asked her, but she only tilted her head in confusion. Realizing she did not know what he meant, he pointed to her wings. "Dragons. It's what we call you. Only dragons have wings like that."

She looked over at her wings as she outstretched them, examining them, then turned back to Eric. Eric remembered something: her silhouette outside the motel. "You were outside the motel, weren't you?" Her eyebrows furrowed; she had no idea what he just said. "If it wasn't you, then who was it? Aren't you and Borrit the only ones who escaped?" he asked her.

Her eyes widened when he said Borrit's name. "You know Borrit?" she asked him, speaking to him for the first time.

Her voice was soft and sweet and made her seem younger than she looked, much like her large eyes did.

He nodded. "I haven't met him, but my friends have."

Something changed in her eyes and her expression softened. "I want to show you something," she said. "Can I?"

Eric hesitated, but eventually nodded. She walked toward him; Eric noticed that the barrier was not forming around him as it did in his meetings with James. When she reached him, she looked past him and he slowly turned to see what had her attention. Suddenly he was facing a group of about fifty people he did not know. They

stood a few feet away from him, all facing forward stiffly, a vacant look in their eyes. He noticed the scales on their skin.

"Are they all dragons?" he asked, shocked.

She said nothing but stared at the group of their wings spread until he was just inches away. Before the girl could answer him, the dragons began to speak.

The man he was staring at suddenly said, "Ryan Heart."

The sound of his voice made Eric jump back in shock. Then he heard names spoken from every direction. Peyton Vale, Enrique Villa, Evan Briggs, Leila Ricci…

Names were spoken one by one, some overlapping each other, filling the room with echoes until they were all silent again. Eric took a step back and stared at the crowd. He turned to look at the girl, who was staring at him as if trying to study his reaction. The people disappeared so it was only the two of them again in the darkness.

"What do you want me to do?" he asked.

She turned to look off in the distance. Eric tried to see what she was looking at. Finally, his eyes found the lighthouse which seemed to appear from nowhere. The white building was quaint, a single story with the small light at the center, and a brown roofing.

"You want me to go here?" he asked her.

She nodded again.

"Why?" he asked as he tried to take in every detail of the lighthouse.

"I need to show you something," she said.

He looked at her again, fixated on her big blue eyes, finally realizing who she was.

"You're the girl who helped Theo," he said.

He saw the flash of another emotion in her eyes. He thought it might be relief from learning that Theo was alive.

"Come in two days. I'll wait when it's dark. Come alone," she said.

At this moment, it occurred to Eric that he did not know where this lighthouse was, but before he could ask, he was being awakened.

Eric was startled awake by someone moving him. Groggy from sleep, his eyes searched for the source until they landed on Neil.

"We have to leave," Neil said.

"What's going on?" Eric asked.

"You won't be training today. There's someone we are meeting with. I want you to come with us."

Eric walked to his closet to grab something to change into. "Who?"

"Harrison."

"The blacksmith?" Eric asked, recognizing the name from his conversation with Theo.

"He's dropping by for a visit. He says he has something to show us. Since it is clear I cannot leave you unsupervised, you will be joining us."

Theo sat in his home, waiting for Neil and Eric. He stared at the door to the guest room where Shawn was still sleeping.

Theo wondered if Shawn had noticed the pictures of Leanna throughout the house, or if he had found the name familiar when they had discussed her death. He wondered if he was too tired to notice, or if it had been too long for him to remember. What mattered was he knew Leanna, and it was time to tell Neil. He planned to after their visit with Harrison.

Neil and Eric arrived and stepped into Theo's office where Evangeline and Harrison would arrive just moments later.

Neil introduced Eric to Harrison, but Eric was preoccupied with his own thoughts. He wondered if he should tell Neil about his plans to meet the dragon girl, but quickly dismissed the idea, knowing Neil would never allow him to. His instincts told him the girl would not react well to someone else, and he was not sure if Theo would have better luck arranging the meeting.

"I have some gear for you to look at," Harrison said, shaking Eric from his

thoughts. He pulled out a simple gray jumpsuit, as well as a cuff with a clear textured gemstone in pieces across the band as if sprinkled into the molten metal. Harrison explained what he had brought. "This is the material the firemen wear. I got my hands on a few rolls and Terra helped me sew it into this, so you can wear it underneath your clothing."

Neil picked up the cuff, his eyes wide.

"Is this what I think it is?" he asked Harrison.

Harrison smiled. "Britstone."

"How did you get this?"

"A friend of mine called about a month ago, said he found something interesting in the mines somewhere in Europe. He couldn't tell me where, but he managed to smuggle it to me for a fair price. It helped that he doesn't know what it is. Anyway, I fashioned a cuff out of it and wanted to see if it still works with the metal. Judging by your reaction, I say it does."

Neil turned the cuff in his hand. "I can feel it as if an extra layer of skin has formed around my body."

Evangeline examined the cuff. "What does it do?" she asked.

Neil answered. "It acts as a shield against magic. It is extremely rare, and it does not last long but, in a battle, it can be a huge advantage."

"The cuff should make it hold together longer. I only have enough for maybe a dozen or so, but I thought it could be of use. In case anything was to happen."

"How long would it take?"

"A few days, maybe?"

"Thank you, Harrison."

Harrison nodded. "As for the cloth, I can deliver them as they're made. You can let me know how many you think you'll be needing."

"Actually, I'm going to be in and out of Luxwick quite a lot this week," Neil said.

"You're leaving?" Eric asked, trying to hide his relief. He wondered if he would be able to sneak away now to find out where the girl would be waiting.

"We will," Neil clarified. "I should help the others search for Borrit's whereabouts as well. We still don't know what his motives are, after all."

"Actually," Theo interrupted. "I have something I need to tell you. I was hoping we could talk after this."

"Oh," Neil said, surprised. Eric watched the silent exchange with curiosity before turning to Eric as if trying to determine what to do with him.

"Eric and I can take a trip into town while you two talk," Evangeline offered.

Eric held in a sigh, knowing he had no chance of arriving at the meeting with Evangeline as his keeper. He thought he had kept his expression neutral, but quickly noticed Harrison staring at him strangely.

Harrison stepped forward and grabbed his bag from the floor. "Perhaps he can stay with me instead. I can put him to work, have him help me with the cuffs. How does that sound?" Harrison asked Eric.

Eric hesitated, wondering if it would be easier to sneak away from Harrison. "Yeah…" Eric finally answered. "That sounds cool."

"Wonderful," Neil said, surprising Eric with his quick agreement. "Why don't you return home and pack your things for the next few days. We'll meet you at the portal in a few minutes."

Eric nodded and left. When he reached his room, he immediately pulled out his laptop to see if he could find the place where the dragon girl wished to meet. He thought it must be in Seattle since that was where Theo met her, so he typed the words 'Seattle lighthouse'. The lighthouse he saw in the dream was one of the first images in the search results, providing the location.

WEST POINT LIGHTHOUSE, SEATTLE

He wrote down the address and grabbed his backpack, running straight to the portal where Neil and Harrison were waiting for him.

Neil walked with them to Harrison's home and stopped at the front door.

"Call me if you need anything and stay with Harrison at all times.

Understood?"

Eric nodded, feeling guilty for lying. "Understood," he said.

"Alright," he said, squeezing Eric's shoulder. "I'll come get you in a few days."

"I'll take good care of him," Harrison assured him before they were left alone.

Eric wondered if he would manage to sneak away from Harrison before the time when he had to meet the dragon girl. Because the drive had taken two full days, Eric knew his only option was to take a flight. After all, two days was exactly how much time he had to get there and even if he secured the transportation, he knew if he left right away, Neil would find him before he ever reached his destination. That left him only one option, to wait until hours before and purchase a plane ticket with his emergency cash. He hoped the amount in his bag would be enough.

When Eric stepped into Harrison's home, he was immediately put to work. Harrison brought him downstairs to his workshop. When Eric stepped through the door, he felt strange, and a chill spread across his skin briefly. He froze at the top of the stairs until the feeling passed.

"It's the celocus," Harrison explained as Eric reached the bottom of the stairs.

"Celocus?"

"A gem, mutated by magic long ago. It conceals magical energy. The walls are filled with it."

When Eric saw the small drawers that filled the back wall, he noticed the labels with various names, most of which he did not know how to pronounce.

"Are all of those magic stones?" he asked.

"Not all. The materials free of magic have their uses. Come here."

Eric joined Harrison at his workbench where he what appeared to be the britstone he had used in the cuffs. The stone was in large pieces.

"How handy are you with your powers?"

"Neil's been teaching me, but I'm not that great with them yet."

"I need you to break this stone into pieces. I could give you a hammer, but I imagine it'll be much easier without it, if you can manage on magic alone."

"You want me to break it with magic?"

"That's right."

Eric looked at the britstone, then at the size of the space. He had not practiced any destructive magic yet, and he had hardly practiced outside the safety of the training rooms.

"Eric," Harrison called. "It's alright. You won't hurt me."

"I broke Theo's arm my first week of training."

"And I'm sure you've mastered the cause since then. Your mother used to crush stones for me all the time when she was a teenager."

"She did?"

"I watched her do it. She would levitate the stone in the air with both hands, then push her hands together while clenching her fingers as if she were crushing it. How about you try it, and I'll stand on the other side of the room if it makes you feel better. How's that?"

Eric considered it and nodded. He watched Harrison move to the opposite side of the room as promised. Eric faced the stone so his back was to Harrison, hoping if any stray fragments flew, they would be stopped by his own body. He focused his energy on one of the large pieces of britstone. It rose shakily, clattering against the table before going up. He held it in the air, leveled to his chest. Eric slowly pushed his hands together, feeling the pressure against his palms instantly. He continued to push, slowly adding more pressure as soon as he was sure the stone wouldn't explode from the force. The stone began to crack, tiny fragments falling from it as it did. The cracks spread, spiderwebbing across the stone chunk until it finally crumbled and Eric released it, watching the now small fragments fall back onto the table. He felt Harrison's hand on his shoulder.

"Well done," Harrison said, patting Eric. "Only six more to go."

While Eric worked on crushing the stones until the pieces were small enough, Harrison prepped the furnace and crucible to melt the steel. As they worked, Harrison told Eric about the many ways Leanna would assist him.

Once they were dressed in their protective gear, Eric watched in awe as

Harrison melted the steel using the furnace and crucible, mixing the britstone with it. He then poured them into the prepared mold.

"When the metals cooled, we can remove the cuffs from their molds. Tomorrow we'll get to work with filing and polishing them. Why don't you go upstairs and shower while I clean up."

That afternoon, they ate the dinner Terra had left them and went to bed, both tired from the long day's work. Eric would have to meet the dragon girl in twenty-four hours. He wondered if it was too soon to leave, but he knew if he did not try then, he would never manage to sneak away on time. Just before midnight, he searched the directions to the airport on his phone and grabbed his bag, quietly leaving the guest room. Just as he was reaching for the front door, a light was switched on.

"Where do you think you're going?" he heard Harrison say from behind him. Eric turned slowly until he saw him, standing in the kitchen doorway.

"I need to meet someone."

"In the dead of night?"

"Please don't tell Neil," He begged.

"I knew when I saw you that you were up to something. I just wasn't sure what. So, tell me, who is it that you need to meet?" When Eric did not answer, Harrison continued. "If you tell me, I may even keep your secret."

Eric knew he didn't have a choice but to tell Harrison the truth. If he did not, he would be back with Neil before morning.

"There was a girl who saved Theo. She told me to meet her tomorrow night, after dark."

"Where?"

"A lighthouse in Seattle."

"And just how were you planning on meeting this girl a thousand miles away?"

He hesitated to tell him. "I was going to fly there."

Harrison laughed, apparently amused by Eric's plans. "You didn't think this through," he said. "Eric, you're a minor. Even if you managed to purchase the plane

ticket, you are required to be checked in by an adult to board the plane alone."

Eric's face fell as he learned he would have never made it onto the plane.

"How important is this?" Harrison asked.

"I don't know… but it feels really important."

Harrison considered his answer, eventually nodding. "There's still plenty of time before then. I'll book a flight."

After purchasing the tickets for a 5 P.M. flight, Harrison sent him to bed, but Eric could not manage to fall asleep.

He remembered the names and thought it was time to search them. Each name he typed brought countless public profiles and records to his browser, giving him no indication as to why the names were important. Growing impatient, he typed five of the names together.

Ryan Heart. Peyton Vale. Enrique Villa. Evan Briggs. Leila Ricci.

He was shown results he was not expecting, containing not just one, but all of the names he had just typed. When he clicked the first result, he found himself staring at a webpage with images of the people he saw in his dream, but their faces were fully human, free of scales. Eric looked at the headline at the top of the pages: Strange Disappearances.

Eric stared at the images, wondering if it was a coincidence that the people he saw in his dream were the same as those on the webpage. He decided there was only one way to test if the dream was real. Eric scrolled back to the top of the webpage and typed in the name "Shawn Ward," and clicked the search button. At the top of the search is an image of the man he had met, the Shawn sitting in Theo's living room waiting to return to his family.

Everything Shawn had shared became clear. Rows of cages with screaming and thrashing, the heat that filled the room, the machine Shawn was hooked up to, the blood transfusion. Eric knew what it meant, but he could not accept it to be true, so he tried to come up with another explanation. Eric shut his laptop and thought of everything he had learned but it was difficult to think of another possibility when not even Neil knew the species existed until they found out about Borrit. If this was the

information the girl wished to show him, he wondered why she needed to meet him in person.

The next day, Eric and Harrison continued to work on the cuffs, filing and polishing them until it was time to leave in the car Harrison had ordered. While in the back of the car, Harrison handed Eric something. It was the piece of celocus Neil had given him to check, attached to a rope necklace. "Put this on, just in case. It will conceal your magic."

Eric put on the necklace. When they boarded the flight, he was so tired, he fell asleep just after takeoff and spent the duration of it in a sleep filled with dreams and free of any visitors.

Eric was startled awake by the sound of the pilot announcing they would be landing soon.

It was 9 P.M. when they arrived in Seattle and the sun had already set. Eric wondered if she was already there. As promised, they went straight to a car rental location and Harrison drove Eric to the lighthouse. Harrison parked as close as they could get, but Eric was concerned when Harrison exited the car as well.

"She said to come alone."

"I'll let you speak to her alone, but there is no chance I'm letting you out of my sight. Understood?"

Unable to risk being taken back home, Eric did not argue. Eric saw the girl before Harrison did, standing on the lighthouse grounds. He stopped him.

"She's over there," he said.

"Stay in my line of sight," Harrison ordered as Eric continued to walk along the path toward the girl.

When he was just a few feet from her, she turned, but her eyes did not meet his.

She was staring at the car where Harrison sat.

"It's okay. He's a friend. He can't hear us; he's just waiting for me."

"Did you figure it out?" she asked him.

"They're all humans," he said.

Her head tilted slightly as she stared at him. "Were," she said quietly.

A knot formed in Eric's throat. "He's turning humans into dragons?" he asked.

She nodded.

"How?" he asked her.

She shook her head. "I can't tell you. He'll know. I have to show you."

"If he's turning humans into dragons, I have to tell my friends. They can make sure no one-"

"No!" she said. "You can't leave."

Eric could see the panic in her eyes. He raised his hands defensively until he saw she had calmed down.

"You want me to come with you?" She nodded. Eric glanced back at Harrison who was watching them, and then turned back to the girl. "You won't come with me?"

"I can't," she said.

He could tell that when she said she couldn't, she meant it. He nodded.

"Okay…" He opened his phone and typed the quick text to Harrison, hoping it would ease his concerns, although he knew it wouldn't.

She needs to show me something. I'm going with her. Tell Neil I'll be careful. Give him my notes.

He hit send and dropped his phone on the ground because he had thought it was best to eliminate the possibility of being tracked. That and he knew he had to leave Neil with something, even if it was simply the notes he had saved about the monster rising from the grave that he knew was Borrit.

"I'm ready," he told her. He heard Harrison yelling his name, but he ignored it. She reached for him, her arms wrapping around him, and they disappeared, no longer standing in front of the lighthouse.

CHAPTER 20
Ghosts of the Past

Neil left them and returned to Theo's office where he was still waiting.

"What is it?" Neil asked.

"It's about Shawn," Theo said. Rather than continue to explain, he led Neil back to his home where Shawn was eating breakfast. Neil and Shawn watched Theo curiously as he, without saying a word, walked to the wall of pictures and removed one of the frames containing a photo of Leanna. He stared at it for a moment, the frame tightly in his grasp. Then he approached Shawn with it, holding it out to him. Shawn took it carefully, glancing at Neil to see if he knew what was going on, but Neil did not understand what was happening either.

When Shawn looked down at the frame, he stared at it, unsure of who he was looking at. His confusion turned to familiarity, and Neil finally understood what was going on.

"You knew my daughter," Neil said, shocked.

Shawn looked at him bewildered, before returning his attention to the photo as the memories returned.

"She was my neighbor. But.." He looked at Neil and Theo. "Eric's her son?" Neil could see each emotion he was experiencing on his expression as he likely recalled their conversation about Borrit. "But you guys said..." he shook his head. "No. She moved. She didn't die."

"It's my fault you don't know," Theo interrupted.

Neil recalled seeing Shawn just as Theo had.

"The night she died, you called the police," Theo said. Shawn, having no memory of it, shook his head, but Theo only continued. "We sent the police away, then I made you forget."

Shawn stared at the photo again, taking it all in.

"Is that why they took me?" he asked.

"I don't know," Theo answered.

"How did you know it was her?"

"Bad days make for better days," Theo said, repeating the quote Shawn had said. "She was constantly saying those words to me."

"So why tell me about her now?" Shawn asked, setting the picture down on the table.

"Because you might have noticed something," Neil concluded before Theo could answer. "Would you be willing to try another memory session?"

Neil left and returned with the ingredients as well as an old photograph.

"Do you recognize this woman?" he asked Shawn as he handed him the photograph. The photo was of Leanna, Theo, and Ivy Morgan, the woman who took Eric. When the photo was taken, Leanna was twelve-years-old, and Theo was fourteen. Both were smiling with Ivy Morgan between the two. Ivy was twenty-four at the time.

"Who is she?" Shawn asked.

"Her name was Ivy. She worked with us, but a year after this photo was taken, she joined our enemy."

"Why would he know Ivy?" Theo asked.

"The Celocus stone I discovered at the orphanage. It had to have been placed by her, but the stone was ours. I was told it was checked out by Leanna months before her death."

Shawn stared at Ivy, but he did not recognize her. It did not help that the photo was taken ten years before she died.

Neil prepared the ingredients to begin the memory spell. "If there is any chance you saw her, even if was brief, the memory will be brought to the surface. I only hope I can see it clearly enough."

With the sage and quartz prepped, he began.

"Study the photograph. Burn her face into your mind and inhale the sage," he

instructed as he lit the match.

As instructed, Shawn stared at the photo until he felt he could see her with his eyes closed. Then he inhaled the sage and lay back on the couch.

At first, Shawn saw nothing. Then the memory began to build itself. He found himself riding his bike home, then suddenly he was there putting his bike away. The memory was hazy. There were details he remembered clearly such as the sunlight on his face, and the smell of the charcoal grill one of his neighbors used every Saturday. As he closed his backyard shed, his attention was caught by raised voices, and for the first time they did not belong to his parents.

Shawn made his way toward the fence that connected his home to Leanna's. The voices grew louder, but he could not recall what they were saying, only that they were both women, and one was Leanna.

Suddenly the memory took him to her front door as he approached it. The door opened and there she was, the woman from the photo, Ivy Morgan. She was older and dressed in a hood, but there was no questioning that it was her. She glimpsed his way briefly as she rushed past him.

Shawn was pulled from the memory as the physical toll became too great. Theo already had the pain medication ready for him to take, which he gratefully accepted.

"She was there," Neil told Theo. "Ivy was at Leanna's home. Their conversation was strained, but the memory is too old to make out what they were saying."

"When was it?" Theo asked.

Not aware of the answer, Neil turned to Shawn, hoping he could piece together an estimate.

Shawn tried to remember, sorting through all the bike rides he took just to get away.

"Sometime in the summer, I think." There was something about the memory

that seemed to bother Shawn. "Wait," he said. "Put me back in."

Neil shook his head. "It's too damaging."

"I think I saw something else, I just can't…"

"We can try again tomorrow, after you've had sufficient rest," Neil told him.

The next morning, Neil returned to search Shawn's memories again as promised. This time Evangeline was there as well since the previous memory session was so recent. He handed Shawn the photograph, but Shawn rejected it. "Not her," he said. "The stone."

Neil was surprised. "Can you retrieve…" Before he could finish his sentence, Evangeline was gone.

When she returned, she handed Shawn the blue stone, the celocus. Shawn studied it.

"Yeah. I've seen this before," he told Neil.

"Where?"

"In her kitchen."

Unlike the memory of Ivy, this memory was almost clear for Shawn. His parents were having a big fight. It started with his mother angry about the dishes and escalated as it usually did. Tired of the yelling, Shawn looked out his window and noticed the light was on in Eric's nursery. He snuck out his bedroom window, using the key Leanna had loaned him to let himself in through the front door.

As he opened the front door, he saw her walking down the stairs.

"I heard them fighting all the way from Eric's room," she said as she reached him, offering a comforting hug. "What's the fight about this time?" she asked as she led him into the kitchen.

"Just the usual bullshit," he said.

It was while she was making a pot of coffee that he saw it. He was sitting at the kitchen counter when at the corner of his eye, he saw the small black box half open on the table. He had only reached for it out of curiosity at the time. He never expected

it to be important someday. When he moved the lid, he found himself staring at the blue gem. The gem was not on its own, but hanging from a rope necklace. He grabbed it, studying its blue color unlike anything he had ever seen.

"What is this?" he asked.

She turned, startling when she saw what he was holding. She grabbed it, surprising him as she quickly placed it back in the box and closed it. "It's just an old family heirloom."

"Sorry-."

"No," she stopped him. "It's okay, I just forgot I had it out," she said. "You have nothing to apologize for." He watched her place the box in one of the kitchen drawers.

Shawn woke from the memory and was immediately put to sleep by Evangeline. They moved to Theo's office so that Shawn could sleep peacefully.

"What did he see?" Theo asked as soon as they were through the door.

"He was right. Leanna had the stone in her possession. It's clear she wanted no one to know about it. The strange thing is the stone was crafted into a necklace."

"And you're sure it's the same stone from the orphanage?" Evangeline asked.

"That stone was checked out by Leanna. It must be the same one."

"Has Harrison said anything since you brought it to him?"

"No," Neil answered. He pulled his phone from his pocket and sent Harrison a text message asking about the stone's dating. "I need to store the memories before they fade," Neil said, leaving them.

"Has anyone returned with news?" Neil asked Roman when he arrived at the angel tower just after he stored Shawn's memories.

Roman shook his head. "No signs of anything so far. It would be helpful if we knew exactly what we were searching for."

"I couldn't agree more," Neil said, sighing.

"Most of the available angels are still searching the surface. I asked Cyrus if

I could speak to Adan, but he refuses to let any of us cross into Hell."

Neil nodded. "I understand his reasons. A dragon escaped without Adan's knowledge, so opening the gates for anyone is too risky."

"What's our next course of action?" Roman asked.

Aaron stepped forward. "I think we should inform the elders. Unlike us, most of them know about the dragons, so they're more likely to spot a disturbance than we are."

Roman nodded in agreement. "I'll assign addresses," he said before turning and walking off, gesturing for those who had gathered to follow him.

"What do you plan on doing?" asked Evangeline.

Neil saw the charred footprints on the stairs in his mind. "I want to see Leanna's home," he said. "Eric's with Harrison, so now seems to be the best time."

Evangeline and Aaron nodded, knowing this would be the first time Neil had set foot in the home since he'd found Leanna's body in the nursery.

"I'll go with you," Evangeline said.

Neil declined. "There's no need for you to concern yourself with me."

"I'm not," she said. "I just want to see it too, the damage he left... I never saw it myself."

"Do you mind checking out a camera from storage, then? I'll meet you outside the portal."

Evangeline left him and Neil walked to the portal by himself, the image of the stairway crowding his thoughts. In less than ten minutes they were standing on the front lawn of the home. It looked exactly the same. He had hired someone to maintain its outer appearance. A woman stood on the lawn of the home next door with a hose in hand as she watered her flower bed, her eyes wide in surprise. Neil swiftly wiped her memory of them before disappearing into the house with Evangeline close behind. The thick layer of dust that had settled over the years nearly choked them upon entering the home. Neil looked at the furniture he had bought with Leanna and turned away from it, remembering his purpose for returning. When he reached the stairway, the memory of that night surfaced, but he suppressed his emotions.

Evangeline was in shock at the sight of the damage. She took pictures of the charred footprints on the carpet and the shattered glass from the photographs that had hung on the wall. Neil slowly walked up the steps and stopped in front of the nursery door, carefully pushing it open. When he saw the nursery looking exactly as it did, the memory of that night became overwhelming. He stepped aside, closing his eyes, and leaned against the wall, rubbing his face. Evangeline walked forward carefully, her eyes fixed on the blood-stained carpet.

"You never had it replaced?" she asked.

"No…" Neil said. "I couldn't bear the thought of returning. I only hired someone for lawn maintenance, so others would see the home is not abandoned…"

Evangeline knelt down and took pictures of the blood-stained carpet with shaking hands. "Why did you want to come here now?"

Neil thought, his eyes fixed on the carpet, then shrugged. "I suppose I wanted to confirm it with my own eyes."

She lowered the camera and stared at the stain. "Roman told me he asked Cyrus about the dragons."

"And?" Neil asked.

Evangeline turned to face Neil, letting the camera hang against her chest. "When it happened, when Adan set his power free and the sorcerers and dragons came to be, it wasn't just a negative reaction that differentiated sorcerers and dragons; those who became dragons had tainted souls."

"You're saying their evil was manifested?"

"His power brought the states of their souls to light. That's why the sorcerers were left alone to be observed by Cyrus while the dragons were brought down to Adan's own creation, Hell."

"Why are you telling me this?"

"Because this," she said, gesturing at the blood-stained carpet, "was done under his orders, and I want to know how Malphilus is capable of controlling someone that is considered a tainted soul."

Neil looked down at the blood, avoiding Evangeline's eyes.

She continued, "You said you knew him once. What was he like?"

He felt as if his throat was closing up. Malphilus was a part of his life he had always kept locked away; the thought of sharing his history scared him. "When Borrit was set free," he explained. "It had already been over twenty years since Malphilus and I had parted ways. I don't even know if he's even the same man anymore…"

"Are you?" Neil was surprised by her question. "Are you the same man you were ninety years ago before he betrayed you?"

He sighed. "Mostly, I suppose…wiser, I hope."

"Then it's safe to assume the same applies to him. Although wise is not a word I wish to use when describing him." She reached for his hand, which had been clenched in a tight fist, and opened it, forcing him to loosen his grip. "Come on. We've spent enough time in this room. If you're going to relive the past, it should be somewhere with memories that aren't so tainted."

She teleported them downstairs to the living room.

"That was a waste of energy," Neil said as he looked around.

"Sure, but it beats walking down those stairs again."

Neil shook his head. "It's a miracle Cyrus allows you to remain with us. If he monitored you personally for a single day, he'd have you moved to another region."

"Yeah, well, that's what Aaron's for."

Neil sat on the couch and looked over at the coffee table, which was covered in a thick layer of dust.

"So first, tell me. Would he have been capable of freeing a beast?"

Neil shook his head. "Not alone. When I knew him, he was more powerful than me but not that much. I cannot fathom the idea that he knew dragons existed when he had no contact with the angels or the gods."

"So, there is a breach we have yet to discover… Okay, let's assume that he or one of his minions stumbled upon Borrit. How would he tame him? By force?"

Neil shook his head. "Force is not something he uses as a motivator, but as punishment that he rarely needs."

"Then, how would he do it?"

Neil thought for a moment although unwillingly; he had always been desperate to forget the man who betrayed him. "One thing I learned the day our friendship ended was that he is a manipulative man. He knew how to read me and therefore how to behave to get what he desired. He most likely knew what to offer."

"What could he possibly offer a beast?"

"Power? Freedom? Revenge? Theo said Borrit knew where he came from, so he most likely knows who put him there."

"And the girl? The one who brought him to Shawn?"

"She was not shown to me."

Evangeline looked down at the couch and thought, twisting the chain of her bracelet between her fingertips. "She's actually the one I've been wondering about." When she looked back up at Neil, he could see both concern and curiosity in her eyes. "I didn't see her either, but Theo said she looked... young. Not just physically, but the way she behaved. Do you think it's possible for them to breed?"

"You think she is Borrit's child?"

"That's what's been bothering me. The only witness we have saw Borrit years ago and there was no girl with him."

"Immortals cannot reproduce, we both know that. I am proof that is not exclusive to angels and gods."

"But what if he found a way? With her?"

He sighed and leaned forward, resting his elbows on his knees. "If he did, we could only hope she was an exception... and a good one at that if her desire to help Theo was genuine." He stood, eager to leave his current environment. "We should return and see if there's any news."

They both knew that if there was any news, Aaron would call Evangeline, but she did not say it because she understood he wanted to end the discussion before it could get personal. In the many years that Evangeline had known Neil, this was the most he had shared about his past. So, she stood and reached for his hand instead, with the intention of taking him straight to the portal. She changed her mind at the last second and they appeared in a place he did not know. At first, he was confused, but

when he looked up at the building to his left and saw the sign, he knew exactly where she had brought him.

"I thought we were returning to the portal."

"We were, but I changed my mind." She looked up at the sign for the Sunnyvale diner then back at Neil. "You have to stop pretending Malphilus doesn't exist until you can't. We can't keep playing this guessing game."

"What game?" Neil asked, trying to feign ignorance.

"You know, sometimes it's hard to believe you're more than twice my age," she said, making Neil wince. "The childish game where we spend decades two steps behind him because you refuse to share your past with anyone but Cyrus. You can't pretend he wasn't your friend forever. Someday you will be standing in the same room as him. I hope that when that day comes, we're there with you."

He knew she was right. For decades, Neil had avoided the topic, wishing that Malphilus would someday disappear, but he knew that was impossible.

Knowing she was getting to him, she continued. "I know you have always believed that he is only a threat to you, and therefore not a cause for concern for anyone but those close to you, but that clearly isn't the case anymore. He has gathered far too many followers over the years, but the fact that he worked to possess such a creature means that this is beyond whatever feud you had all those years ago." She stopped to calm down. Her voice softened when she continued. "You have to see what we do if we have any chance of learning his true motives."

Neil looked up at the diner, then closed his eyes, sighing. He nodded making Evangeline feel relieved. "You're right," he said, stepping closer to the diner's back door. "I do need to remind myself that I know him." He stared at the faded logo on the back of the metal door. "There's so much I've missed..."

The regret in his voice surprised Evangeline. "You've seen this place?" she asked cautiously.

Neil nodded. "I'm not entirely sure, but I believe so... just not through my own eyes." He turned to face her. "Not that it matters anymore. I cannot give any information that has not already been brought to light. All I can recall is fire..."

Evangeline sighed, closing her eyes. "So, it really was him that night, wearing his mask." He nodded silently. "Alright then. Let's go tell Aaron and Roman." She held out her hand again and teleported them to the portal. When he tried to walk away, she kept hold of his hand. "I'm not saying you have to share everything. I would never force you to share almost two hundred years of personal history when even I have years I wish to keep private," she said. "But you do need to tell us the important details, even if it's just a little at a time." She let go of his hand and vanished, waiting for him on the other side of the portal.

Before joining her, Neil thought about her words. For most of his life, he believed that the only person who he would never outlive was the one who had betrayed him, so keeping his past to himself came naturally. Sometimes he forgot that was not the case anymore because he had Aaron and Evangeline. They stayed by his side not because Cyrus sent them but because they wished to.

The angels continued to watch out for any imbalance of power caused by Borrit, but nothing had come up. Neil was not sure if the quiet was a good sign or the calm before the storm. He turned away, desperate to escape to the one place he could, his sleep, somewhere the angels could never escape to again.

It was in the middle of the night when Aaron realized Evangeline was not at the tower anymore.

"Evangeline?" he whispered, calling out to her. When he heard her answer, he followed her call and found himself in one of the lounges where the sorcerers often rested. She was sitting on the couch with her hands on her lap and her eyes closed.

"What are you doing?"

She kept her eyes closed and her head tilted down. "Praying to the God of Heaven."

He sat next to her. "You still pray?" he asked.

"Sometimes... I suppose I think it's easier to keep him in the loop... assuming he hears any of it over the chatter."

Aaron nodded, understanding her reasons. "Did you scold Cornelius?" he

asked her.

For once, she did not seem pleased with herself for taking the initiative. She had done it many times before with Theo and Roman, but for some reason being blunt with Neil was different for her. She nodded sullenly. "I told him what he needed to hear," she said quietly.

Aaron did not say anything in response, but simply put a comforting arm around her shoulders and sat quietly by her side.

Neil's peaceful sleep was cut short by the sound of his phone ringing. He reached for the phone and stared at the screen with bleary eyes. The caller ID read Harrison's name. He answered.

"Did you determine the dating?" Neil asked.

–Cornelius, I'm sorry," Harrison said. Something in his voice woke Neil completely. –It's Eric... He's run off."

CHAPTER 21
Nebula

Eric opened his eyes to a bright light above his head, blinding him. For a moment, he had forgotten where he was, but quickly recalled everything. The girl had transported them to a room where he had eventually fallen asleep.

He lay on a soft mattress on an old bed with a metal frame. The room, which the girl had said was her bedroom, was a small windowless room with solid white walls. Only a solid metal door was at the center of one of the walls.

"You're awake," she said, startling him. He turned quickly to see the dragon girl standing in the corner of the room to his left. She must have teleported in because there was no way she was there when he had first awakened. Her wings were tucked behind her back. She stared at him, unblinking. Despite the limited space, she tried to distance herself from him as if she was afraid of what would happen if she came to him. Her vibrant blue eyes stared at him widely to convey her hopefulness but her stiffness revealed her fear.

"Don't you sleep?" he asked her.

She shook her head. "Not since I grew up."

"Grew up?" he asked, confused. "I thought you guys were all created, except Borrit." He wondered what that could mean, but knew there was only one possibility. "Were you... born like this?" he asked. She did not answer him, but continued to stare, making it clear she did not wish to answer him. "Why did you need me here?"

"I have to show you."

"Show me what? The people he turned? The ones from the dream?"

"Everything... about Borrit, about us."

"Why can't you just tell me?"

She shook her head slowly. "Because you have to see it. If I tell you, he'll

know. He always knows." She stepped forward, raising her hand. He realized she was holding something for him.

"I brought you food," she said, handing him what appeared to be a sandwich from a vending machine, before quickly distancing herself again. "When you're finished, put that on," she said, pointing to the pile of clothing on the small table. "I'll come back in twenty minutes, then we can go."

She vanished without further explanation. Five minutes later, he had finished his food and was tossing the plastic container into the trash bin. He stood and walked to the table where the attire he had been instructed to wear was. On the table was a gray button-down shirt and a white mask. He had seen a similar mask once before, in the dream he had of the woman who turned out to be Ivy Morgan. Knowing that the mask was what the enemy wore made Eric feel strange wearing it, as if he was committing an act of betrayal. When he was dressed, the girl appeared in front of the door.

"Ready?" she asked him.

"Are you sure they won't notice I'm not one of them? They're going to be able to tell I'm younger than they are," Eric said.

"I've seen younger," she said, surprising Eric because he could not imagine a child among Malphilus' followers. "If anyone asks, you're here because you wanted to see the base and I promised I would show you. Don't give them your name; they won't know it and they won't want it anyway. Let's go," she said, grabbing him by the arm and teleporting.

They appeared again in a small hallway in a concrete basement-level building. "Stay behind me and act like you're supposed to be here, and they won't even care you're there," she said before walking toward a door. He did as he was told, straightening his back and walking with his head held high to express confidence, hoping to imitate the way Aaron and Evangeline walked.

When they stepped through the door, Eric was shocked by the sight of a large group of dragons marching in the same direction. He watched them, all on the opposite side of a large open space, walking to the open door, a sorcerer with a mask monitoring

them, most likely their handler. He recognized many of them from the dream the girl had showed him.

"Were they really all human?" he asked quietly so only she could hear him.

"Yes," she answered.

"How?"

She walked him to another corridor and down the stairs, where a masked sorcerer appeared to be standing guard.

"Blue…" he said, looking behind her to see Eric. He raised an eyebrow in curiosity. "You brought a friend?"

"He wants to see where we came from. I told him I could show him; is that okay?" she asked.

The man nodded and stood, removing a key from his back pocket and unlocked the large metal door. "You know the rules. Don't touch the cages, and when you're done, knock three times and I'll open the door." He opened the door, the sound of screeching filling the hall, and stood aside as the girl walked through. When Eric walked past him, he smirked. "Have fun," he said before closing the door and locking it again.

What was waiting on the other side startled Eric. Rows of large cages filled the space, some with humans and others with dragons. The dragons thrashed in their cages, yanking on the chains that kept them secure, while the humans, however few there may have been, appeared to be weak, most likely having been there for days. Most did not notice their presence. The few that did stared with narrowed eyes, uninterested in their arrival.

"Oh my God," Eric whispered.

"The process is long and dangerous, but the people who survive it become his slaves."

"Process?"

She turned to face him. "I showed it to your friend," she said, referring to Theo. "It's his blood; Borrit's blood. If he puts enough of it in them, it turns them, but it takes a long time and it only works if they're a match. The man we woke up, his

blood wasn't gone yet so I could undo it."

One of the dragons in a cage next to Eric lunged for the bars, startling Eric. He nearly fell as he stumbled back, his heart racing in fear, but the girl remained unfazed, staring at the dragon with her usual emotionless expression.

"Let's go back to the room. We can talk there," she said, walking back to the door and knocking three times as instructed. As they walked past three dragons being marched back to the cages, he noticed the girl staring at the female dragon in the group. She appeared worried, as if she cared for the female dragon. Without a word, she proceeded to walk to the hallway then reached for Eric and teleported them to the room.

She stepped up to the edge of the bed and sat, her legs crossed underneath her. Eric sat on the other side of the bed and faced her.

"Why not let them go yourself?"

The girl looked down. "I was going to, but Lydia said it was a stupid idea."

"Lydia?" Eric asked, having never heard the name.

She looked up at Eric, her eyes bright with an emotion Eric could only call sadness. "She was a sorcerer here."

"Was?"

"Borrit had her watch me when she first moved here. She's the only one who knew when I stopped growing. She told me to keep it a secret just in case so that I could go out at night…. Anyway, she was in charge of guarding your friend; she's the one who caught him. I was going to let all them out, but she caught me and told me that the people in those cages and the other dragons aren't like me. They can't think for themselves, they aren't in control, they just do what Borrit tells them. All they know is how to burn and kill, and if I had opened the cages, that's all they would've done, only outside. She didn't tell me I was wrong, though. I guess he talked to her when she was guarding him, because she started telling me that she thinks we might be on the wrong side…"

Eric remembered everything Theo had told them. "Is she the one who opened the cage?" he asked.

She shook her head. "She didn't know my plan changed. I stole the key when she wasn't looking. I was going to take him to the guy who was being turned so they would have someone to tell them what Borrit's doing. After, I was supposed to talk to your friend again."

"They why did you contact me? How?" he asked, confused.

"It was supposed to be him…" she explained. "There's this plant Lydia gave me, it's a way to call someone through my head but it needs something to work, a part of the person or something connected to someone. Lydia made the potion for me." She leaned to the side and pulled the mattress corner up enough to slip something out from underneath. When she opened her hand, she revealed a small pendant with a thin chain. She held it out and dropped it into Eric's already open hand. When Eric took it, he saw it was a small pendant in the shape of a wolf's paw. It reminded him of the painting in Theo's living room. "I thought it was his…"

"I think it was my mom's," Eric said.

"Why didn't she see me then?"

Eric stared at the pendant. "She's dead… You can't call a dead person, so it probably called me instead because I have her blood in me." He slipped the pendant into his pocket. "What did you mean was?" he asked again.

The girl looked guilty. "When I let your friend…"

"Theo," Eric told her.

"When I helped Theo and the human get out, Borrit was mad. He wanted to know who opened the cage because he didn't believe that Theo got out by himself."

The girl let the memory play out as she told Eric. Every dragon and sorcerer at their location entered the large open room they were summoned to and Borrit appeared at the top of the stairs. His eyes glowed with rage. He descended, his footsteps charring the concrete steps.

"Two prisoners got out today," he said, unable to control the fire igniting in his throat. "No magic can break the cage. No fire can burn it." He stopped at the bottom of the steps. "Someone here opened the cage."

The dragon girl stood to the side, hiding her fear. She watched him closely, hoping he would believe that the prisoners escaped on their own since the only assistance they had was opening the cell door.

Borrit smirked. "No one wants to confess?" He teleported to the side of the room, only a few feet from the dragon girl. He grabbed the nearest sorcerer by the throat and lifted him. The man struggled, grabbing onto Borrit's arms in an attempt to loosen his hold. The girl watched in shock. "Someone must pay. I do not care who." His jaw glowed from the fire and he opened his mouth, ready to expel the flame on the frightened sorcerer. The girl was about to step forward and confess when another voice spoke.

"It was me," a voice in the crowd said. The girl's eyes widened in recognition of the voice. She turned in time to see Lydia step forward. "I opened the cage."

Borrit turned and let his fire extinguish, dropping the man to the ground. He fell with a thud and another sorcerer helped him up as he desperately refilled his lungs with oxygen. Borrit turned and looked at Lydia with surprise and anger.

"You?" he asked, walking to her until he was inches from her, looking down on her.

"I'm sorry. I let my emotions cloud my judgement. I was empathetic and that was a mistake."

The dragon girl watched from behind Borrit. She saw Borrit's hand starting to glow. She knew what it meant because she had seen it before, only once, and she never wished to see it again. She moved to step forward, but she saw Lydia's hand go up at her side, making the girl stop. Suddenly she knew. Lydia left the cell unguarded on purpose; she let her take the keys. Turning herself in was the plan all along. She knew because she could see the determination in her eyes.

Borrit raised his glowing hand. "You know the consequences of betrayal."

Lydia nodded and looked over at the girl, locking eyes with her. She smiled sadly, then the smile turned to shock as Borrit drove his hand through her abdomen. The girl watched as the life drained from Lydia's eyes and she drew her last breath, slumping on Borrit's arm. He let her drop to the ground and walked away. Everyone

immediately proceeded with their day, some even stepping over Lydia's body, but the girl stayed still, her eyes fixed on Lydia. She was confused when she saw the blue ribbon of smoke leave from Lydia's parted lips. She watched it in awe as it rose to the heavens. She did not understand it because she had never witnessed it.

She sat on the bed with Eric, the image of the smoke still fresh in her mind.

"It was probably her soul," Eric told her.

"Her what?" she asked.

"I haven't seen it before but Neil told me about it. When people like us, sorcerers, angels, probably dragons too, die, their memories are reviewed in Heaven and if they were good people, their souls rise to heaven."

"What's Heaven?"

"I don't really know... but it's a good place. If her soul went up, then that means she's there."

"So, she was accepted? By your people?" she asked him.

Eric nodded and she looked relieved. "I was wondering," Eric said. "That guard... He called you Blue. Is that your name?"

The girl tensed; her blue eyes wide.

"If we're going to do this... if I'm going to help you, to help the people in the cages... I need you to trust me. We need to trust each other or nothing's going to happen. Can you trust me?"

She stared at him, but nodded.

"Everyone calls me Blue. It's what Borrit named me because of my eyes..." She paused, trying to think of a way to explain. "There's this woman, a dragon like me. I talk to her sometimes, when Borrit isn't there... Sometimes she's normal, like she's awake. Well, she says she's my mom."

"I don't get it. Does that mean you were born like this?"

She seemed unsure. "I guess... I asked her about it once and she said that when they took her, I must have already been in her stomach."

"When they turned her, you were turned with her... the first-born dragon."

She nodded. "Well anyway, that woman, my mom. She said she gave me a name and it's Nebula."

"Nebula, how old are you?"

She looked at him with confusion. "Theo asked me the same question, but I don't know what that means."

"I mean… how many years have you been alive?"

"I don't know."

"I have one more thing I want to know. What do you want us to do?"

"I want you to help me stop him."

"From what?"

"That's what I've been trying to figure out."

Eric ran his fingers through his hair and turned so he could lean against the wall. "I need to tell Neil all of this. They need to know what we know."

She shook her head. "I can't let you leave. I don't know if I'll be able to go outside again."

Eric tried to think of a way to contact Neil. First, he wondered if he could get to a phone, but realized it would be a risk if someone heard them. Then he had an idea. "The plant you used to contact me…"

Nebula shook her head again. "I told you she made the potion for me. I can't make it, and you need magic."

"Did you see her make it?"

"She had a paper she was reading before she made it…"

"Can you find it? So I can make it myself?"

Nebula disappeared, answering Eric's question. Eric waited patiently in the room for her to return, unsure of how much time had passed. What felt like an hour passed before she appeared again with a pocket notebook in her hand. She handed it to Eric. He flipped through the pages until he found a page titled 'Dream Root'.

"What do you need?" she asked him. "I tried to read it, but I don't know what a lot of that stuff is."

The spell is simple, surprising Eric. "Do you have the plant?"

Nebula walked to the mattress corner and pulled out a pouch, tossing it to Eric. He peered inside and saw a small bundle of what appeared to be a dried-out flower, violet on the ends.

"Did she use something to crush it?"

Nebula disappeared again and appeared with a mortar and pestle. Eric took it and pulled the dream root from the pouch. When he counted the stems, he realized they only had enough for two visits. He took what he needed for the spell and put it in the mortar and pestle, crushing it into a fine powder.

"What else do you need?" Nebula asked.

Eric looked over the notes and read over the list. "Water and Evran's powder, whatever that is, are the only things on there."

Nebula disappeared again. Five minutes later, she arrived with a three-inch jar of an emerald green powder and a bottle of water. "Is that everything?"

Eric nodded and followed the instructions. First, he took what he thought was a tablespoon of Evran's powder and mixed it into the mortar along with one dream root. He used the pestle to mix them together as best as he could until the dream root was coated in the metallic powder. According to the notes, the next thing he needed was an object of the person he wished to contact. He thought, searching his pockets for something, He looked down at the bracelet on his wrist and thought of Neil, but realized he had been given his mother's so that would not work. Then he remembered the necklace, the celocus stone Harrison gave him. He realized that since Harrison had made it, it might just work. He removed the necklace and placed it at the center of the mortar, then put his hands over it.

"What are you doing?" she asked.

"It says I need light, but it has to be magic so I'm creating an orb." He tried to picture the light forming between his palms. Finally, a small orb of light formed. Nebula watched in awe as he lowered it into the mortar. The powdered mixture glowed, then changed colors, the emerald green shifting into a deep violet. Eric let the light die and carefully removed the necklace, putting it back around his neck and under his shirt.

"What now?" Nebula asked, staring intensely at Eric.

Eric grabbed the water bottle and poured it into the mortar, watching the violet powder swirl in it. "Now I drink it," he said, taking the mortar and drinking the mixture until it was gone. The taste of ash overwhelmed his taste buds and burned his throat. He struggled to keep himself from gagging but just managed. He dropped the mortar and covered his mouth, making sure the mixture did not come back out.

"Did it work?" she asked, her stare still as intense as ever.

Eric took a deep breath and wondered the same thing. Then his head spun, his body gave out from underneath him, and his vision faded to darkness.

CHAPTER 22
A Crack in the Earth

While Eric was finding answers with Nebula, Neil was in a state of both rage and fear.

"How could you take him to her?" Neil asked Harrison, struggling to keep his voice steady. Harrison had not called Neil from Seattle, but when he arrived back on his flight home. After Eric was gone, when he calmed down, his instincts had told him that Eric going with the girl was the right thing. Now it was his job to calm Neil down.

"Because I trust his instincts," Harrison said.

"He's thirteen years old, Harrison, he isn't even old enough to drive," he said through his teeth.

"He sent me a message just before he left with her. He said to tell you he would be careful and to make sure you look at the notes on his phone," Harrison said.

"Where did you take him?" Neil asked.

"If I tell you, can you promise me you won't go after him?"

"Of course not!"

"Then I won't tell you, not yet. You and I both know he must be safe, otherwise, Malphilus would be waving him in front of your face. It's better that you don't try to find him."

Annoyed, Neil held his hand out. "Give me his phone."

Neil took it and left, going straight to the angel tower to speak to Evangeline. The moment Evangeline saw him, she rushed toward him. Neil wondered just how murderous his expression must have been for her to rush to him with such concern.

"Eric's left with the dragon girl."

"What?"

"Apparently the dragon girl contacted him. Who knows how she managed that, but he's left with her and he left notes for us," Neil said waving the phone at her.

Impatient, Evangeline swiped the phone from his hand and opened his notes.

"There's a link to an article," she said before clicking on it. "March 3rd, 1956. Teen claims to have seen a man rise from the dead. There's a picture."

Evangeline showed Neil the photo with the dark silhouette. Just as Eric had, they recognized the form as Borrit.

"Where?"

"Riverview Cemetery in Los Altos. Do you think this is where he escaped from?" she asked him.

"The only way to know is to see for ourselves. Have you traveled to Los Altos?"

"No, but I can get us close," she replied, teleporting them immediately to an alleyway. She walked out onto the street and called a cab to the cemetery. When they arrived, Evangeline turned to Neil, troubled. "You feel that?" she asked him.

Neil nodded, "Power" he said quietly.

"I've never felt anything like this," she said. "It's almost… crippling."

Neil walked toward where he felt the overwhelming power was coming from. They walked, searching with their phone flashlights until Evangeline spotted something. She saw the patch of grass, completely dead. On its surface was a strange crack. They walked toward it, the weight of its presence almost crushing them as they neared it.

"Are you alright?" Neil asked.

Evangeline nodded. "You?"

Neil took a deep breath and nodded. "Yes, it's just… overwhelming."

Evangeline agreed. "This is it, isn't it? The point where Borrit escaped from Hell. The heat that's radiating from the ground…" She looked to Neil with concern. "It can't be anything but Hell underneath."

"I need you to call for Aaron," Neil said.

Evangeline nodded, sending a message. Aaron appeared, concerned.

"What's wrong?" he asked. It only took seconds for him to feel the weight of the crack, his eyes closing as he adjusted to it. "What is that?" he asked Evangeline. When she turned to Neil, Aaron did the same and waited for orders.

"I need everyone searching to make sure there are no other cracks like this one on this Earth."

Aaron was confused. He looked at the crack, then at Evangeline.

"He found it, Aaron," she said. "Eric found the place where Borrit escaped."

Aaron's eyes widened as he took in the crack. "A crack in the wall between Hell and Earth in a graveyard…" he said. "How fitting."

"If this was here before his escape, we need to know if there are more."

"What do we do about this one?" Aaron asked.

"Tell Cyrus. He'll know how to close it.

Rather than return home to sleep, Neil threw himself into work, searching for more breaches with the others.

"You need to rest," Evangeline told him.

"I need my grandson back under my roof," he said quietly.

"Everyone will be on alert for his return. You're no good to him like this," she said gently. Neil closed his eyes and rubbed his aching head. He glanced at his wrist, at the bracelet Leanna made him.

His phone began to ring. He grabbed it quickly, hoping it would be Eric, but saw Terra's name instead. He answered.

"Terra?"

"Come quickly. It's Harrison, he collapsed."

Aaron heard every word and reacted quickly, teleporting Neil to the portal. They both rushed into the house and into the kitchen where they found Harrison on the ground unconscious with his head propped onto Terra's lap.

"Harrison?" Neil called, shaking him, but he did not stir. Aaron pressed his hands to the sides of Harrison's head, his healing magic radiating from his palms as he checked him.

"What is it? Exhaustion?" Neil asked.

Aaron looked confused and surprised.

"What?" Neil asked again.

"He's…" he said, pausing as if he was questioning his own assessment. "Dreaming…" He removed his hands and looked to Neil.

Harrison opened his eyes and was perplexed by his surroundings. He slowly stood and looked at the concrete floor of his own basement. He stood and walked up the stairs, confused when he opened the door to pitch-black darkness. Stepping into it, he turned and realized that the basement door was gone.

"Harrison!" someone called out. His name echoed in the darkness. When Harrison turned, he saw Eric standing just a few feet from him.

"Eric!" he called out in surprise, running to him. "Is this real?" he asked, stopping.

"Sort of," Eric said. "I'm in your dream."

"How?"

"I don't have time to explain. I need you to tell Neil that Borrit is making other dragons."

"Making them?"

"Yeah, he's kidnapping humans and he's turning them into dragons. He's been doing it for years. Not all of them survive, but the ones that do work for him. He's been using his blood. That's why Shawn was getting the transfusion; he was getting turned into a dragon."

"How do you know this?"

"Because I've seen them, the dragons that were created."

Harrison's face paled. "She took you to their lair?"

"It's okay. They don't know I'm here, but don't tell Neil."

"Are you coming home yet?"

"Not yet. Not until I figure this out. Tell them I'm okay and that the dragon girl, Nebula, is keeping me safe. If I leave now, she won't be able to let me in again."

"Eric…"

"I'll reach you again when I have more," Eric said.

Neil sat in the armchair in Harrison's living room, waiting anxiously for Harrison to open his eyes. Three hours had passed and Harrison had yet to wake up, but Neil still refused to sleep. Evangeline kept busy in the kitchen, preparing tea to help Neil relax. The pounding in his head began, growing stronger and he knew he was no longer alone.

"Spare me the torment, Malphilus," he said quietly.

"Cranky today?" his voice replied as an echoing whisper in his head.

Neil grabbed his head in pain, knowing that it was only worse due to the sleep deprivation. Then the pain stopped, and his eyes turned cold, his expression vacant as he lowered his hand, dropping it to his side because it was no longer him sitting in the armchair.

Evangeline stepped into the living room with the cup of tea in her hand. When she saw the expression on Neil's face, she stopped, disappointed. "It's you again," she said.

Sitting in Neil's body, Malphilus smiled. "Is it that obvious?"

"You feel different," she said, "And your eyes, they're dead."

He stood and walked to her, stopping just inches from her. "Sorry to disappoint you," he said, still smiling.

"Why are you doing this?"

"Doing what?"

"Why can't you just leave him alone? What's your goal out of all of this, out of using the dragons?"

His smile turned to a scowl. He leaned forward so his face was an inch from hers, so she could feel his breath on her. Then he whispered. "Figure it out."

He stepped back, stumbling. Now returned, Neil reached for his head again, closing his eyes.

"Where was he this time?" she asked, surprising him because he had not realized she was there.

Neil looked up, shaking his head. "Underground? I barely got through the door before I was brought back." He paused to catch his breath then asked, "Did you speak with him?"

Evangeline nodded. "Briefly. It was nothing worth mentioning." Neil walked to Harrison. "He's still sleeping?" she asked.

"Yes…"

"What is it?"

"It just feels strange."

Before she could ask what he meant, they noticed a change in Harrison's breathing and turned to look at him. Harrison opened his eyes slowly, taking a moment to adjust to the light, then he tried to move. Evangeline helped him into a sitting position then let go when he was steady. He thanked her as she stepped away.

"Are you alright?" Neil asked. "You collapsed so suddenly." Harrison stared at Neil in surprise, but said nothing. "Harrison?" Neil called out, trying to get his attention.

Harrison looked at Neil, reaching for the back of his neck. "I think…" he said hesitantly. "I think I just saw Eric."

Neil and Evangeline both stiffened.

"What?" Neil asked.

"Eric… I just saw him, in a dream?"

"Do you mean like a vision?" Evangeline asked.

Harrison shook his head. "No, as in I just spoke to him, or more like he spoke to me."

"How is that possible?" she asked.

Neil stared down at the floor as he searched his own thoughts for answers. Then realization came across his eyes and he whispered, "Dream root."

Hearing the words from Neil's mouth seemed to carry meaning for Harrison because he smiled. "Of course," he said.

"What did he say?" Evangeline asked.

"He said to tell you that he's safe. He's still with the dragon girl. Her name is Nebula, but that's not all. He said he's seen what Borrit is doing, what he tried to do with the young man who was saved. Borrit is using his own blood to turn humans into dragons, using them as his slaves."

Neil stared at Harrison in shock. "Did he say why? Did he tell you how many?"

Harrison shook his head. "He said he would reach me when he has more information."

Neil leaned back in the armchair. "He's not coming back yet ?"

"No," Harrison said sympathetically.

"He's in Seattle?" Neil asked tensely.

Harrison nodded. "He says no one knows he's there and that the girl is keeping him hidden."

He turned to Evangeline. "Gather everyone into the conference room immediately. Aaron, Roman, Theo. Get Shawn and Esme as well."

A few minutes later, everyone was gathered.

"It must be serious if even I was invited," Esme commented.

"I'll get straight to the point. Eric used dream root to contact Harrison." Seeing the confusion on their faces, he explained. "Dream root is a rare herb that can be used to visit someone in a dream. It requires DNA or an object that carries a connection to the person being contacted. He delivered new information with it." Neil looked at everyone. "He's infiltrated their base."

Everyone in the room was immediately either in shock or disbelief.

"You're telling us," Roman said, "that a child managed to sneak into their operations base unnoticed?"

"He had help," Neil answered. "A girl, Nebula, took him there; she's hiding him." He looked to Theo and Shawn. "She's the dragon girl who helped you two escape."

"How do we know this isn't a trap?" Roman asked, clearly irritated that they were relying on a teenage boy. "Malphilus or Borrit could have sent her. How else would she have been able to contact Eric? How would she even know him?"

Neil tried to think, shaking his head. Then, Theo spoke up. "You said he used dream root?" he asked.

"Yes."

Theo sighed. "I usually carry around a pendant with me. I had it the day I went to Seattle and I haven't seen it since…" He looked straight at Neil. "It belonged to Leanna."

Neil sighed then smiled bitterly. "If she used it to try and contact you, it could have tried to connect to Leanna and found Eric instead… How typical."

"What information did he give you?" Aaron asked.

"According to him, Borrit has been kidnapping humans and using his blood to turn them into dragons. He's creating an army, but his motive is unclear."

"Is such a thing even possible?" Evangeline asked. "To mutate a human using blood alone?"

"Who are we to say what is possible when even our own creation was accidental."

Roman spoke up. "Can we truly know his information is correct? He could have been misled."

"What choice do we have?" said Aaron. "If he's wrong, that doesn't change the fact that we have a major problem on our hands with just one escaped dragon. If he's right and we choose to ignore it, we could be ambushed by dozens of creatures we don't even know how to trap." Roman sighed, knowing Aaron was right. He leaned on the chair. "What do we do?" he asked looking to Neil.

"What we were doing already; we prepare for the worst," Neil replied. "It is all we are able to do with what little information we have… Eric is our best chance. Let us pray he is able to uncover the truth before it is too late."

CHAPTER 23
Borrit

Eric opened his eyes and found himself staring up at the ceiling. This time he woke already aware of where he was. Feeling her gaze on him, he turned his head to see Nebula on the chair, her large blue eyes unblinking.

"Did it work?"

Eric sat up and leaned against the wall. She appeared next to him on the bed, making him jump, her legs crossed underneath her and her wings spreading slightly. She stared at him, waiting for an answer.

"It worked," he said.

"Did you tell them everything?" she asked.

"Everything I know," he said. "But I need to find out more."

"Are you sure they can stop him?" she asked, doubtful despite having reached out to them in the first place.

Eric told her what he knew. "I've only known them for two months…"

"Months?" she asked. When Eric saw her expression, he knew she had no concept of time.

"I haven't known them for that long," he clarified, "but I know that they're good people and I know that they're strong and smart. If anyone can stop him, it's them, but only if they know everything first."

She stared at him for a moment longer, then nodded. "Does that thing hide your magic?" she asked, pointing to the pendant.

"How did you know?"

"Because I didn't feel anything when you made the light, and usually magic feels strange to me."

"Yeah, it hides it."

"I have a place I used to like to hide in sometimes when I was bored," she explained. "There's a hole in the wall and there's this box that goes up and down and at the bottom the wall opens to the room where Borrit likes to be."

"That's perfect," Eric said. "If I hide there, maybe I can find out what he's planning." He got up quickly, ready to go but stopped when he saw her hesitation. "What's wrong?" he asked.

"I have to go to practice," she said.

"And?"

"So, if you go there, I won't be able to get you until after I finish."

He realized she was saying he would be alone behind the wall to what was essentially Borrit's office with no backup and no escape route. The idea of being alone so close to the monster that murdered his mother frightened him, especially since he used to have nightmares of him, but his task was too important to let fear stop him. His need to prove to Neil that he could be helpful was even more motivating.

She looked down at his chest, then studied his face. "You're scared," she pointed out.

"I'm fine," he said, trying to hide it from her,

"I can hear your heart. It's faster now," she said.

Eric looked down in embarrassment. "I'm fine," he repeated. "I need to do this. Please, take me there. I won't get caught and you can come and get me after you're finished."

She hesitated, then looked as if she had remembered something. "Promise?" she asked.

Eric nodded. "I promise."

"Wait here. I'll make sure no one's there," she said before vanishing. It was only a minute before she returned and, without warning, took him by the arm and teleported again. He barely managed to grab his mask from the blanket in time and found himself falling on the ground with a thud, still in a sitting position.

"A little warning next time, please?" he said while putting his mask on.

"Sorry," she said, helping him up.

"So, where's this secret door in the wall?" he asked, looking around the four-hundred-square-foot concrete storage room.

She indicated a metal panel on a part of the wall that stuck out more than the rest. She slid it open to reveal a space large enough for Eric to climb inside.

"Your secret door is a dumbwaiter," Eric said, walking to it.

"A what?" she asked.

"People use it to move things to different rooms," he explained before climbing into the cramped space, keeping his knees to his chest.

"When I lower you, the opening will be on the other side," she told him.

He nodded, shifting so his back was against the side.

"There's this little hole you can look through, but be careful because he might see you."

"I'll be fine," he said, trying to reassure both of them. "I'll see you when you're done."

She looked at him once more. Her stare was as intense as usual, but in the short time he had spent with her, deciphering her expressions had already become easier. He could tell by how her eyes were open slightly more than usual that she was worried, and her unblinking expression told him she was studying him, most likely to see if his confidence was a lie, which it was.

"I need to do this," he told her. She nodded and pressed a button on the wall, then closed the door from the outside. When it clicked shut, he heard the mechanisms work. The dumbwaiter lowered slowly, eventually stopping.

Just as Nebula said, on the sliding door was an uneven hole the size of a dime. When he looked through it, he saw that the room was dark. When he focused his hearing, he knew for sure that the room was empty. He thought he should take the opportunity to search the room. Knowing that the more he thought about it, the more afraid he would get and the more time he would waste, he opened the sliding door and stepped into the room.

The silence made his fast-beating heart seem louder than it was. He was suddenly afraid that Borrit might hear it. He tried to relax. Once his shaking had

stopped, he created a ball of light with his hand, letting it sit on his palm to illuminate the room which was surprisingly well organized. A desk sat against the back wall and rows of books filled a metal bookcase by the door. He stared at the spines of the books, noticing most of them were burned, some more charred than others. The books were mostly studies on astronomy; the more used books seemed to focus on the lunar cycles, which puzzled Eric.

He left the bookcase and moved to the metal desk. He opened one of the drawers on the left side, but it squeaked, making him stop. He took a moment to listen, confirming it had not been heard. He opened the drawer as slowly as he could, but nothing was inside, so he moved on to the next drawer. In the fourth and final drawer down, he found a small notepad. Careful not to move it, he leaned closer to get a better look at the blank page and noticed indentations in the page, most likely of what was written on the previous page. Eric forced the light he was holding to float next to him on its own, then slowly tore the page off. He looked around for a pencil, but could not find one. He heard footsteps approaching.

Eric quickly folded the paper, careful not to crease where the writing was. He slipped it into his pocket then climbed back inside the dumbwaiter. Once he was in, he waved his hand to put the light out and shut the door. He worked to quiet his heartbeat again, taking deep even breaths. Just as he had slowed it, the door opened and Borrit entered. Through the small hole, Eric could see the glow of his fire as he walked to a lamp on the wall and touched the top of it, leaving a flowing flame in its place.

After he let the flame that enveloped his hand die out, he stopped and stood very still. Eric watched as he slowly turned toward the dumbwaiter. His eyes began to glow. Eric remembered what Nebula told him, to be careful because he could be seen. Eric moved his head back and listened as the silence shifted to footsteps, slowly coming closer to where he was hidden. He quieted his breathing as much as he could, knowing that holding his breath would only quicken his heartbeat. When he heard the footsteps stop close to his ear and the heat began to spread through the cracks, it became more difficult to stay quiet. He thought he was doomed, but the sound of the

door opening brought relief as the heat ceased.

"What?" Borrit asked, stepping away from the dumbwaiter.

"I have the maps you asked for," the sorcerer said.

"Leave them," he said.

Eric heard the rustling of papers being placed on the desk. "Before I leave, Malphilus wants to know if you have everything you need."

Eric stiffened at the mention of Malphilus and wondered what it was that Borrit needed. Humans?

"I will be ready," he said. Then Eric listened to the footsteps fade but just as he heard the door opening, Borrit spoke again. "Get Blue," he said.

The door closed and Eric waited nervously for minutes before he saw her appear through the hole. He noticed her glance shift to where he was hiding briefly while Borrit was not looking.

"You needed me?" she asked.

"I was told you left your room two nights ago."

Eric wondered if she had been caught, or if he was heard after all.

"I couldn't sleep, so I walked around for a little while," she answered. Her voice remained flat, never wavering. It was impossible to tell if she was nervous.

"Blue," he said, walking closer to her. He placed a hand on her head and caressed her face. He smirked. "I remember when you were born. You have grown so much." He released her and moved to his desk, leaning forward onto it. "I think you are ready."

Nebula stared at him. When he did not add anything, she asked, "Ready for what?"

"Ready to know everything," he said. Borrit's eyes glowed as he raised his hand to stare at his palm, and the glowing spread to it. "I only remember being this," he said. "I was in that place with fire and thousands like us, beneath the ground, trapped in cages." He let his glow die out and looked at Nebula again. "Then one day, I was free." When he saw the confusion on her face, he laughed. "One day when I was in my cage, I saw something I had never seen. Darkness. I reached for it and I crawled

out from the ground and outside was that man."

Malphilus, Eric thought to himself.

"He told me about gods, about the ones who put us in cages. Three powerful men who created us and then when they did not like us, they put us underground."

"Why are you telling me this?" Nebula asked.

Borrit smiled. "Because I want you to be there, next to me. I want you to see them when I set them free. Our brothers and sisters who are trapped."

Eric's stomach dropped when he heard those words. Hundreds at least, maybe even thousands of dragons were down there, and he planned to set them loose on Earth.

"When I escaped, that man promised me revenge. We will have it soon." He paused to study her. "You will not have to hide anymore."

Nebula stared at Borrit with cold eyes. "What do I have to do?" she asked.

He shook his head. "Nothing. You will be a witness, nothing else."

Her head tilted slightly to the left, which Eric knew meant she was thinking. "Will he be there?"

Borrit smirked and his eyes glowed for a split second before returning to their deep red color. "No," he said to Eric's frustration. "He had better things to do. This is our fight. Let me show you…" He held his hand out to her and she took it, vanishing with him. Five minutes passed before they reappeared in the room, making Eric wonder where it was that he took her.

"I will summon you when it is time. You may leave now," he told her.

Nebula stared at him, then vanished. Borrit walked to the table and looked at the maps the sorcerer brought, studying them carefully. When he was finished, he piled them and vanished. Eric listened for sounds. When he was sure no one was around, he carefully opened the dumbwaiter door and walked to look at the maps. There were five of them, all of locations across Texas. Eric read the names of the five locations over and over again, trying to memorize them.

Then the sound of someone teleporting frightened him. Eric turned quickly, fearing the worst, but was relieved when he saw a pair of big blue eyes. Nebula stood in front of the door with an unfamiliar expression on her face.

"I thought you were Borrit," Eric said, trying to calm himself down.

"What are you doing outside the wall?" she asked. Eric realized this new expression was anger.

"I had to see what the maps were of," he said.

She grabbed him and teleported him to her room. "What if Borrit came back?" she asked him.

"Then I'd be doomed?"

"You would be dead or tortured," she said, her anger rising.

"I'm sorry," Eric said quickly. "I know it was stupid, but I got something that might help." he removed the paper he took from his pocket. "Do you have a pencil?" When she did not respond, he looked at her, not surprised to see a blank expression on her face. "It's like a pen, but wood. Something to write with."

"I'll go check Lydia's room," she said before disappearing. Five minutes later, she returned with about a dozen writing utensils in her hand and dumped them onto the bed. He searched them, pulling a pencil from the pile, pleased that the tip was dulled. He walked to the table and laid the paper down, then with the pencil he softly shaded it, revealing the writing that was on the torn-off paper.

"What's that?" Nebula asked.

"It's a date," he said. He looked at her, feeling he had the information he needed. "I need to use the dream root again."

It took less than a minute for Eric to repeat the process of the spell before he was sitting in the same place as he was only a few hours earlier with the violet mixture in front of him. He stared at it before plugging his nose and chugging the mixture, letting the now familiar liquid burn down his throat. It only took him seconds to drift off.

When he opened his eyes, he was sitting in the same room, only it was darker. He stood and left through the door, entering the pitch-black darkness ready to wait for Harrison to get there. Minutes later, a confused Harrison appeared thirty feet in front of him, searching his surroundings.

"Eric?" he called out.

"I'm over here," Eric answered. Harrison turned toward him, and they approached each other.

"I assume you have information since you're here," he said.

"I have a lot. It'll be faster this way," Eric said. He reached for Harrison's head, pressed his palm to his face, and let the spell take over. He implanted his memories into Harrison's mind. Every important detail he heard and saw would now be in Harrison's memories as if he had seen them himself. The maps of the locations in Texas, the fresh dragons in their cages, what Borrit told Nebula, and the date he found. When he was finished, Harrison jerked away from Eric's hand and reached for his head, which was throbbing–something that surprised him in this dream state.

"Sorry, but we don't have time for me to help you memorize everything and I don't have any more dream root to do this again."

When the throbbing calmed, he looked up at Eric with wide eyes.

"The date?"

"February 25th," Eric confirmed.

"That's in three days," Harrison said, paling.

"You need to tell Neil as soon as you wake up. He has to figure out where Borrit is going before the 25th."

"Will we be expecting you soon?"

Eric shook his head. "I have to stay with Nebula," he explained.

Harrison sighed. "Neil won't like this."

"He won't have a choice," Eric said. "Please just tell him, and fast."

Eric ended the dream and sat up on Nebula's bed. She stood at the foot of the bed, waiting expectantly.

He waited for his vision to focus, then he told her. "It's up to them now."

She nodded once, but Eric could see she was nervous.

CHAPTER 24
Adan

When Harrison woke, he was in his desk chair. It did not take him long to refocus, grabbing his laptop from his center desk drawer and opening it. He searched maps of the locations he saw in Eric's memory. Alpine, Marfa, Fort Davis, Valentine, and Marathon, all locations in Southern Texas and, what concerned him most, all in the desert. Once he had printed the maps, he took them and grabbed his pendant from his drawer, throwing it around his neck, then rushed to the portal.

No longer worried an angel would get close enough to realize he was human, Harrison rushed straight to the Angel Tower. He was barely crossing the lobby when Esme ran in front of him.

"What are you doing here?" she asked him.

"I need Cornelius, now. It's an emergency."

Esme grabbed him by the shoulder and teleported to the conference room. "Wait here," she said, leaving and returning less than a minute later with Neil.

Neil rushed to Harrison, knowing his emergency could only be about one thing. "He contacted you, didn't he," he said.

"It's bad, Cornelius," he replied. "We need the others here. They'll need to hear this."

Panicked, Neil only looked at Esme. "I'll get the others," she said, disappearing. In the meantime, Harrison laid out the map printouts.

Roman and Aaron arrived first followed by Evangeline and Theo.

"We have a problem," Harrison said.

"Who are you?" Roman asked.

"We don't have time for introductions," Harrison said. "Borrit is planning to free the dragons from Hell."

"How do you know that?" Aaron asked.

"Eric used the dream root to contact me again. He transferred his memories to me so it's all inside my head. He saw Borrit speaking to the dragon girl, Nebula. He told her of a man who promised him revenge on the gods."

"Malphilus," Neil said without hesitation.

"When he escaped Hell, Malphilus must have told him the story of his isolation. Borrit told Nebula that soon, their species will be free, and they will get their revenge."

"There are likely thousands of them," Roman said. "It was miraculous for him to escape."

"That's just the thing; there might be something else about that day we don't know," Harrison said. "Eric got into Borrit's office." Harrison noticed Neil tense. "He had dozens of astronomy books. The most worn ones were about the lunar cycle. He also had maps brought to him." Harrison gestured to the printouts he had placed on the table. "All locations around one region of Texas."

"Then all we have to do is figure out where he's going?" Aaron asked.

"We don't have much time," Harrison said. He looked at everyone, fear in his eyes. "Eric also found a paper with a date written on it: February 25th."

Hearing the date, just three days away, Neil stood silently thinking to himself. He clenched his fists at his sides.

Aaron stared in shock. "We have to go to Cyrus."

"No," Neil said, angrily.

Everyone in the room looked at Neil in surprise, but no one argued with him, not even Roman.

"We don't have time for this," Aaron said. "We have to go to Cyrus, Neil, we have no choice."

"No. I'm finished with the secrets and his lies," he said, shaking his head. "We will not go to Cyrus. We will go to Adan." When he saw everyone staring in disbelief, he continued. "You heard the story. The dragons are Adan's responsibility, and he cares about the humans. Cyrus is too protective of him. We have to go to him

directly."

"As much as I agree with you," Roman said, "none of us have met him, so how do you expect us to reach him?"

"Aaron has," Evangeline said quietly. Aaron closed his eyes the moment she said it and sighed.

"You've met Adan?" Roman asked.

"Once, just before we were introduced to the sorcerers," he admitted. "Cyrus introduced me."

"If you've been there, then you can teleport to him. You can speak to him," Roman said.

Aaron sighed. "I'm not sure it would do any good. Cyrus is still keeping him in the dark about Borrit. Maybe it's for a good reason."

"Aaron," Evangeline said, grabbing her brother's arm. "It's like you said. We don't have time to argue. He's the best option for unfiltered information."

Aaron stared at Evangeline, seeing the determination in her eyes. "Alright," he relented. "I'll talk to him."

"I'm coming with you," Neil said.

Aaron gritted his teeth. "I was waiting for you to say that. You know you can't be teleported across dimensions."

"I also can't die, remember?" Neil said. "I'm coming with you."

"I can't win this one, can I?" Aaron asked.

"Eric's still in their den, so not a chance."

Aaron muttered, "Stubborn old man," making Neil smile a bit. Aaron leaned against the table and looked at Harrison. "What exactly are we asking, besides the obvious?"

"Tell him about the dates, the one when Borrit escaped as well as the one three days from now. Tell him about the lunar cycle books and the map locations. He may be able to make a connection that we haven't."

Neil dug into his pocket and pulled out his cell phone. He handed it to Evangeline. "Just in case Eric gets his hands on a phone." He turned to Theo. "Gather

all our combat-ready sorcerers now and tell them the situation. They must prepare for the worst." Theo nodded and turned to leave, but Neil stopped him. "Theo!" he called. Theo turned to face him again. "No going off on your own," he said.

Looking guilty rather than frustrated for once, Theo nodded. "I won't. Promise." Then he turned and left.

"Esme, I need you to do the same with the angels."

"On it," she said before disappearing.

"Roman and Evangeline. I need you to go and speak to Cyrus."

"I thought we established going to him was a waste of time," Roman said.

"I know, Adan is who we need. That's why I need you two to distract Cyrus and make sure he does not interrupt us."

"Understood," Roman said. He glanced over at Harrison one last time before turning and walking away.

"Wait a bit before you go," Evangeline said before following after Roman.

Neil turned to Harrison. "You know what to do. We're going to need flame-retardant gear more than ever if we are really expected to face them in the middle of a desert."

"Cornelius, there's one more thing," Harrison said. Neil waited expectantly. "Eric said it was the last of the dream root. He said he plans on staying with the girl."

Neil sighed. "Of course he does."

"I was concerned as well, but when he transferred his memories to me, I understood why. Nebula is different from the others."

"Different how?" asked Aaron.

"She was born there, born as a dragon. One of the humans that was turned, she must have been in her womb when the transformation happened. She looked about eighteen or nineteen, but mentally…" He shook his head. "Her knowledge of the world is practically a child's." Neil and Aaron shared the same expression of concern. "She needs him," Harrison explained. "He's becoming her guide in all of this and she trusts him. He can't abandon her."

Neil ran his fingers through his hair and nodded. "I understand," he said. "As

much as it pains me to admit, I suppose it was for the best that she found him rather than Theo."

Harrison nodded. "He'll be okay with her," he said before leaving only Aaron and Neil in the room.

"Ready?" Neil asked Aaron.

Teleporting to a separate dimension with Neil was the last thing Aaron wished to do. Although Neil would not be killed or suffer as much as a mortal would, they did not know what he would experience, as it had never been done. "No, but I know I can't talk you out of this, so let's go."

Neil nodded. Aaron grabbed Neil by the arm, his grip tighter than usual, and thought of the place where he met Adan.

Normally teleporting with the angels was quick and painless. The first time Neil was introduced to the angels was when one named Ivan came with orders to bring him to a portal to meet Cyrus. Even the first time, the experience was only slightly disorienting, watching the scene change. Once, Neil teleported on his own; it took a physical toll, but it was still quick.

This time was different and the warnings they had received now made sense. Neil watched as the room warped, twisting in front of him, and he felt as if he were being twisted with it. Flashes of blue light clouded his vision and when Aaron's grip tightened, he knew he was feeling the struggle. Neil reached a point where he could no longer hold back his scream. Then the new scenery solidified and his scream ceased, but he did not feel grounded. Cold sweat ran down his forehead and neck. Before he could focus, Neil felt himself being pulled. He knew it was for good reason because when he stopped, he found himself on his knees in front of a bucket, expelling whatever was left in his stomach.

Neil felt Aaron's hand on his back, supporting him as he steadied his breath.

"Still worth it?" Aaron asked.

Neil laughed, but it came out hoarse, burning his throat. "Honestly, I've experienced far worse," he said as Aaron helped him to his feet, bringing him to a wall so he could lean on it for support.

"I don't want to know what could've been worse than that," he said. The sound of fast footsteps distracted him from Neil. "I really hope they're with Cyrus, because Adan already knows we're here."

Neil turned slightly, his hand still on the wall for support, Aaron in front of him, holding up his left side. They stared at the white wall and watched as a hole opened at the center. A man who could only be Adan stepped through it.

The man was tall, possibly six feet. His hair was jet black, slightly long, combed back behind his ears, and his beard neatly trimmed. He was dressed in dark gray pants and a matching long-sleeve shirt, with what resembled a sleeveless black overcoat, buttoned down at the front of the waist.

He looked at them bewildered. "How did you get in here?" he asked, but when he saw Aaron, he was surprised.

"Did my brother send you?"

"No," Aaron answered. "We came of our own accord."

Adan looked between the two of them. "You, I understand," he said to Aaron, then he turned to Neil. "But how did you possibly manage to get in here? There is no doorway and teleporting a man like you would have ripped you to pieces."

"Well, I can confirm it was far from pleasant," Neil said. "But I am no man."

Adan stared at Neil for a moment, focused on something. "It's you," he said. "You're that man Cyrus found, the demigod. Am I correct?"

Neil straightened, barely managing to maintain his balance and took a step toward Adan, holding his hand out. "My name is Cornelius Alewar. The others call me Neil," he said.

Adan stared at him for a moment, then shook Neil's hand, never breaking eye contact. "Adan," he said. "Although I am sure you knew that." He released his hand. "Now state your purpose before I report you for entering a restricted area."

"We are here about the dragons," Neil said. When he saw that Adan was not familiar with the phrase, he clarified. "Hell's fiery monsters."

Adan stiffened. "How do you know about them?"

"Because one escaped to Earth," Aaron said.

Adan paled. "That is impossible…"

"If you need proof, then please allow me to show it to you," Neil said. Before Aaron could stop him, he was placing the memory Theo showed him into Adan's head. Adan stepped back quickly in shock, having trouble coping with the fact that the creature he had dedicated his life to keeping contained had slipped past him. "Cyrus has been too busy trying to protect you to be honest with us, but we need your help, Adan. I would not be here if it were not urgent."

Breaking free from his shock, Adan nodded. "Come with me," he said, turning toward the wall he came through. It opened and he waited for Neil and Aaron to go through it before following them.

Adan took them down the long, narrow hallway and opened the next wall. They stepped through the opening into an octagonal room.

"Now tell me everything," Adan demanded.

"Earlier this year we noticed a strange imbalance of power on Earth," Neil explained. "When we went to investigate, we discovered a fire, small but abnormal. Cyrus told us he knew nothing that could cause it, but recently one of our sorcerers encountered a creature we did not know existed. He claimed he came from what he described as the 'fiery place down below'."

"What did you call him?" Adan asked.

"A dragon. It's a creature of fantasy the humans write stories of, one we now realize was based off your creature," Neil said. "One of the elders told us your story, the story of our creation."

"Thousands of years spent here, trying to keep my worst creation from destroying what I love, and you're telling me that one escaped without my knowledge?" Adan asked, clenching his fists.

"The place he escaped through, it was linked to Earth's surface, a spot in a graveyard where the ground is dead and warm. The other demigod, Malphilus, helped him escape from the outside, but this occurred sixty years ago. We came to you because he had plans to set the rest of his kind free. He wants revenge, Adan. My grandson, Eric, is currently underground with the dragon, Borrit. He gave us

information about his plans. Borrit has been creating dragons by putting his blood into humans. Eric managed to get into his office. He found books about the lunar cycle, maps of one region of Earth, and a date, just three days away. We were hoping you could make sense of it."

Adan thought for a moment. "How many years ago did he escape?"

"Sixty," Neil said.

Adan thought, as if trying to dig up a memory within the thousands of years' worth that he carried. Then his eyes darted up. "The eclipse," he muttered.

Aaron was confused. "There wasn't an eclipse that day."

"No. I don't mean that kind of eclipse," Adan said, shaking his head. "There are things in this universe even we do not understand. Every sixty years, there is an eclipse that cannot be seen by human eyes, but gods can." He turned to Neil, "You may be able to see it."

"I don't understand. What does an unseen eclipse have to do with the breach to Hell?"

"The eclipse interferes with our power on Earth's surface. He must have escaped from just beneath it," he said.

"He has dozens of dragons by his side now. How are we going to stop them from breaking through when the next eclipse happens?" Neil asked.

"You can't," Adan said bluntly.

Neil and Aaron stared at him in shock. "But you can," Neil said in a low voice, making Adan's eyes meet his. "They are your creations, after all. You got them here, can't you create more cages?"

Adan sighed, breaking eye contact. "I cannot."

"Why not?" Neil demanded.

"The first time was different. I sealed them in their cages all at once, I cannot risk the rest getting out."

"If you leave him be, they may get out anyway."

Adan looked up. His eyes, filled with rage, locked with Neil's. "I think it's time you see what I see," he said thickly.

Neil was confused. Then Adan's dark eyes glowed blue, and Neil and Aaron's eyes did the same. Suddenly Neil and Aaron saw something they could not see before, a brightness.

Neil looked past Adan and what he saw shocked him. The walls behind Adan were gone, behind them they revealed Hell. Thousands of cages filled the black surface. Inside each of those cages was a beast, raging. Thousands of dragons thrashed in their cages, releasing fire, setting the surface ablaze.

"This is insane," Aaron said, approaching the wall.

"Do not step too close. It is quite hot near the barrier," Adan said. Neil and Aaron stood just outside the barrier, their eyes scanning the area but unable to see the end of the cages. Adan approached Neil, stopping just three feet behind him. "Don't you see," he said. "This place… I am the only one who can keep it from falling apart more than it already has. These cages draw from my power. If I leave them their barriers are vulnerable." Neil turned to face Adan. "That eclipse is all the more reason for me to stay, because this place will need more power than ever with its outer defenses vulnerable."

"Then what can we do?" Neil asked.

"Stall," Adan said. "The eclipse will only last an hour at most. If you can prevent him from accomplishing his goal during that time, we will be able to say the worst has passed. What happens after, I cannot say." Adan stepped closer. "You have an advantage, Neil, you will be able to see the eclipse just as he can, you will see its light shining onto the surface and know which area to protect. My brothers will be unable to help. If they leave their posts, they will be weakened by its effects. They are better off where they stand at full power so the angels can draw it from them… Just remember one thing," he said, shifting his gaze between Neil and Aaron. "The only ones capable of wounding them are other creatures like themselves."

CHAPTER 25
Calm Before the Storm

When the night came, Eric was left to rest in Nebula's room. It took him longer than usual to drift off in the dark room, which did not surprise him. Nebula, unable to sleep, sat in her chair across from the bed. Not a second passed when he no longer felt her piercing stare. Then a familiar feeling hit him; the sudden tiredness that weighed down on him and forced his eyes to close.

It was time to see James.

Eric opened his eyes and found himself in the dumbwaiter. He slid the door open and stepped out onto the darkness, letting the dumbwaiter disappear behind him. He turned, searching for James, stopping when he saw him in the distance.

"Do you just stand here when I'm gone?" Eric asked as he walked toward him.

"Why? How much time has passed for you?" he asked.

"Since the last time? Two weeks," Eric answered.

"Feels more like an hour," James said. He looked down at the ground curiously. With his hands in his pockets, he shifted his weight from his heels to his toes and back again, swaying. He furrowed his brows. Then the blue flame surrounded Eric and he nodded. "There it is," he exclaimed.

Eric looked down at it and then back at James.

James smiled. "So, how are things?"

"I've been getting help from a girl."

James' eyes widened in amusement. "Got yourself a girlfriend?"

"She's a dragon, and she's helping me with the dragon from your vision," Eric said, rolling his eyes. James' expression shifted to something he did not recognize, his eyes narrowing.

"You befriended a dragon?" James asked, now serious.

"Not exactly…" Eric said carefully. He stared at James, unable to figure out what he was thinking. "She came to me for help."

James smirked. "You're just full of surprises, aren't you? A dragon coming to you for help…" James paced in front of the barrier. "So, what are you doing? To help?"

"What he's doing is in less than two days. The only thing I can do is get all the information I can. My friends have to do the rest."

"And have you?"

"Have I what?"

"Have you gotten all the information you can get? His plans? His motives? His means?" James stopped pacing and stood as close as he could to Eric. "His methods?"

"I think so," Eric answered.

"You don't sound very sure."

Eric and James stared at each other, neither breaking eye contact. The distant rumbling caused them to break their eyes away from each other. James looked back and studied Eric's expression.

"Be careful out there," James said. "See you next time."

Eric turned back. "See you then," he said, just before he was opening his eyes back in Nebula's room. Eric slowly got up, unsure of what time it was, but he could guess it was morning because Nebula was not in the room. As he let himself wake up, he thought of what James had said.

Nebula appeared and turned on the light. She joined him on the bed and held out a packaged blueberry muffin in one hand and a banana in the other. "Breakfast," she said. He took it and ate it with her staring as usual, something he had surprisingly grown used to. When he finished, he balled the plastic in his hands and tossed it into the trash can along with the banana peel. Eric's gaze shifted to the mask on the table.

"Can we walk around the base today? There's something I want to check," he said. When he turned to look at Nebula, he noticed a hint of confusion on her face.

"I thought you said we couldn't do anything more."

"I know…but I want to make sure."

Nebula stared, then her eyes darted to the mask briefly, before turning back to him. Finally, she nodded. "Just give me a minute so I can tell them I'm skipping training."

"Will they be okay with that?" Eric asked, surprised.

"Borrit wants me to stay with him tomorrow, so they won't care," she explained. "We have to stay out of sight, though. Most of the sorcerers left last night."

"Why?" Eric asked, concerned.

"I don't know. He doesn't tell me that stuff."

Eric leaned back, thinking to himself, but he could not figure out why Malphilus would call back his sorcerers. Borrit said it was his mission, that Malphilus would not be there, but why would he take resources that were supposed to be going to something he clearly wanted to happen? Dismissing the question, Eric stood as Nebula disappeared to let him get dressed in private. When he was finished, as if hearing his sudden lack of movement, she appeared again as he was tying the mask.

"Ready?" she asked him.

Eric nodded as he tied the last knot and straightened the mask over his eyes. Nebula took his arm and teleported them to the storage room and where the dumbwaiter was.

"What did you want to look at?" she asked, unable to make suggestions as she had already shared what she was able to. Eric thought back, then remembered something,

She must have learned his expressions as he had learned hers, because she seemed to understand what he was thinking.

"What did you remember?" she asked him.

"I've been wanting to ask… where did Borrit take you when I was hiding in the dumbwaiter?"

"I don't know. He didn't really say much.

"Can you take me there?"

She shook her head. He understood when she first told him she could not take him outside the base because she had not much experience outside, but now they were discussing somewhere she had been. Then he realized why she was hesitant.

"Nebula…did he tell you that you can only teleport here?" he asked her.

She tilted her head slightly. "What do you mean?" she asked.

"Do you know you can teleport anywhere you've been before?"

She shook her head. "No, I can't…" she insisted.

Eric sighed. "He probably told you that so you wouldn't leave. How did you get to the lighthouse?"

"I walked."

He stepped forward and gently took her hands. "You can do this, Nebula. All you have to do is think really hard about the place where Borrit took you to and we can go there."

She stared at him, considering what he was saying, then nodded. She closed her eyes. After a minute, Eric felt the air change and realized they were in the middle of a desert. When he examined the area, he was disappointed that there were no landmarks or indications of civilization in sight. Not trusting his survival skills enough to search for any, he looked at Nebula. "Let's go back," he said. She obeyed.

When they were back in the storage room, she made sure no one had walked in. "If that's all you wanted, we should go back."

"Wait," he said, stopping her. "When you told me about your mom, you said that sometimes it's like she's awake. What did you mean by that?"

Nebula appeared confused by his question's relevance, but she answered. "You saw the others," she explained. "They're different than Borrit and me. They don't speak, they just fight and follow orders. Well, sometimes, but only sometimes, when I'm next to her she starts to talk."

"Is she pretending? The other times when she doesn't talk?"

Nebula shook her head. "It's weird… It's like she's in pain when she talks, like she has to try really hard to do it."

A crazy thought entered Eric's head. Nebula did not need to see his

expression to know it was because she could hear his heart beating more rapidly than usual. "No," she said, answering his thought.

"I have to," he said.

"No," she said again, more fiercely, her blue eyes glowing slightly.

"Nebula, please. If you could just get her alone, maybe if I can see it for myself-."

"It's dumb and dangerous."

"All of this is," he said, waving his arms. "But I'm here anyway."

She clenched her fists then closed her eyes. When she opened her eyes, they had returned to her original color. She walked to the dumbwaiter, stopping in front of its closed door. Her hand glowed; she was about to use her fire. She held up her hand to the door and used her finger to burn a hole through it about the same size as the one in Borrit's office.

"You can watch from here," she said, gesturing to the newly burned hole.

He obeyed, climbing inside the dumbwaiter. Once he was safely inside, he peered through the hold to watch as she disappeared. Five minutes later, she appeared again, this time with her mother.

Her mother thrashed and clawed at Nebula, who did her best to keep her still, both hands pressed firmly to her mother's side. Her mother's skin glowed as her fire ignited within her and she breathed fire onto Nebula, but she was still unfazed.

"Calm down," Nebula said. She repeated this over and over again, wrapping her arms tighter around her mother, but it did not work. She only became more violent, trying to free herself from Nebula's hold. Nebula tightened her jaw, then sighed. "MOM, STOP!" she yelled. This seemed to work. Her mother stilled, her breathing heavy as her fire went out and her eyes darkened. Nebula loosened her grip and stepped away from her slowly, keeping her body between her and Eric, ready to grab her if she became violent again.

Her mother turned to look at her. Her face softened with a look of recognition mixed with shock.

"Nebula…" she whispered. She was in pain as she fought to stay focused,

constantly reaching for her head. "You grew again," she said.

"I'm not going to grow anymore," Nebula said quietly.

Nebula's mother looked at her, pained. She stepped forward, opening her arms, but just as she was about to wrap them around her daughter, she stepped back in pain, her hands shooting to her head.

Nebula did not fret as her mother dealt with what must have been excruciating pain. Instead, she watched silently, her eyes closed because she knew this would happen. She watched her mother hunch forward in agony, saying 'no' over and over again. Then the pain seemed to stop because her mother stilled and dropped her arms to her sides. She slowly lifted her head, resuming her original expression.

She stared coldly, then she lunged.

In Luxwick, the angels scrambled to prepare for what was coming, knowing their help would be needed. Suddenly the sound of someone teleporting startled them: It was louder than usual. They saw Aaron appear with an arm on the ground and the other held by Aaron. Esme ran to join them.

"Is Evangeline back yet?" Aaron asked her.

"Not yet," she answered. "What did he say?"

Neil looked up to see that all the angels and sorcerers in the room were waiting to hear from them. The room was silent, the only noise coming from Neil as he tried to catch his breath. He swallowed and pushed himself off the ground, Aaron and Esme helping him. He stood on shaky legs, his arm around Aaron to keep himself from falling.

He finally addressed the room. "We cannot turn to the gods for help. This struggle is up to us. An eclipse will cover the desert approximately between one and two in the morning on February 25th. Only I will be able to see it. We only have until then to prepare for this fight. According to Adan, this eclipse will affect the power of the gods. Even if the gods were to join us, they would only be as powerful as the rest of us. If Adan comes, Hell will be weakened. If Cyrus comes, the angels will be left powerless. Even I may be weaker than you during this time. Our enemy is stronger

than us; killing them will not be a possibility."

He could see the concern on their faces: The more he spoke, the more hope they lost. He continued. "But if we do nothing, that door will open and there will be nothing we can do to stop them. Even Adan would be powerless, as they would destroy our Earth. We are the humans' only hope so we must stop the dragons from accomplishing their goal until that eclipse passes and Cyrus is able to come down."

An angel in the crowd expressed his concerns. "With all due respect, Cornelius, he has done nothing to stop them so why would he now?"

"Although I don't agree with his decisions, Cyrus kept his knowledge of these creatures to himself to protect his brother. However, now that Adan is aware of the situation, I expect his help to return the dragons to their cages."

Another angel rushed into the room. "Roman and Evangeline have returned," she announced.

Soon after, Roman and Evangeline stepped through the door, both surprised by and concerned about the obvious tension.

"Did he find out about our visit?" Aaron asked.

Evangeline shook her head. "Cyrus is clueless, so Adan must have kept quiet."

Neil nodded and turned to look at the many faces still sharing in his direction. He slowly stepped away from Aaron, who only released him once he was sure Neil was steady, although his legs still trembled slightly. He stepped in front of the others so he could focus on them.

"I want you to understand that I do not expect you to face them, not for me. For once, we are following the orders of Adan, not Cyrus. If you choose to continue your day-to-day operations, I completely understand."

"Don't be stupid," Esme said, at the front of the crowd. "We want to help, we all do." The other angels and sorcerers expressed their agreement.

Neil was relieved. "Very well," he said. "Our priority will be to contain the dragons, to keep them from their goal as well as protecting the nearby civilians from them. I will inform you all when the eclipse has begun."

With that statement, they dispersed to continue their preparations. Roman approached Neil. "I'm the only one they have not seen," he said. "I can take a team around the area to keep watch for suspicious activity."

Neil nodded. "That would be best. Take the inexperienced; we'll need the others to prepare as best as they can."

Roman nodded and stepped away, calling out for various angels to follow him.

With just hours before the eclipse, Neil walked to Harrison's home. He rang the doorbell then glanced at his watch. It was 10 P.M., leaving them just three hours. When there was no answer, he looked to the windows, noticing they were dark. When he listened in, he realized there was no movement inside the house.

Suddenly, headlights illuminated the scene. Harrison's car was pulling into the driveway, the lights blinding Neil. Harrison stepped out and rushed to meet Neil at the front door.

"Where… " Neil began to speak, but was cut off by Harrison, who was in a hurry.

"The cuffs are finished, and Terra used up all the cloth. There are enough for about two dozen of your soldiers to wear," he assured Neil. He stepped past him, unlocking the door and letting him in. "I had to go into town for a meeting. I think you'll be pleased to see what it was for."

Harrison walked into the kitchen and pulled a small package from his jacket pocket. He took the package, carefully peeling away the brown paper, leaving him with a satin cloth. Neil watched as Harrison pulled away the overlapping corners to reveal a familiar dried plant.

"Dream root" Neil whispered.

"I have a friend in town who had a few left over. I managed to convince him to sell me the one, but it's only enough to use one time."

Neil stopped him to hug him. "One time is enough. Thank you."

Harrison smiled and hugged him back. "It's the least I could do," he said.

Neil released Harrison, who handed him the bundle. "I will gather what I've made and bring it to Luxwick. Now go see your boy."

Neil nodded and took off, desperate to speak to his grandson. He reached Theo's office in record time, knowing he kept Evran's powder, the ingredient he needed for the dream root spell, in one of his drawers. Remembering the spell from long ago, Neil performed it in his kitchen and brought the finished substance with him to his couch. He drank it and welcomed sleep.

Eric, who was in Nebula's room, fell asleep as well. Thankfully, he was alone, because Nebula might have panicked at the sight of him suddenly losing consciousness.

He stood in the darkness and searched for James, but was surprised to find Neil instead.

Neil rushed to him, embracing him when he was within arm's reach,

Eric stood in shock. "How did you-?" he began as Neil released him.

"Harrison got his hands on some dream root," he explained.

"Good," Eric said. "There's something I need to tell you. I saw Nebula's mom today. She talked to her in front of me and there's something that's off about them."

"Off? Off how?"

"The dragons, they're all like animals, but with Nebula's mom, it's like suddenly she was human. It wasn't for that long, but she was normal for a while. I don't know how, but he's controlling them, all of them."

"You're saying they aren't willing?"

"I'm saying that right now they're dispiteous, but I think they could go back to being humans," Eric explained. "You can't let them get put in Hell with Borrit."

"Dispiteous... How do you know that word?

"I... heard it somewhere. Why?"

"It's just quite... archaic." Neil shook his thought away. "I will inform the others, but now I need you to listen to me. In just a few hours, Borrit will be marching his dragons to open a door to Hell. When that happens, you get out and you find a phone so you can call one of us."

Eric shook his head. "No, I'm not leaving Nebula."

"Then take her with you," Neil demanded.

"Borrit wants her with him. She won't be able to leave."

"What exactly do you expect to be doing?"

"Borrit has some volunteers who stayed to help. I can walk with them."

Neil's eyes went wide with fright. He grabbed Eric by the arms. "Please, Eric, I understand your concern, but you can't expect me to be alright with you walking among them."

"I promise to try to stay safe, but if I think I can help then I'm going to."

"Eric!"

"I'll be okay," Eric said, before they were both pulled from the dream.

Neil sat up, his jaw tightening as he tried to suppress his anger. He clenched his fists and pounded it against the couch. On impact, his magic sent the furniture around him sliding in all directions away from him. He closed his eyes, and took a deep breath, and looked at the time. It was 11:15 P.M., less than two hours before the eclipse.

Not wanting to waste any more time, he rushed out the door to go with the others.

At half past midnight, Eric sat in the room having just put on his mask when Nebula arrived.

"Ready?" she asked.

"Yeah," he replied, standing to fix his shirt. She was staring, with a question in her eyes. "What is it?"

"Do you really think we can be humans again?" she asked.

He thought of a way to word his answer, not wanting to give her false hope. "I think they can all get their personalities back and that might mean they can be humans again if Borrit is gone…"

She nodded. "Let's go. The sorcerers are getting ready in one room. Remember, act like you belong there. Grab a weapon even if you aren't going to use

it. Then just do what they do, and you'll be okay."

Eric nodded, but he knew that she could hear his fast-beating heart. Thankfully, she chose to ignore it and teleported him just outside the door. She gave him one last look then disappeared.

Inside the large room were multiple sorcerers in their masks, preparing for battle. Doing as Nebula instructed, Eric entered the room with his head held high and walked straight to the weapons, taking one of the belts and securing it to himself, then filling it with throwing knives. Another sorcerer walked up next to him. Eric guessed that he was not much older than him. The young man was smiling widely, so excited that it was unsettling. He watched him as he took some metal wire and rolled it, clipping it to his belt.

"Wire?" Eric asked.

The sorcerer looked at Eric, his smile widening. "Never used it before?" he asked. When Eric shook his head, the sorcerer raised it. "It's light, but it hurts. You get it around their necks and strangle them with it."

Eric nearly shuddered at the thought, but he stayed calm as the sorcerer secured the wire to his belt.

"What made you volunteer for tonight?" Eric asked.

"No way I'm missing the fight of the century," he answered.

"Aren't you afraid, though? That the dragons will kill everyone?"

The sorcerer smiled. "Exactly. The humans will burn, and we'll be the ones on top."

Eric noticed the sorcerer instinctively reach for his neck, bringing Eric's attention to the scars there, most appeared to be cigarette burns. For a moment, he understood how someone so young could speak of genocide with a smile if his scars were the result of abuse. It was clear he craved revenge.

CHAPTER 26
The Blood Moon

Eric stood in the room with the other dozen sorcerers, waiting patiently as they practiced with their weapons, all seeming pleased to be there. They lined up, straightening themselves. Eric quickly joined them, realizing there was a sorcerer at the front facing them, most likely their leader. The group marched out of the room together and Eric followed, staying in formation with the rest of them, making sure to stay at the very back. When they were approaching the next door, Eric noticed the dragons marching toward a different door.

He took a quick glance forward. When he saw that no one was facing his direction, he carefully slipped away and followed the dragons. He watched as they crossed into another room and rushed to the doorway, standing just outside it. With his back against the wall, he carefully peered over the door frame to see what was happening inside. Dragons filled the room; they were all calmer than usual, like obedient soldiers with their backs straight waiting for orders. Their usual anger had been diminished and replaced with cold stares.

Borrit appeared on the left side of the room, facing the dragons. Nebula appeared and joined him at his side. Borrit studied his soldiers carefully. Eric focused on amplifying his hearing.

"Today they will finally serve their purpose..." he said to Nebula.

Eric watched them, noticing something in Borrit's hands; a small rounded stone. It was three or four inches long, perfectly smooth, and a deep red color. Each time Borrit stroked the stone, it glowed slightly. When Eric looked at the dragons, he noticed the same glow in their eyes. At that moment, Eric felt another set of eyes on him. When he turned, his eyes locked with Nebula's. He jerked his head down, gesturing at the stone in Borrit's hands. She looked down at it, nodded subtly, then

turned her attention to Borrit.

"That rock," she said. "What is it?"

Borrit smiled. "This," he said, raising the stone to show her. "Is the leash for my pets." Hearing this sent chills down Eric's spine. This one small object was controlling the mutated dragons. Then he saw the scar on Borrit's hand. A blood tie? He wondered. He needed to get to a phone, to call Neil and share what he had learned.

He turned to run in the other direction but crashed into something. One of Malphilus' sorcerers grabbed Eric by the collar and dragged him into the room with the dragons.

"You've got a spy outside," he announced, tearing off Eric's mask. Borrit and Nebula stared at Eric and Eric could see fear in Nebula's expression. Eric struggled, but the man was too strong. He felt defenses turned on as his magic was released. With his free arm, he knocked the man back, but the man recovered in seconds and wrapped his arm around. Borrit smiled. "You are that boy… his boy," he said.

Eric shuddered. His cover had been blown and the beast somehow knew who he was.

Borrit stood and looked at the sorcerer. "Guard him until I need him," he ordered, and the sorcerer gladly grabbed Eric by the hair and pulled him away from the room. Eric looked over his shoulder just long enough to see Borrit take Nebula's arm and teleport, the dragons disappearing after them.

Neil left his home ready to face what was coming, ready for it to end so that Eric would return to Luxwick where it was safe. He walked straight to the portal, sending a message to Evangeline on the way to meet him on the other side. The moment he stepped out on the other side, she was there, ready to take him where he wanted.

"You seem motivated," she said, grabbing his arm and teleporting them to the desert in Texas.

"I just spoke to Eric," he said once they had arrived.

"Really? What did he say?"

They headed toward the nearest town, where Roman was posted. Neil spoke as they walked. "He believes the dragons can return to their human forms. He is also refusing to leave and insists on walking with them."

Evangeline sighed. "That Collins blood must be strong," she said, referring to his birth father.

"I've noticed," Neil said.

When they reached the outskirts of Fort Davis, they found Roman standing at the base of one of the mountains.

"Anything?" Neil asked him.

Roman turned to see them, shaking his head. "Nothing so far."

Neil joined him and looked out, finding it impossible not to enjoy the view of the night sky across the open land. The thousands of stars only distracted him for a moment before he was pushed back to reality. Neil slumped as an overwhelming feeling of nausea hit him. His hand automatically reached for his stomach as his heart beat quickly. He felt as if his throat was closing, causing his breathing to hitch.

"What's wrong?" Evangeline asked, reaching his side.

Neil hunched forward, feeling as if he needed to vomit again, but nothing happened. Then suddenly, he saw it: a red tint in his vision. He slowly straightened, Roman and Evangeline helping him stay on his feet. When he looked up, he saw a sliver of red light across the edge of the moon, creating a thin red crescent. He stepped forward, breaking away from their grasp, and looked up at the moon from under its red glow.

"Do you see that?" he asked.

Roman and Evangeline looked up, but did not know who he was referring to.

"See what?" Roman asked.

Neil sighed. "It's starting, the eclipse."

Neil stood at the base of the mountain with Roman, staring up at the partial eclipse that only he could see, at least until he could no longer bear its effects and dropped to the ground so he could save his energy. The moon was now one quarter covered by the deep red fog that tinted its light.

Evangeline appeared next to him and followed Neil's gaze, concerned that they could not see what he saw. "They're on their way here now."

"Good. It won't be long before that moon is completely covered."

"What do you see?" she asked him, staring up at the moon.

"It's just… a red shadow, almost like a cloud. Everything is tinted red."

"A blood moon," she said.

Neil nodded and tried to stand, struggling under the imaginary weight the eclipse had on him. Despite his efforts to hide his struggle, Evangeline noticed. "Should you really be out here tonight?" she asked. "Maybe it's better if you stay in Luxwick until it's over."

The angels and sorcerers began to appear in pairs, sorcerers with their weapons ready. When he saw Theo and Shawn with Aaron, he focused on them and shook his head. "I need to be here," he said before leaving to join them. Just as he was reaching them, Theo noticed him and waited for the orders he knew he was about to receive.

"Get the inexperienced soldiers and volunteers to surround the town and put up a barrier. With the eclipse's light over the desert we have no reason to believe they would strike the town, but they are unpredictable. We have to assume one or two may wander off. We cannot allow any civilians to pass through or even catch a glimpse of what is going on." Neil turned to Shawn. "Why are you out here? You should be in Luxwick."

"I wanted to help, if I can," Shawn answered nervously.

Neil nodded and tried to think. When he looked at the mountains, he had an idea. "Theo, do you have any Bluetooth ear pieces in your office?" Theo nodded. "Binoculars?" he asked, and Theo said yes, now understanding where he was going. "I can't have him out here, but he can be our eyes."

"I'll get him set up," he said, leaving with Aaron to get what he needed.

It did not take long for Theo to round up the younger sorcerers as well as those who were not as fit for battle to surround the nearest border of Fort Davis. They stood in one long row just outside the town and held their arms out, their palms facing

forward. They looked at each other, acknowledging that they were ready with a short nod. Then they let their magic spread, the blue light leaving their palms and joining to create a magical wall in front of the town.

Neil watched the barrier go up, then he felt something strange. The sorcerers around him scrambled and the angels tensed. He turned around. Although he had seen Theo's memory, and although he knew what to expect from everything Eric had told him, he was still surprised when he saw dozens of dragons appear with masked sorcerers.

At the front stood Borrit, who was taking in the sight of his obstacle, apparently amused by it. Borrit looked up at the moon, which was now half covered, then forward. His eyes found Neil's in an instant. He tilted his head, studying him. His eyes glowed and then the fire spread to his jaw.

As Neil looked at the beast, all he could think about was Leanna. This was the creature that had ended her life, and tried to end Eric's. He injured Evangeline and Theodore and taunted Theodore about Leanna's death. Seeing him for the first time brought all his anger to the surface. Then he was distracted when he looked to Borrit's left and saw a girl there with big blue eyes staring ahead. Her eyes met his, locking on him. He realized that this girl was Nebula. She stared at him until Borrit leaned over and whispered something to her. She took one last look at Neil then teleported. Then Borrit set his pets loose.

Masked sorcerers charged toward them, and the sorcerers and angels took charge. The field erupted into chaos as the two sides merged, sorcerers fighting sorcerers and angels who worked to protect those on their side, making use of their teleportation abilities. Before he knew it, a sorcerer in front of Neil was attacking him.

The sorcerer sent a throwing knife at Neil's head, but he blocked it before he could reach him. The sorcerer continued his attacks, getting nearer and nearer with each strike. Normally, Neil would be able to defend himself with ease, but the eclipse was weakening him more than he expected. When the sorcerer moved to punch Neil, he could not deflect it in time. The sorcerer's fist contacted Neil's stomach. On instinct, Neil sent another wave of his magic, the light knocking the sorcerer back. Feeling his

magic was weak, he fought the sorcerer directly, dodging his attacks as well as getting a few in himself. The sorcerer caught him by surprise when he waved his knife. Unable to dodge, Neil's side was grazed by the blade. Before he could react, the sorcerer pushed both his hands forward, sending Neil flying and landing on his back. Neil threw his arms in front of him to form a shield, but he could feel it weakening. Each blow to it sent him stumbling back down before he could jump to his feet.

The sorcerer used his full power to attack and Neil was sent onto his back, his arms falling to his sides. The sorcerer was about to send his knives toward Neil, but someone else's magic knocked them aside. Theo stepped in front of Neil, his attacks sending the sorcerer stumbling back instead. Neil quickly jumped to his feet.

"Go talk to the dragon girl!" Theo yelled to Neil as he used his arm guards to shield himself. "She's on the mountain. Go find out where Eric is!" Theo got close enough to the sorcerer to knock him unconscious then yelled for Aaron, who appeared by his side. Theo turned to Neil and yelled. "GO!" turning to fight the next sorcerer who had reached him.

Aaron grabbed Neil, teleporting him just outside where the fight was. "Where do you need to go?" he asked.

Neil scanned the mountain, finally seeing Nebula's shadowy figure and pointed to her. "Up there. I need to speak to her."

Aaron teleported Neil to the mountain, twenty feet from Nebula, who had her back to them, watching the fight. Neil stepped toward her when she called out. "Stop there," she said, not turning to face him. Neil and Aaron stopped. "If you come to me, he'll see you and he'll know. We can talk from here."

Neil and Aaron crouched to ensure they could not be seen from below.

"You are Nebula, correct?"

"Yes," she answered.

"Eric, my grandson, he was with you. He said he would be among Malphilus' men, but I know he is not because he would have moved to our side by now. Where is he?"

She turned her head slightly but did not face him. "Borrit found him. He's

okay, but Borrit had one of the sorcerers take him to guard him. He's probably in one of the cells."

"Send him straight home, please. I will not have him anywhere near this," Neil said.

Aaron nodded and disappeared, leaving Neil alone with Nebula.

CHAPTER 27
A Scorched Earth

After Eric was dragged away by the sorcerer, he tried to fight but his attempts were useless. In the end, he only managed to get in one good hit before the sorcerer grew tired of the fight and pushed Eric to the ground, pinning him on his stomach. Eric felt as if his heart had stopped when he felt something being wrapped around his wrists, tightening so he could not separate them. He would not be able to use magic, not with his level of experience. The sorcerer then picked Eric up off the ground and practically dragged him the rest of the way and threw him into a cell.

This is where Eric had been since the start of the eclipse.

Eric sat in his cell with his back against the wall. He had spent most of his time trying to untie his wrists, but the effects of the Seraphinum stone in the call walls were draining his energy. The sorcerer sat in a chair outside his cell, his mask now off and tossed to the ground. He stared at Eric, rarely blinking, making Eric uncomfortable and frightened.

A loud noise startled him and caused even the sorcerer to turn his head in its direction. He glanced at Eric, then stood carefully and reached for one of the throwing knives in his belt. He opened the door and stepped through it, leaving Eric alone.

Minutes after the sorcerer's departure, Eric heard a struggle outside, followed by a silence. He tensed as he stared at the open door, terrified that whoever was outside may be an enemy. He was relieved when Aaron appeared. Aaron rushed to the bars and gripped them, frustrated by the effects. He disappeared, then reappeared with bolt cutters. He cut through the cell's lock, dumped the bolt cutters, and rushed to Eric, untying him.

"How did you know I was here?" Eric asked.

"Nebula told us," He said, helping Eric to his feet.

"Us?" Eric asked.

Aaron sighed as he pulled Eric outside the room with him. "Neil's pissed, by the way. You said you would be careful." He then teleported Eric just outside the portal and yelled. "Go home!"

Remembering the stone, Eric called out, "Aaron, wait…" but it was too late. Aaron was gone as quickly as he arrived, frustrating Eric. Instead of going through the portal, he rushed back outside and ran straight to Harrison's home.

When Eric arrived at Harrison's house, he used his magic to unlock the door.

"Harrison?" he called out as he rushed up the stairs to his study.

"Eric!" Harrison said as Eric burst through the door. "You're alright?" he asked.

"Can I use your phone?" he asked, frantically.

Harrison handed his cell phone to Eric, who dialed Neil. To his frustration, Neil did not answer.

"Do you have any angel's phone numbers on here?"

"Why?" Harrison asked, confused by Eric's panic.

"I didn't get the chance to tell Aaron something important. I need to talk to one of them."

Harrison shook his head. "I don't have anyone but Cornelius."

Eric groaned, frustrated. Then he realized he did have an option, although not a very good one.

"Do you have anything that could give me a boost?" he asked. Harrison stared at him in confusion.

"I have some mutated quartz…" he answered, regretting answering when Eric rushed past him and headed for the basement. Harrison chased after him. "What are you planning on doing?" he asked as Eric scanned the various drawers.

"I have to get over there," he said. Before Harrison could say a word against it, Eric was opening the drawer with the quartz. As soon as he took it in his hand, adrenaline surged through his veins. The blue magic surrounded his feet as he focused his mind on the patch of desert where Nebula had taken him.

Harrison realized that Eric planned to teleport straight into the warzone.

"Eric, NO!" Harrison screamed, grabbing onto Eric just as he was teleporting.

They landed together on the hard ground on their backs. Eric let the stone slip from his hand, knowing the magic was gone from it. He tried to catch his breath, his hands shaking from the amount of power he had just used. Harrison was to his left, exhausted as well.

When Eric looked up at the moon above him, he swore he could see the slight tint of red surrounding the moon, but when it faded, he decided it was just his imagination. When he turned his head to the right, he saw a faint light, most likely from the fires the dragons were creating. Knowing he did not have much time, Eric pushed himself to his feet and ran full speed toward the light.

"Eric, wait!" Harrison yelled behind him, but Eric continued to run, picking up the pace.

On the battlefield, Theo stayed near the front as he took on the enemy sorcerers, doing his best to injure them without needlessly killing, hoping they would retreat when their wounds became worse.

Meanwhile, Shawn lay on his stomach up on the cliffs, a pair of binoculars in his hand and the earpiece on and connected with the one Theo was wearing. During Shawn's lookout duty, he scanned the battlefield doing as Neil told him: to be their eyes. When he looked further ahead from where Theo was fighting, he noticed the dragons retreating. Most but not all of them were gathering up ahead, circling a section of the land.

"Theo, something's going on out there," Shawn told Theo.

Theo got close enough to the sorcerer he was fighting with to knock him with his elbow.

"What?"

"It's the dragons, they're all standing in a circle. I think they're getting ready to open the portal," he said.

"Where?"

"Straight ahead, about thirty yards from you."

Theo turned to the sorcerers behind him. "The dragons are our priority. We have to push through. Spread the word so the angels know!" he yelled.

Theo turned and ran forward. He fought the enemy sorcerers, only suffering from minor attacks until he neared the front of the fight when he heard Shawn again.

"Theo, behind you!" Shawn warned.

When Theo turned, Borrit was in front of him. Before Theo could react, Borrit wrapped his hand around his throat. He pulled him closer, so their faces are just inches apart. Theo struggled to breathe, his hands reaching for Borrit's. He felt sharp pain where Borrit's fingers were squeezing.

Borrit smiled. "I thought you learned," he said.

Theo kicked Borrit's knee as hard as he could, making his grip loosen just enough to allow him to break free. Borrit reached to grab him again, but he dodged and pulled one of his throwing knives out, tossing it in the air and aiming it at Borrit's head. Just as the knife was about to reach Borrit, he grabbed Theo by the wrist. The knife fell to the ground as Borrit twisted Theo's arm and burned it, causing Theo to cry out in pain. Theo dropped to his knees, his arm still held up by Borrit as he burned through his flesh, his eyes glowing.

Esme appeared behind them and attacked Borrit, forcing him to release Theo. Borrit turned to face her, surprised by the interference, but he welcomed it, charging at her. She fought Borrit directly, trying to avoid his still-glowing hand. Her strength almost matched his as she successfully blocked his attacks and got in a few herself, focusing her strength on his throat and chest in hopes it would hinder his ability to breathe fire. He aimed to punch her, and she ducked, barely avoiding his attack, and used the opening to punch his throat, knocking him back.

His expression changed to anger. Growing tired, he caught her closed fist as she threw another punch at him. "Impressive," he said, smirking. "You are wasted here," he said before letting go and continuing his attacks, stepping up his game. Esme was barely managing to keep him from killing her and she could tell because his fire was building up. She struggled not to stumble. When she realized if it continued, both she and Theo would die, she evaded him and rushed to Theo, who was finally on his

feet, and teleported. When they vanished, she felt a strange weight, as if she was being dragged down. Theo felt it too, the extra seconds that had added to their teleportation.

When they appeared in the nearest town, she realized that Borrit was holding on to her as well. She teleported to the cliff, not daring to leave him near civilians.

They appeared on the cliff, ten feet from the surface, and dropped, rolling apart. Borrit was the first to recover, immediately aiming for Esme, but Theo shielded her with his magic long enough to bounce him back. She jumped to her feet and fought him as Theo attacked him from behind. The rage was visible on Borrit's face as he thrashed, knocking them both back. Theo was launched ten feet and the air was knocked from his lungs on impact. He rolled to the ground, struggling to recover, when a shadow crossed over him. Borrit stood over him with his eyes glowing and Theo watched as Borrit's hand began to glow. Feeling that his time was up, he closed his eyes and reached for the shield pendant Leanna gave him years ago. The unmistakable sound of a gunshot broke him from his prayer.

When he looked up, Borrit was looking at something behind him. Theo saw Shawn standing at the edge of the cliff with a gun pointed at Borrit. He pulled the trigger over and over again, clumsily firing every bullet in the direction of Borrit's chest, hoping none of the bullets hit Theo, but Borrit charged at him. Borrit was just in front of Shawn when Evangeline appeared behind Shawn and took him away. At the same time, Esme grabbed Theo and teleported as well, leaving Borrit alone on the cliff.

At the front, many of the dragons were now standing in a circle with their hands joined. They could see the red glow of the moon igniting the ground. They spread their wings, creating a barrier around them. Their eyes glowed as they summoned their fire together and it began to burn the ground. When they had used all of their fire, they waited again, letting it build up in their chests, weakening Hell's barrier with each blow.

Nebula, who was still watching from the cliffs, heard Harrison yell in the distance and tried to listen. Hearing Eric's name, although faint, she turned to scan the darkness. Finally, she saw Eric running toward the warzone. Relieved he was okay,

she nearly teleported to him but came to her senses and scanned for Borrit just in time to find him looking straight in the direction Eric was running from. Her chest pounded as she watched him looking at Eric with eyes filled with rage. When Borrit turned and his eyes locked with hers, she saw their glow was brighter than ever. Her heart felt as though it had stopped completely. He knew Eric was out of his cage because of her, he always knew. She could feel his rage all around her despite the distance between them.

She kept her expression the same as always, hoping he would think he was mistaken and turn his attention away from her and let Eric alone. When he turned away from her again, she believed he would return to his task, or at least she did until he rubbed his thumb over the stone, making it glow. She was confused as one of the dragons who was fighting off sorcerers stopped and turned around, his eyes vacant. When she had asked Borrit about the stone earlier that afternoon, she did not know its purpose. She only knew it was important because of the way Borrit protected it. With her limited knowledge, she had guessed that it made him stronger. She watched as the dragon disappeared and reappeared ten feet from Eric, forcing him to stop running. The dragon charged at Eric and he barely managed to block its attacks. The dragon moved behind Eric, forcing him to turn around. Knowing he could not fight the dragon, Eric stumbled, throwing up his shield to stop himself from being burnt. Each time his shield came up, he believed he was successfully protecting himself, but Nebula knew that if the dragon wanted to kill Eric, he would already be dead. The dragon was waiting too long between his attacks for them to be deadly.

When she looked behind Eric, she realized what was happening. Borrit was using the stone to control the dragon like a puppet, guiding him to force Eric directly in his path. He wanted to exert Eric's energy but what Borrit wanted more was to make it clear to Eric that his life was ending. He wanted to kill Eric himself, but in his favorite way, an arm right through him. Eric tripped over his own feet, falling on his back, and scrambled to stand, but his magic was spent.

Unable to watch any longer, Nebula swallowed back her fear and let the fire in her throat rise, filling her lungs. She teleported behind Borrit and released her fire,

aiming for his wings. Borrit screamed as Nebula burned him. Before he could try to stop her, she was tearing at his wings.

Borrit's scream boomed across the desert, surprising everyone who was occupied in their battle.

Hearing the roar, and confused by Nebula's departure, Neil walked to the edge of the cliff to see what was happening. When he saw Eric, he paled and ran quickly to the base of the cliff.

Borrit grabbed Nebula by the throat with one hand. Her eyes focused on the stone in Borrit's hand, she freed herself from his grip long enough to sink her teeth into the hand that held the stone and grabbed it, knowing Borrit could not teleport with his damaged wings.

"Eric!" she yelled as she threw the stone in his direction.

Eric turned to see her throw it, not noticing the dragon who was attacking him had stopped. Eric rushed to the stone, his feet slipping on the dirt. Before he had reached the stone, Borrit tossed Nebula aside and turned to face Eric. He was already summoning the fire from his lungs.

Still a distance away, Neil saw everything happen as if in slow motion. His heart was caught in his throat.

Just as Eric closed his fist around the stone, Borrit opened his mouth to breathe his fire. Eric looked up just in time to see the bright fire headed toward him.

"NOOO!" Neil screamed.

With no time to react, Eric could only close his eyes. A weight crashed down on him, knocking him to the ground, the gravel scraping his cheek as he landed. The weight pinned him to the ground and the heat swallowed him, but for some reason it did not burn. An ear-splitting scream filled his eyes, which he realized was coming from whoever was on top of him—the person who knocked him off his feet and now had their arms wrapped around him to protect him. He was not feeling the burning, because someone else was burning in his place.

Harrison.

Harrison screamed so loudly that everyone on the battlefield heard it. With

his weakened power instinctively protecting his own body, there was nothing Eric could do to stop it.

The screaming stopped and Eric was left in darkness. The smell of burning flesh overwhelmed him as he lay underneath Harrison's shaking body. Harrison's arms, which had been crushing him before, were now weakening because he was losing strength. Eric stared at the ground next to him in shock, his eyes wide.

"It's alright…" Harrison barely whispered before his body stilled completely.

Eric twisted and slipped out from underneath Harrison's limp body. He knew Harrison had followed him, but he never imagined that this would happen. Eric shook, unable to stop the tears as he stared at Harrison's vacant eyes.

The dragons were now rampaging since they were not being controlled, but the noise barely registered in his ears as he looked at the stone in his hand. He struggled to his feet and looked at Borrit, who was barely being held back by Nebula. Dozens of sorcerers were scattered on the ground wounded as the angels struggled to reach them so they could take them out of harm's way.

Neil, who had not moved, looked at the stone in Eric's hand. Eric tightened his grip on it. He saw the pocket knife on Harrison's belt. Eric lifted his hand, summoning the knife to his own hand, and opened it. Remembering the scar on Borrit's hand, he placed the stone on the ground, sliced his own palm and let his blood drip down. When nothing happened, he looked up at Nebula, who now had other sorcerers with her, keeping Borrit back as well.

"Nebula!" he called.

She turned away from Borrit. When she saw the look in Eric's eyes and the bloody stone on the ground, she somehow knew what he wanted her to do. She breathed fire at the stone to let it glow as Eric barely managed to shield himself. When she was finished, Eric picked up the hot stone, surprised its heat brought him no pain.

Neil watched as a strange red glow crossed Eric's eyes. At that moment, the dragons stopped thrashing and went completely still. They all turned at once, their new target clear to everyone who watched. Neil realized that Eric was now in control and that he was sending the dragons to Borrit. They began to charge.

"Get back!" Eric yelled to those surrounding Borrit. They did as they were told and watched in shock as the dragons charged toward their leader, not understanding what was happening. Borrit looked at Eric in anger, but he could not reach him because the dragons were blocking his path. Realizing Eric's intentions, Neil came to his senses.

"ERIC, STOP!" he yelled. The dragons stopped, just inches from Borrit, surrounding him. In the same moment, Eric turned and locked eyes with Neil. Tears were still spilling from his bloodshot eyes as he looked at Neil, making Neil's throat tighten. "Do not force them to do this," Neil said quietly.

Eric stepped back and released the stone, letting it float in front of him. Then he put his palms in front of him, facing them toward each other. He curled his fingers and pushed his hands together, crushing the stone just as he had done with the britstone. Using whatever strength he could muster, Eric crushed the stone to pieces, the shards falling to the ground. He stumbled but kept himself from falling as the dragons regained their senses, staring around in shock. Most of them turned to look at Eric.

"Do whatever you want to him," Eric said.

Some of the dragons simply stared at Eric in surprise, but those who felt braver and angrier turned to Borrit, their anger and grief for all the time they had lost taking over. Eric looked away as they charged at Borrit, but he saw the fire and heard the raging screeches coming from Borrit as they tore him apart. When he looked up again, he saw Borrit's blackened body fall to the ground and instantly break apart into ash. The ash glowed red for a few seconds, then slowly sank into the soil, disappearing.

The dragons who had decided he needed to be stopped stood around where his ashes had sunk, trying to catch their breath. Nebula stared at the ground in shock. When she turned to look at Eric, he saw something he had never seen before: The corners of her mouth lifted slightly. She smiled at him in relief because he had done it.

Borrit was dead.

CHAPTER 28
Human

Many people on the battlefield froze, although the sorcerers who marched for Malphilus began to flee. Some managed to teleport but the rest were seized by the angels and teleported away to be dealt with accordingly; they were too dangerous to be left to roam.

Eric and Nebula stared at each other with the same question in their eyes. What do they do now? But before either of them could reach a conclusion, something distracted them, as well as the sorcerers and angels who were left standing. The dragons hunched forward at once, some with their arms around their middles as they dropped to their knees, unable to hold themselves up. Eric and Neil looked at the dragons with concern, unsure of what was happening. They all seemed to be in pain, a few even letting out screams of agony. Then they began to claw at their backs desperately. Eric watched in shock as the wings on their backs shrank, withering away. The angels moved to help them, but the heat from the dragons' bodies forced them to step away. Slowly, the dragons' wings turned to ash and fell, sinking into the ground much like Borrit's body did.

Their borrowed power was returning to its rightful place in Hell now that the connection to Borrit was lost. A minute passed before every mark of being a dragon faded from their skin and they were left on the ground, gasping for air. They crawled forward, using palms that now looked human.

Realizing the dragons were human again, the angels rushed to help them. Eric smiled in relief. Nebula, he thought would be human too, but when Eric turned to look at her, his heart sank and his smile disappeared. Although her reddened eyes had slowly become blue again, she looked down at her raised arms, staring at them as if waiting for the scales on her skin to fall off as they did for the others, but they did not.

She looked up, her eyes locking with Eric's. She was crying. Her blue eyes were now red from tears for the first time. She was confused by the liquid that spilled from them as she moved to wipe them away. They both realized why she was the only one who did not become human. Although the others were changed back, she was still a fetus when her mother had the blood transfusion. Unlike the others, she was born a dragon so she had no human form to revert to. She was a creation of Borrit, as if he were her father.

"Nebula?" a woman called faintly in the distance. Eric and Nebula both turned to see her mother, yards from them and still on the ground searching for her daughter, her weakened state stopping her from rising to her feet.

Eric realized Nebula was looking at him with horror. She looked to her mother again in panic, then back at Eric. He realized what she planned to do.

"Nebula, don't," he called out, but he was too late. She disappeared before he could convince her to stay. Eric grabbed his hair, frustrated with himself for not being able to do anything and willed his tears to stop.

Neil ran to Eric and grabbed him by the shoulders. "What were you thinking?!" he yelled. He did not know how much more he could take of his constant worry for Eric.

Eric knew he should answer, that he should be explaining exactly why he was there, but he could not get the words past his trembling lips. His throat tightened and he tore his gaze away from Neil, trying to hold it together, but instead found himself staring at Harrison's still body. Neil followed Eric's gaze. When he saw Harrison, he pushed his anger aside and pulled Eric into his arms. Suddenly, he was unable to scold Eric for his recklessness. His anger was calmed and replaced with grief.

"This wasn't your fault," he whispered to Eric. When he felt Eric trembling, he squeezed harder, almost crushing him. When he felt a sudden wave of strength returning to him, he looked up at the sky and noticed the moon was mostly uncovered. "It's over now," he told him.

Looking over Eric, he saw that Theo, Shawn, and Esme had arrived and were standing just a few feet away, watching them. Neil stepped back, putting his hand on

Eric's shoulder and giving it a gentle squeeze with his eyes focused on them.

"We need to gather the humans somewhere private so they can be tended to," he said to them. Then he looked over at Harrison and released Eric's shoulder to approach the body. He stopped in front of it and knelt, pressing a hand gently to Harrison and closed his eyes. When he opened them, he saw Harrison's soul slipping from his parted lips. The others stepped closer, watching it as it slowly rose to the sky.

"Thank you…" Neil whispered, hoping the God of Heaven could hear his gratitude for accepting Harrison as one of them. Evangeline knelt down next to Neil, placing a hand on his back.

"The body needs to be brought back," he said. "We need a proper ceremony. Our way."

Esme nodded. "I'll take care of it," she said, turning her attention to the dozens of humans still recovering from the reversal. Neil nodded and stood, returning to Eric's side, and they stared at the humans who were scattered among their own people. Aaron and Roman reached the front of the crowd and stood in front of Neil, waiting for orders.

"Does anyone know a private place where we can take them to be tended to?" he asked them.

Roman nodded. "There is a nearby warehouse, but it's not ideal."

"It will do," he said. He turned to Eric. "I don't suppose you would agree to go home now…" Eric shook his head, making Neil sigh. "Stay close to me, then."

Roman teleported them to a warehouse, then returned to the others. In small groups, the humans were gathered and walked to the inside of the warehouse, all too weak to question where they were being taken. Some of the angels arrived with lights, setting them down around the room so that everyone was able to see. Neil walked over to the large boxes that were piled along one of the warehouse walls and climbed on top of it, turning to face the humans who were now all standing or sitting in front of him. They focused their attention on him.

"I'm sure you must all be very confused…" he said. "My name is-."

"Neil," one of the humans said. Neil turned to the teenage boy. "We know.

He told us," he said.

When Neil looked to the others, he saw a recognition of some sort in their eyes.

"How much do you know?" Neil asked.

The boy answered. "Not much. The only thing any of us really learned was when he was telling us what to do. Even then, most of it's hazy. I don't know about everyone else, but I have no clue how long I was there." He looked between Eric and Neil. "What's the date?" he asked.

Neil hesitated, wondering if he should ease them into how much time they had lost, but Eric stepped in.

"February 25th, 2016," he said. Each reaction was different, some shocked, some grieving, but the one emotion they all seemed to share was understanding. When Neil looked down at Eric, all Eric said was, "They need to know." Neil nodded in understanding and returned his attention to the crowd.

"I imagine for some of you it's only been months. For others I'm afraid the time you lost may range from years to even decades." They stayed silent, allowing him to continue. "I won't lie to you. Returning to your lives will not be easy. None of you have aged since the day you were turned."

One of the women stood. "What do we do, then?" she asked, shaking her head.

"My people can help. No matter what, you cannot return to your normal lives. We will arrange for you to start fresh somewhere else, a new name, a new identity. As for your families, our kind has an ability to alter human memories. You all have the option to be put in contact with your families to see if they would be willing to begin new lives with you and to keep the circumstances of your age a secret. If they are unwilling, we can simply make them forget meeting you. Unfortunately, we are unable to alter your memories of what happened to you. Which is why we have a favor to ask of you." When they said nothing, he continued. "No matter what you choose…no one can know any of this. Where you were, what happened to you, the fact that all of us exist, it must be kept a secret. The time you spent in captivity is far too long for us to

help you forget, so asking you of this is all we can do."

Slowly, each of the humans nodded or promised to never speak of what happened.

Neil searched their expressions for a hint of untruthfulness, but they all appeared to be genuine. "I expected this to be more difficult," he said.

Someone else spoke. "If it weren't for you guys…" he shook his head. "I don't even know what would have happened, but it probably would've been really bad. It's not like telling people would help any of us. We'd be freakshows."

The humans stared at Neil in silence, exhaustion creeping over them. "The night has been long. After you have been examined, you will be taken somewhere to rest for the night. Then in the morning we can work on what comes next. One step at a time."

The angels approached the humans one by one to heal them of their wounds.

Evangeline walked through the crowd, to the teenage boy who had spoken earlier.

"Josh?" she asked carefully.

He turned to face her, confused that she knew his name. For Evangeline, seeing him made her feel as if she was back in high school, greeting him at the diner when he spent his afternoons at the counter. He looked at her, recognition crossing his eyes.

"I know you…" he said.

She smiled. "Not personally, but yes. My brother and I went to school with you and your brother."

"You were always at the diner," he said, his eyes traveling down to look at her coat then returning to her eyes. "So, you're not human?"

"I was," she said. "But I haven't been for a very long time." She walked closer to him, slowly reaching out to touch him until her hand was around his arm. She healed him. His shoulders slumped and he exhaled.

"What did you do?"

"Healed you…" Ignoring his surprise, she continued. "I spoke to your brother

recently."

Josh looked at her as his emotions threatened to bubble to the surface. "How is he?"

For Evangeline, seeing Josh again was the strangest thing. He was the same teenager who went missing during a fire all those years ago, but he had matured so much. Although she was sure that she and Aaron had matured as well, seeing the change in someone else seemed odd.

"He never really got over what happened, not completely." When she saw the guilt cross his face, she took his hand, forcing him to look at her again. "He has children now. Grandchildren too."

His eyes widened in disbelief. "He's a grandfather?" She smiled, nodding. He sighed, having trouble hiding his own smile, but then he shook his head. "I can't go back."

"Why not?" she asked.

"It's been so long; all it would do is mess with his life."

"On the contrary, I think it would bring him closure."

"What about his family? I can't stay in town. I can't make him leave them either."

"You are his family… We'll figure this out. I promise," she whispered. He finally relaxed, slowly wrapping his arms around her as tears filled his eyes.

Shawn leaned against one of the warehouse walls, and Theo took the spot next to him.

"You ready to go home?" Theo asked Shawn.

A smile spread over Shawn's face. "I never thought I'd hear you ask that," he said.

Theo put his hand on Shawn's shoulder and gripped it tight. "You've had to wait long enough."

Shawn nodded. "As excited as I am, do you mind if I shower first?"

Theo laughed before straightening his back, briefly scanning Shawn's body, which was covered in dirt and soot much like everyone else.

"That's probably best," he agreed, gesturing for Shawn to follow him as he headed for one of the angels.

Neil spent the rest of the night watching as the humans were tended to; there was nothing he could do to help unless asked. Roman stepped away from Nebula's mother, leaving her with another angel. She had clearly given up on her daughter returning to her, so she sat on the ground with a blanket wrapped tightly around her. Roman walked to Neil.

"Is that the girl's mother?" Neil asked him.

Roman nodded. "The dragon girl is actually what I came to discuss."

"What is there to discuss?"

"We both know she did not perish. I saw her flee as well, so what are we going to do about her?"

Neil stared at Nebula's mother while he considered his answer. "When Theo first told me about her, he described her as a child." He looked over at Eric, who was sitting on the floor just a few yards away. "Eric seems to think so too…"

"There is no way Cyrus would allow her to roam," Roman pointed out.

Neil nodded. "You are correct. Cyrus will want her in a cage like the others…but she proved she was on our side, and I cannot see a child like her down there. I saw what it was like."

"What are you suggesting?"

"That we look the other way for as long as we can. Cyrus does not know she exists, so I think it is best that it remains that way."

"Won't Cyrus know the next time he searches your memories?"

"It's difficult, but I can keep the memory from him if I try hard enough." When Roman did not reply, Neil looked at him in surprise. "I was expecting an argument."

"I've grown tired of arguing…" Roman said.

Neil looked at Roman curiously, wondering if the events of that night had finally gained his trust. Hoping that was the case, Neil turned back to the crowd and stayed silent rather than question the unity that had just formed.

Exhausted, Eric fought sleep as he sat on the ground. When it became more difficult to keep his eyelids from closing, he jumped to his feet, hoping that moving around would help. Then he saw a figure at the corner of his eye.

When he turned toward the warehouse door, he saw it slowly crack open and a shadow cross it. Eric watched the silhouette walk past the windows; it felt familiar. He turned to look at Neil; when he saw that he was busy speaking to Aaron and Roman, Eric snuck away to the door. Taking one last look behind him, he slipped through the door, into the moonlight.

He walked in the direction he saw the silhouette go until he was at the edge of the warehouse wall. He stepped around the corner, stopping when he saw a man with his back turned to him. Eric stared at him, wondering if his eyes were deceiving him. He knew this man.

"James?" he called out. The man turned around. Sure enough, it was James standing in front of him. Eric's eyes widened. "You're real…" he said.

James looked down at his own body then let his eyes travel to Eric's feet, smirking when he saw the blue flame was not present. "Must be…" he said. He took a few steps closer to Eric. "Nice to see you in the flesh."

Eric was too overcome with surprise to respond, unable to tear his gaze away from James as he took in every detail of him as if he appeared any different than he did in the dreams.

"You know," James said, "it's rude to stare."

Eric could not look away. "Sorry," he said quickly.

"Don't fret. It must be strange meeting face-to-face."

"Definitely," Eric said.

"So, how did your...dilemma turn out?"

"We did it," he said. "We stopped him. He's dead."

The smile on James' face disappeared, replaced by a scowl. When he saw Eric tense, he reverted back to a smile. "You should be careful. It's always the good people who get hurt the most." He searched Eric's eyes. "But I'm sure you've already learned that lesson."

Before Eric could process what, he had just said, James' body jerked forward and he gripped his head in pain.

"What's wrong?" Eric asked quickly.

James shook his head. "Just a headache. I get them often." He held his head between both hands and suddenly looked up at Eric. When their eyes locked, pure horror crossed his face. He gasped, taking a step back. "ERIC, RUN!" he yelled. Eric jumped back as James hunched over again. James grabbed his head. "Sorry," he said. "I wasn't feeling like myself."

Eric's stomach sank as he stared at James with understanding.

"You look like you've seen a ghost," James said.

"You're him," Eric said.

James looked confused. "Who do you think I am?"

"Malphilus…" he said.

James' smile grew wider, almost sinister. "Smart too. Wonderful."

Eric was pushed back as Neil appeared in front of him, his breathing heavy. Neil threw his arms forward, attacking Malphilus with magic, but he only blocked it with ease.

"Don't look so scared, Cornelius. We were just getting to know each other."

Aaron grabbed Eric and Roman was there too. Looking around Neil, Malphilus looked straight at Eric.

"See you soon," he said. Then he disappeared and they were all left standing, staring at the spot where their enemy had just vanished from their sight.

Acknowledgements

Since I was a kid, I've always loved writing stories. I first started writing this book when I was sixteen years old. Inspired by Harry Potter, I began to write notes of my own young boy in a world of magic and as the years passed, it began to take its own shape. This book was nine years in the making, and I am proud to finally have it printed.

Thank you to the incredible freelance editors, Nick Hodgson (Reedsy) and Penny Fletcher (Guru) whose services made my self-publishing journey possible. Nick was the one who edited my first draft, and she did such an amazing job guiding me through every strength and weakness in my writing. Her work pushed me to improve my story in a way that I didn't realize was possible. Penny helped me with my final draft, polishing my manuscript, resulting in a final draft I was happy with, and ready to share with the world.

A huge thank you to my high school English teacher and former boss Caley O'Neil who was always there to help me when I needed her. When I wrote the first chapter in 2014, a draft that changed drastically over the years, she was the first to read it. She gave me the confidence to continue writing this book and to work hard to improve my writing each day.

Thank you to my mom, Isabel, for reading my book in its entirety when I finished writing the first draft, despite amount of boring passages and typos it contained at the time.

Writing this book was wonderful, and its thanks to the public resources available that I was able to finally self-publish this book. I have a long collection of notes for story ideas, but this is the first I managed to finish, and I am looking forward to continuing Eric and Neil's journeys.

Thank you for reading, and I hope you love their story as much as I do.